I0586563

Review

When I pick up a novel by Stefan Vučak, I know I am in for a thrill ride. His books seem to have a life of their own. They take readers by the hand and lead them through a landscape of political upheaval, intrigue and scandal. I have enjoyed his previous book, *Cry of Eagles. Strike for Honor* certainly did not disappoint me. He has created realistic situations, lifelike characters and convincing dialog that place readers in the midst of what could be a disastrous political situation. If Stefan Vučak's previous books set a high bar of excellence, *Strike for Honor* has surpassed that bar.

Readers' Favorite

Books by Stefan Vučak

General Fiction:
Cry of Eagles
All the Evils
Towers of Darkness
Strike for Honor
Proportional Response
Legitimate Power
Autumn Leaves
All My Sunsets
F/X-26
28th Amendment
Night Sirens
Broken Rose

Shadow Gods Saga:
In the Shadow of Death
Against the Gods of Shadow
A Whisper from Shadow
Shadow Masters
Immortal in Shadow
With Shadow and Thunder
Through the Valley of Shadow
Guardians of Shadow

Science Fiction:
Fulfillment
Lifeliners

Non-Fiction:
Writing Tips for Authors

Contact at:
www.stefanvucak.com

STRIKE FOR HONOR

By

Stefan Vučak

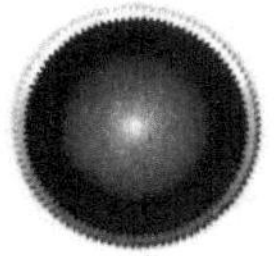

Note:

This is a work of fiction. All names, characters, places, and events are the work of the author's imagination. Any resemblance to real persons, places, or events is coincidental.

ISBN-10: 0-9942923-8-4
ISBN-13: 978-0-9942923-8-4

Dedication

To Daniel ... grasping at life's opportunities

Acknowledgments

My thanks to Susan Stevenson for helping to guide me through the National Transportation Safety Board procedures.

Cover art by Laura Shinn.
http://laurashinn.yolasite.com

Chapter One

A distinctive pealing blare tore the dawn silence as a warship announced its departure. Vincent Pacino could tell the difference between a man-of-war and a civilian tub. He raised an eyebrow and shrugged. The ship out there would not be the only one leaving this morning. He tried not to let the thought spoil the moment.

Placing his cup on a black saucer, he sighed with contentment and sat back against the chair. He patted his trim stomach and grinned.

"Ah, that was good."

Linda peered at him over the rim of her mug, holding it between both hands. Her large deep brown eyes shone with amusement, and the right side of her full mouth lifted. He wanted to climb out of his chair, reach for her and squeeze her until her helpless squeals were reduced to loving surrender. Apart from wearing a dashing white uniform, he still didn't know what she saw in him, but he would not question his luck.

"I don't know where you put it," she said candidly and shook her head in bemused wonder.

Framed by short raven hair, her soft round face glowed with suppressed laughter. Despite her seemingly cheerful demeanor, there were lines of concern in the corners of her eyes. Vin pretended not to see them. Besides, nothing he could do about it right now. He could only hope she wouldn't hurt too much while he was away.

"Despite your unfailing efforts to turn me into a pear, my sweet, this body will never give in," he declared comfortably.

The small table between them lay littered with remnants of

their breakfast. His usual fare of two fried sausages, accompanied by eggs done over-easy, with toast to mop up the remains, didn't seem extravagant to him. Two cups of strong black coffee generally bedded the whole stuff down. It took fuel to power his five-foot eleven frame.

Some of his fellow officers doing penance in Yokosuka went native and turned up their noses at traditional American cuisine, never giving up trying to seduce him with superbly cooked local fare. Despite embracing all things Nipponese, one or two still harbored a secret weakness for Big Macs, which made Vin roll his eyes. Still, he admitted to developing a taste for Fukagawa-meshi and gourmet sashimi. There simply was no accounting for taste.

Linda's eyebrows arched as she lowered her mug. "A pear?"

Her soft contralto, mixed with an exotic touch of Southern accent, never failed to enthrall him.

"It's all that bracing sea air keeping me in shape, or maybe the extracurricular activities we indulge in after hours," he said with a lewd smile.

She giggled and tossed a piece of toast at him. "You're crude, Lieutenant."

"Guilty, ma'am." Vin's grin faded. "Will you be all right? It's only an eleven-day deployment, but I hate leaving you alone, especially when—"

She waved him off. "We've already packed most everything, and Leighton has the paperwork. We're not lugging furniture or appliances. I'm a navy wife, remember? I've done this once or twice before."

"So you have, my sweet. I'll check with Leighton before we shove off."

"I have it under control, Vin," she assured him in a patient voice. "Don't worry about it."

A friend, Commander Leighton would square away all the Housing Services Center red tape. Vin didn't want to handle last-minute snafus because some fool rating forgot to forward his Detaching Endorsement L20/L01 form.

Knowing when to give up, he reached across the table and grasped her right hand. The skin felt smooth and cool, and he loved running his fingers and palms over it, constantly amazed how a woman's skin seemed to have a texture unlike anything else, made to be loved.

"I'll try not to, but this isn't a routine rotation. If it weren't for the FTX—"

"I know what a Key Resolve exercise is. We've been through one last March."

The annual joint Field Training Exercise, conducted by the Combined Forces Command within the Korean Theater of Operations, was a defensive rotation to test rear area security and stability. It also made a firm demonstration to deter war with the Democratic People's Republic of Korea. Pacifists on both sides of Congress claimed it as a needless provocation. Perhaps it was, but as a serving naval officer, Vin believed in the value of positive deterrence. At any rate, nobody sought his opinion. They just told him.

He glanced at a copy of *US Today* beside him and Linda frowned.

"You worried what the North Koreans might do?"

"I'm always worried what those fanatics might do," he muttered sourly and pointed at the headline. "It's been a couple of years since Sung Kang-dae and his henchmen ousted 'Glorious Successor' Kim Jong-un after his father's death in 2011, and he's still consolidating his position. Besides, Jong-un was only a kid. Imagine someone like that made a four-star general and commander of their armed forces, for God's sake!"

"Only twenty-six or twenty-nine at the time?"

"Nobody knows for sure and the PROK isn't telling. They're a secretive bunch, but a seasoned old bird like Sung would not sit back and allow someone so inexperienced to become Supreme

Leader. Despite talk of political and economic reform, Sung is a military hawk and things haven't changed much in that country. Not so you'd notice."

"You think they might interfere when they supposedly sank *Cheonan* in 2010?"

Vin pursed his lips and shrugged. "They could, but I hope not, and they'd be crazy to try it. From all accounts, Larry Tanner is having a good round of what everyone is saying are favorable talks with their government to lift sanctions and open up trade. The country's a basket case. Why aggravate the situation with stupid posturing?"

"Ideology," Linda murmured.

"Yeah. Think how much blood has been spilled around the world over that one!"

"It would ease tension if they simply shut down their nuclear facilities at Yongbyon."

"It certainly would. Sung said he'd do it, citing its construction as an outdated policy by Kim Jong-il, and an unwarranted drain on the country's resources. All true, but they haven't made any moves to shut them down yet."

"But if Tanner is hopeful—"

"I reckon he's one of the best Secretaries of State we've had in some time, but it's hard to figure what Sung really wants."

"He wants to hold onto power and not be beholden to anybody. I'm talking about China and Russia," Linda added wryly and Vin grinned.

"You got that right, my sweet. Anyway, that's all high politics and way over my pay scale. It's not my worry. I simply don't feel happy running out on you like this."

"Vin, cube it, okay?"

He squeezed her hand and grinned at her characteristic expression. Two years younger than him, at twenty-four, she had maturity and poise of someone older. Navy life had toughened her, made her more self-reliant and confident. That independence helped steer both their careers through some demanding times, with a lot of love in between.

His posting to the 7th Fleet base at Yokosuka, Japan, had been a promotional leg up, but it also created a degree of strain on their personal life. A navy career was never easy on a relationship. After eighteen months on USS *Curtis Wilbur*, his application to attend the Naval Postgraduate School at Monterey, California, for a master's in Systems Engineering, had come through. It meant twelve months on shore away from salt and spray, but it would be worth it. On graduation, he would also receive another half stripe. A lieutenant commander at twenty-eight wasn't bad going and fitted his planned career curve. The fact that he finished fourth in his class at Annapolis, and had so far ticked all the right boxes, did not hurt his fast-track path either. In today's right-sized navy, every tick counted. There were far too many lieutenant commanders wiling away their time with shore appointments, and Vin wasn't planning to join them.

"Your Dad has us squared away with an apartment in Monterey, and my Mom is seeing to the furniture and the curtains," Linda said easily. "We'll be arriving in style. I hope you like chintz. You go ahead and enjoy your manly games with the Koreans and don't worry."

"Manly games? Never mind." He chuckled and patted her hand. "I knew I could count on you. Chintz or not, we'll have some serious time together once we're in Monterey. It's a promise."

"I won't mind it at all," she said softly, a world of expression in her voice.

He sighed, understanding her completely, but there wasn't anything he could do about her loneliness. Not right now. Navy life had always been tough on wives, and they would just have to work it out.

"Yeah. I know this hasn't been easy for you, has it, my sweet?"

"Yokosuka and Tokyo were interesting, and teaching math and science at Kinnick High filled my days, but it'll be good being home again. At least the school's on the base and I was spared having to commute somewhere else."

Vin nodded. A huge 570-acre complex, the Yokosuka Naval Base provided military facilities for 25,000 people and housing for 19,000 American personnel. Although the figure is somewhat lower these days, as some had elected to leave following the massive earthquake off Sendai in 2011. However comfortable, for her, home was still Norfolk, where he managed to snag her after a whirlwind courtship during his posting there with Fleet Forces Command. Monterey might be on the other side of the continent, but from Japan, it amounted to the same thing…almost.

"Besides, I'll be able to take my master's in education at California State while you're doing yours," she added and lifted her chin, daring him to challenge her, which he did not intend doing. She was also a dedicated professional and not only a curvy body.

"Right! Enough of this jawing." He slapped the table with both hands, stood up, and patted down his service blues dress jacket. There would be time to talk after the Field Training Exercise. He glanced behind him and frowned. "Where's my duffel bag?"

"In the car," Linda said and hastily piled stuff into the dishwasher, then grabbed her brown leather bag from the credenza.

"My girl! Let's do it."

Vin picked up his visored cap, jammed it on his head, and strode out of the narrow kitchen. He heard a click as she locked the apartment door and they walked down the corridor toward a bank of two elevators. He pressed the down button, clasped his hands behind his back and stood at the at ease position. He wasn't even aware he did it. After years of service, it was habit, the reaction coming automatically.

Outside, even though late February, the air had a lingering

crispness that made Vin's skin tingle. Crowded by nine-story tenement towers and lesser buildings, the open parking lots were clearing as duty personnel made their way to various administrative offices and support facilities. Civilians would be opening shops along Main Street and other establishments. This morning, more than the usual number of cars were heading toward the docks to board Fleet ships made ready to steam into the Yellow Sea where they would meet their Korean counterparts. Other cars would be streaming in from Ikego Hills, Negishi Heights and surrounding suburbs, impossible to house everyone on the base.

The sun still struggling to clear the housing complex, dark shadows shrouded the parking lot. Small mounds of snow huddled in corners. Linda shouldered her bag and ambled toward a dark red Honda Civic parked two rows back in the designated lot for their apartment tower. Dressed in a cream knee-length skirt and smart business jacket, she looked trim and attractive. Admiring her legs, Vin allowed himself a moment of distraction.

The front and rear lights blinked and the car gave a beep as she deactivated the security system. She opened the driver door, tossed her bag onto the rear seat, and climbed in. Vin got into the passenger seat and buckled up. After glancing at him to make sure he had his seatbelt on, she pressed the starter button.

Following a line of traffic heading toward the docks, most of them with Navy registration tags, Vin felt a building excitement at the prospect of going to sea again. His ten-day leave over, only granted because of his pending relocation Stateside. He couldn't help it. The sea ran in his blood and the deeps had his soul. A sailor, the open ocean his first love. A strange love that captivated his mind ever since his father took him to Halona Point to gaze at the majestic Pacific rollers that traveled all the way from Antarctica, to smash themselves against Oahu's shores.

Kenneth Pacino, a young lieutenant commander serving with the 3rd Fleet out of Pearl, also shared his yearning and faraway look, focused on the deep blue of a clear sky and unbroken expanse of ocean. Vin loved his father and cherished their moments of intimacy, but those moments were far too brief when they came, and infrequent. He did not understand why his father had to be away so often and for months at a time, resenting his absence. His mother tried to explain it to him once, and although he only partially understood, it was with intellectual detachment. It wasn't until he stood above Halona Point, watching the creamy rollers march in, allowing the soft tropical breeze to flow around him, smell the iodine-laden air, he decided that he would also sail the deeps. When his father took him aboard his *Spruance*-class destroyer, the conversion became complete. He would follow the family tradition and join the Navy.

But he still resented those long gaps between their reunions.

He took a quick look at Linda's profile, relaxed as she concentrated on her driving, and his eyes softened. The sea might be his first love, but she had fulfilled something else, a part of him that by joining made him complete. His love for her of a different order, and he had been startled when he realized he had room in his heart for her and the tug of an open sea. As a Navy brat herself, it made things easier, but he knew she pined for him when his ship had to sail. Sometimes that created a pull within him from opposite directions, but he could not be with her always and remain what he was, no matter how much he wanted to.

After he got his master's, did he want to ask for a shore billet, devoting himself to applied research in advanced weapons? They talked about it fleetingly, but Vin yearned for command of his own ship above everything else. A shore assignment would never get him there. At best, it would make it a long proposition. Right now, the sea ran in his veins and he needed to be there, no matter how much his heartstrings dragged at him. She understood his need, because that's what he was, which only made it worse.

He would make it up to her once they were in Monterey.

As they neared the docks, he could see tall loading cranes cluttering the harbor docks. Navy personnel were everywhere: officers, ratings and toiling gangs. Across the water, two tugs crowded the sleek 567-foot-long USS *Shiloh*, CG-67, a *Ticonderoga*-class Aegis cruiser, getting ready to depart. Her functional boxy superstructure and rear helicopter housing didn't make her graceful, but her business was dealing out death, not stand in review.

Linda pulled the car to a stop before a guarded gate at Sherman Pier and switched off the engine. She looked at him and her brown eyes turned misty. He reached for her. With a strangled sob, her arms were around his neck.

"There, my sweet. It's only an exercise," Vin murmured softly into her short hair after swallowing a lump.

She pulled away and dabbed at her eyes. "I told myself I wouldn't get emotional."

He smiled and brushed her cheek with a finger. "It's all right. You can be emotional for both of us."

"Just don't be a hero, okay?"

"You're talking like I'm off to a war."

"With North Korean boats shadowing you, no one can tell what they'll do."

"I'll have a powerful ship under me with all the missiles and guns I want to fire. They'd be crackers to try something."

"If they do, make sure you duck. That's an order, Lieutenant."

"Aye aye, ma'am." He pulled her tight and their lips met. Her soft mouth opened and the first touch of her velvety tongue made him feel all prickly. Joined in a dance of abandon, he wondered what the hell he was doing trading her for the sea. Having to come up for air, he broke the moment and looked deep into her eyes. "Keep that thought," he said and gave her a quick peck on the cheek.

She tittered and fisted him on the shoulder. "Dirty old man."

"Always, my sweet." He glanced at the digital watch on his right wrist and sighed. "Got to go. Love you."

"Me too," she said, clearly distressed despite the brave little smile she gave him.

He wanted to say something comforting and endearing, but words would only make it trite. Abruptly, he unclipped his belt, opened the door, stepped out, and slammed it shut. As he made his way to the rear of the car, its trunk lid popped open. He retrieved his dark blue duffel and walked toward the guard post without looking back. He heard the Honda accelerate away behind him.

Saying goodbyes had never been his strong suit.

A marine, the semi-automatic on his right hip within easy reach, stepped out of the small windowed shack and saluted.

"Morning, sir."

A second marine inside the shack watched them both. Vin could see three M16A2 rifles mounted on the back wall. He returned the salute, slid the duffel to the ground and dug out his wallet. He handed the ID card to the guard who passed it to his buddy. After a computer check, Vin got his card back and the marine saluted again.

"Give 'em hell, Lieutenant."

Vin saluted with a grin as the gate rolled back on its tracks. "Cocked and locked," he said and picked up his bag. He paced slowly into his world and breathed deeply. The green water smooth with hardly any wind.

Walking down the pier, he barely registered the background noises permeating the air like a pervasive blanket: cars, forklifts, trucks, prime movers, and the constant hum of machinery—a harbor readying itself for a major deployment.

Tied portside, a thin thread of gray smoke lingered above USS *Curtis Wilbur's* rear stack. The warship's sharp clipper bow cleaved the air as it rose into a clear sky. Massing 6,900 tons and 505 feet long, painted drab gray, the *Arleigh Burke*-class guided missile destroyer was a powerful ship. Armed with multiple Mk 41 vertical launch cells that could launch Tomahawk or Standard attack missiles, Evolved Sea Sparrows for defense, VL-ASROC antisubmarine missiles, five inch/54-caliber main gun, torpedo tubes and a Phalanx CIWS close-in defense system, the ship could hold its own. Two MH-60 Sea Hawk helicopters housed in a stern hangar extended its reach when sub hunting. Pushed by four GE gas turbines powering two shafts, going better than thirty-six knots, the ship also demonstrably fast.

Admiring the ship's sleek lines, he once told Linda he couldn't wish for more.

Behind the ship, tied along its starboard side, lay a sister destroyer, *Mustin. Lassen* and *Fitzgerald* were laid up for major maintenance and would be missing the scaled down FTX, no doubt to the chagrin of their skippers. Apart from them, everybody else also prepared to head out, except the carrier USS *George Washington.* She would also miss this exercise, a deal to appease the North Koreans. As the Fleet's deputy commander, Rear Admiral Kenneth Pacino—due to get his third star in the fall according to the grapevine—would be running the exercise from his command ship, USS *Blue Ridge*, LCC-19. Vin wondered what his old man was doing now. Probably giving his chief of staff ulcers, he mused sardonically.

Despite the fact that both of them were at Yokosuka, he'd had limited contact with his father. Their respective duties simply made socializing on a grand scale impossible. To make up for it, his mother visited when he and Linda were in port, valuing being under the wing of an admiral's wife. It wasn't patronage, merely taking practical advantage, and Vin would have been nuts not to accept the social benefits his father's position offered. That's as far as it went, and neither would have it otherwise. The older Pacino never used his rank to advance or influence Vin's career. Still, it was nice to know he had one admiral in his pocket if needed.

As he approached the destroyer, its arching side looming beside him, the offset gray-black DDG-54 painted prominently on its bow, Vin figured life could be a whole lot worse. He paused beside the gangway guarded by two marines and returned their salutes. Without being asked, he held out his ID. The marine looked at it carefully and made a tick on his clipboard.

Vin shouldered his bag and climbed up the gangway. When he reached the weather deck, he looked up, saluted the colors and then saluted Lieutenant JG, Minny Couper, standing her stint as Officer of the Deck. She looked confident these days; a far cry from her initial eager, trusting phase when she first came on board. Wanting to make a good impression, she micromanaged and drove her team to distraction, which forced Vin to remind her she was there as a manager. The chiefs were there to look after the sailors.

"Permission to come aboard, sir," Vin said formally. Couper returned his salute.

"Permission granted, sir."

Vin stepped on the steel deck and quickly looked around. There weren't many people about, most of the activity being below decks.

"What's the word, Minny?"

"Set to shove off at ten hundred, as per the advertised schedule. You've got the afternoon watch in CIC."

"Everybody on board?"

"Just about, but—"

"I know. Koslov hasn't reported in."

"Not yet, and Commander Linnen is something pissed," Couper agreed equitably, clearly not overly agitated at the prospect of Koslov getting a reaming.

"Well, it wouldn't be a deployment if the XO wasn't pissed at somebody," Vin said comfortably and walked toward an open hatchway leading into the ship's bowels.

Commander Deron 'Sheet' Linnen was a good officer and cut the crew a lot of slack, but he didn't have much time for any prima donna. Senior Chief Koslov's last-minute departure antics definitely fitted into that category. Every ship had a character and Koslov was *Steel Hammer's*, as they commonly referred to the ship. How people came up with such names, Vin couldn't figure it. They might as well have called her *Glowing Hammer* after the Fukushima reactors went into a meltdown. *Curtis Wilbur* and several other ships happened to be in port at the time. Rumor said that everything in Yokosuka received a dosing, although according to the official poop, tests showed nothing. The men still joked about it, and he knew other ships had requests for transfers, but none from *Wilbur* went. The men liked how Captain Tyler Woods ran things. For that matter, so did Vin.

He squared everything away and raided the wardroom for a coffee, then went topside. Standing beside the ASROC torpedo launcher, he watched the hands single up the bowlines. At ten a.m. sharp, the ship's horn blared, sending up a plume of white steam from the forward stack and tugs eased the warship away from the wharf.

Time to do some paid business.

* * *

Sung Kang-dae pursed his thin lips and stared across the wide table. His small black eyes bulged slightly from a podgy flat face, gave nothing away. Not a tall man, dressed in a drab gray jacket, narrow collar clipped tight around a powerful neck, he nonetheless exuded palpable power. His arrogant, domineering gaze accentuated the impression of instant retaliation if he were contradicted. A hard man to warm up to, Tanner reflected.

Seated on either side of him, the Foreign Minister and the Minister of Public Security, deferred to the Supreme Leader without moving, carefully watching everything, their faces equally inscrutable. They hadn't said much so far, but both were definitely 'players', powerful men who didn't feel they needed to prove themselves. They were the ones who got things done and knew it.

Behind the dictator, a thin nondescript individual acted as interpreter.

Sung spoke rapidly in the Hangul dialect, his words brooking no opposition, each point emphasized by tapping the table with a clenched fist. He did not want to appear to be giving away anything, certainly not to a nominal enemy.

"These concessions in no way imply that the Democratic People's Republic of Korea is prepared to bow to anyone! Our sovereignty must be respected at all times," the translator grated.

Larry Tanner kept his face impassive as he listened, his hands folded over the table. The polished surface glinted from two elaborately cut chandeliers mounted on deceptively delicate gold chains. Of course, the chains could not have been gold to support the weight of the crystal. Needless extravagance, but that was only one contradiction in this torn, wretched country. The bare table devoid of anything that might distract the flow of conversation.

Everything in the room was large, including the wide windows and table. Frosted glass softened the bright sunshine outside and rounded the sharp edges of conversation. On the wall behind Sung hung a square black-and-white picture of Kim Il-sung, the Eternal President, the man who sought to create a dynasty in his name. The eternal butcher would be more accurate, Tanner thought, but he wasn't here to pass judgment. His job was to represent the United States and its interests. If successful, wider global interests would also be served, but that would merely be a bonus, icing on the cake.

"Mr. Chairman, the United States has always been prepared to respect your country's sovereignty in the family of peaceful nations," he said smoothly, reminding Sung the objective of this meeting—dragging North Korea from the brink of total disintegration and shoring up his own power.

"If that's the case, Mr. Tanner, why does the United States

demand that I dismantle the Tongch'ang-dong missile facility?"

"Sir, your defense posture does not require development of missiles with a range of nine thousand miles, like your Taepodong-2. Such long-range weapons have only one function, to project a strategic threat."

"You would deny us a credible defense posture?"

"Your country is not threatened, sir. Not even by the United States."

"The rhetoric of your past presidents lends a lie to your statement, Mr. Secretary."

"The rhetoric of President Walters is not a lie."

Beside him, Marian Cromatry, Under Secretary of State for Economics, Business, and Agricultural Affairs, shifted slightly to signal his disquiet and alarm at the prospect of annoying the Supreme Leader. Cromatry worried about his portfolio and agenda, which was commendable, but Tanner was required to maintain a global perspective. During the exhaustive and often frustrating talks to date, overlaid with diplomatic protocol and tedious formalities, Tanner *had* walked softly, but firmly, gauging the mood of the North Korean leader and his ministers. A hardliner in the mold of his predecessor, Kim Jong-il, outwardly unyielding, Sung nevertheless appeared to be a pragmatist and a realist, confirming the dossier he had read.

Whether Sung liked it or not, and he undoubtedly didn't, the PROK leader had to face the unpalatable truth that maintaining an unworkable ideology would ensure the country's continued slide into poverty and increased unrest. Faced with widespread starvation and economic collapse, despite token attempts at limited market liberalization, not having anything to lose, the people would eventually rise up. The rebellion might be crushed, but the glorious Juche maxims of Kim Il-sung would be exposed as hollow oratory that they were, particularly the Songun—army first—doctrine. If one wanted to live well and have a privileged life, he joined the armed forces, but not everybody could be in the Army.

Sung could no longer parade his military might with stomping boots and rumbling missile carriers in the '60s-style Soviet demonstrations for the benefit of domestic and international media. It simply didn't wash anymore.

Russia might be a reluctant ally at best, but it had problems of its own. Wary of getting embroiled. China, although an active supporter, it shifted its focus to the world's economic stage and no longer willing to automatically shield an extremist regime. Sung and his ministers knew all that, hence the talks, albeit reluctant ones.

Across the table, Sung's yellow face equally impassive, but it was a mask. His clenched fist betrayed inner tension. Both were playing for high stakes with big chips. No one wanted to blink first. With Sung, however, if he lost, he would also probably lose his head.

"I am prepared to review our intercontinental missile program, provided we reach an acceptable agreement that guarantees our security, but I demand tangible results first!" the interpreter said.

In a gesture of conciliation, figuratively speaking, Tanner pushed his pile of chips to the center of the table.

"To show our good faith, sir, the planned Foal Eagle land exercise has been suspended. With the announcement to scale down your military forces and desire to defuse tensions across the peninsula, your southern neighbor is more than willing to avoid giving the impression that this year's joint land exercises are in any way an expression of aggressive intent toward your country."

Sung spoke rapidly after the interpreter finished translating Tanner's statement.

"That is welcome news and appreciated, Mr. Secretary, but we also want the Key Resolve naval deployment canceled. It's an unwarranted and blatantly provocative intrusion into our territorial waters. We don't object if our misguided neighbor wishes to undertake routine training evolutions of its vessels. However, those exercises don't require the challenging presence of your 7th Fleet."

"I assure you, sir, the exercise with our South Korean friends is in no way meant to be anything but a peaceful rotation and evaluation of our tactical doctrine," Tanner said smoothly, a blatant lie, of course.

Given Sung's smirk when he heard the translation, the dictator also recognized the diplomatic doubletalk. Both knew exactly what the annual Foal Eagle/Key Resolve exercises were about. The naval parade of strength a clear demonstration of America's intent to crush Sung should he be so foolish to engage in open conflict. The PROK regime may have extended a first tentative gesture of reconciliation toward the West, but clearly, Sung wanted it done on his terms.

It was all about saving face. Although rattling the nuclear threat had a hollow ring these days and the man knew it, his ballistic missile posture more credible. Kim Jong-il may have been ready to see his country immolated for the sake of some ideological purity, but the men who held power now were not so ready to throw away the gains they had made and now enjoyed simply to prove a philosophical point. Acceding to Sung's unreasonable demands would also make America appear weak, opening itself to more debilitating claims. What was required here was firm determination to act. Sung was buying and America was selling—at its price. If pushed too far, Tanner could always walk away and everybody knew it. Just as everybody knew he wouldn't, but he might, and that's what kept Sung in line.

He gazed unwaveringly at the Supreme Leader, reminding him he now pushed too hard, then cleared his throat.

"As you know, sir, Key Resolve is scheduled to commence in three days' time, as communicated to your National Defense Commission. Its deployment readiness is too advanced for the exercise to be rescinded. However, in anticipation of successfully concluding our introductory talks, the scope of the exercise has been scaled down to five days only. In recognition of the mutual value of our discussions, I want to announce that normal air operations, supported by our carrier, USS *George Washington*, have also been canceled. The ship will remain in port."

Sung's eyes flickered briefly in surprise. After a moment, he spoke rapidly.

"That is indeed gratifying, Mr. Secretary," the interpreter declared. "Much remains to be resolved between us, but your visit here is a first encouraging step. When I hear the United States Congress announce that America is lifting its economic sanctions and is prepared to normalize trade, encouraging other countries to do likewise, we shall begin immediate shutdown of our uranium reprocessing and plutonium extraction facilities as a prelude to converting our reactors to purely civilian use. We shall also invite the International Atomic Energy Agency to monitor the shutdown and conversion program. We're a peaceful nation and have no need of nuclear weapons—provided our security interests are not threatened."

Tanner allowed himself a small smile, which Sung saw. The bastard could afford to be magnanimous, since he already held more than sixty nuclear warheads. At least that's what CIA's intelligence claimed. Whether he could launch them or not a moot point, which nobody wanted tested. Still, dismantling their uranium reprocessing and enrichment plants would be a positive move. It would also ease the enormous economic drain the facility imposed on the country. Regardless how distasteful it might be to Sung, the bean counters and financiers were slowly taking over, as they had already done elsewhere in the world.

"The President will be delighted to hear this, Mr. Chairman. You understand, resolution of your dispute over the Northern Limit Line might take some time to settle."

Sung gave a dismissive gesture. "Although an important issue to be addressed in the future, it should not stand as an impediment to fostering a growing cooperation between our respective countries and the world community at large."

"I appreciate your patience, sir. On the matter of your arms sales to Iran, Syria, and Yemen, this is something that troubles us greatly. These countries are open supporters of terrorism and declared enemies of the United States. Curtailing this trade would do much to ease a worldwide problem."

When the Supreme Leader heard the translation, he leaned back and laughed. "Mr. Tanner, I'm willing to engage in meaningful discussions, but I would appreciate if we dispensed with hypocrisy. Everybody is selling arms to everybody else. It's merely business and a valuable source of revenue for us, as it is for America." Sung gave a disarming smile. "Besides, after that unfortunate incident with Israel, not something a supposed ally would do, I thought Iran was now your friend." He stood up and gave a small nod. "I look forward to extending our conversation to mutual gain this afternoon, Mr. Secretary." He stood up and marched out without giving Tanner a chance to respond or stand. The interpreter hastily scrambled after him.

Tanner watched him leave, having to admire the wily devil. Everything Sung said was blatantly true. He had advised Walters not to raise the issue of arms sales, but the president remained adamant. Still young, the man had a lot to learn. What worried him was the president's predilection for running foreign policy initiatives on his own, bypassing the State Department. He didn't mind initiative, but it needed to be tempered by facts and firm guidance—his guidance—something Walters did not always welcome. Tanner had to give the man his due, though. With a flair for international politics, Walters had shown that he could hold his own with prickly foreign heads of state. The way he handled Sharron Ibrahim last year during the Valero crisis had been an exemplary display of diplomacy. Walters always cut to the heart of any issue, Tanner had to give him that.

When the door closed after Sung and the interpreter, the Minister of Public Security shifted his considerable bulk in his chair and smiled warmly. Clearly, he did not share the hardships of his countrymen. The atmosphere in the room immediately became lighter simply due to the body language of the two ministers.

"I'm afraid, sir, the Supreme Leader will not be joining us for lunch. He has pressing matters of state requiring his attention. However, I am at your disposal and look forward to continuing our talks this afternoon," he said in soft English with barely an accent, his attitude polite, but friendly. "Which includes the limitation of our weapons trade. You must understand, sir, it's a sensitive topic for us, but in this case, I must side with the Supreme Leader."

"I acknowledge that America is not a shining example of restraint, Mr. Minister," Tanner said ruefully, "and neither is the rest of the developed world, but actively helping Iran upgrade its missile technology is seen as going a little too far."

Kham Chang-uk grinned and shrugged. "You help your friends, do you not? But this is something for us to discuss later, yes?"

The Foreign Minister also smiled from his seat. "Indeed, we have much to go over, and it's fortuitous you're here at this time."

The talks so far were guarded and at times tense, but Sung Kang-dae seemed genuinely keen to get America onside, from necessity rather than choice, Tanner reminded himself, with a large helping of self-interest thrown in. It did not matter what his real objectives were. With Kim Jong-il out of the way, and having ousted the former dictator's youngest son as successor, Sung was unfettered by his predecessor's repressive policies. Those who objected were ruthlessly removed. The man did not want to embrace any version of democracy. He did not crawl cap in hand to China nor Russia either, which the American administration was gratified to see. Hardliner or not, he was not blind to the desperate plight of his people and the sorry state of the country. A case of simple expediency, not a change of ideology. Feed the people and stay in power.

It was up to the United States to work within those parameters. Tanner had bet his chips and called on Sung Kang-dae to show his hand or fold. As he looked at the two men across the table, he got the unmistakable impression that he had missed something. They looked smug and pleased with themselves.

"I appreciate the opportunity, gentlemen, to make the first tentative steps that might lead to a more normalized relationship between us."

Kham laughed openly. "We're alone now, Mr. Tanner. You can dispense with diplomacy, sir."

Tanner stared at the Minister of Public Security. "I'm not sure I understand," he said cautiously. What was he missing?

Kham shot a quick glance at the door. "Our plans are almost complete and we'll make our move soon. Once Sung is out of the way, we can talk seriously."

Tanner felt himself stiffen and his diplomatic mask came down with a clang. "You're planning to depose the Supreme Leader?"

"Don't act surprised, Mr. Tanner. Mr. Zardwovsky must have kept you updated."

Tanner fought to keep dismay showing on his face. After achieving what he thought was solid progress with Sung, he now faced a palace revolt that threatened to undo everything. A revolt apparently supported, and perhaps even orchestrated, by the CIA, regardless of any perceived benefits such a revolt might realize. Did the president keep something from him again, or was this another one of Raymond Grant's initiatives? Either way the implications were staggering.

"Well—"

"It's simple, really. We stood with Sung Kang-dae to unseat Kim Jong-un and his collective leadership. The young man was out of his depth. We hoped Sung would usher in real progressive change, but nothing substantive has happened. He used this time to consolidate his own position. If we're to avert national disaster, and perhaps open conflict with our southern neighbor and your country, we must act now before Sung becomes too entrenched."

His mind whirling, Tanner pulled himself together. "And who will replace him? You?"

Kham laughed with genuine mirth. "I don't aspire that high, sir. We intend that Premier Tung In-san be the Supreme Leader. This, after all, is what America wants and why you're here, is it not?"

"Yes, it is," Tanner mused slowly, not sure if the Korean was wise to voice blatant treason so openly. He glanced meaningfully around the room and Kham grinned.

"Rest assured, sir. The room is 'clean', to use your vernacular. No one can overhear us. There are certain privileges to my position."

Tanner believed him. He gathered his composure and gave a weak smile. "I am glad to hear that. I would hate to have our conversation, ah, misinterpreted?"

Kham smiled knowingly. "We cannot afford misunderstandings or ambiguities. Rest assured, the Reconnaissance General Bureau men will not be barging in on us. Now, shall we have lunch? We won't be interrupted and you'll be able to talk freely."

Confronted with another and extremely unwelcome dimension to his visit, Tanner found his appetite suddenly gone.

* * *

Barely touching the horizon, the bloated sun colored the wispy clouds with red and orange fire. Clearing the security barrier, the official cavalcade of four cars sped along the apron toward the sleek, specially modified blue and white Air Force Two, a military version of the Boeing 757 with a range of 6,900 miles, waiting on the taxiway, easily able to make the return Pyongyang to Seattle leg of almost 5,200 miles in one hop. He would have to make a refueling stop at the Lewis-McChord AFB before continuing on to Washington, he didn't mind that too much. He would be home.

Armed guards stood around the large aircraft, facing out, watchful for any disturbance. Given the nature of the North Korean society, Tanner did not expect placard-waving protesters, glad to see the aircraft as a symbol of home soil. He'd had enough of oily diplomacy, veiled threats and starched smiles. The slightly overdone traditional *kim chee* dish at lunch probably didn't help either. A sample of Kham Chang-uk's oblique humor?

A light sprinkle of snow covered the open tarmac, the crystals glittering in the fading light. Nobody seemed to mind it.

Preceded by a security car, his limousine stopped beside the ramp and an officer hurried to open the door. He stood at attention and saluted. Tanner climbed out and nodded to the man. A pervasive smell of jet fuel hung in the air and he could hear engines spool up. A small passenger jet roared down the longer active runway, lifted and climbed into settling darkness, booming as it disappeared. The low Sunan International Airport terminal brightly lit, an island of modern architecture in a sea of squalor and abject poverty.

When driven from Sung Kang-dae's residential palace on the outskirts of Pyongyang, what he had seen of the neat city impressed him, but he saw only what they wanted him to see. Then again, Tanner didn't need a tour. He already knew what North Korea looked like from endless briefs.

Kham stepped out of his black limousine and strode toward him. Tanner extended his hand and smiled warmly. He had come to have a lot of respect for the manipulative minister and hoped their paths would cross again. Kham gripped it firmly and grinned.

"I wish you a safe return to America, Mr. Secretary." He

glanced at Cromatry. "And you too, sir."

"I found our talks most productive, Mr. Minister," Tanner said wryly, not glancing at the official photographers crowding around them.

"Until our next meeting, Mr. Secretary," Kham said with a broad smile.

Tanner turned and began walking along the red carpet leading to the ramp. The honor guard along both sides snapped to and presented arms. Tanner climbed the steps and paused at the hatch a story above the ground. He turned and waved, waited for the camera flashes to die down, then entered the aircraft.

Colonel Grissom saluted. "Welcome aboard, sir."

"It's good to be aboard, Bill. Are we cleared to go?"

"Just give the word, sir."

"Then let's get out of here," Tanner told the pilot and turned to Cromatry. "Come with me."

They walked down the hard gray carpet while a rating closed the door and buttoned up. Tanner got to his private office and heard the engines spool up. Inside, he moved behind the desk, lowered himself into a soft leather seat and sighed.

"God, I'm glad that's over, but we got what we came for, I think."

"A bit more than that, wouldn't you say?" Cromatry said wearing a whimsical look as he stood before the desk.

"You can say that again. If I heard Kham right, we have got a new can of worms."

"You heard him right. He's talking about a coup and the CIA is in on it."

"Sounds like it, doesn't it," Tanner agreed.

"I can't believe it."

"As much as I hate Sung and what the little turd stands for, at least we've been working with him and making some progress. He is a known quantity, but this? The mess could blow the lid off the President's entire diplomatic initiative. Remember what happened when they deposed Kim Jong-un? It took us a year to put in new feelers to Sung. I don't relish the idea of doing it all over with Kham."

"He seems more receptive to enter into a reciprocal dialogue with us than Sung," Cromatry pointed out reasonably.

"Perhaps, but we don't know what he wants."

"From what Kham hinted, Grant apparently knows what he wants."

Tanner ground his teeth in frustration. "You know what really sucks? The idea that Grant sought fit to enter into a diplomatic deal with Kham. Who the hell is running our foreign policy around here? Me or the CIA?"

"Lending a helping hand, perhaps?"

"But under my direction, damn it!"

"I'm happy for you to handle it. I for one won't mourn if Sung is popped off."

Tanner snorted. "If it were that simple, I would give Kham a loaded gun myself, but it isn't. If he goes ahead and China finds out that we've been behind it, there'll be a stink."

"You'll have to talk to Grant."

"For sure, and I looked like a fool not knowing what the hell he was on about." Tanner raised a warning finger. "Not a word to anybody about this, okay?"

"You got it, but—"

"I'll talk to the President. Prepare a summary of the last two days and we'll go over it after dinner, only on the substance of our agenda, nothing else. One hint…"

Cromatry grinned and paused, one hand on the door handle. "The boss would have told you about the CIA if he knew, wouldn't he?"

Tanner thought it over. Walters liked to conduct some elements of his foreign policy himself, but on something this big?

He could not accept the possibility the president would be running a double agenda without him. Walters simply wasn't experienced or sneaky enough, although he picked up things fast. Perhaps too fast. That's what Washington did to people. It made them manipulative and devious.

"I would like to think so."

"Well, I'm glad I'm not in your shoes," Cromatry said and walked out.

The C-32 bumped slowly along the taxiway as it headed toward the start of the runway.

Tanner stared at the closed door, then shook his head. A good man, Cromatry tended to treat his duties with a marked lack of gravity. Then again, a healthy dose of cynicism might be the thing to maintain perspective. Right now, cynicism wasn't a bad way to look at things. Cromatry ran his department well, which made up for a lot of sins. Tanner would simply have to factor in this latest development and prepare policy options for the president like he always did. The problem in this case, he was short of options.

Damn the CIA, and damn Grant.

On days like these, and there were far too many of them lately, he wondered why he allowed himself to be talked into taking this job. After his stint as ambassador to China in the previous administration, he had been shocked that Walters wanted him, a staunch Republican, to be his Secretary of State. Nevertheless, the appointment gave him a certain sardonic glow of satisfaction knowing the president couldn't find anyone in his party to do the job.

He served his country and that had to cut across party lines, didn't it?

Tanner leaned across the desk and stared at four small wall clocks showing world times: three-thirty in the morning in Washington. If he rang the president now, it would only make him grumpy and yelled at. Anyway, Walters could do nothing in the middle of the night.

The aircraft turned, lined up, roared down the runway, and Tanner was pressed into his seat. Moments later, the nose lifted and the lumbering jet staggered into the sky.

Meeting the Supreme Leader in his palatial residence had been a historic first, given the prickly relations between the two countries. Tanner did not need to study Sung's ideology. The man was a hard communist and nothing would change him, but that also provided a degree of predictability. Of far more value, the meetings during the last two days gave him an insight into the man's psychology and character. Clearly ruthless to have clawed his way to ultimate power, Sung nevertheless suffered from a disease that afflicted all dictators—insecurity. Although not always true, most totalitarian regimes were either overthrown by a popular uprising or toppled by internal treachery. Sung's overtures to America were blatantly designed to forestall both possibilities, something Tanner used to his advantage.

Lavishing twenty-six percent of its national budget on the military, and an unknown amount on its nuclear and missile programs, simply wasn't sustainable, not when the gross domestic revenue and international trade continued to shrink and could not recover because of ongoing sanctions. Not that simple, of course, but he hadn't allowed the little bastard to intimidate him with bluster. Tanner's instructions from the president were clear. If North Korea wanted economic help and opening up markets, they would need to take demonstrable action to disarm. Previous administrations tried appeasement and gotten nowhere for their pains. Actually, he helped design the current administration's position policy, bringing the young president around to his point of view after several heated discussions. Thankfully, Walters was a man prepared to take unpalatable advice after having his naïve idealism blunted by a dose of realpolitik.

America no longer sought to automatically support questionable governments merely on the basis that they might have neighboring totalitarian or religious regimes, often one and the same thing. He only needed to look at Pakistan as a prime example of such a failed policy. Having created the Taliban, it had now turned on its creators, somewhat ironic and appropriate in his view.

After doing some paperwork, he showered, changed and felt half-human again. He dined alone, not in the mood for Cromatry's genial banter, and he had a lot to think about. He caught up with the Under Secretary after a glass of nice red Burgundy and they went over the economics side of their visit. At least that part went well and Sung appreciated an increase in American food aid without any of the usually attached strings. By the time he got back into his office, it was eight a.m. in DC. No use putting it off any longer and he really didn't want to.

He sighed and picked up the white phone.

"Yes, sir?" the rating from the comms bay answered.

"Get me the President."

"Yes, sir!"

After a couple of minutes the phone gave a trill and Tanner picked up.

"I have your line, sir."

"Thank you." Tanner replaced the receiver and picked up the brown encrypted secure phone. "Mr. President?"

"Larry, you know what time it is here?" Samuel Walters demanded bitterly. "This couldn't wait until I've had at least my second cup of coffee?"

Tanner broke into a smile. "It couldn't."

"You're spoiling my breakfast and making me upset. That's not a good way for me to start my day. My doctor tells me I should take up stress management. You're not helping, you know. Okay, what is it? Or did you call just to irritate me?"

Tanner broke into a smile. The president allowed him a lot of liberty, but he couldn't push it too far. "Sir, we have a situation."

Chapter Two

President Samuel Walters crossed his legs, chewed his lower lip, and leaned back against the striped beige sofa positioned next to the great seal. Impeccably dressed in a dark blue suit, white shirt and yellow tie, black hair neatly combed back, he knew he presented an image of a confident executive, which his chief of staff approved. If you cannot have substance, at least have the image, Cottard always drummed into him during the election campaign. That was over two years ago, a lifetime away. The unfortunate fact for his Republican opponents, this Democratic Party presidential nominee had both.

Walters remembered as though it were yesterday, Manfred Cottard walking into his office to announce that in his opinion, the senator from Michigan should run for the White House. Walters was so startled, he dropped his pen and gaped at the political strategist, completely taken aback by the preposterous idea. At fifty and barely into his second term, his worry was getting reelected to the Senate, not claw for the presidency. Besides, he didn't have the socially approved background, business connections or old money support necessary to last through the primaries, let alone a six-month slugfest once the nominees were announced.

Cottard had not been fazed at all. He merely wanted to know whether Walters wanted to translate his political agenda off the Senate floor and make it national policy, a vision for a different America. With the sales pitch done, Walters became convinced and willing to test the political landscape by doing some sample polls. Cottard shook his head, leaned forward and stared hard at him. 'You're either committed or you're not,' he said. He had no time for weathervane politicians.

Walters regretted listening to the driven man scores of times since, but he got the White House. In hindsight, a questionable prize at best. Almost halfway into his term, he already soured fighting partisan politics.

"What's next?" he demanded from his chunky, powerful chief of staff. In a purely unconscious gesture, Cottard rubbed the underside of his nose with his right thumb.

"The Foreign Ownership Bill—"

"I want that bill in the House tomorrow, Manfred. Tomorrow, not next month."

"We're about through editing it," Cottard said soothingly, but Walters ignored his slightly condescending attitude.

"If someone wants to sell off his twenty million-dollar plus farm or factory, from now on, he'll have to get federal approval. That goes double for foreign investments in our financial institutions."

"We live in a free country, Mr. President. It's hard to tell someone not to seek overseas investors or sell when he's getting a good price."

"And this obsession with short-term profits is killing us," Walters grumbled sourly. "China is waging economic war against us and it's time we fired a few shots back. If we're not careful, we'll wake up one day and find somebody else in control of our economy."

Manfred Cottard shrugged. "It's simply free market forces sorting themselves out."

Walters stared hard at his chief of staff. "That's crap and you know it. While those Harvard idea balloons plot their graphs, the United States is losing its manufacturing capability and vital skill base, becoming reliant on the likes of China, our enemy, political and economic. Their point would be valid if the world was a single integrated market system, but it isn't. Economic theory doesn't take into account national strategic interest."

Cottard smiled and raised both hands in surrender. "You won't get an argument from me, but the Republicans and the southern states will howl if you go ahead with this, pointing out to more government red tape and intrusive meddling in private affairs."

"Let them howl. Besides, the bill provides tax offsets for compliance. You only have to look at what those Chinese bastards have done to our rare earths industry. They bought us up and once they gained control, they shut down the plants, forcing us to buy the rare earths from them on their terms and prices. They've now introduced export quotas, for Chrissake!"

"Our companies are waking up to what's going on, Mr. President. We bought a lot of those mines back and the processing plants are coming back online," Cottard said with quiet authority.

"But it's not happening quickly enough. I want that bill in force before we sell off the whole damn country. I tell you, Manfred, the next war will be over energy, like the one we fought with Iraq. Water and food scarcity will be another motivator."

"If we do have a war, I hope we don't hash it up like we did there or in Afghanistan," Cottard said dryly and Walters chuckled, allowing the tension to ease out of him. It wouldn't do anybody any good if he worked himself into a coronary.

"Yeah. Not our finest hour, was it? It cost us almost two trillion dollars, and for what? Simply to bolster our military-industrial complex. The Taliban are back and they've taken Pakistan as well. Instead of fixing things up, we destabilized the entire region, perhaps irretrievably. Anyway, we're out of there now and those places will have to make it on their own."

"You mean clean up the mess we made for them?"

"True, but Bush will have to wear that legacy. I won't have the Republicans push it in front of my door, for sure as hell, I'll not send our troops to fight guerilla warfare terrorism again."

"Especially since the Republicans created the mess to begin with."

"You got that right. If we have to fight, we'll let the SEALs or the Delta Force do it one-on-one. Make it personal, in your face, I say. Let's not forget the global financial meltdown while we're at it, which the GOP caused by deregulating oversight controls and then blamed the resulting mess on us. Bastards! We managed to slowly climb out of that hole, and I don't want them shoving us back into it by any talk of blocking this bill."

"I don't think that will happen, Mr. President. They're still cowering after your handling of Israel's sabotage of the Valero Texas City Refinery. With a seventy-two percent job approval rating, you're riding high."

"That rating won't last and we both know it. It's got to slide sometime. I'll make a decision, or fail to make one, which will piss somebody off, and those numbers will disappear. However, while I *am* riding high, I want to push our legislative agenda for all it's worth. Besides, we campaigned on energy, national resource security policy platforms and cutting the deficit. It is time that we delivered."

"I'm not arguing, Mr. President, and last year's civil service and military budget cuts were substantial."

"It cost me some popularity with the Joint Chiefs, but it was time we injected some rationality into weapons procurement. We've got to stop wasting billions on duplicate research and development. We must push standardization into our programs."

"I agree, but it also cost you popularity with Congressmen who have major military contractors in their districts," Cottard said dryly.

"Nothing but pork barreling, plain and simple, and the voters saw through it. Get that bill moving, Manfred."

"It will be on the floor tomorrow."

Walters studied his chief of staff. A profoundly insightful political strategist and tactician, Cottard tended to be overprotective sometimes. The idea of risking the presidency by doing what was in the national interest didn't always sit too well with the chief of staff. Cottard claimed that you had to hang onto power, no matter what. Getting kicked out of office wasn't going to achieve anything. That's where Walters drew the line. The whole idea of seeking office was to pursue a legislative agenda he campaigned on, and if the Republicans blocked him, the people should understand where the blame lay.

"See to it."

"I take it you also want to push the Strategic Energy Initiative Bill just as hard? You'll have the Natural Resources Defense Council and a lot of environmentalists lining up against you."

"Screw them! We've been coddling those groups for too long. If they had it their way, they'd turn all the farms into prairies and reforest the rest. We'd be living in zoos, not the wildlife. Oil, coal, and uranium will continue to be our primary energy resources for at least the next fifty years. Especially oil, and not only because we need gas to fill Joe Citizen's car. We have strategic industries dependent on the stuff. I support renewable energy initiatives, but they can't carry the base load, not now, and certainly not at an affordable price."

"The greens lobby won't see it that way."

"Are they going to pay my electricity bill if we shut down coal-generated power stations? Are they going to pay for replacement plants? And what about the impact on support industries using that power, which incidentally maintains our standard of living, and theirs? Those groups are good at protest marches and grand visions, but very short on practical application; all the while enjoying the benefits our supposed profligate economy brings them. Hypocrites!"

"You cannot ignore them, Mr. President. Like it or not, the environmental lobby represents a significant voting block you cannot afford to alienate."

"I know." Walters looked gloomy and sighed. "Damnation! I don't want to turn Alaska into a polluted wasteland, but we're nuts not to exploit what's under there while subjecting ourselves to OPEC's fickle moods. You told me yourself a number of times. Much of our foreign policy has been compromised by having to cater to Arab demands simply to secure our oil supply. Well, that's going to stop, and bringing Iran onside is an important first step. I want the SEI bill to go through."

"Yes, sir, but we aren't doing too badly, and the balance has shifted since we became a major shale oil producer. The General Electric thorium reactor at Sunol has been running for nine months now without problems. The concept has proven sound and justifies further Congressional support."

"That should plug the greenies for a while," Walters grumbled. "Why is it that California can do stuff while the other states are digging in? We should build thorium rectors everywhere."

"Two more are under construction, but these things take time."

"Except that we haven't got time. India and China aren't dragging their heels with their thorium programs."

"They don't have our system of government, sir," Cottard said dryly. "Are you still planning to revoke China's most favored trading nation status? I have to tell you, we'll be heading for trouble, economically and diplomatically."

The president set his mouth and ran his hand through his hair. "We'll wear it, but they've gone too far. They're refusing to float their currency, pegging it against the dollar, despite rulings by the WTO. That single move gave them an unbeatable balance of trade advantage. Not only against us, but the Europeans and everybody else. You've read the briefs. They want to establish a basket of currencies for trade in oil and commodities, designed to displace the dollar and weaken us further. If that weren't enough, they're conducting a cyber war against every level of our government, military, and corporations. With three trillion in reserves, they're also manipulating the international bond market. You expect me to smile and give them a well done?

"We shifted our industries to them in search of quick profits, which gave them instant access to sophisticated technologies, and they're copying it in blatant disregard of intellectual property laws. We lifted them out of the nineteenth century into the twenty-first without having to pay the necessary R & D along the way and the bastards are now shafting us. Why go into a shooting war when you can win the economic one. You have to admire their pragmatism, though. Wasn't it Carl Marx who said the West would give communism the tools to defeat us?"

"And we've been doing it," Cottard agreed with a wry smile and rubbed his nose.

"Marx must be laughing in his grave, as are the Chinese. It's an initiative the Vice President is passionate about and one I happen to agree with. Get those bills moving, Manfred."

"Yes, sir." The White House chief of staff locked his fingers and frowned. "Mr. President, the UN is voting tonight to re-impose sanctions on Iran because they kicked out the IAEA inspectors, and we still haven't told Prichard what to do."

Walters groaned and his shoulders sagged. "Why the hell did they have to pop off that underground nuke? It almost derailed everything."

"President Hamadee Al Zerkhani may have been willing to open bilateral talks, but it didn't mean he trusted us," Cottard said softly. "And the Ayatollahs could have told him to do it. Don't forget, they are the real power over there."

"Mmm. Maybe I *should* have bombed his ass after the Valero incident. The wrong guy would have been hit, but it would have removed a destabilizing threat."

"You don't mean that. Israel represented a regional threat, and what's more, they still do. Every time an Arab country upgrades its military, Israel wants to nuke them. Abdon Sayar's Labor and Kadima Party coalition is still holding and they're keeping their promise to clear out settlements from the occupied territories, which has eased tensions with the Palestinians, but it doesn't mean the right-wing zealots in the Knesset, or his generals, are happy. Should his government fall, we could still see a return to a more militant posture."

"And we'd be facing a nightmare," Walters said with a scowl.

"Open warfare at least. They might not go as far as to revoke Palestinian statehood, but they could finish what Mossad failed to do with Valero and strike at Iran's nuclear installations themselves. Iran knows it. You also know why they carried out that test. They wanted to let everybody know that security is still their primary priority, and a nuclear deterrent will achieve it. You didn't actually expect to change centuries of history with a couple of sympathetic talks with Al Zerkhani, did you? If you want to know what I think, Israel is just as radical as the Ayatollahs. More so. If there is a war in the Middle East, it won't be started by Iran."

Walters stared at his chief of staff. "You always did have good political sense. I sometimes wonder whether you would have made a better Secretary of State."

Cottard gave a lopsided smile. "Tanner is doing a great job for you there. I like my current work well enough not to want to change. Seriously, sir, you should continue supporting Iran. While everybody is focused on Israel's protests, don't forget Pakistan. They're a much more credible regional threat now that we're out of Afghanistan."

"I know. The Taliban have infiltrated the government and they've become more militant and extremist. As a Shi'ia state, I can see why Iran views Pakistan's nuclear-armed Sunni regime a far more potent strategic threat than Israel."

"There you are. Let the Israeli lobby pound the table. They won't be getting much traction."

"I shudder to think what India is making of all this."

"Worried as hell, I'd imagine. Those incursions into the Kashmir last year didn't help either."

Walters exhaled loudly and wagged a finger. "No matter what we do, the Republicans will still look to make cheap mileage out of it. I guess this is where my approval rating will take its first hit. Tell our UN Ambassador to veto any move to impose sanctions on Iran. Tell him to drop a subtle hint to Israel to tone down their hawkish rhetoric. While you're at it, I want Congress to announce the lifting of sanctions against North Korea. Better give Granger a heads-up, but he's to keep his trap shut until after Prichard has had his say."

Cottard grimaced. "It would be kinder not to tell the poor man anything. He's got to stand in front of the press gaggle pretending ignorance. They'll give him hell once they find out he's been holding out on them."

"Granger is a good Press Secretary and a tough man. He'll handle it," Walters said without any outward sympathy and rubbed his eyes. After a moment, he leaned back. He could talk to Cathy about everything, but some things she wouldn't understand fully, and there was also a question of security. It would be unfair to unburden himself completely to her. Even though his chief of staff was a friend, there were limits. After all, he *was* the president, but he needed to talk to somebody. Slightly ashamed at this display of weakness, he pulled himself up.

Stop whining. You knew what you were getting into. Instead of feeling sorry for yourself, do something about it.

Yeah, shoot the House majority leader. Although a Democrat, the man could be a cranky, whining obstructionist.

"You know, Manfred, sometimes I think there is a lot to be said for an isolationist policy. Everybody looks at us to solve the world's problems while figuring angles to stab us. If that weren't bad enough, our partisan party system isn't helping any either. We're ruining our country on misguided ideology."

Cottard remained silent for a moment, clearly aware of a change in Walters' mood. "I wouldn't want to live under a Chinese system, but you've got to admire their determination and pragmatism. Sometimes there are advantages to a totalitarian regime. Especially when you want to get things done."

"It seems to be working for them, all right," Walters said moodily. "Still, for all the progress they've made, I can't help feeling that it's all window dressing. They improved the economic lot of their people simply to keep them quiet while they pursue their policy of globalization."

Cottard snorted. "Isn't that what we've been doing? Sam, you cannot afford to get swept up trying to right the world, or you'll end up losing perspective. You need to focus on protecting America and its interests first and foremost. If that means alienating some country or interest group, so be it."

"Better be blamed for doing something than sitting on your hands moaning about it. Is that it?"

"The people put you into the Oval Office to make decisions, not win friends," Cottard said firmly. "Sometimes you go a bit far, but at least you're sticking to your policies."

Before Walters could reply, a knock came and the door to the outer office opened. A middle-aged woman, her peppery hair tied up in a bun, stepped into the Oval Office, her hand on the door handle.

"Excuse me, Mr. President. The Secretary of State is here, and Admiral Stone is on his way."

"Thank you, Unice," Walters said and gave Cottard a meaningful look that said their conversation would be taken up later. "Show the Secretary in."

"Admiral Grant will be here in ten minutes, sir."

"Good…Come in, Larry." Walters motioned to the tall man waiting outside. "Help yourself to a cup."

Larry Tanner ambled in and sat beside Cottard after giving the chief of staff a polite nod.

"There's snow outside," he complained stiffly as he poured himself a cup. He stirred in a sugar cube and took a sip.

"You'll live," Walters murmured indifferently. He had bigger issues to worry about than snow in Lafayette Square. "Wasn't there snow in Pyongyang?"

"How was the flight?" Cottard queried with his usual amused smile. "Apart from being long," he added to forestall a predictable rejoinder.

Tanner gave him a pointed look. "It *was* a long flight, and it gave me time to think, something I would encourage you to do," he said and faced the president. "Have you spoken to Grant yet?"

"He'll be here in a minute. We'll have his version of the story then," Walters said.

"I hope you'll fire his ass. He undermined our entire North Korean initiative just as we might be getting Sung Kang-dae onside."

"Sung only has one side—his. Getting rid of him could simplify not only our position, but theirs as well. However desirable the outcome, I have to agree that Grant appears to have gone way beyond his brief."

"He was told to provide an intelligence assessment of their regime, not orchestrate a coup," Tanner said bitterly.

After another knock, the door opened and Vice Admiral Graham Stone walked in.

"Sorry for the delay, Mr. President. You caught me reading an interesting article in a North Korean newspaper about Tanner's visit."

Walters smiled at the formidable presence of his National Security Advisor. The way the retired admiral handled his job sometimes raised eyebrows, but his slant on the international political landscape, coupled with awesome knowledge of all things military, made him invaluable. He and Tanner complemented each other well.

"Anything we should know?"

"The official party line is to go soft on America," Stone said as he eased his bulk down. "Sung might actually deliver on his rhetoric." He glanced at Tanner. "You read it the same way?"

"It could all fall apart if Kham Chang-uk messes things up," the Secretary of State snapped, clearly still feeling the miles.

"Gentlemen! If you want to brawl, do it outside," Walters said firmly. "But Graham is right, Larry. How do you read Kham? If he's going to jump, we'll need to know how to react."

Tanner crossed his arms in his lap. "You want to know my assessment? The Minister of Public Security is young, smart, ambitious, and knows his country won't survive if they keep following Kim Jong-il's modified Juche doctrine, which Sung is determined to do."

"Political independence, economic and military self-sufficiency, Mr. President. Within the framework of army first," Stone added quietly and Walters nodded.

"I got the gist, Graham. So, he and—"

"The Foreign Minister, Yeum Ling-chol," Tanner supplied.

"—the Foreign Minister," Walters said, neatly sidestepping the jawbreaker name, "wants to seize the initiative before Sung becomes too entrenched and moves in on them. Tung In-san wouldn't be a bad choice for a Supreme Leader, and we might get more out of him than Sung is promising now. Anything special I need to know about him?"

"Tung is the WPK Central Committee General Secretary and a compatriot of Kham and Yeum. They all belong to the reformist faction and only sided with Sung to topple Kim Jong-un and the ruling committee because the system wasn't working."

"Like that's new." Stone snorted and Tanner shot him a cold look.

"Sung has tolerated minimal economic liberalization, but he doesn't want to rock the boat too much for fear of undermining the power of the generals loyal to him. Army first, as Graham said. Even so, some of them already consider he's gone too far and wants to clamp down. Most of them are old school and don't enjoy the prospect of losing power if a more progressive regime steps in."

"Which makes the position of the reformists somewhat precarious," Walters mused.

"You got that right," Tanner agreed. "Getting into bed with Kham Chang-uk and the others was a shotgun marriage for Sung, which he will want to dissolve sooner rather than later. He must see Kham as a threat. Yes, I think Kham will jump."

"Which way are the reformists leaning?"

Stone cleared his throat. "They're primarily pro-Chinese, Mr. President. They want to maintain friendly relations with the Russians, but China has the money and is a growing power."

"Can't say I blame them. When exactly are they planning to pull off this takeover, Larry?" Walters demanded.

Tanner shrugged. "They didn't say, but I got a very strong impression it won't be long. If they wait, Sung is bound to clean them up."

"Sung is giving us almost everything we're asking for, and it could all be undone by Grant's version of policy making. Even if Kham and his faction succeed, it will generate a period of instability that could undo the lot if China decides to step in."

"I concur. It would take some time for things to settle down and dialogue to reopen."

"Let's say everything does go smoothly, there is no guarantee the new regime will remain friendly to us once this Tung In-san character takes over, regardless of what Kham might have told you now. Like you said, China has the money and they wouldn't want one of their satellites aligning itself even partially with the West."

Tanner inclined his head in acknowledgment and shrugged. "True, Mr. President, but a peaceful Korean peninsula would be to their advantage as well. They might be more pragmatic than we give them credit. Kham is a straight shooter and didn't walk away from his China leanings. He simply doesn't want to antagonize a powerful neighbor, and he cannot irritate China too much by being radical. Besides, working with the West wouldn't be a betrayal of their Juche doctrine. You only need to look at China to see what a more market-oriented outlook has done for them.

Mao's philosophy didn't work, so they changed it. We can only hope that Tung In-san will adopt the same pragmatism—if he gets in."

Walters stared at the tall man, always impeccably dressed, thick brown hair neatly combed, he figured he hadn't made a bad bargain with his SecState. The eyes captured attention; icy blue, they gave very little away and saw everything. Tanner's competence obvious, if sometimes irritating, making him wish that he'd left the man in Beijing where he could continue annoying the Chinese.

"I'm like a donkey caught between two bales of hay," he said with heavy irony. "Sung may be a son of a bitch, but at least he is a known quantity."

Another knock caused heads to turn.

"Admiral Grant is here, sir," Unice announced.

"Show him in," Walters said decisively, stood up and sat down behind his *Resolute* desk, facing everybody. The significance of the move not lost on Cottard and Tanner as they exchanged glances. Grant wasn't going to enjoy this encounter.

The sixty-four-year-old vice admiral marched in like he boarded a battleship. He paused when he saw the Oval Office full and looked at Walters.

"You wanted to see me, Mr. President?"

"I did. Take a seat."

Grant cautiously sat beside Stone, his guarded look made it clear he was not among friends.

"I trust you had a productive trip, Mr. Secretary?"

"Very," Tanner said coldly, his dislike obvious.

Walters pulled back his shoulders. "I won't beat about the bush, Admiral. So I'll ask this straight out. Who told you to initiate a power spill in the North Korean leadership?"

Grant blanched and patted the back of his head, clearly gathering his thoughts.

"Mr. President, your brief—"

"Was to gather intelligence for me. Nothing else! I make the decision how that intelligence is used, not you."

Grant lifted his chin and his eyes flared. "Stone ordered Zardwovsky to penetrate every level of their government and the National Defense Commission. It also meant getting inside the Supreme People's Assembly. Inevitably, along the way we would come across dissenting ministers."

"But no one gave you the authority to organize a coup!" Walters snapped.

"We didn't organize anything, sir. Least of all a coup."

"Then where did Kham Chang-uk and Yeum Ling-chol get the money to buy supporters for one?"

"We helped strengthen their faction, Mr. President. We bought them, I don't deny it, but we haven't financed a takeover."

"That's not what Kham told me, Raymond," Tanner said softly. "It seems Zardwovsky didn't think so either."

"If he orchestrated something, he acted outside my authority and I shall take appropriate steps," Grant declared and puffed himself up with indignation.

"I find it difficult to believe as CIA Director, you wouldn't know what one of your most senior executives was doing," Walters told him bluntly. "The money involved didn't come from petty cash. You must have known."

"Mr. President, I can assure you—"

"If you didn't know, it doesn't say much for your leadership of a vital national security agency, Admiral. In fact, it tells me you lack the necessary character and administrative ability to exercise such responsibility. This is merely the last in a series of incidents where your performance has been less than exemplary, which compromised not only our security, but embarrassed this Administration. Accordingly, I will relieve you of that burden and accept your voluntary resignation. You will remain at Langley until your replacement is appointed. In the interim, if you say or do anything that compromises the Agency or this Administration, I'll have you tried for treason. That's all."

Ashen faced, Grant slowly stood up. "Mr. President—"

"You overreached yourself, or allowed a subordinate to overreach himself. Both are unforgivable. What is even more unforgivable, you jeopardized this Administration's foreign policy in a misguided belief that you or someone under you knew better than this office how to conduct it. Regardless of the desirability to oust Sung Kang-dae, it wasn't your decision to make! You have also accelerated a situation that might be maturing too quickly. There are broader implications to be considered than merely getting rid of Sung."

Grant clenched his jaw, nodded stiffly and stepped out. He did not quite slam the door.

"Mr. President, was it wise to fire him now?" Stone asked diffidently. "I agree he had it coming, but it could send a wrong signal to Kham Chang-uk and unsettle whatever he has in mind, or force him to act when we're not ready."

"Then we'll have to get ready."

"Sung might also start thinking about his flank and do something drastic to his opponents. We're not prepared to deal with either eventuality."

"You and Larry handle Kham, but I'm still not sure whether we should support him."

Tanner sat up and looked at the president with alarm. "Regardless of how Grant went about it, to depose Sung would be in everybody's interest, sir. China isn't exactly enamored with him, although they're providing a lot of his financial and military support."

"Not as much as he would like," Walters countered. "I agree they don't care for his belligerent military stand either, bad for business. Right now, China is more interested in economic expansion than bolstering a bankrupt ideologue. However, I meant it when I said a regime change right now could be counterproductive."

"If we don't support Kham, we'll be condoning what amounts to an internal massacre when the RGB finds out what's going on, if they haven't got an inkling already. It will permanently embitter the whole reformist movement and drive North Korea firmly into the hands of reactionary hardliners, which will leave the issue of a peaceful Korean peninsula hopelessly tangled for decades to come."

Walters regarded his Secretary of State with mixed feelings. The man cut an imposing figure and his firm features testified to a life of enviable accomplishment. What tended to rub Walters the wrong way, when Tanner made a statement on international affairs, that's how it was, and left little room for disagreement. Tanner's presence conveyed absolute authority, not necessarily such a bad thing, especially since Walters was still coming up to speed handling the international arena. Tanner did not always agree with him and wasn't reticent at saying so, but when Walters made a decision, he accepted it and carried it out with detached efficiency.

Tanner was right about Kham, though. Sung would initiate a purge and could become openly aggressive simply to discourage further dissent. Not a desirable outcome. To take the expedient course would build on a fragile relationship with Sung, but others in North Korea would remember America's treachery, and Sung won't live forever. Freedom was not the sole province of the West and others were entitled to the same opportunities and dignity of life. Those rights applied to all mankind. He could not in clear conscience withhold that from the North Korean people simply because supporting a repressive regime guaranteed an illusory peace for the peninsula. That kind of expediency only succeeded at alienating everybody and diminished respect for America as a democracy. He would be damned if he went down that path, but he might be forced to.

"I am aware of the pitfalls, Larry, which is why I'm pissed at Grant for starting something we're not quite ready to deal with, but we'll talk about that later. First, we need to know exactly what Grant's been doing. Get Zardwovsky in and grill him. I'll leave his fate to the new director. And Graham? Call, what's his name, the CIA Chief of Staff—"

"Stan Tankard, sir."

"Tell him to revoke all Grant's access privileges and security clearances. That goes for Zardwovsky as well. I don't want them sabotaging things before the new director steps in. The CIA has played like it's a law unto itself for too long. It's time we cleaned things up at Langley, and I know the man to do it."

The image of Mark Price, lean, hard-featured, dark brown hair untouched by age, powerful hands, gave the impression of a man who had faced adversity and death and beaten both. Every time he saw him, he was struck by the man's capability and confidence. Rather young to head the agency, but the job needed new ideas and determination to implement them. The old fossils who held the post to date saw it as a career sunset job, and look where that got him.

Chapter Three

Vincent Pacino liked the middle watch. As the junior Tactical Action Officer, his duty station normally in the Combat Information Center, he enjoyed his stints as Officer of the Deck, conning the big destroyer. With almost everything automated, there wasn't much conning to do. Standing watches also helped him retain his surface warfare officer wings. Out of habit, he glanced at the Electronic Chart Display Information System screen and checked the radar plot. They were still three hundred nautical miles from their staging position off Deokjeokdo Island, where they would join the massed ships of the South Korean navy. After thirty-six hours at sea, steaming at an easy thirty-two knots, they would reach Initial Point in eleven and a half hours, 0930 advertised time, and that's when the fun would begin.

Somewhere in the darkness around him were three sister destroyers: *John S. McCain*, *Stethem*, and *McCampbell*, with the lead ship *Cowpens*, a missile cruiser, trailing astern. He could see them plainly in the plot even though they were invisible to the naked eye. *Shiloh* had steamed ahead to confer with the leading element of the South Korean force and help coordinate the meeting engagement.

With two hours still to go on his watch before getting relieved at 2400, he could look forward to a good night's sleep. Tomorrow, when the mostly computer-simulated exercises would kick off, he expected to spend a lot of time in the Combat Information Center. He wouldn't mind it at all. Running *Curtis Wilbur's* Aegis command and decision, and weapon control systems, was like playing an advanced Warcraft video game. The difference here, the kills were real. How far the joint exercises would push realism would be up to the command ship *Blue Ridge* and his old man. Then again, with North Korea apparently prepared to talk again, Key Resolve could turn out to be nothing more than steaming up and down the western seaboard of the peninsula.

Either way, he hoped they would get to squirt off some SAMs and pop off a round or two from the main gun to see if the damned things worked.

With the bridge darkened, lit only by green navigation and radar displays, the watchstanders were almost invisible. The ship barely whispered as it cleaved the cold Yellow Sea water. Outside, it was completely black, a perfect backdrop for the dense profusion of stars arching above them. Even in the most remote wilderness on land, the stars were never so brilliant or packed into such glowing ribbons of pearly light. The tropical seas were the best, where a ship's bow wave and wake produced a magical blue-green phosphorescent blanket from the disturbed plankton.

Sailing through the night, the rest of the world did not exist. Only the endless ocean and the ship. The deeps had changed Vin's perspective and rearranged his priorities. Out here, he only faced the sea and what it could throw at him. The worries that dogged him on land paled into trivial insignificance. An illusion, of course, but it helped him focus on really important matters: his career and Linda.

Not that he had done badly with his career. After commissioning as a raw ensign, he spent twelve months on USS *Nicholas*, FFG-47, an *Oliver Hazard Perry*-class frigate, part of Task Force 20, U.S. Fleet Forces Command, based at Norfolk, Virginia, doing all the odd jobs junior officers were delegated which no one else cared for. The experience challenged him and he learned a lot, least of all about himself. With rank, he had authority, but rank did not automatically convey leadership. The ship's senior chiefs were patient and kept him from making the obvious bloopers. Some of his old man's suggestions and guidance also helped.

Promoted to lieutenant, junior grade, they shipped him to Newport, Rhode Island, where he attended a seventeen-week Surface Warfare Officers School, Division Officer course, followed by a seven-week Anti-submarine Warfare Officer upgrade. Linda remained in Norfolk during that time, but did manage to visit a few times. The SWOSDOC core program was a ball-buster and he could not afford to be distracted too much. Newly married, separation came hard, but the program gave him a serious step to further his career and he meant to succeed. Third-generation Navy, bilging out never entered his mind.

Once the courses were done, he had no time to relax. In typical Navy humor, he hardly saw Linda when he again shipped out. After six months of sea duty and seasoning as a Division Officer, he underwent a twenty-four-week Department Head course, by far the most demanding and in-depth professional training any surface warfare officer would attend during his career. So they told him. They had not been wrong. He finished second in his class with two broad stripes of a full lieutenant and immediately shipped to the 7th Fleet base at Yokosuka, Japan.

Linda…

So far, given what navy wives put up with, he figured he hadn't done badly in that department either. It would be good getting back to the States, though.

At 2300 a rating brought him coffee. As he sipped the hot fragrant brew, real navy java, it brought a jolt of adrenalin that helped him focus. Enough commercial shipping in the area kept him awake and on his toes, literally. Thinking about hitting the bunk, Vin was glad to see Lieutenant Couper come to the bridge at 2355. He quietly gave her a rundown while the middle watch took over. He returned the younger girl's salute and gratefully went below. He peeled off his uniform, ignoring his dozing roommate, and sank into his portside bunk. He fell asleep to the soft hum of shipboard machinery.

Low cloud obscured the horizon when Vin went up to the

forward weather deck the next morning to take in some fresh air. The sun still low, it colored the sky red as it struggled to burn through the overcast. The glassy sea had a silver metallic sheen, the water creaming on either side of the sharp bow. Created by the ship's movement, the wind stirred his hair.

Satisfied that everything was all right with the world, he went below to the wardroom and snagged breakfast. Off watch officers talked about the coming exercises and what waited for them personally. The word was that the captain would hold a last-minute pep talk with all senior officers at 0830, and Vin didn't want to miss it. He saw the published program they'd be following over the next five days, but the thing very short on detail, and deliberately so. A naturally mean and sadistic person, Admiral Kenneth Pacino probably wanted to test the captains of his ships as much as evaluate tactical doctrine under field conditions. At least that's how the scuttlebutt poop had it. He knew how his old man's mind worked and the rumor could be true. That was okay with Vin, as long as they got to shoot some live ordnance.

The wardroom loud as always, filled with good-natured banter and occasional laughter. Everyone looked forward to doing what they were paid to do—fight their ship. There weren't many other reasons to be in the navy. It certainly wasn't politics or a juvenile desire to place one's life to protect his country. Adventure drove them, pure and simple. True for the ratings anyway.

Although technology made front-line ships more powerful and sophisticated and reduced the need for quantity, it still took men and women to run them. Some of the concept designs Vin had seen were virtually automated weapons platforms capable of being controlled from land-based command centers that required only skeleton maintenance crews to man them. This wasn't revolutionary technology. NASA had done it for years with their Mars rovers. Advanced computer decision support systems and bright-eyed analysts playing virtual what-if scenarios on yard-wide screens would soon supplant the role of a traditional commanding officer as a theater tactician.

The concept of unmanned cruisers not new, and certainly possible with emerging system integration and stealth models. However, it was hard to win friends on shore from a computer console that might be thousands of miles away somewhere else. Then again, a warship's business was not to make friends, but project power and enforce a country's foreign policy. Vin hoped his career would be long over before such ships went into general service, even though he longed to be part of the design process that would bring them into reality.

The age of fighting sail and the crash of broadsides, whether from cannon or missile, was fast coming to an end. If naval architecture saved sailors' lives, he did not consider it such a bad thing. If warfare was reduced to nothing more than an elaborate virtual reality video game, would it encourage conflict and make death too impersonal? After all, the objective of warfare was to obliterate your enemy and eliminate his ability to retaliate. That inevitably meant wiping out his population and infrastructure. Could there be such a thing as a limited war between major powers, especially when one considered the impact on intertwined economic frameworks of everyone concerned?

There was a lot to be said for jousting knights settling the outcome of a dispute between two nations on a neutral field of honor. Then again, the concept of honor merely disguised the inevitable brutality of any conflict—to dismember your opponent any way you could, colored banners and trumpets notwithstanding.

War wasn't about national honor anymore, if it ever was, but the balance sheet bottom line, the only thing that concerned the multinationals. A competitor wasn't a hostile nation, but another corporation to be destroyed. If the conglomerates had it their way, *they* would dictate all government policy. They *would* be the government. They taught him that one at Annapolis.

Vin allowed himself a wry grin. Philosophy and warfare, never comfortable companions, but made for fascinating reading nonetheless.

At precisely 0830, Captain Woods walked into the crowded wardroom. Commander Linnen swept his eyes over the assembled officers and snapped to.

"Attention on deck!"

Woods walked to the front, nodded to Linnen, and clasped his hands behind his back. Forty-two and only five-foot six, he nevertheless exuded command presence. His piercing black eyes cut and probed everything they focused on, impersonal like a radar sweep. Although a fairly easygoing skipper who did not fuss over the little things, he left that to the XO, no one cared to test the limits of his geniality. A cobra only has to bite once to make its point. *Steel Hammer* had a reputation to maintain and Captain Woods intended adding to it.

"Sit. I won't keep you long," he said briskly, his voice strong and resolute. There was no need to shout in the small confines of the room. "You've undoubtedly checked the ship's datanet looking for your individual assignments and what we can expect from this year's joint exercises with our South Korean friends, and found nothing. Apart from today's rotation, I haven't found anything either and *Blue Ridge* isn't telling. It looks like Admiral Pacino is keeping his cards close to his chest this time and intends throwing a surprise or two at everybody." He paused as his eyes sought out Vincent. "Unless, of course, you have some inkling what's in store for us, Lieutenant?"

Faces turned and Vin gave what was hopefully a disarming smile. Everybody knew his old man, and that inevitably generated a bit of friendly ribbing and some envious comments, which he had learned to ignore and live with.

"Sorry, Captain. I'm as much in the dark as you are."

"Mmm," Woods grunted in a tone designed to convey maximum skepticism, which produced the expected chuckles of disbelief from everyone. He lifted his arms to restore order. "All right, I won't push it. If the Admiral does decide to give you a heads-up, I would appreciate knowing about it."

"Aye aye, sir," Vin said with a smile.

"Okay, to business. We will enter the ops area at our scheduled time of 0930 hours. Our orders are to team up with a ROK DDG *Sejong the Great* and FF *Masam*, and conduct a sub hunt on their diesel boat, SS *Lee Sunsin*. As you know, when running quiet, a diesel is damn near invisible. It's an ideal littoral defense platform, designed to interdict coastal approaches, and we need to get past it. We'll also be up against two of their patrol killer guided missile boats loitering somewhere forward of our advance line if we get the sub. They won't be bashful about hitting us if we break through—simulated, of course.

"We'll be in real-time contact with *Blue Ridge* over the JMCIS link, but *Curtis Wilbur* will have initial tactical command. If we nail the sub, command will pass to *Sejong* to prosecute the PKGs as we attempt to penetrate their screen. Once we've all had our fun, *Sejong* will then run another sub hunt exercise. During these evolutions, I'll rotate your responsibilities to give everyone an opportunity to gain proficiency in several tactical areas. Commander Linnen has the duty list."

Woods paused and swept his eyes over the group.

"Although this is a peaceful rotation, there will be live fire shoots of our weapons systems. We need to make sure the missile launchers and guns haven't rusted up on us." The comment brought another round of chuckles and smiles. "As with previous Key Resolve maneuvers, our North Korean friends might decide to show their displeasure at our presence and insert one or two of their Romeo class subs or an OSA II missile patrol boat into our engagement area simply to be a pain.

"You may have seen on the news the political overtures the United States has extended to North Korea, which might lead to further easing of tensions across the peninsula. That's all very well, but the diplomats are nice and cozy in Washington and we're here. Without air support from our carrier, we'll have to rely on our own defense systems. I'm not expecting anything, but while we're having fun with our ROK friends, we don't want the PROK boats slipping inside our twenty-mile exclusion perimeter and crashing the party. The Rules of Engagement are clear. If they breach the outer perimeter, they will be warned off. At fifteen miles, we're authorized to lock them up and paint them as targets. At ten miles, if they bring up their missile radars, they get a final warning. At five miles, we're cleared to engage."

The news received with some shuffling of feet and nervous coughs. Woods allowed the sentiment to run its course.

"I know what you're thinking. Five miles won't give us much reaction time, but that's the way it is. There will not be another *Cheonan* incident, not on my watch."

Vin knew what happened in March 2010 during the Foal Eagle/Key Resolve exercise. Everybody did. The sinking of the *Pohang*-class corvette, presumably by a PROK submarine, increased tension between the two Koreas and served as a poignant reminder that the 1950s war was by no means over. Not as far as Kim Jong-il was concerned. After some saber rattling by both sides and further trade restrictions imposed by South Korea, tensions had since eased. Normalization of relations, if that was the correct term, eased tensions even further, following the ascension to power by Sung Kang-dae. Economic and diplomatic friction may have been reduced, but the PROK military were still prickly as ever. No telling what one of their theater commanders might do, or a ship's captain.

"That's all," Woods said, glanced at the exec and walked quickly out of the wardroom.

Linnen stood up and looked at the assembled officers.

"Your duty postings for this evolution are now on MIDS. Study them. At 0930 hours, I expect you all to be at your assigned station. Look sharp and we'll show the ROK guys how real business is done. Dismissed!"

Vin smiled as he looked at the exec's gangly frame, the service blues uniform wrinkled and sagging like it hung on a skeleton. The XO wanted a ship of his own, and a successful execution by *Curtis Wilbur* during this rotation might help him get it. Uncle Sam didn't build too many new ships these days and there was a long line of officers waiting their turn to step into another man's ship before their promotion window closed and they wound up paper shuffling in the Pentagon. Vin shrugged philosophically as he walked out of the wardroom. It wasn't his problem, or something he needed to worry about yet.

In his quarters, he plugged himself into the Multi Information Distribution System and scrolled down the list until he came to the URL link attached to his name. When the window opened, he leaned forward and frowned. He was due as OOD for the afternoon watch, followed by a stint in CIC in the first dog watch.

"Lovely," he muttered at the prospect of doing eight hours straight. Well, the evening watch still two hours off, he would have the rest of the night to himself. He noted that he had another stint in CIC tomorrow during the forenoon watch and shrugged. It could have been worse. He could be doing heel-and-toe watches, but it looked like the skipper didn't want everyone going that far yet. Anyway, he only had four more days to go on this brisk spring cruise and he would head off for sunny California. At least he hoped it would be sunny.

* * *

The 7th Fleet command ship USS *Blue Ridge* cleaved the mercury water with its blunt bow and shouldered off the rolling seas in a welter of flying spray, its 18,800 metric tonnes hardly swaying in the long swells. It looked like a small cargo tramp, and only its traditional gray paint identified it as a military vessel. An old ship on its last deployment, making way for a modern new vessel, it nevertheless continued to serve. Once the breaker's yard got to work on it, no one would care about its proud history. The first stars winked shyly overhead. Clouds smeared the sky red where the sun had sunk.

Rear Admiral Kenneth Pacino stared intently at the arrayed 600mm flat screens of the Joint Maritime Command Information System, slowly lifted the thin gold-plated clutch pencil to his mouth and worried the end. The Tactical Flag Command Center situated in the midships-positioned superstructure quiet, the silence interrupted by the soft throb of ship's machinery that could be felt through the bones. Console operators slouched over keyboards, monitoring two separate exercises, occasionally issuing instructions into their thread-like mikes that hung from slim headsets.

Relaxed in his padded leather chair mounted behind the watchstanders, he could observe everything and issue orders without being in the way. Everyone and everything in the darkened complex there to serve him and keep him informed. From the sophisticated communications system able to patch him to any Naval, Marine, ship or land-based establishment around the world, and a battery of computers that presented him with an integrated picture of air, surface and sub-surface contacts, everything designed to support and augment his decision-making capability. He could be in a land bunker rather than on a ship as far as his senses could tell.

Right now, Pacino watched a developing scenario of three Blue Force vessels stalking a South Korean Red Force submarine attempting to sneak past them, enabling it to launch a simulated attack on *Blue Ridge*. In this part of the exercise, the ROK DDG *Sejong the Great* in tactical command. He nodded with satisfaction as he took in the disposition of the three ships closing fast on the red submarine's suspected position. It shouldn't be much longer, he thought comfortably. After all, a standard evolution that didn't take a whole lot of tactical strain to execute. Although the ROK destroyer driver was competent, the evolutions lacked the smooth precision exercised by Captain Woods when he commanded the little flotilla earlier in the day. Arranged in a shallow V to prevent the red sub from flanking them, Woods had positioned a ROK ship on either beam and his MH-60 Sea Hawk attack helicopter sanitized the area along their line of advance.

All the ships had their Prairie-Masker acoustic countermeasures system working, making their movement almost totally silent to the sub's passive sonar and hydrophone sensors. The Sea Hawk was under no such inhibition, dunking its sonar head and MAD gear in a checkered pattern as it searched for the sub, occasionally letting go with a full sonar blast that must have rattled the sub crew's ears. Apart from squirting off an anti-air missile at the pesky MH-60, which the red sub wasn't equipped with, it simply had to take it. Inevitably, the helicopter found its quarry and that ended it. Woods allowed the ROK DDG to launch a simulated ASROC torpedo and the exercise umpire on *Blue Ridge* judged it a valid kill, an exemplary evolution.

In the current round, Pacino demanded that the submarine be prosecuted without helicopters or active sonar. That made things a lot tougher for the Blue Force, but as he explained to *Sejong's* grumpy captain, war was neither fair nor predictable. Sometimes you were forced to fight with one hand tied behind your back, which was tough crumbs. Suck it up and deal with it. When the captain complained that Woods had it all his way, Pacino asked if he would complain as much if he were facing a PROK sub? They sure as hell wouldn't give him a program before launching an attack. Whether the ROK captain was mollified or not, he didn't give a toss. The look he got after that exchange from the Korean three-star admiral observing the proceedings hadn't been brotherly. Pacino controlled this exercise and he wanted every piece of doctrine, every ship, officer and rating, put through as much stress as was possible in the five days allocated to Key Resolve. Not nearly enough time, but that's all he had to work with. Bending the ROK admiral's nose out of shape hardly bothered him. The Korean might look on these proceedings as parading the flag to his northern brethren, but Pacino definitely didn't. If the *kim chee* hit the fan, it would be Americans who'd be laying it on the line. *Damn it all!*

In his opinion, a moaning officer was a nine-to-five desk jockey and he had no time for cocktail warriors. The *Sejong* captain would get a downcheck from him with a note that an attitude adjustment was in order. What that might do to the man's career was something for the ROK Navy Command to sort out. Besides, those people looked at things differently. They were just a littoral outfit anyway.

The fact that his own performance might also be under scrutiny by the Commander 7th Fleet never entered his head. Unless he did something drastically unthinkable or dumb, his third star assured. Third star or not, it didn't influence how he conducted this exercise. He was a professional testing his tools. If one broke or bent under the strain, he wanted to know about it now rather than find out under combat conditions when ships and lives could be lost at the hand of an incompetent.

Admiral Pacino acknowledged that he was a driven man, but he wasn't obsessed or fanatical about it. He simply demanded the best out of himself and those fate had placed in his way to command. A surgeon may worry himself over the health of his patient during a procedure, but that didn't preclude him from secretly relishing the cutting that accompanied his humane act. Like most dedicated military men, Pacino abhorred war, but if he needed to shoot, he was the consummate ruthless warrior. Confronted by an enemy, it was his duty to remove the threat using skill, guile, and every advantage modern technology offered. Chivalry? That was for romantics and throb writers. There was nothing chivalrous about blasting a man to bits.

The far left screen showed the broader tactical picture in IR mode, the view provided by a prowling MQ-9 Reaper staged out of Osan Air Base. The unmanned aerial vehicle was a successor to the General Atomics triumphant Predator program. Pacino noted with interest the maneuvering of the PROK *Najin*-class frigate and an accompanying *Sariwon*-class corvette. An OSA II missile patrol boat far off to port, close to Deokjeokdo Island. All were shadowing the Blue Force, but kept a discrete distance. He didn't like the North Koreans nosing around the exercise area, but as long as they stayed outside the posted exclusion zone, he had no grounds to grumble. They were simply being a nuisance and knew it. Those guys had to keep pushing until something gave. The frigate, though, probably the command ship, had positioned itself directly in the line of advance of the Blue Force and appeared happy to stay there. It would be interesting to see what *Sejong the Great's* grumpy captain would do about it.

Sejong shifted to port slightly and Pacino frowned. Why did he abandon the engagement area? Unless the red sub withdrew, sooner or later the three Blue Force ships would have it on a plate. Was the ROK captain attempting a flanking finesse to dazzle his superiors? If so, a pointless gesture. Pacino firmly believed in a doctrine that said, if you got a working solution, prosecute it. Don't fiddle for a sweeter position and risk losing an existing tactical advantage. That's how you got your ass shot off.

A yeoman brought him coffee and tea for the ROK admiral. Pacino nodded to him and took a thirsty sip. He had been glued to his seat since 1400 hours and his body had stiffened up. He wouldn't have minded dinner, but he did not relish the prospect of entertaining the dour faced Korean admiral, not if lunch was any guide. He should have left *Blue Ridge* tied to its pier in Yokosuka and conducted the exercises in comfort, but there was nothing like being underway to add realism to proceedings. Could the ROK admiral be seasick?

He needed a brisk jog around the ship's top deck, but that was impossible. All the topside spaces were strictly off limits to everyone, and that included the 7th Fleet deputy commander. Men moving about interfered with the ship's communication systems, or some such crap. Pacino wondered why modern technology couldn't distinguish between a jogging sailor and an incoming missile. Sometimes, he simply felt out of touch with today's game console warfare.

Earlier, he tried to chat up the Korean admiral, feel him out about the latest North Korean overtures to the West and cancellation of this year's Foal Eagle exercise, but the man appeared to have a spike up his butt and rebuffed all overtures at cordiality. Did the three-star resent that a mere two-star was in charge of Key Resolve? If so, he could take it up with the Fleet commander or the State Department.

"Admiral, we might have a situation," Commander Rileigh said as he looked up from his multi-function screen.

"Talk to me," Pacino ordered, quickly scanning the display. The exercise Tactical Action Officer pursed his lips.

"Sir, SS *Lee Sunsin* is in grid C-6, but I have *Sejong the Great* way over in E-4. *Curtis Wilbur* is getting awfully close to the PROK corvette. More accurately, the corvette is closing on her."

"Yeah, I saw *Sejong* veer off. Patch into her CIC," Pacino growled, wondering what the hell the Korean had in mind.

In the center screen, the ROK DDG's Combat Information Center real-time link showed a definite acoustic signature coming from its towed array sonar. They had a submarine in their teeth, but it couldn't be *Lee Sunsin*, not in that position.

"Sir! *Sejong* has launched its helicopter."

Pacino frowned. It was a direct contravention of standing orders for this exercise. It looked like the DDG captain wanted to show up Woods that he was just as good. Dumb. He must know the sub he chased could not be Red Force. He didn't like the implication.

"Sir, *Wilbur* just warned off the corvette," the comms watch commander announced.

Pacino's mouth twitched as he noted the PROK ship shift to port. A very sensible move under the circumstances, he mused and turned to Rileigh.

"Commander, order *Sejong* to recall its SH-60 immediately and steer one-one-zero. Tell him he might be in contact with a PROK submarine. Expedite!"

"Acknowledged!"

Pacino looked at the ROK admiral. "I would advise that you reinforce my order, Admiral."

The short Korean officer lifted his head and looked back coldly, his small black eyes devoid of expression.

"My commanders know their duty, Admiral. Do yours?"

Pacino stared at him, not believing he had heard right. The man playing one-upmanship now?

"We're engaged in a peacetime exercise, Admiral Chin, not a hostile confrontation. *Sejong* is contravening the ROE and needlessly risking an engagement."

A fleeting smile touched Chin's mouth, but not his eyes. "Don't worry, Admiral Pacino. *Sejong the Great* will merely deliver a friendly warning to the PROK submarine."

Pacino snorted and turned to the comms commander. "Have they acknowledged?"

"Negative, sir."

"Order it to withdraw now and issue a cancel alert to all Group Bravo units. This exercise is over. Contact the PROK frigate and warn them that their submarine is in violation of the stated exclusion zone and request they withdraw immediately!"

"Aye aye, sir!"

"Too late, Admiral." Rileigh pointed at his screen.

The ROK Sea Hawk hovered, then veered off sharply. A few moments later, the screen showed a rising plume of water. The Reaper's IR image clear and crisp as a HD television picture.

"Sir, *Sejong* reports dropping a reduced yield depth charge five hundred yards from what they say is a PROK Whiskey-class submarine…Sir! We have a torpedo in the water!"

Pacino slammed the palm of his right hand against the armrest and shook his head at the ROK Admiral, now a little pale. From being a friendly exercise, the situation had suddenly assumed an altogether unwelcome realism. The tension in the Command Center almost palpable and heads turned, everyone waiting for what might be an inevitable confrontation.

"And you just got a PROK version of a friendly warning, Admiral!" Pacino snarled and turned to the comms commander. "Pull back *Wilbur* and *Masam*. Now!"

"Sir, no response from the PROK frigate."

Pacino ground his teeth. Everyone playing stupid games of dominance.

"*Wilbur* is under missile attack from the corvette! CSS-N-8 Saccades!" Rileigh reported, then a few seconds later, he looked up, face grave. "*Sejong* has taken a hit on the port bow."

In the center tactical screen, Pacino saw two black objects streak away from the PROK corvette and speed toward the American destroyer. Nothing he could do but watch and pray that Woods would get his ship and men out of this alive. *Wilbur* was equipped with the latest Aegis systems, software and countermeasures, and Woods was a very capable captain, but sometimes none of that was nearly enough, not when you only had seconds to react.

One missile became a puff some three thousand yards from the destroyer as it descended to five yards above the water in its terminal phase, downed by the ship's Sea Sparrow anti-air missile. A moment later the second one disappeared, but on the screen, it looked awfully close to the ship. Pacino felt his mouth go dry and his stomach gave a flutter. There must have been damage. Double-spaced plating protected most of the superstructure and hull to suppress shrapnel penetration, but the countermeasure could not protect the ship from a close detonation; and Vincent was aboard that ship. If something happened to him…

This was supposed to be a peaceful exercise!

"Sir, *Curtis Wilbur* has taken the corvette under main gun fire," Rileigh announced wearily. "They report damage along the port side, but they can still maneuver."

Pacino bit down on his pencil, the situation totally shot now. Under the Rules of Engagement, Woods was perfectly entitled to defend his ship, regardless of the political quagmire this action would undoubtedly open for everybody. The damage report worried him, but until he got more information, he could only wait and stew. No matter what happened, he promised himself that he would carve the *Sejong* captain's ass for this.

Plumes of water surrounded the PROK ship and there were explosions. When the broken ship slid beneath the waves, the Tactical Flag Command Center very quiet. The fun had truly gone out of the day.

Furious, Pacino slowly turned and glared at the ROK admiral.

* * *

Commander Rae Dong-yul checked the glowing amber screen and frowned. This was the third time in five minutes that he had stood over the radar plot, staring at the three bright blips slowly converging on his position. Actually, he approached them. This much attention on the loitering imperialist ships could indicate nervousness on his part, but a glance at the watchstanders keeping a rigid eye on the helm, threat and target acquisition systems, assured him they saw nothing unusual at the commanding officer monitor the enemy vessels.

The exec, stationed at the weapons fire control console, cleared his throat. "Comrade Commander, we're being painted by the American AN/SPS-73 surface search radar."

"Nothing from their AN/SPY-1D Aegis system?" Rae demanded sharply. The search radar could be ignored, but a squirt from their weapons system would be another matter.

"Negative so far, sir."

"Do you think they have detected *Kurung Thae*?"

The Whiskey-class diesel-electric submarine shadowed the large American *Arleigh Burke*-class guided missile destroyer with its accompanying ROK destroyer and frigate as an interdiction measure in case the enemy violated the Northern Limit Line and strayed into PROK home waters. So far, Rae saw no indication that the enemy ships intended any such maneuver. With Deokjeokdo Island in front of them, the imperialist ships were nowhere near the NLL. The capitalists were unpredictable and he wasn't going to take any chances of them slipping past him.

Newly promoted after serving as executive officer on an aging Russian *Krivak*-class frigate, he fully intended to make sure his precious *Peryong Lam*, an upgraded *Sariwon*-class corvette, equipped with the latest Yingji-82 anti-ship cruise missiles, did not fail the homeland or the Supreme Leader. He turned and stared at his executive officer.

"Contact *Laan Ghae* and ask them if the imperialists have any submarines in the area."

"At once, Commander!" the younger man said briskly and strode toward the communications shack located behind the nav plot table.

Rae sighed, wishing the exec wouldn't be so gung-ho. *The man was young and he would get weary of it in time*, he told himself, *and ease up*. The trouble with the new crop of young officers these days, everyone eager to charge into battle with the imperialists, oblivious to the fact that such an encounter was likely to be terminal. Contrary to official propaganda, the Korean People's Navy could not match itself against the imperialists. Rae wanted more professionalism in an officer and less breast-beating about the Supreme Leader. Although, he wasn't about to say that aloud.

Turning his attention to the matter at hand, it was possible the enemy was engaged in an antisubmarine exercise. The vectored tactics of the three ships certainly suggested this, but whose submarine were they hunting?

The exec emerged from the comms shack. "Sir, *Laan Ghae* reports that we have a ROK *Chang Bogo*-class diesel submarine approximately eleven kilometers starboard of our position, slowly moving east."

"Any other contacts?"

"Nothing else, sir."

Rae didn't like it. It brought the two submarines uncomfortably close together. Was *Kurung Thae* playing a game of its own, stalking the ROK boat and possibly the surface combatants in an impromptu exercise? If it was, it introduced an unstable variable into an otherwise peaceful evolution by the imperialist force. Preventing the enemy from encroaching on the sacred home waters, deliberately or not, was his bound duty and honor, but to knowingly provoke the enemy without cause would be foolish.

He bit his upper lip and nodded. "Contact *Laan Ghae* and recommend they withdraw our boat from the immediate tactical area."

He knew Baye Mangjul, commander of the *Najin*-class frigate, very well. Both had studied tactics at the Shanghai Gaochang Temple Naval Academy. His friend now a captain and a squadron commander, primarily due to family influence. Nice to have a minister for a father. Not exactly envious, those were the breaks, but it sometimes rankled that the purity of the Workers' Party should be contaminated by nepotism. However, Rae wasn't that idealistic or naïve not to accept reality or manipulate the system to his advantage. Everybody did it.

The exec stepped out of the comms shack and grinned, which lit up his otherwise stern face. "Do you want their exact response, sir?"

Rae smiled and shook his head, knowing perfectly well what *Laan Ghae* probably suggested he do with himself.

"The abridged version will do."

"They said we should mind our own business…sir."

Chuckling, Rae checked the radar plot while the exec resumed his station. He had done his duty by alerting the squadron commander, who was almost certainly aware of the tactical situation as he was. He didn't like the developing scenario, but he was not responsible for the disposition of PROK forces in the area. Within the bounds of his orders, he would do what was necessary to safeguard the security of the homeland.

The radio operator came out and looked anxiously at Rae. "Comrade Commander, we received a warning from the American destroyer, advising us that we have crossed their thirty-two-kilometer exclusion zone. They request we withdraw."

"Very well," Rae said calmly and the operator stepped back.

"We're in international waters and have as much right to be here as they do. More so!" the exec protested sharply and Rae turned to study the young lieutenant.

What he said was theoretically true, but reality seldom conformed to theory. The American was probably being friendly, not wishing him to get tangled in their exercise. Besides, Rae operated under strict orders and his ROE were clear. Unless the imperialists crossed the NLL, he merely shadowed the enemy. He had no problem following those orders at all. Testing himself against the powerful American DDG was not his idea of heroism. What would happen to his elderly parents if he were no longer there to support them? His sister certainly would not be able to, not with two young children of her own and a husband on a disability pension after an accident at a munitions factory. No, he needed to be sensible and survive.

"Have we been painted?"

"Nav radar only, sir."

"Very well. Helm? Maintain course and speed."

"Maintain course and speed. Aye, sir," the quartermaster acknowledged in a neutral voice.

A quartering sea sent a burst of white spray from the bow,

which smeared the armored glass of the bridge. In the west, the sun had dipped below the horizon, coloring the high clouds in bands of red and yellow. The first dog watch would be over in an hour or so and would give the crew relief, but there would be no rest for Rae or the exec. He took the duties of the sea phlegmatically. A commanding officer now, not a lowly lieutenant who could rely on predictable routine.

"Helm? Warn me when we approach the imperialist force within twenty-four kilometers."

"Acknowledged, comrade Commander."

Although naval intelligence knew all about the American AN/SPY-1D radar, it would do no harm to record its emissions. They could have changed, and new information was always useful to have. Anyway, it gave his crew something constructive to do. If the Americans were exercising, so could he.

As he stood with his hands clasped behind his back, he felt the throb of power from the engine room. The corvette not a large ship, only sixty-two meters in length with a crew of thirty-eight officers and men. At six hundred and fifty metric tonnes, her maximum speed of eighteen knots woefully inadequate to close on a target or get out of trouble. Apart from a deck gun and depth charges, her primary offensive weapons were four side-mounted canisters, each carrying a variant of the Chinese Yingji-82 anti-ship missile, codenamed CSS-N-8 Saccade by the Americans. Radar and infrared capable, delivering a 165-kilogram warhead at Mach .9, it would cause terrible damage to a ship's fragile superstructure—any ship. At least that's what he had been told. He had seen one fired only once. Even with the Juche policy of army first, missiles cost money and his homeland didn't have a lot of them to waste on frivolous target practice.

Peryong Lam lifted its sharp bow and crashed through a dark roller, sending a wall of water and spray flying aft, smearing itself against the forward windows. A discolored red patch remained over a black sea where the sun had been. Rae swayed as the ship pitched, easily compensating for the motion. The bridge lights came on and he blinked.

"Comrade Commander, we're now within twenty-four kilometers off the American warship," the quartermaster announced quietly.

"Very well. Port ten. Steer one-zero-zero."

"One-zero-zero, aye, sir."

"Sir, we're being painted by the AN/SPY-1D," the exec warned, looking excited.

"Record all transmissions. Has the American changed course?" Rae demanded, wishing the exec wouldn't be so keen to test himself or the ship.

"Negative. Still holding at three-three-zero," the exec said after a glance at the radar plot.

A young ensign looked up from his sonar console at the port side of the bridge and pushed back a bulky headset.

"Comrade Commander! Hydrophone effects! We have a depth charge explosion."

The radio operator emerged from his shack. "Sir, *Laan Ghae* reports that *Kurung Thae* is under attack by a ROK destroyer. They order us to go to action stations."

"Very well. Acknowledge," Rae said calmly, despite his tense stomach, and glanced at the exec. "Ready the missiles, but do not bring up the targeting radar."

"At once, Commander!" The exec smiled and pressed buttons on his console, clearly relishing the prospect of engaging the imperialists. "All canisters at ready state, sir."

Rae nodded and bit his upper lip. Was *Kurung Thae* under actual attack, or was the enemy prosecuting a ROK submarine as part of their exercise? *Kurung Thae* had no business being so close to the engagement area in the first place. If the situation was not handled properly, someone could end up making a horrible mistake. He hoped it wouldn't be him. He glanced at the radar plot and glared at the quartermaster.

"I told you to steer one-zero-zero, you fool!"

The unfortunate man blanched and hurriedly spun the small wheel to the left. "One-zero-zero, aye, sir!"

Rae grunted and glared at the man. The idiot had gotten carried away by the momentary excitement and allowed the ship to close on the American destroyer.

"Sir! The American has brought up its AN/SLQ-32 jamming radar," the exec announced, looking anxiously at his commander, some of his assurance looking a little ragged.

"Comrade Commander, the American is turning to starboard, steering three-four-zero," the chastened quartermaster said.

Was it to avoid an engagement, Rae mused and somewhat relieved, or merely being prudent, not wishing to provoke one? Either way the American had signaled its intention—do not approach closer. He was quite happy not to do so, finding his palms suddenly sweaty. He checked the radar plot. *Peryong Lam* had shifted to port, opening the range gate between the two ships.

The radio operator emerged again. "Comrade Commander, *Laan Ghae* advises that *Kurung Thae* has launched a torpedo at the ROK destroyer." He clamped his hand to his headset and looked up, his face pale under the bridge lights. "We're ordered to close on the nearest enemy vessel and engage."

Commander Rae Dong-yul stared at the youngster for a moment, and felt the weight of the world on his shoulders while worst case scenarios flashed through his mind—all terminal for him and his ship. Mangjul could not be so rash to order something like this. It didn't make any tactical sense.

"Ask them for disposition of any enemy submarines in the area," he snapped, wondering if behind the facade of his uniform, he lacked the physical courage of his convictions. "The enemy could have carried out a mock attack on their own submarine."

The radio operator disappeared, not looking convinced, and Rae fumed and tapped his fingers against his thigh. This was ridiculous. Why would the imperialists attack now? They were engaged in a peaceful exercise. *Kurung Thae* had gotten too close to the ROK ship and probably mistaken for one of their own. That must be it. At least he hoped so. The alternative did not bear thinking about.

"Comrade Commander," the exec hissed beside him. "Shall I bring up the targeting radar?"

Rae glared at him. "Attend to your station!"

"Sir!" The young lieutenant snapped to attention, abashed by the fury of his commander's response.

The ensign looked up. "Comrade Commander! Hydrophone effects! A torpedo strike! It sounds like a ship breaking up."

Rae almost groaned. Beset by personal doubts and a strong suspicion that *Laan Ghae* had overreacted, he felt helplessly swept into a situation that could end tragically for everyone. Didn't the squadron commander see this?

The radio operator's eyes were round with fear as he emerged from the shack. "Sir, a ROK destroyer has taken a torpedo and *Laan Ghae* has ordered us to open fire on the imperialist force."

"Ask them to confirm that *Kurung Thae* has been attacked," Rae demanded in a tight voice. This was fast getting out of hand.

The radio operator spoke quickly into his mike, then looked up and shook his head. "Our submarine has withdrawn without incident."

Rae reached for the operator's headset and yanked it off. He brought one earpiece to his head.

"Commander *Peryong Lam* to Commander *Laan Ghae*."

"At once, Commander!" the other operator said in a strained voice.

After a few seconds of crackling static, Rae heard the familiar voice of his friend.

"Commander Dong-yul, what can I do for you? Your orders are not clear?"

"Sir, how close was the depth charge to *Kurung Thae*?"

"Five hundred meters according to their report. Why?"

"Sir, I submit that it inadvertently or deliberately strayed into the imperialist's exercise zone and assumed the attack was made on them, when in reality it could have been launched against a ROK submarine, or it could have been merely a warning. Now that *Kurung Thae* has withdrawn, why are we prosecuting?"

"My orders are not to be questioned, Commander. Carry them out!"

"Sir! The imperialists have not made subsequent runs against us."

"For the last time, Commander. Carry out your orders! And I shall address your insubordination once we're back in port."

If we ever get back, Rae mused, but he did not dare say that aloud. Not like his friend at all, ordering something so stupid. Numb, he pulled off the headset and held it out to the operator, who took it and quietly shrank back. He looked at the quartermaster, resigned to the inevitable end of this stupidity.

"Starboard twenty! Steer one-two-zero. Increase revolutions for eighteen knots. Exec? Ready missile canisters one and two and lock on the American DDG."

He gave his orders in a flat voice, devoid of emotion, thankful others could not feel the lead ball of dread that materialized in his belly. Glancing around the bridge at the tense faces, they seemed to have worries of their own. He did not believe in any god or saint, but he fervently wished he were somewhere else.

"Steering one-two-zero, sir!" the quartermaster announced crisply as the ship swung to starboard, the throb of power clearly audible with increased speed. Water creamed on either side of the bow in a tall plume.

"We have a target lock on the enemy vessel, Commander. Range, sixteen kilometers and closing," the exec said, not looking so confident anymore, or ready to lay down his life for the Workers' Party.

The radio operator rushed out. "Comrade Commander! A

message from the American vessel warning us to break missile lock."

Rae looked at the exec. He really had no choice, and it was so futile. With his ship crawling through the water, his only hope was that a cruise missile strike would take out the American before *Peryong Lam* was sunk, the most probable outcome.

"Fire the missiles."

Pale, the exec stared at him for a moment, then turned to his console.

From the forward port canister, a jet of bright yellow-white flame shot toward the stern as the Yingji-82 booster ignited, sending the sleek six-meter cruise missile streaking into the air. *Peryong Lam* was momentarily buried in a black column of toxic exhaust smoke before its speed carried it clear. Seconds later the starboard missile lifted from its canister.

Rae watched the two tails of fire arc up, then flatten as the boosters dropped off and the missiles headed east toward the unseen American destroyer, now skimming some ten meters above the water. At less than sixteen kilometers separation and out of their boost phase, flight time would be something like forty seconds. Not much time for the American ship to react, but it would. He was certain of that.

"Sir! The American has fired chaff and is jamming," the exec said, looking anxiously at his commander. Any thought of glory destroying the imperialists had long faded from his troubled eyes.

Rae nodded, then shot a hard look at the quartermaster. "Hard a port! Steer zero-nine-zero."

"Zero-nine-zero, aye, sir!"

Peryong Lam healed sharply as the corvette made a radical turn to disengage.

"Sir, the American has fired Evolved Sea Sparrows against our cruise missiles!" the exec reported urgently. "One of our missiles has been destroyed."

Far on his right, Rae saw a bright orange flash. A moment

later, a second flash below the horizon outlined the masts of the American destroyer, hull down. The blast looked awfully close and he wondered if the missile had hit, but he couldn't see any secondary explosions to indicate one. The American close-in defense system had probably picked off the missile and might at this very moment be targeting *Peryong Lam*. Even at his maximum speed, it wouldn't mean much against a Harpoon anti-ship missile.

"Both cruise missiles destroyed, Commander. The last one very close and the enemy could be damaged."

"Ready missile canisters three and four!"

Right then, a column of white water grew in front of *Peryong Lam* and the ship plunged into it, the exploding shell going off with a muffled crack. Before the ship could emerge out of the wall of spray, a much sharper detonation occurred close on the starboard side. Another column of white lifted and the ship shook savagely. Shrapnel peppered the bridge and armored glass exploded, showering the watchstanders, bringing with it frigid air.

Commander Rae thought he heard someone scream as a lance of fire stabbed into his right side and the bridge lights went out. He gasped for breath and felt something warm run down his thigh. He instinctively glanced at the radar plot. The American had not bothered to waste a missile on him, shelling him from its main gun tube! Making radical turns could save him yet, despite the gun's twenty-four-kilometer range. Against a radar-controlled gun and his slow ship, a hollow hope. Before he could give the order to maneuver, there was a shattering crash and something slammed into him. He could hear the roar of the flames as darkness descended.

A searing flash blossomed over the ship's stern that ripped the starboard canister to shreds. The missiles' liquid fuel ignited, setting off the solid rocket boosters in a ball of fire forty meters high. Two more columns of white water leaped up on either side of the stricken vessel. Its stern ripped away, the ship reared up, smashed back into black waves and wallowed in the swell. The bow slowly lifted and what remained of the ship slid backward into the dark waters. Bubbles of air and steam burst to the surface, then the sea swallowed everything. Only an oil slick and some debris marked the spot where the ship went down.

* * *

Finishing his stint as Officer of the Deck for the afternoon watch, Vincent Pacino handed over to Lieutenant Bishop, and with a nod at Commander Linnen, raced down the companionway to the mess. The serving counter busy, he managed to squeeze in past two sailors with a mumbled apology, and grabbed a greasy slider—beef hamburger—between two warm buns, a small bucket of fries and a tall glass of pink bug juice. He gulped down half the mixed fruit juice, relishing the tangy taste, before he sat down at one of the empty tables. The mess getting crowded fast and cheerful voices filled the air, mixed with laughter and friendly taunting. Normally, Vin would eat in the wardroom where messroom specialists—waiters—served the officers, but he didn't have time to indulge in the personal service. It was not unusual for officers to grab a quick meal in the mess. Linnen himself was known to snag an odd sandwich here.

Half a dozen hungry bites demolished the hamburger. Vin paused for breath and cleaned up most of his fries and downed the rest of the juice. Heaving a sigh of contentment, he shoved the remains into a disposal bin and hurried down a gangway, walking briskly along the corridor that led to CIC. He glanced at his wristwatch and winced: 1802 hours. He hoped the skipper wouldn't be there as he opened the hatch and stepped into the ship's combat center.

"Ah, Mr. Pacino has graced us with his presence at last," Captain Woods remarked dryly from his center seat.

The comment generated smiles and chuckles from the officers and watchstanders.

"Apologies, Captain," Vin mumbled, glad his red face could not be seen in the darkened room.

Woods stood up and pointed at his chair. "Judging by the smudge of ketchup on your chin, it's not hard to guess where you've been." That caused another round of chuckles.

Vin automatically probed his chin, but couldn't feel anything, and realized the Old Man was having a little fun at his expense.

Woods laughed and patted him on the shoulder. "The watch is yours, Mr. Pacino. I'm going to do what you've just done. Don't shoot up anybody while I'm away."

"No, sir."

"Mr. Pacino has the watch," Woods announced and hurried out.

Vin lowered himself into the still-warm seat and quickly scanned the two main screens of the Aegis Combat System that showed the tactical disposition, weapon systems status, countermeasures, search radar and navigation plot. He knew the parameters of the exercise, but being in CIC gave him a different perspective. He glanced at the sonar and anti-submarine warfare desk, the screens were clear. He then gave the engineering display, damage and fire control stations a cursory look. It wasn't information he needed to know.

In the tactical plot, *Sejong the Great* stood approximately eleven thousand yards on their starboard beam, with *Masam* loitering eight thousand yards to port. He could just make out the smudge of Deokjeokdo Island far to port. *Blue Ridge*, the exercise target, well to starboard over the horizon, safely behind the line of advance. Vin looked more closely at the towed array sonar readout—nothing. Wherever SS *Lee Sunsin* hid itself, the Blue Force hadn't spotted it. Could it be hugging the bottom, waiting for the searching ships to run over it, giving her a clear run to the target? If she was and had everything shut down, they would never hear her. Around here, the Yellow Sea had an average depth of only 144 feet, going to five hundred at some places. He glanced at the fathometer: 162 feet, well within the capability of the Korean boat.

He noted the PROK missile corvette tooling around on their port side, but still outside the twenty-mile outer perimeter, if only just. He didn't worry about the PROK frigate or the PKG thirty-one miles off their port beam. Besides, *Sejong* was much closer to both. He gave a mental shrug. On this ops, it called the shots.

"Got it all wired in, Lieutenant?" Lieutenant Commander 'Patch' Blazer asked quietly and Vin nodded.

"Yes, sir. I'm worried if the Red Force sub is lying doggo underneath us."

"We'll have to listen hard then, won't we?"

As the junior TAO, Vin was content to command the CIC watch, but Patch, as the Tactical Action Officer and senior officer present, would immediately take over should Vin falter during any Blue Force maneuver called by *Sejong*. With situational awareness clear in his mind, he felt ready for anything. Playing the Aegis systems was one big interactive video game, and he played it like no one else on board the ship. The string of 'Superior' in his fitness report attested to his skill. He might be good, but Patch still held one unshakeable advantage over him—experience. With more exercises like Key Resolve, Vin figured he would be able to match himself against the hotshot commander with no trouble. Was that why the skipper left him in charge? The Old Man could be devious when he wanted to and reading him not easy.

Whatever the reason, Vin occupied the hot seat now and would make the most of it.

The afternoon evolution while OOD on the bridge interesting, watching *Steel Hammer* charge around, the sea foaming around it as they closed on the Red Force sub. The exercise had a detached feel, though. The Old Man ran everything from CIC, even steering the powerful destroyer from below, leaving the topside watch to Commander Linnen. If they provided panorama screens in CIC, there wouldn't be any need for a topside watch at all, Vin mused wryly. As the watch dragged on, he hardly had anything to do. The bridge repeater screens gave him a degree of situational awareness, but not the same thing as being in CIC where the action was. Still, standing topside watches added to his proficiency and ticked another little box on his Fitrep 1610/2.

At 1830 hours, Captain Woods walked in and his eyes flickered at Commander Blazer, who didn't waste any time clearing out, glad to have an opportunity to attend to personal hydraulic problems and grab a meal before getting back. Senior officers did not stand watches, but were expected to be on duty as required. Vin figured that over the next four days, he would stand quite a few watches.

He started to get up, but the captain motioned for him to keep his seat and took Patch's chair.

"Carry on, Lieutenant."

"Aye aye, sir," Vin said, only mildly conscious of the captain's presence beside him.

He had done this shit before and wasn't at all intimidated. He felt alive and all his senses were in tune. The ship seemed to talk to him and he was part of it, its guiding brain and will. This is what he was meant to do.

As he studied the evolving tactical situation—still no sign of the sub—aware of every movement the three ships made, he sat up as the corvette crossed the twenty-mile exclusion zone.

"Comms? Warn the PROK ship to stand off," he ordered crisply. The captain gave no indication that he had heard.

"Aye, sir."

As the corvette maintained its course, Vin didn't hesitate. "Bring up the AN/SLQ-32 and do a sweep," he ordered.

At the same time, using the control joystick mounted on the right armrest, he shifted it right until the digital compass read three-four-zero that swung *Wilbur* a little to starboard. A moment later the PROK ship swung to port, which made him feel a whole lot better. Someone over there wasn't paying attention or merely wanted to yank his chain.

When *Sejong* suddenly put on a burst of speed and turned slightly to port, Vin frowned. What were they doing? And why hadn't they communicated their intention?

From the MQ-9 Reaper live feed, he watched as *Sejong* launched its SH-60 in clear violation of exercise rules. Besides, the red sub wasn't supposed to be anywhere near where *Sejong* headed. Was it?

"Comms? Query *Sejong* and ask them to clue us in as to what they're doing."

"Aye, sir." A few moments later the petty officer turned and looked at Vin. "No response, sir."

"Mmm." Vin glanced at Woods. "Should we contact *Blue Ridge*, sir?"

"What would you suggest, Lieutenant?" the captain asked mildly, his black eyes inscrutable.

Vin had a ready answer, and then paused. This was an exercise and the captain sought to exercise everybody. As the junior TAO, Vin should be advising the captain, not that the skipper needed his advice. Besides, with its God view of everything, the command ship probably knew what was going on better than he did.

"Negative, sir. *Sejong* is the evolution commander. Although their action is unauthorized, we should wait and monitor the tactical situation."

"Carry on, Lieutenant," Woods said, giving no indication whether he agreed with Vin's assessment or not.

Unbelievably, he watched as the SH-60 dropped a depth charge. One minute later, the comms operator looked at him.

"Sir, *Sejong* reports a torpedo in the water."

Vin tensed and his heart beat faster. The ROK DDG had deliberately launched on what was likely a prowling PROK sub, thereby throwing the exercise program out the hatch. The fact that the thing had no business being in the engagement area at all made no difference. The situation was quickly getting very hairy.

Two minutes later the shadowing corvette changed course sharply to one-two-zero, which would bring it closer to *Curtis Wilbur*. A preliminary to an attack?

"Sir, *Blue Ridge* has ordered all units to withdraw. The exercise is canceled."

"I should damn well hope so," Captain Woods growled.

Vin pointed at the tactical screen and stared at the captain. The Aegis Electronic Warfare System was warning them the corvette had established a missile lock. "Sir…"

"I see it," Woods said quietly. "Comms? Warn that ship to break off missile lock and sheer off." With that order, he took effective command. "Announce action stations."

Immediately, the Claxon clanged and a coldly metallic voice came from the 1-MC speaker. "All hands, man your battle stations! This is not a drill!"

To Vin, this version of the video game had become very real, relieved that he did not have the responsibility for playing it out.

"If you don't mind, Lieutenant?" Woods said beside him and Vin hastily got up. The captain took his seat and immediately changed the ship's course farther to starboard.

"Bring up the Sea Sparrows and the main gun to ready state, and enable the Phalanx CIWS."

Still standing, Vin watched with dread as the corvette launched two Saccade anti-ship cruise missiles from a range of ten miles. At Mach .9, after jettisoning their boosters, flight time would be a bare forty seconds. Suddenly, everything happened too fast. He felt his face drain as he stared with morbid fascination at the tactical screen. Why were they doing this? Their sub wasn't hurt. More lives could end here, but he still felt a degree of detachment. *Only a video game*, he told himself.

"Vampire! Vampire! We have incoming missiles!"

"Fire chaff and enable autonomous defense," Woods snapped, allowing the Aegis freedom to defend the ship as it saw fit. This was electronic warfare and human reactions weren't fast enough. Maneuvering the ship out of the question, not against subsonic missiles and at such close range.

Vin bit his lower lip and watched as the two CSS-N-8 missiles bored in on *Steel Hammer*. He could feel the ship shudder slightly as the Aegis fired chaff rounds from the forward M-130 dispenser, followed by a ripple of four Sea Sparrow anti-air missiles. On the screen, he saw two blips target each oncoming threat. Agonizing seconds dragged by as the Aegis system waited to see if the Sparrows would hit. Three thousand yards from the ship, one cruise missile suddenly blossomed as the Sea Sparrows hit, but the second one had evaded. The Phalanx engaged immediately, throwing seventy-five armor piercing tungsten penetrator rounds per second from the Vulcan six-barreled Gatling gun.

"Take the corvette under main gun fire," Woods ordered instantly, turning the ship sharply to starboard to reduce its aspect.

At three hundred yards, Vin thought the Saccade would hit and braced himself. With the destroyer's 505-foot length, the missile had a lot of hull to aim for. This close the ship couldn't possibly evade, but then the missile suddenly detonated. The Phalanx had done its job, but left it a fraction late.

Hypervelocity shrapnel continued along the missile's trajectory and peppered the destroyer's port superstructure and hull. Burning fuel followed, splashing against the ship's side. *Steel Hammer* shuddered, but otherwise appeared unaffected. Molten fragments penetrated the ship's double-spaced steel plates and sprayed the CIC's interior. Consoles were ripped apart and men screamed. Lights flickered and cut wiring arced and spat. Without thinking, Vin threw himself at the captain.

Something slammed into his right side and back, and he gasped as lances of fire consumed his body. Slumped across Woods, his legs gave way and he folded to the deck. *You aren't supposed to get hurt in a video game,* he thought wryly. Pain burst in his head and everything faded.

Chapter Four

Admiral Pacino watched the empty sea where the North Korean corvette went down, unable to believe this was happening. In a mere few minutes a reckless act had developed into a major international incident, and it happened on his watch. It didn't matter that he wasn't personally responsible, the chair experts and second-guessers would nod their heads sagely, pointing out that this latest American aggression only confirmed their view that the annual land and sea exercises were a wasteful anachronism standing in the way of resolving a prickly standoff between the two Koreas. With no war to fight, the Navy was trigger-happy and its commanders undisciplined. Instead of increasing its presence in the Pacific, the United States should be scaling down, defusing tensions rather than adding to them.

No one would care that a rogue Korean captain had launched the first attack. All they would see is a powerful American destroyer sinking a small North Korean vessel. The tree-huggers and pacifists would love it. Pacino sighed, suddenly weary of it all. It was true what they said that truth was the first casualty of war. This wasn't war, exactly. Only perception counted these days. Perception created by the media and self-interest groups. Just when America was getting somewhere with the North Koreans, this had to happen. Not that he gave a damn one way or another, thankful that he wouldn't be handling the political fallout for this.

With a deep scowl, he looked away from the Korean admiral in utter disgust. If the ROK Navy Command wanted to play mind games with their northern neighbor, they could do it on their own time. *Damn it all!*

"Comms? Issue a Sierra Romeo Charlie to all units."

The communications commander stared at him for a moment. "All units to return to Point Charlie, aye aye, sir."

Admiral Chin climbed out of his chair and stood before Pacino. "Admiral, you don't have the authority to cancel Key Resolve! That decision must be made by both Fleet commanders."

"And I've halved your problem, Admiral," Pacino told the little man, his voice cold and gravelly. "You have a lot to answer for and I'll make sure you pay for this. Your presence is no longer required in the Command Center…sir."

Chin opened his mouth to say something, then snapped it shut, his small black eyes blazing with fury. He pursed his lips and stomped toward the hatch. Pacino watched it close after him with a clang. The little shit!

"Order *Masam* to close on *Sejong the Great* and render assistance."

"Aye aye, sir," the comms commander replied soberly. Everyone looked concerned and somewhat shocked at the horrible and speedy turn of events. "All ships acknowledging Sierra Romeo Charlie."

"Very well. Make to *Curtis Wilbur*. If able, search for survivors." In the chilly northern waters this time of year, any survivor would not last long. Still, the gesture had to be made, regardless how futile. It all seemed so pointless. What was worse, no one would appreciate it.

"Aye, sir." A few moments later the commander looked up. "*Wilbur* has acknowledged and is proceeding."

"Ask her to report status," Pacino demanded woodenly. Waiting, he watched the destroyer change course on the tactical screen. The PROK frigate had not made a move, so far. Waiting for orders?

"Sir, *Wilbur* reports shrapnel damage to port superstructure and hull. All fires suppressed. CIC took a hit and there are casualties. Two dead."

Pacino's stomach twisted at the thought of Vincent being one of them. Woods would have said something, wouldn't he? No, he was focused on his duty. Time enough for details and sentiment later. Everyone still had a job to do, and that included him.

Commander Rileigh turned from his screen. "Sir, the PROK frigate is making for the sunk corvette's position."

"The frigate just warned *Wilbur* to stand off," the comms commander announced.

Pacino nodded. The law of the sea demanded that preservation of human life took precedence over all other considerations. Unfortunately, the people who wrote that didn't have the North Koreans to contend with. He noted that *Wilbur* still maintained course. Regardless of any political consequences, it would take the PROK frigate much longer to reach the area. However unlikely, it was possible that someone had survived when the corvette went down. *Wilbur* was doing the right thing. He hoped the PROK frigate would see it in the same light. If not, there could be more bodies to fish out, and they would be North Korean bodies.

"Commander Rileigh, direct the Reaper to descend and focus on the corvette's position."

"Aye aye, sir," Rileigh acknowledged, then issued instructions to the Reaper's operators, located in the aft part of the Command Center.

Moments later the IR image shifted as the drone closed on the sunk ship's last known position. Pacino could see nothing but black rolling swell. If anyone was alive in there, the body heat would clearly identify the person. The sea was empty, but he had known that all along. Pointless, all so pointless.

Wilbur quickly closed on the corvette's location and launched a boat. Without further messages from the PROK frigate, the destroyer waited as the area was swept for survivors. With the frigate closing rapidly, the destroyer finished its search and retrieved her boat.

"Sir, *Wilbur* reports no survivors. They are withdrawing."

Pacino watched as the graceful destroyer slowly swung to starboard and put on revolutions.

"Comms? Advise the PROK frigate that we found no survivors."

"Aye, sir." The comms commander issued the message, and then slowly lifted his head. "Admiral, Captain Woods advises that Lieutenant Vincent Pacino has been severely injured. He launched his Sea Hawk with orders to make for Kunsan with the wounded."

Vincent!

Pacino grunted from the physical pain that suddenly churned his guts. He always knew that serving in the navy, even in peacetime, was dangerous. Innumerable things could turn around and bite if not handled properly. That did not take into account normal hazards of the sea. He had known it all intellectually, understanding that his son ran the same risk as anyone else on board a warship, but he had not been prepared for the emotional impact. He had seen others hurt and killed, and sympathized, but it was a detached, impersonal thing. The thought of his son mangled or disabled was like his own body had been torn up. It gave him a dramatic demonstration of the pain others suffered when hearing of a loved one wounded or lost.

He wanted to ask how badly Vin was hurt, but refrained. The fact they medivaced him, told Pacino it couldn't be trivial. He took a deep breath, emotions churning, and looked at the comms commander. "Thank you," he said quietly.

Everyone had heard, but the looks of helplessness were submerged as they turned pointedly to their screens and consoles. There was nothing they could do for him, perhaps glad that it wasn't one of them on the stretcher. Pacino had to deal with this himself, shutting out the anguish and desire to lash out. Compartmentalize and move on. This wasn't the time to get emotional and fall apart. Besides, admirals were not supposed to get emotional.

Setting his mouth in a tight line, he understood what Woods was doing. *Curtis Wilbur* simply wasn't equipped, and neither was *Blue Ridge*, to handle major medical trauma. Flying the wounded to the American Kunsan Air Base made sense. The installation was on the western side of the Korean peninsula and only some ninety miles from the exercise area. At its top speed of 170 mph, the MH-60 Sea Hawk would get there in forty minutes. The helicopter could have made for Seoul, a bit farther, but that would have involved getting civilian authority involved. Right now, such action not very advisable, and Pacino applauded Woods' foresight.

He climbed out of his seat and glanced at the exercises umpire. "Captain Roberts, advise the bridge to set course for Point Charlie, then proceed to Incheon where the fleet will await further orders. While anchored, they are to maintain constant readiness CIC watches. Arrange for Admiral Chin and his staff to be airlifted to the ROK Naval Headquarters at Chinhae. I want him off this ship without delay."

The grizzled captain nodded. "Aye aye, sir!"

"Download all logs and Reaper footage and have them ready for me in half an hour."

"You got it, Admiral."

"One more thing, Captain. I want a total media blackout on this. Not a word is to go out without my say-so. Clear?"

"Understood."

Pacino walked out of the Tactical Flag Command Center and made his way toward his quarters with heavy feet. Ruth would take this badly. As the only child, Vin had everything dotting parents could provide, even when Pacino wasn't always there for his son. His absences had hurt the boy, and every time Pacino came ashore from sea duty, he needed to get reacquainted.

Understandable resentment as Vin didn't understand why his father was not home like other dads. He understood that his father was in the navy, and that meant being away a long time, but Pacino knew that Vin resented him because he wasn't there when the boy needed him.

The change came when Pacino took his young boy on board his *Reliant*, a *Spruance*-class destroyer. He remembered like it were yesterday. The light shone in Vin's eyes as he gawked at the guns, radar mast and boxy superstructure. On the bridge, Vin sitting in the captain's chair, lord of everything he saw, the young boy transformed. When he confided with quiet determination that he too would one day command a ship, Pacino did not doubt at all that his son would. Ruth hadn't liked it, but thankfully, was wise enough to recognize Vin's unshakeable resolve. She hoped that he would grow out of what she considered a childish fantasy, but Vin never did.

Pacino opened the door to his cabin and decided he would call her in the morning. Nothing would be gained by telling her now, and possibly some harm. He wouldn't ruin her night. Anyway, in the morning, awake and refreshed, she would be better able to handle the shock. He would also have more information by then to tell her. At least he hoped so. He sat down in his little office, the hum of ship machinery soothing him, and stared at the yellow phone on the desk and finally pulled it toward him. Still the Key Resolve commander on station, there were responsibilities to discharge.

He would mourn later.

Picking up the handset, he punched in nine for the communications center.

"Yes, Admiral?"

"Put me through to Vice Admiral Owen."

"Aye aye, sir!"

He didn't have long to wait. Although almost 1930 hours, the

Commander, U.S. 7th Fleet, wouldn't be far from a phone. As Pacino knew, their respective jobs owned them. Their duties gave little time to either of them to enjoy the few privileges of their rank.

After listening to mindless background music, the line clicked.

"Kenneth? How you doing up there? It's only been a day and you're already bothering me." Owen gave a short barking laugh and Pacino smiled. The two of them got along, provided everything ran smoothly, which he endeavored to ensure.

"I hate to interrupt your evening, Admiral, but we have a situation," Pacino said quietly.

He could clearly picture the sixty-one-year-old wizened officer slipping into his official persona. His deep gray eyes would squint and Owen would lean forward slightly as he concentrated.

"The short version first," Owen demanded crisply, all traces of geniality gone.

"A ROK DDG driver violated exercise parameters and dropped a depth charge on a loitering PROK sub. One of their corvettes rippled off Saccade cruise missiles at *Curtis Wilbur* and got sunk for its trouble. We have casualties. I've suspended Key Resolve and we're regrouping before heading to Incheon, pending any decision to resume Key Resolve."

It took Owen a few seconds to digest the information and assess the political ramifications, then gave a weary sigh.

"Ah, shit!"

"Yeah, that's what I said," Pacino agreed. "Admiral, I think they told the ROK commander to wave the flag at the North Koreans. Admiral Chin as much as admitted it."

"Asshole! What have you done with him?"

"He's being bundled off the ship and ferried to Chinhae."

"He couldn't have liked it when you pulled the plug on Key Resolve," Owen growled. "Which was the right thing to do, by the way."

"Thank you, sir. Although I'd like nothing better than to

string the ROK captain from the yardarm, I think the North Koreans were also spoiling for a fight. Talks or no talks, we need to slap down those guys hard, Admiral. Both of them."

"That decision is not part of your job description, Kenneth."

"We've been going soft on everybody for too long and we're reaping the reward of appeasement."

"I'll pass that insight to the CNO. This fiasco will make him see red anyway. It won't make the President or Tanner happy either. They think they've got North Korea in the bag."

"They could have a problem, sir. Judging from what happened tonight, some of the PROK generals clearly disagree."

"It could've been a spur of the moment decision, you know. Anyway, that's for the President to sort out. You mentioned casualties."

"Captain Woods reported two dead and an unknown number wounded. He's dispatched them to Kunsan in his Sea Hawk."

"They've got the facilities," Owen agreed without argument. "Get one of your DDGs to lend you a Sea Hawk and get yourself to Kunsan, Admiral. I'll cut orders for one of their F-16s to ferry you back to Yokosuka the minute you're feet dry."

"Aye aye, sir," Pacino acknowledged.

"Keep a lid on this, Admiral. We need to sort things out before we face the press."

"Already done."

"You know, Kenneth, this isn't a can of worms, but a bucket of snakes!"

"You got that right."

"You got stuff for me to look at?"

"Within fifteen minutes, Admiral."

Owen sighed again. "Okay, let's get into the long version. I'll need to know what I'm talking about when I get Parker out of bed."

When the connection broke, Pacino stared at the phone, then slowly replaced the handset. *Blue Ridge* gently shifted under him as the ship rolled in the swell. Owen had his problems, but right now, they were insubstantial, something that didn't really matter. Pacino imagined his son, strapped down in a helicopter, flying through darkness. Would he find life when he touched down at Kunsan?

Without willing it, Vincent's life flashed before him in a cascade of blurred images in no particular order. There were flashes of laughter, pain and transformation from carefree boyhood into serious manhood. Unfortunately, there were also too many blank gaps when duty took Pacino away.

"My boy…" he whispered brokenly and felt his eyes sting. His throat tightened and he tried to swallow, but it went down hard.

* * *

Mark Price left his Chevy in the West Wing visitor parking lot and walked briskly toward the entrance. He squinted at a gray sky covered with patchy cloud that watery sunshine struggled to brighten. A light sprinkling of snow stood piled in corners, glinting in the light. The morning air crisp and lingered like cigarette smoke as he exhaled. Tomorrow already March and late to be seeing snow. He shook his head, not understanding it.

Weather wasn't the only thing that baffled him. The call last night from the White House chief of staff had been a surprise. That the president wanted to see him also came as a surprise. He had talked to Walters about carving up the Department of Homeland Security, thinking it was one of the president's passing pet notions, but Walters had dispelled that at their first meeting. Price raised some of the ideas his friend Thomas Meecham advocated, not taking them very seriously, but Walters had been receptive. When he thought about it, Meecham was right. The FBI already had legislative jurisdiction for internal security of the United States. DHS was merely another bloated bureaucracy, created by Bush in a knee-jerk reaction after 9/11 that sucked in resources and people like a vacuum cleaner, and likewise, delivered dirt at the other end. Give more authority to the FBI and the job of protecting America would be done, and would free badly needed money. A simple, neat solution. Unfortunately, politicians and bureaucrats rarely liked simple, neat solutions. It undermined their credibility for obfuscation.

Price had voiced less radical options to streamline the organization without involving total dismantlement, but he agreed with the president. DHS had grown into a monster and some of its arms needed chopping. His last talk with Walters over a month ago, he thought he was done. Any change to DHS would require detailed planning and impact analysis, not something to be done overnight. Even with the president's urging, the process bound to take some time. Was Walters ready to discuss a proposal? If so, he would probably want to do that with Ed Bishop, the DHS Director, unless the president wanted to use him as a sounding board first.

As Director, National Operations Center, the business end of DHS operations, as Price called it, he held a very responsible position, but departmental reorganization wasn't part of his job description. The fact that he was chummy with the president had already ticked Bishop off, much to the amusement of Colin Forbes, Director, Office of Operations Coordination, and Price's boss. Pissing off the DHS director not exactly career enhancing, but if the president asked him to come in and talk, Price wasn't about to say no. Anyway, he had things to air, and if he was going to bitch, might as well do it to someone who could do something about it.

The Secret Service checked him in with a polite nod and an entry in a logbook when they saw the unrestricted access badge pinned to his left lapel. He quickly made his way through the West Wing. Still short of eight o'clock, the corridors were already filled with hurrying civil servants, some in deep conversation, others wore anxious looks as they clutched folders for imaginary protection. Armed guards stood unobtrusively around corners and doorways, ready to step in should a disturbance interrupt the business of government. Passing the formidable Ms. Davies, the chief of staff's stern-faced guardian, Price found himself in the Oval Office reception area.

Unice looked up from her flat computer screen and flashed him a smile. "Good morning, Mr. Price. How was the drive in?"

"It's murder on the Beltway," Price said. She always asked him the same question and he always gave her the same answer.

"You found a parking spot, sir?"

"The Chairman of the Joint Chief's slot was empty. If he decides to come in, he'll draft me and bust me to private. At my age, I'll look real silly with a crew cut lugging a fifty-pound pack."

Unice chuckled as she picked up the phone. "I doubt he would do anything that drastic…Mr. President? Mark Price is here…Very good, sir." She replaced the receiver and nodded. "You can go in."

"Thanks, Unice."

He strode to the heavy white door, pulled down the handle and stepped in.

"Ah, Mark! Good of you to come." Walters waved at him from behind his desk.

"Good morning, Mr. President."

"Grab a seat."

Price was puzzled to see Manfred Cottard and Graham Stone sitting on a sofa, both looking relaxed. Only mild curiosity, as he saw both often enough not to feel intimidated.

"How are you, Mark?" Stone queried pleasantly as he leaned over the coffee table, filling a cup from a silver pot.

"Not too bad, thanks," Price said cautiously, having expected a private session with the president.

He didn't mind the elderly admiral at all. Without his help, the Israelis might very well have gotten away with their sabotage of the Valero refinery. What also made him valuable was his extensive knowledge of all things military, coupled with sharp political awareness, probably a prerequisite of his position as the National Security Advisor. Security these days meant far more than simply dealing with military threats.

"Here, you'll need this." Stone held up a cup and saucer.

Price looked at him suspiciously as he took the cup and sat on the opposite sofa. Taking a sip of the fragrant brew, he held the cup in his lap.

"Right, now that we're all here…" Walters cleared his throat. "I have been very impressed with how you handled the Valero Texas City Refinery incident, Mark. Despite your unorthodox approach requiring the kidnapping a senior Mossad officer and making him spill his guts, which by the way nailed the Israelis, Graham here has been singing your praises, but you didn't need them."

"I was one man in a team, Mr. President. Thomas Meecham deserves most of the credit."

"That's why he's now in Washington, rather than enjoying Houston's less than salubrious climate. Having the John the Baptist scroll mess dumped in my lap last July, and getting a call from the Pope himself demanding that we return the thing, perhaps Meecham should have stayed in Houston. Never mind. Valero was a neat job, but what I also liked was your clinical evaluation of the Department of Homeland Security and your suggestions how to clean it up. You didn't have a personal agenda and you presented options not necessarily to your liking, or mine. That was good. You analyzed the problem and gave me several alternatives how to solve it. Some I didn't care for, but that doesn't mean I didn't need to hear them. What I valued most, you shied away from injecting personalities, concentrating on the national need and function. I wish others in my Cabinet practiced the same philosophy, but that's another matter."

Walters paused and Price met the president's penetrating eyes without looking away. He always cut it the way he saw it, and that had probably cost him his CIA job as Deputy Director of Operations. Zardwovsky's thinly veiled hostility hadn't helped. He wasn't a team player, the fat shit complained more than once. What his boss said, Price wasn't polishing the right Company egos, or ingratiating himself enough with Zardwovsky. In plain English, he didn't play the office politics game acceptable to the powers that be. When Zardwovsky tried to shaft him after a mission went belly up, making it like it was all Price's fault, they were never going to be pals.

"How fixated are you on your job with DHS?" Walters asked mildly, his eyes glittering with amusement.

Price wasn't entirely sure where this was heading, but the president clearly relished the come-on play.

"It's had its moments, but I think my department is humming now." He wasn't bragging, merely stating a fact, something that Walters could easily verify.

"Colin Forbes said the same thing, and I have a lot of time for Forbes. He'll be busy implementing some of the changes you and I talked about. DHS will not be totally dismantled, and the FBI will get more authority as you recommended. I imagine the news isn't going to thrill Ed Bishop a whole lot. If he can't handle it, nobody is indispensable. I like the way you operate, Mark, and I want you to sort out another problem for me. That's why I'm asking if you'd be willing to consider a new position."

"It would have to be a real challenge to contemplate a move, sir, and I like working for Forbes."

Cottard and Stone smiled broadly, and Walters chortled with genuine humor. "Oh, it would be a challenge, all right. I want you to take the job as the next CIA Director."

Well, crap!

The buzzing in Price's ears suddenly got louder. He lifted his cup and took what he hoped would look like a normal sip. He needed a moment to steady himself. Boss the CIA? The place needed a shakeup and some serious branch pruning, which he had advocated for years. Was he the man to do it? Could he overcome the enormous organizational inertia, entrenched bureaucracy, stifling procedures and poisonous infighting, focusing on what the agency was really about? Whoever took this on seriously would not be loved, a given. He would need to wear a flak jacket, and probably a 24/7 bodyguard, to avoid being assassinated. The president wasn't kidding about the job being a challenge.

"You did say *next*, sir?"

"I did. Raymond Grant wasn't up to it and decided it would be better if he made room for someone else," Walters said dryly and Price suppressed a smile.

Grant had gotten the chop! Not that he grieved or anything. The shithead had it coming.

"Oversight?" Price asked, looking directly at the president.

"The normal Congressional mandates still apply. Apart from that, you'll have complete autonomy, provided you deliver. Cottard and Stone have a few suggestions you might want to consider, but that's all they are...suggestions. You'll have a free hand to address problems this Administration has identified that need fixing. How you fix them, and anything else that's come unstuck, will be up to you. As a former operative, I imagine you have a few ideas of your own about that place. If you take the job, you'll face opposition not only on the Hill, but within the Agency itself, and that's where the real challenge will lie. Slotting you in there is sure to get some noses out of joint, which you'll have to deal with. I need someone there who can give me reliable intelligence, not a rehash of CNN news a day after it happens. What do you say? I think you're up to the job, but I won't shove you into it. If you don't think you can cut it, tell me now. I sure as hell don't want to find out the hard way."

Price admired the president's straight shooter approach, which wasn't altogether surprising from a former fighter pilot. He was being rushed and Walters probably knew it, but it could also be a test if he could think on his feet. The president needed a decision maker, not another obfuscating politician.

Clean up the CIA? Man, put him in a pit of rattlesnakes instead! Zardwovsky would be one of the first to go, not just because he hated the man's guts.

"I do have one problem, Mr. President."

"Let's have it."

"I don't want to be fighting the NSA every time I want SIGINT information. When I was there, the CIA always had to claw to get anything out of them, and I don't believe things have changed since. It got so bad, the Company was forced to build its own earth receiver stations to capture signals intelligence, but it's a crazy duplication of effort and cost. I certainly had my share of grief with them while at DHS."

Walters stared at his National Security Advisor. "How about it, Graham?"

Stone winced and shrugged. "He has a point, sir. There have been complaints, and not only from the Agency."

"I'm giving them what? Eight billion a year? The CIA gets half that…less. For that, all I get is lousy HUMINT analysis. What the hell are they doing with all that money? Talk to Trent Bruster, Graham. I want this nonsense stopped or I'll issue an Executive Order and there'll be some changes with the management structure over there. NSA serves the national interest, and it does that by providing signals intelligence to whoever needs it! I thought this information hoarding crap was sorted out after 9/11."

"I'll get on it, sir," Stone assured him.

"Another thing. Organize a summary audit of the place. I want to know what's going on over there."

"I'll look into it."

"While you're at it, I want your brief on all our intelligence agencies. They've had six months to write one. I want to see where we can rationalize procedures, use of assets, and cut duplication."

Stone winced and shifted in his seat. "You'll be stirring a hornet's nest here, Mr. President."

"So? I placed everybody on notice, Graham, and they know it. If they cannot demonstrate a core reason for existing, they're gone."

"Yes, sir."

"Get something on my desk within a week." The President turned to Price. "Satisfied?"

Price blinked at the speed this was done, but Walters was like that. He gave a wry smile. "I'll find out the hard way, won't I, sir?"

Walters chuckled. "Talk to Graham if you strike a problem. So, what's it going to be, Mark?"

Price didn't have to think hard or weigh up his options. The job would probably age him before his time, but what a challenge! If he could get Meecham in as the FBI liaison, at least some of his problems would be solved.

"I'll do it, Mr. President, and thank you for your confidence," he said with resolve, already running over the table of organization.

"Outstanding! You've got a day to pack your things and clean out your office. I want you at Langley tomorrow for a handover with Grant. Once you're fully briefed, show him the door."

"About Mr. Forbes…"

"You can say your goodbyes with a clear conscience. I've already clued him in. Before you start steamrolling, we have a situation in North Korea that Grant created for us. Perhaps I should have mentioned it before you said yes. When you hear what it is, you might want to change your mind."

Price smiled. "Let's hear it, sir, and then I'll let you know."

Walters laughed. "Want to back out already? Cottard and Stone will fill you in. Take him away, boys. Good luck, Mark. You'll need it."

The phone rang and Walters picked up. "Yes, Unice?" He listened, nodded slowly, and suddenly looked weary. "I'll join them in the Situation Room." He replaced the receiver and stood up. "It looks like we have another development with North Korea. We've just sunk one of their ships. You'll have to rearrange my schedule for the day, Manfred, and make the necessary apologies."

"Of course, Mr. President."

Stone stood up and stepped to the president's desk. "What happened?"

"I don't have any details. Jason McDonald and Admiral Parker are here to fill us in. Let's go. You too, Mark. This now definitely concerns you."

Price slowly rose, wondering what was going on. A North Korean ship sunk? He was already dealing at a level far above his previous position and wondered whether he had made the right decision. His operational awareness had been jerked from the comfortable confines of Homeland Security to the world stage, and he felt the cool breeze. He braced himself and took a deep breath. The scope might be huge, but like any job, it was a mosaic of layered tasks. As long as he handled one piece at a time, he wasn't going to be overwhelmed.

"I think we'll also need Tanner, Mr. President," Cottard said and slowly rubbed his nose.

"Get Unice to call him," Walters said briskly and strode toward the door.

Price walked behind Stone, the National Security Advisor moving quickly, showing none of his age. Two Secret Service agents followed them, keeping a watchful eye on the president. As they made their way down wide stone stairs, Price eagerly wanted to see the Situation Room, the tactical nerve center where the National Command Authority did business.

Downstairs, a floor beneath the Oval Office, an impeccably dressed marine sergeant opened a polished wooden door and snapped to attention. Walters walked through without giving him a glance. When Price stepped into the gloomy interior, the two officers inside stood up smartly. Walters sat down at the head of the long polished table and everybody made themselves comfortable. The marine closed the door behind them. Price sat next to Stone and took in the place at a glance, absorbing everything.

The cave-like rectangular room had subdued lighting coming from ceiling cornices and down lights focused on the table. Apart from three speakerphones, the dark surface bare. A giant LED screen, showing the Yellow Sea and the Korean peninsula, took up most of the far wall, flanked on either side by smaller screens. Tucked against the right corner sat what looked like a communications console. The place smelled of warm electrical circuits. Cool air-conditioning kept the room from feeling cozy. Price figured the president didn't come here to be cozy.

He turned his attention to the two officers across the table. He had seen General Jason McDonald, Chairman of the Joint Chiefs of Staff, on TV and the papers, but first time in the flesh. The man was huge, probably six-foot four, square head, thick neck and a powerful body that had not gone to seed. At over six-foot two, Price not a small man, but the general dominated the room. Dark brown eyes stared at him unwaveringly, doing an assessment of their own. Price decided he would need to study this man carefully.

The four-star admiral sitting beside the general visibly shorter and trimmer. Above a high forehead, the peppery hair combed straight back. Wearing rimless glasses, the naval officer bore the same intense look of all 'can do' people. The six rows of ribbons on his left breast attested to achievements gained under fire and adversity—another tough customer to be reckoned with.

Just then, the Secretary of State rushed in, slightly breathless, and sat down next to the admiral.

"Before we start, some introductions are in order," Walters said sharply. "Next to Stone is Mark Price. You may have seen him before. He'll be taking over from Grant, subject to Congressional approval, which he will get. I don't own both Houses for nothing. Get to know him. For your benefit, Mark, the man taking up most of the table is Jason McDonald. His term as Chairman of the Joint Chiefs will expire at end of the year, to the relief of many in the Pentagon, I should imagine, but a man who gets things done. Don't hesitate to use him. Beside him is Admiral Wayne Parker, Chief of Naval Operations. Next to him is my Secretary of State, Larry Tanner. You guys can chat later and swap lies."

Price gave McDonald a rueful grin. "If you're wondering who took your parking spot, General, you can blame me for that."

"That was *your* beat-up Chevy?" McDonald looked outraged. "Next time, I'll have it towed away!"

The president crossed his arms over the desk, his eyes hard. "Fight it out later. Okay, General, let's have it."

"The bare bones first, Mr. President," McDonald said in a deep voice after giving Price a glare. "Last night, at approximately 1845 hours local during a routine Key Resolve exercise, a ROK destroyer dropped a depth charge near a prowling PROK sub. Suspecting a genuine attack or just being trigger-happy, it squirted off a torpedo and hit the destroyer. A loitering PROK corvette rippled off two Saccade anti-ship cruise missiles at one of our DDGs and got sunk instead. Admiral Pacino immediately suspended Key Resolve and the 7th Fleet contingent is steaming for Incheon."

Price could hardly believe it. Well, crap! This certainly was a development. He looked closely at the president for a reaction. The man appeared calm, evaluating the situation and the implications. Price wondered how Walters did it, juggling what must be a thousand problems running a government, yet still managing to look cool.

"That's almost four hours ago our time, General," Walters said thoughtfully. "Why wasn't I notified earlier?"

"It took time to get all the information together and have Admiral Parker updated, sir," McDonald said without flinching.

"There is something else you need to know, Mr. President," Parker added in a firm voice and everybody looked at him.

He had a presence, Price decided. But then, everyone in the room had it. He wondered mildly if he projected the same authority, then gave a mental shrug, not giving a damn. His results would do the PR image for him.

"This wasn't enough, Admiral?"

"The South Koreans may have been pursuing an agenda of their own," Parker said softly, no need to shout. The air-conditioning whispered in the background.

"And we know this how?" Walters demanded.

"Admiral Chin, the Korean Key Resolve commander, as much as admitted it."

Walters passed a hand through his hair. "What the hell was that PROK sub sneaking around the exercise area for anyway? We told them what we were doing. It looks like both sides were out to score points. Casualties?"

"Nine dead and eleven wounded on the ROK destroyer, sir," Parker said. "It's under power and steaming for Incheon. We have three wounded and two dead on the DDG from a close Saccade detonation. There were no survivors from the PROK corvette. They normally carry a complement of thirty-eight."

"What a mess," Walters said and sighed.

"Mr. President, Admiral Pacino wants the Koran Navy Command to press charges against the ROK destroyer captain and Admiral Chin," Parker added. "He also advocates punitive action against the North Koreans."

The president smiled without humor. "Commendable sentiment, and under different circumstances, understandable. Your assessment, Admiral?"

"We're still evaluating the details, but the situation is clear enough. Personally, I think Admiral Pacino has a point. The

South Koreans have grown arrogant, baiting their neighbor unnecessarily, confident that whatever mess they create, America will bail them out. I'm not questioning our Pacific deployment posture, but I submit, sir, the ROK destroyer driver would not have taken the action he did without full authority from Admiral Chin."

"And he in turn would have been given the green light by Seoul," Walters said wearily. "Speculative, but plausible. The North Korean response?"

Parker shrugged. "They were shadowing our ships with a missile frigate, a corvette, and an OSA II patrol boat. When we dropped our depth charge, the sub captain, or the squadron command ship more likely, may have made a unilateral decision to retaliate. Given their regimented command structure, I would lean toward the latter, but I'm not discounting the possibility that this was a planned response."

"And Chin pulled the trigger. What does the Korean Navy Command have to say?"

"So far, nothing. They're probably still digesting the situation. We have a press blackout for the moment, but this is bound to get out soon."

"Okay, Admiral…General. I want all the facts and details by eleven. I'll see both of you upstairs, then. As of right now, this year's Key Resolve is canceled."

"Sir, do we pull back the fleet?" McDonald asked

"No, keep them at Incheon for the time being. In case we want to make a statement or something."

"Statement?"

"Like parading them outside the North Korean naval base at Haeju Bay, General!" Walters snapped sarcastically.

"Very good, Mr. President," McDonald said and his mouth curved in a lazy smile.

The two officers stood and quickly walked out of the room. When the door closed behind them, Walters smashed his fist against the table.

"Damnation! We've been propping up South Korea for over sixty years and they pay us back by being real dumb. Sung Kang-dae was supposed to keep a low profile with this year's Key Resolve."

"It might not be him at all, Mr. President," Stone said pointedly. "A lot of his military are not enamored with the idea of easing their posture vis-à-vis the West, or the very real prospect of being trimmed down. We have a number of vested interests at play over there."

"I agree," Tanner said thoughtfully. "Talking to Sung, although he would have preferred Key Resolve canceled altogether, he didn't make a fuss over it. I couldn't see him sabotaging our talks by taking an aggressive stance after we've given him Foal Eagle."

"So, one of his admirals decided to wave the flag?"

"Possibly more than one. That flag may not have been entirely for the South Korean benefit either."

"A warning to Sung, eh? The PROK generals like their cushy positions and want to keep them." Walters smiled and shook his head. After a moment, he looked at Price. "This is probably way over your head, Mark, and I don't expect your input right now, but this development makes it imperative that you get up to speed. Graham...Manfred, when we're done here, don't let him leave the building until he knows what you know."

The National Security Advisor gave Price a wry smile. "If you want to bail out, now is as good a time as any."

"I didn't mean for you to discourage him," Walters said with a hollow grin.

Price pulled at his chin. "Those talks you referred to, Mr. Secretary," he ventured, sorting out the jumble of information that landed on him. "I gather we're making some sort of peace overtures to North Korea?"

"It's more in the nature of a carrot and the stick, Mark, and it's Larry to you. If that were all, this sinking incident would be merely a regrettable blip, but we also have a possible palace coup in the offing designed to depose Sung."

The possibilities marched in Price's mind and something clicked. He turned and looked at Walters.

"Mr. President, the plotters, could they be behind this? Taking advantage of an unexpected situation to weaken Sung's authority and move in?"

Walters stared at him, then slowly nodded. "A novel interpretation, Mark." He glanced across the table. "Larry?"

Tanner gave Price a thoughtful look. "It certainly is a novel interpretation, Mr. President, and makes more sense than having to deal with a rogue admiral or two, although I'm not discounting the possibility. Kham Chang-uk could not have anticipated what happened, but positioning that PROK sub to hassle our forces might have been deliberately provocative. He does have a number of senior military officers in his pocket, and he did say the takeover plans were almost complete."

"Something for you and Mark to look at," Walters said.

"Since Admiral Parker raised the possibility," Price added softly, "how committed is South Korea to normalizing relations with the North? There could be elements within their own military not too thrilled at the idea and the prospect of subsequent reduction in American weapons handouts, and the strategic support we provide. We're virtually paying for their defense posture. It's striking how similar their behavior is to the Israeli Defense Force's resistance to peace overtures with the Palestinians."

Walters frowned. "You're saying the South Korean government might not have known anything about this?"

"Yes, sir. Then again, perhaps they did. Would Admiral Chin have acted on his own?"

"You're full of ideas this morning, aren't you? Larry?"

"Both scenarios are possible," Tanner conceded reluctantly, a worried frown creasing his brow.

"Look into it. Okay. How do we contain this?"

"It might be an idea if you called Sung, Mr. President," Cottard said firmly. "I'd also talk to the Korean president, Samun Man-shik. Both might be pissed at what's happened and we need to find out what they're going to do about it. However, we can't let this distract us from our discussions to normalize relations with North Korea."

"I agree. Before I start calling anyone, I need facts, which McDonald will hopefully have when I see him. In the meantime, arrange for me to talk with the families of the two dead men."

"Yes, sir."

"Mr. President, this is something I think I should handle. Talk to Sung, I mean," Tanner said evenly. "I know how you enjoy running off on your own, but in this case an unguarded word could have unfortunate consequences. Besides, I know both men and Sung now knows me."

Walters gave him a nasty grin. "You don't trust me to be diplomatic, is that it?"

"Not exactly, but—"

"I'll talk to Samun and you can have Sung, okay? I've dealt with Samun before."

Price could tell Tanner wasn't happy, but the Secretary of State gave in with a gracious nod. There wasn't anything else he could do anyway. Watching the byplay, it gave Price an interesting insight into a government at work.

"Some sort of coordinated media position might be to everyone's advantage before both sides overreact," Cottard prompted.

"Which they will anyway," Walters said grumpily. "Prepare something with Granger and let me see it. Keep the Vice President in the loop. This also brings me back to my original question. Should we support Kham and his faction? If we don't handle this right, the whole thing could degenerate into an acrimonious slinging match that could derail any overtures with Sung."

"That's a decision only you can make, Mr. President," Tanner said soberly. "You can do what's morally right and face possible upheaval in North Korea if Kham's faction takes over, but which in the long run will stabilize the region. The pragmatic option could usher a period of stability and progressive reform, however slowly, but at a cost of more purges if we betray Kham."

"And significant diplomatic damage to the United States by propping up what we know is a brutal dictatorial regime," Walters added thoughtfully.

Price closely studied the president's reaction, and only saw firm resolve, but to do what? He had seen Walters willing to castigate Israel over the Valero incident and reach out a conciliatory hand to Iran, both unpopular moves in some quarters, at home and abroad, but his actions were vindicated by demonstrable stabilization of the Middle East region. Would the president be prepared to do the same thing with South Korea, or would political expediency prevail once again simply to achieve a formative relationship with North Korea?

He definitely needed to get an update from Tanner. If this were mishandled, more than Kham Chang-uk's head would be on the block.

* * *

Sitting in the back seat of his official car, Admiral Pacino gazed absently at traffic flowing along Main Street, and at stores and restaurants on either side. Dusk slowly settled and bright streetlights softened the sharp angles of the buildings. Despite the chill in the air, lots of civilians and military types moved along the broad sidewalks, going shopping, strolling or having a meal out. The Yokosuka naval base was large, with facilities to match. All a blur now, a distraction, and he wasn't paying attention.

The cluster of apartment buildings that made up the housing complex loomed in front of him and the driver slowed down. Taking a left turn, the sedan crept toward the tenement entrance and stopped. The driver immediately stepped out and hurried around the car to open the door where Pacino sat. He set his mouth in a tight line, climbed out and looked up at the nine-story building, lights shining from most of its windows.

"I'll be waiting here, Admiral," the petty officer announced crisply, standing at attention.

"Thanks, Neil," Pacino said softly and made his way toward the entrance, feeling his stomach tense. This would be ugly, but it wasn't something he could delegate.

On his way from Kunsan, he had lots of time to think, perhaps too much time. Under normal circumstances, he would have enjoyed the exhilarating flight in an F-16 Falcon, but last night, he only wanted to get it over with. Regardless of any personal feelings, as deputy commander of one of the largest naval fleets in the world, Admiral Owen expected him to act accordingly. When they met, the bare facts of the incident were quickly disposed of. Records from *Curtis Wilbur* and *Blue Ridge*, supported by damning video from the Reaper UAV, were irrefutable. What took time was discussing the whys and preparing follow-up recommendations for the Chief of Naval Operations. This was beyond Owen's authority to resolve summarily, the admiral happy to pass it up the line to Parker.

Then the call came from the Kunsan base hospital.

He didn't get home until almost midnight. Confronting Ruth turned out to be one of the toughest things he'd had to do in all his life. Not a pleasant night.

A soft *ting* from the right elevator and Pacino stepped toward it as the two-door panels slid back. Inside, he pressed the sixth floor button, faced the door and clasped his hands behind his back. The doors closed with a sigh and the elevator surged up.

In the brightly lit corridor, he walked briskly over the hard carpet and paused before apartment 605. He clenched his teeth, reached out and pressed the doorbell button. He heard the chime inside and waited. A few moments later the lock clicked and

Linda opened the door. Her face lit up with obvious pleasure.

"Kenneth! This is a surprise. What are you doing here? I thought you were out boating somewhere in the Yellow Sea."

Pacino removed his braided cap and tucked it under his left armpit. "I was, but there has been a development. Can I come in?"

She frowned and stepped aside. "Of course."

He walked in and waited for her to close the door.

"I'm fixing dinner," she said brightly, but he could see tension around her eyes. "A chicken stir-fry. You can be the official taster. Come inside and I'll fix you a drink."

"Linda..." He hung his cap on a hook beside the door, reached for her hands and held them. Color drained from her face and she tensed, her large eyes staring at him tragically.

"It's Vin, isn't it?" she whispered and bit her lower lip. "What's happened to him? He isn't..."

"No, he's alive, but he's been badly hurt," Pacino said gruffly, feeling her pain, anxiety and torment. He wished this wasn't happening. "*Curtis Wilbur* suffered shrapnel damage from a cruise missile near miss and CIC took damage. There were casualties."

"No!" Her eyes filled and fat tears slid down her cheeks.

He pulled her against him and held her trembling body tight, feeling a lump grow in his throat. Forced to live through it all again, the hurt and anguish just as sharp.

After a few sniffs, she looked up. "Let me go, please. I'm all right." She dabbed at her eyes and searched his face. "How bad?"

Pacino wanted to laugh at the absurdity of that question. How do you describe mangled flesh, broken bones and a body that will never be whole again? How do you make it up to a vibrant woman whose life of promise and a bright future suddenly shredded by an exploding missile? How do you make everyone pay, not only for his hurt, but the hurt suffered by others, and would continue to suffer?

Something of his own pain must have shown, because Linda

reached out with her small hand and gently brushed his right cheek.

"I'm sorry, Kenneth," she whispered. "He's part of you as much as he is part of me."

Pacino swallowed, pushing it all back. "When the missile went off, Vin threw himself at Captain Woods. If he hadn't done that, Woods might very well have been killed. As it is, Vin was struck in the back and right side by shrapnel. He lost part of his liver and a kidney. They're not sure about his spleen."

"My God!" She pressed her knuckles against her mouth and stared at him in horror.

"There is something else," he said slowly, wanting badly to somehow undo it all. "He has a severed spinal cord."

After a moment of incomprehension, the shock hit her and she screamed in agony.

"No! Oh, God, no! No!"

Stricken with his own grief, Pacino gathered her in his arms. She struggled, beating her tiny fists against his chest, shaking her head from side to side.

"I want to see him! I want to see him!"

He stroked her short, soft raven hair and held her. "We'll both go and see him," he whispered to her.

After a while, spent, she sagged against him and moaned. "No. Please no…Oh, Vin…"

Just like that, not one life destroyed, but two; four if he included Ruth and himself. She took it just as badly when he told her. All those deaths, on both sides, and for what? It all seemed so pointless.

His cellphone went off. He dug it out of his jacket pocket and flipped open the lid.

"Pacino!"

"Kenneth, it's David," Admiral Owen announced softly. Something in his voice made Pacino immediately tense and his mouth went dry.

"Yes, sir?"

"Sorry to call you like this, and I wish to heaven that I didn't have to. I got a call from Kunsan. It's your son. He didn't make it. There was simply too much damage."

A tingle ran down his body and Pacino went rigid. He understood what Owen said, but it didn't register, like it happened to somebody else. He closed his eyes tight and clenched his mouth as memories chased each other. Without saying anything, he snapped the lid shut and slid the phone into his pocket. He looked helplessly at Linda, but the words wouldn't come.

"I heard," she whispered brokenly, tears sliding down her cheeks. "This can't be happening. It's a nightmare. Please God…"

Feeling hollow and old, he swallowed hard and cleared his throat. "At least he didn't suffer," he said harshly, his intellectual side doing the talking.

Looking at it objectively, he was right. Had he lived, Vin would have been a cripple, just another poor slob whose life was jerked from under him. What could he look forward to? A lifetime of pity and phony sympathy, gazing at the sea and a future now forever beyond his grasp? Perhaps Vin could have made something of himself. The boy had always been strong willed and determined. Well, Pacino would now never know as he held on, listening to the cold, calculating part of himself. If he weakened just once, his emotions would overwhelm him in a rage of destruction like a burst dam.

He would grieve later.

Vincent…

Linda sniffed, reached out with her hand and wiped his cheeks, giving him a wan smile, tears streaming down her face.

"Admirals aren't supposed to cry," she choked.

"Fat lot you know," he said brusquely, not realizing that he was crying.

"I want to be alone now, Kenneth. Do you mind?"

"I do mind. You're coming with me. Being alone right now is not what you want."

She lifted her head and her eyes flashed. "Is that an order, Admiral?"

"No, Linda. You're upset and you need to be with your family."

"Family? My family is…" She stopped and her mouth gaped as she realized what she had said. Suddenly contrite, her shoulders sagged. "I'm so sorry, Kenneth. I never—"

"I know. It's all right. Forget it. We need to get over this together. I can't force you to come with me, but you really don't want to be alone right now."

"Ruth…she doesn't know," she said brokenly. "Oh, Kenneth!" She clung to him and sobbed. After a moment, she stepped away from him, tilted back her head and screamed. "Damn you all!"

Feeling like screaming himself, he could only wonder what went on in her mind. Did it hurt more now that Vin was dead, cheating her out of their future, or that he would not be with her anymore, even if only as a cripple? Women looked at these things differently. He would have to ask Ruth sometime…after a while.

His calculating side told him it was better this way, but he didn't believe it. As long as there was life and intellect, every person was worth saving. He would have to talk to Ruth about that, too.

Eyes red, Linda wiped her cheeks, glanced down, and patted her slacks. "It'll be better for Ruth if I'm there," she said firmly, a new resolve in her voice. "Give me a moment to switch things off." She made for the kitchen, then stopped. "You want a drink? I could sure use one."

Pacino nodded and followed her. "Me too. Make it bourbon, straight."

"It's the night for it," she agreed grimly.

In the kitchen, she switched off the ceramic cooktop and

pushed a simmering pot to one side. Chopped vegetables lay piled on a glass board. She removed a steel bowl from a drawer and scooped in the vegetables. Sniffing, she brushed her cheeks with a jerky swipe of her hand. She covered the bowl with cling wrap and slid it into the refrigerator.

She glanced at him and smiled, a hollow, empty thing. "Sit down. I'll bring the glasses."

As she disappeared into the lounge, Pacino pulled back a chair from the breakfast table. He sat down and let out a long sigh. Life sucks, he decided. What was it all for, he wondered. Right then, it didn't seem to make a whole lot of sense.

Linda emerged carrying a bottle of amber liquid and two crystal tumblers. She seated herself and poured them generous measures, her hand trembling only a little.

"Ice?"

He shook his head, picked up a glass and held it up.

"To Vin."

She blanched, bit her lip and forced a small smile. "To Vin," she echoed and took a long swallow, then made a face. "And I told him not to be a hero." Her mouth sagged and he could see her fighting to hold back the tears. They spilled over and she let them run.

He tossed back the whiskey in one swallow and exhaled the biting fumes. Glancing at the bottle of Wild Turkey, he reached for it and poured himself two fingers.

She held the tumbler between her hands and searched his face. "What happened out there, Kenneth? You mentioned a cruise missile. The North Koreans?"

"Stupid! All so stupid. The South Koreans started it. They made a mock attack on a PROK sub and it went downhill from there. Everybody overreacted."

"Many dead?"

"On the South Korean destroyer and the PROK corvette that *Wilbur* sunk."

"And Vin," she added softly.

"And Vin. Everybody too eager."

Her eyes were fixed on him. "What are you going to do about it?"

He looked at her in astonishment. "What *can* I do about it? The politicians have it now. We take our orders, go out again—"

"And die again. For what, Kenneth? What's the point of it all?"

He took a gulp of whiskey and clutched the tumbler. "I can't fix the world, Linda, no matter how much I might want to. No one man can."

"So we let the politicians bury it, is that it? All in the name of some higher purpose? Does anybody even count the lives we toss away for that higher purpose, whatever that might be? Does anybody care?"

"I care," Pacino said firmly and meant it.

"Then do something about Vin and the others…on both sides."

He saw the steely determination in her eyes, the demand, and frowned. "What do you expect me to do? File a strongly worded protest with the UN? Go to the papers? I've talked to Owen and he's going to discuss it with the CNO."

She shook her head and exhaled harshly. "Follow the chain of command, right. That will get everybody hopping for sure."

Pacino finished the bourbon and stood up. "Linda, I'd love nothing better than to stick it to both sides, but I'm not a vigilante and there is a lot more at stake here than Vin's life. You ought to know that."

"What could be more important than Vin's life? Tell me that?" She stared at him with contempt and sneered. "I thought you said you cared, but you're like the others, worried only about your precious rank. Everybody can go to hell as long as they don't take away your medals. Badges of death, that's all they are. You're willing enough to pull the trigger when ordered, but when it comes to doing something right and taking the initiative, you hide behind your uniform."

Her words cut into him like a searing knife and his mouth twisted with anguish and anger. He wanted to smash her for daring to talk to him like that. Instead, he leaned forward and glared at her.

"Now you listen to me, young lady! I faced death and I gave orders to kill. It's the price I paid to protect civilians like you! It's the price Vin paid, and he never hesitated to pay it. He's dead and I would gladly swap places with him. If I could, I'd shoot the son of a bitch who caused it, but there is nothing I *can* do. So don't give me any of your cheap melodramatic psychology crap about doing what's right!"

"We write him off then, is that it? A nameless pawn thrown away without regard by faceless Washington men."

Pacino saw his son standing proudly on *Reliant's* deck, jaw firm, his eyes fixed on the sea beyond the ship, voicing his resolve to command a ship just like it, and his heart tore. His eyes stung and he blinked rapidly. He wanted to lash out and physically punish not only the stupid ROK destroyer driver, but also those who had sanctioned his action and the trigger-happy PROK morons who wanted to demonstrate their superiority to the imperialists. Unfortunately, there wasn't anything he could *do*.

Regulations controlled his life, without which anarchy would rule rampant. Couldn't Linda see that? Helpless, knowing that somehow he failed her, failed Ruth and himself, he pursed his mouth to stop from crying out his anger and clamped his fists against his temples with impotent rage. When he finally lowered them and looked at her, his eyes were hard.

"Damn you!" he snarled and slammed his fist against the table. He stood up, turned abruptly, and stomped toward the door. He snatched his cap off the hook and jammed it on.

"Kenneth! Wait!" Linda wailed and her hands embraced him.

Head buried against his back, she shook with uncontrolled sobs. "I'm sorry. It's just…"

Still angry at her, Pacino exhaled slowly, willing himself to calm down. She was distraught and understandably so. They both were. Nothing would be gained by lashing at each other, saying words neither of them meant, but which might be hard to take back later. He slowly turned and embraced her. Running his hand through her silken hair, he kissed the top of her head.

"It's all right, honey," he whispered softly, stroking her hair. "I know it hurts, because I feel that hurt with you."

She slowly lifted her head, cheeks wet, and looked imploringly at him. "Then do something about it. Stop this senseless waste."

A noble sentiment, but alone, what could he do?

Chapter Five

Samuel Walters pushed away the signed paper, leaned back and sighed. By now, he would normally be upstairs in the residence enjoying a snifter of cognac and chatting with Cathy about her day. The goings-on in Korea had ruined it all. On top of which, his decision to veto imposing sanctions on Iran gave the papers a field day, calling his policy unwise, exposing the United States to further terrorism attacks sponsored by a rogue state. Never mind that Iran has never supported Al Qaida, but rationalism seldom counted with the tabloid press or Fox News. The more responsible broadsheets and CNN generally had measured responses, most of them cautiously approving his action. Of course, the Republicans, particularly their far-right evangelical faction, were not at all bashful voicing their 'grave concern at this latest reckless decision by an inexperienced president'.

Sometimes it simply didn't pay to get out of bed.

The media were still scrambling to find out what really happened in the Yellow Sea, but that would soon change when the two Koreas put out their version of truth. McDonald and the CNO had explained it clearly enough. As far as Walters saw it, this was definitely not a case of a lone cowboy shooting it up, but a sponsored directive made at the highest level of the South Korean Navy Command, and by extension, the government. He considered it highly unlikely that Admiral Chin would have acted on his own. Possible, but he didn't believe it.

The North Korean response to the attack on their sub? Any number of scenarios could explain what they did. From outright provocation having that thing out there in the first place, to calculated intimidation. Could this Kham character have set it all up as Price suggested? Those people liked to play their games at many different levels and he could not dismiss the possibility. For Price to have thought of it, fresh into the game, confirmed for him that he made the correct choice for his CIA director. Provided the man could cut it, which only time would show.

Despite the papers and networks eager to beat him up over Iran, that was one policy area he felt happy to field. Last year, Tanner and his team had made demonstrable strides to ease tensions between Iran and the U.S. With trade flowing more or less freely for Iran, Al Zerkhani even hinted at a possible exchange of ambassadors. That would be good for everyone in the Middle East and the world at large, with the possible exception of Israel. Well, if they didn't like it, they and their lobby can squawk. Those International Atomic Energy Agency clowns had overstepped their authority at insisting they see every aspect of Iran's nuclear fuel reprocessing and enrichment plants, forgetting that military considerations notwithstanding, Iran did have legitimate commercial and intellectual property concerns. Walters doubted the usefulness IAEA provided at all, or the money spent on it. Nuclear proliferation was a cat that fled the bag long ago and everybody should stop pretending.

It would blow over.

What happened to America was not likely to blow over anytime soon. The Christian right were becoming far too influential in federal politics, and with the Republicans in particular. Their insidious infiltration into every level of that party worried not only him, but also a growing segment of the population, and that included the international community. The notion of a sectarian-held White House sent chills down his spine. If Americans didn't take care, they would wake up one day to find their freedoms, rights, and what they could say and print, severely curtailed. It might happen, but not on his watch.

This could be something for Kimberly Baker to look at. Getting her on board during his campaign had been one of Manfred's master tactical moves and gained him a lot of women votes. A former Florida governor, the vice president had good connections with the southern evangelical groups, although not controlled by them. A passionately religious woman, she nevertheless clearly understood what separation of church and state meant. With extremists pushing intelligent design into secondary schools, diluting the whole concept of science, Baker's objectivity was just the thing needed to inject some sanity into the subject, if possible. Sending her south to spend some time there could be useful, come the next elections.

A knock on the door made him look up as Unice peered in.

"Mr. Granger is here, Mr. President."

"Show him in, and ask the Chief of Staff and the SecState to see me."

"Very good, sir."

The lanky press secretary strode in and placed several loose sheets of paper on Walters' desk.

"It's started, Mr. President. Copies of morning headlines from the Korean rags—both of them."

Walters picked up the sheets and scanned the headlines. The South Korean tabloids: *The Korean Herald*, *The Korea Times*, and *The Seoul Times*, all bore similar evocative lines:

NORTH KOREAN SUBMARINE ATTACKS DEFENSLESS SHIP!
GRAVE LOSS OF LIFE WHEN SHIP TORPEDOED!
NORTH KOREA MUST PROVIDE REPARATIONS
PUNISH THE EVIL REGIME, SEOUL DEMANDS

Glancing at the translations, the North Korean papers by comparison were almost restrained. The government's *Minju*

Chason and the Worker's Party *Pyongyang Sinmun* both had interesting slants:

IMPERIALISTS SINK PATROL SHIP
UNPROVOKED ATTACK BY SOUTH KOREA
THE SUPREME LEADER WILL DEFEND THE HOMELAND

Walters threw down the sheets in disgust. "They didn't waste much time, did they? Either of them."

"They had all night to prepare, Mr. President. When our tabloids pick this up, everyone will be clamoring for an official White House response. I've got to give them something, or by tomorrow morning the networks will eat us alive."

Tie undone, jacket hanging as though thrown on a coat hanger, sporting an unshaved face, the press secretary right now didn't project an image of a White House in control. Walters wasn't overly concerned how Granger looked. When it mattered, standing in the press room facing the gaggle, Granger was the consummate media professional. Walters felt confident he would put the best spin on the situation as he always did.

"Don't worry. We also have a night to prepare. I'm about to make some calls. When I'm done, Cottard will fill you in and you can give something to the sharks. Okay?"

Granger straightened and nodded. "That'll do it. This morning, he didn't give me much."

"We didn't have much," Walters temporized.

Unice opened the door and stepped to one side. "Mr. Cottard and Mr. Tanner, sir."

"Show them in. . . I'll talk to you later, Jim."

"Thank you, Mr. President," the press secretary said and walked out.

"Oh, Unice. You can make that call now to President Samun Man-shik."

"Very good, sir."

Tanner breezed into the Oval Office in his usual dominant style, taking large strides and sitting down without being invited. He eyed the assortment of pastries on a silver platter and helped himself to a blackberry Danish. Sitting back, he took a large bite and grunted, clearly satisfied.

Walters smiled at him with amused indulgence. "Pour yourself a coffee."

Swallowing, Tanner held up the remains of his pastry. "I will. Why can't I have Danish like this delivered to my office?"

"Because you're not the president, that's why," Cottard said with relish as he sat beside him. "Good thing, too."

"Hah!" Tanner looked searchingly at Walters. "I still think that I should be making these calls, sir. If I fail to make any headway, you're always there as a last resort."

"I'm simply cutting out the middleman, Larry. I also want the South Koreans to know from me that I'm less than impressed with them. It makes a better impression if I say it."

Tanner shrugged, took another bite and poured himself a cup. "Don't say I didn't warn you."

Scowling, Cottard rubbed his nose and sighed wearily. "Mr. President, I got a call from General McDonald. One of our wounded has died."

"Any more good news?"

"Sir, it was Admiral Kenneth Pacino's son."

Walters looked weary. "Damnation! It should have been a simple exercise. Put a call to him once we're done. I want to talk to him."

"Yes, sir."

The white phone rang and Walters pressed the speaker button. "Yes, Unice?"

"I have President Samun on line two, sir."

"Thanks." Walters pressed another button. "Mr. President?"

"Good evening, President Walters. Not entirely an unexpected call, sir," Samun answered in flawless English. Even without his Stanford degree, English was a mandatory language in South Korea.

"And a good morning to you. I wish I were calling under more pleasant circumstances, but events in the Yellow Sea last night your time have spoiled my day somewhat."

"I haven't had an entirely restful sleep either."

"The tone of your newspapers doesn't exactly contribute to calming what could be a volatile situation that seems to have been created by your Navy Command."

"It may look that way to you, Mr. President, but our action represented a legitimate response to a threat against our joint forces. The subsequent loss of life clearly demonstrated the reality of that threat. I hope you're not about to suggest otherwise."

"Nothing would have happened if your destroyer had not initiated its attack."

"We were merely warning off the PROK submarine."

"By violating the Rules of Engagement, which Admiral Chin seemed happy to do. This action may have gravely compromised our initiative to normalize relations with North Korea."

"Mr. President, I've been thoroughly briefed by Navy Command and I fully support their response. The fact that a PROK corvette fired on one of your destroyers should demonstrate the duplicity of our northern neighbor. They're extremists and cannot be trusted. Extending them a helping hand is a futile gesture, as you will find. Your efforts will amount to nothing, as have all previous American attempts at reining in their nuclear and ballistic missile programs, in the same way that you failed with Iran.

"We have a nuclear-armed neighbor who would not hesitate to unleash total destruction on us. The only thing holding them back is our willingness to retaliate with all our might. We provided a clear demonstration of our resolve during last night's exercise, and we gave a pointed reminder to Sung's regime that we will not cower or bow to his threats."

The man was raving, Walters thought and glanced at Larry, who shook his finger in warning. The SecState also looked worried the conversation appeared to get out of hand. Perhaps he was right. The Koreans were running their own agenda and would clearly do nothing to discipline Admiral Chin or the destroyer captain. Well, time to make things clear.

"President Samun, since you consider your defense forces capable of meeting your national security needs, which I am happy to recognize and welcome, it might be an opportune time to review our military commitment. As you know, the United States is running an enormous deficit. Reduction of our presence in your country would constitute a substantial saving for us. Given the strength of your economy and defense forces, I can only applaud your country and your ability to at last stand fully independent. Our withdrawal would also please a large segment of your population."

Larry gaped at him, and then slowly cast a horrified look at the broadly grinning chief of staff. Walters ignored them both. Much of what he said was perfectly true. South Korea had substantial land, sea and air assets, largely supplied and supported by American equipment and technology. Its superiority notwithstanding, it could not compare to the sheer numerical quantity at North Korea's disposal. The country might be destitute, with pitiful industry and infrastructure. Facing destruction of its starving populace would be a relief to Sung. South Korea, on the other hand, with a modern economy and prosperous population, might be less eager to throw it all away in a hollow gesture of defiance. He did not kid when he said that many South Koreans would be glad to see the last of the Americans. In many respects, both Koreas were equally reactionary and shortsighted.

The silence at the other end told Walters that his opposite number might be thinking along similar lines. The prospect of confronting his northern neighbor alone may have suddenly lost its initial appeal, regardless of the advice he may have received. Whether they liked it or not, the stark reality was that South Korea's prosperity existed solely because of the American defense umbrella, and he wanted to remind Samun of that brutal fact.

The Korean cleared his throat. "Mr. President, the easing of tensions and encouraging economic cooperation with our volatile northern neighbor is clearly in everyone's mutual interest. Your ongoing support in achieving those goals is essential. I regret if our activities have in any way introduced a stumbling block to your discussions with Chairman Sung. Perhaps a closer review of Admiral Chin's involvement in last night's regrettable action might be warranted after all."

"I am gratified to hear that, Mr. President," Walters said coldly, making certain Samun noted his displeasure. "What may be beneficial is a conciliatory gesture on your part, sir."

"And what might that be?"

"Call Chairman Sung and offer a formal apology."

"Apologize to that madman? Never! I'll see him rot first."

"You need a peaceful neighbor, Mr. President, and America needs a nuclear-free North Korea. Your gesture would be an act of mature statesmanship. Examine what you want and what's in the best interest of your country. I look forward to hearing what you decide." Walters leaned across his desk and replaced the receiver.

"You cut him off!" Tanner said incredulously. "I can't believe it. You actually cut him off."

"No, I merely reminded him of some stark realities."

"Mr. President, Mark Price could be right, and South Korea used Key Resolve to ensure our commitment to their defense posture, even at the cost of derailing our talks with Sung."

"It's one possibility, Larry. Kham could also have used the exercise to promote his own agenda," Walters said evenly. "Whatever that is. A nice bit of reasoning by Price, though. I want you on the phone to your opposite number in Seoul once we're done here. You won't be going to bed early, but I don't want to put this off. If they don't prosecute Admiral Chin, make it clear that United States will suspend all future Foal Eagle/Key Resolve exercises. I might do that anyway. We'll also be reviewing their equipment procurement programs. If they threaten to curtail our military presence on their soil, tell them that I'm more than happy to bring everybody home."

"Is that wise, sir? It could encourage Sung to adopt a more antagonistic posture. China might also take it as a signal to further expand its political and economic presence in the Pacific."

"It will demonstrate our preparedness to be evenhanded, something that's been lacking in our foreign policy to date. It's time everybody woke up to the realization that World War II happened last century and the political landscape has changed, as have our enemies...and supposed friends. We're in a different global war now: economics and energy. I aim to see us win both, but it's not going to happen if we maintain an outdated defense posture, and the sooner everyone comes to grips with that, the better. Anything else?"

"You're talking about scaling down our involvement with NATO, Mr. President?" Cottard asked in shock.

Walters looked directly at his chief of staff. "I am."

Cottard winced and shifted his legs. "I admit to a certain logic in your position, but implementing such a policy would raise a howl of protest from the Republicans and generate unrest within the military. I won't even contemplate what the Europeans would say."

"That doesn't mean we shouldn't do it. We're bleeding ourselves while Europe reaps the benefits. If the EU wants a unified defense posture against an enemy that no longer exists, let them pay for it themselves. This may cost me a second term, but I trust the American people and their readiness to understand what I'm doing and why. Besides, I don't think the average American on the street gives a toss about NATO. It's an outdated posture. As you pointed out a number of times, Manfred, the people put me in this office to make decisions and govern. They didn't put me here simply to enjoy four years of pomp and ceremony."

"Your attitude might be refreshing, sir, but the Democratic Party may feel differently if Congressmen see your policies costing them their seats."

"They need an attitude adjustment and a reminder why they were elected. If I can convince the people, I expect to win more seats, not lose them. If I can't, then I've got it wrong and somebody else can make the decisions."

Tanner smiled and exhaled loudly. "You may have a short presidency, but it will be an exciting one. I'll give you that."

"It's nice to know that I have your unqualified support, Larry. Shall we call Sung?"

"I've changed my mind. You can have a crack at him first. Your handling of Samun was interesting."

Walters laughed. "Not so good on your feet when the gloves are off, eh? I'll remember that. You've been spending too much time at embassy cocktail parties."

"It's what diplomats do, Mr. President. Clean up messes made by amateur politicians."

"I should fire you," Walters said candidly and touched a button on the phone pad.

"Yes, sir?"

"Put a call through to Pyongyang. Personal for Chairman Sung Kang-dae."

"Er...yes, sir."

Walters glanced at the digital clock on his desk and quickly calculated times. It would be nine-forty in the morning over there, plenty of time for Sung to have downed his coffee or soya, or whatever he drank. Would he take the call, though? Walters could not remember that an American president had ever called a North Korean leader. It looked like this would be a first for both of them.

"I have Pyongyang, sir."

"Thank you, Unice…Mr. Chairman? This is President Samuel Walters."

"Good evening, Mr. President," the translator replied. "This is an unexpected call. What can I do for you?"

Walters pursed his lips, wondering whether he should let Larry take over after all. Sung didn't appear to be in an appeasing mood. Then again, hard to judge from a translator's voice. That was the trouble with phones. They cut out the most important things about a person.

"I'm calling in regard to an unfortunate incident in the Yellow Sea last night, sir."

After a moment, the translator came back. "The incident where you and our misguided neighbor attacked one of our submarines and destroyed a ship that merely observed your provocative naval exercises? I warned your Secretary of State about that."

"Mr. Chairman, what the South Korean navy did is deplorable and indeed provocative, something which I made clear to President Samun. I expect those responsible to be dealt with. As for the sinking of your corvette, however regrettable, it was purely defensive. We were fired upon."

"You can hardly expect me to believe, President Walters, that South Korea will acknowledge this piece of treachery."

"That is exactly what I demanded from President Samun, Mr. Chairman."

There was silence again.

"You sank a small patrol ship that cost the lives of its entire crew! Do you want me to be silent?"

"We lost lives as well. Much needs to be evaluated before we understand everything about this incident beyond the mere fact of the event. Why did your submarine loiter there, sir, knowing it placed itself in danger? Why did your corvette fire on us after the submarine withdrew unharmed? As to the reason why the

South Korean commander disobeyed standing orders and made his mock attack is also something we're investigating. I submit, Mr. Chairman, it would be prudent for you to look into the action of your own navy before events force our hand."

"Are you dictating to me?"

Walters sighed, questioning his sanity when he decided to run for the White House. He had a crippling deficit to bring under control, with no help from the Republicans. Military spending to cut back, especially over-sophisticated weapons systems like the all-purpose fighters that were so expensive and costly to maintain, the Air Force dared not fly them. Fielding an economic attack by China, and this little North Korean shit was pissing in his ear. He should simply bomb their reactors and be done with it.

"Mr. Chairman, we're at a crossroad. What happened last night has the potential to undo positive steps achieved to normalize relations between us. Both our countries would benefit from a more neutral posture. I also understand that such an outcome might not be regarded with equal enthusiasm in certain quarters of your government, or that of South Korea. How do you wish to proceed, sir?"

It took almost a minute before the translator responded.

"I acknowledge what you're saying, Mr. President, and your frank words. As you suggest, it might be wise to look beyond the obvious. I, too, would regard any deterioration in our talks because of this incident as unfortunate. Can I ask if Secretary Tanner will be available should it be necessary for me to contact him?"

Walters let out a slow breath. Sung *was* a realist and a pragmatist. He glanced at Larry, who nodded.

"At any time, Mr. Chairman. To assist you, I shall make available transcripts of all communication logs and video data from our surveillance drone."

"Undoctored, Mr. President?"

Walters laughed. “Undoctored, sir. Everything will be delivered to your National Defense Commission.”

“That would be most helpful.”

“I thank you for hearing me out, sir.”

“And I appreciate your call.” The line went dead.

Walters pressed the speaker button and leaned back against the chair. “Not a very sociable person, is he? At least, he was prepared to consider alternatives. Larry? You heard me. Talk to Admiral Owen and see that Sung gets the data. Let SecDef know what’s going on.”

“If we give Sung our comms transcripts, it will reveal our eavesdropping capability,” Tanner warned.

“You don’t think Sung knows how good our systems are? Or China? Which is saying the same thing.”

“Mr. President, does this mean you’re withdrawing support from Kham Chang-uk?” Cottard asked guardedly.

“One step at a time, Manfred,” Walters said, not pleased at having a dark cloud over what he considered to be two very successful diplomatic overtures. “Call Price and ask him to contact Kham Chang-uk. I want to know what those people are doing. I’m going up to the residence.”

* * *

A light drizzle fell from a gray morning sky, making the headlights of oncoming cars glitter. The wipers made a periodic swish across the windshield as the tires whispered on the slick road. Mark Price drove on automatic. He had been here so often it remained ingrained in his consciousness. What was not ingrained, he had little idea what to do once he arrived at his destination. No, that wasn’t quite right. He knew what needed to be done, all right. What bugged him how to go about doing it. Come in charging with an axe chopping off heads, or take the walk softly approach before exerting his authority? Neither seemed appropriate somehow.

The Company was made up of tough men—at least those who made things happen—who would dismiss him as a political flunkey if he tried the folksy method. Yet cutting a swathe through people, especially when he wasn't entirely certain who needed chopping, would unnecessarily compromise the Company's effectiveness. The place certainly needed a cleanup. Far too many people had grown old doing the same weary thing, treading water until retirement, forgetting their real job. Lack of reliable HUMINT and analysis, the president said, and Price agreed with him. Far too much emphasis was placed on satellite imagery these days and back room second-guessers, instead of having people on the ground getting the raw stuff. What he needed was objective input from someone whose opinion he could trust. The problem he had, were any familiar faces still around since the last time he had been here?

When the large green signboard loomed ahead, he slowed and turned into Potomac School Road, then a right onto Route 123—Colonial Farm Road—that led to the Central Intelligence Agency headquarters, Langley. The thick trees on either side of the road thinned and he could see the familiar complex of buildings emerging on his right. Black clouds hovered overhead, an omen?

At forty-five, Price was very young for his position, something that would undoubtedly not sit well with older men in the Company who perhaps had harbored ambitions of their own, particularly those in the National Clandestine Service. That problem didn't weigh heavily on his conscience. Those people would simply have to get over it. If they couldn't, there were always opportunities on the outside. He firmly believed that no organization should allow itself to become hostage to someone perceived to be indispensable. In his view there were only two classes of people: those who excelled and those who thought they excelled. He always tried to weed out the latter quickly. That approach had worked for him at DHS and he saw no reason why it shouldn't work here.

Clearing out his desk yesterday afternoon, with Mary clucking sympathetically over him, Price was excited at the prospect of shaping the Company in a new mold, but also feeling unavoidable nostalgia at leaving a post that now worked with quiet efficiency. His elderly secretary, somewhat bulky, her peppery hair in permanent disarray, tried to hide her dismay that he was leaving, while maintaining an air of cool detachment. It didn't work.

He looked around his bare office and the packing cartons on the desk, he picked up his slim leather briefcase and closed the door for the last time. Without saying anything, he gave Mary a hug and walked out. He offered her a position as executive assistant and hoped she would accept. An efficient assistant was worth her weight in platinum. With Mary, that said a lot. Colin Forbes wished him well and that was it. He had not seen Ed Bishop. According to Forbes, the man took Price's appointment as a personal affront. Lots of people would once the news got out.

He took the second turnoff right, drove past the open expanse of the parking lot on either side, and headed for the main entrance. Tall oak sprinkled the compound. Flanked by two blocky buildings, the curved atrium, known as the bubble, seemed out of place for its stark utilitarian purpose. Heavy green-tinted glass made the windows appear like black eyes. After going through a check at the main gate, he parked his Chevy in a vacant visitors slot and got out. The drizzle eased and stopped, but it left the air chilly, smelling of snow. He squared his shoulders and marched toward the entrance, nodding to the statue of Nathan Hale, hanged by the British for spying.

Inside the gray-marbled lobby, his footsteps echoed as he walked over the round CIA seal toward the security counter. Along the left wall was a statue of William J. Donovan, director of the Office of Strategic Services, the forerunner of the CIA.

Inscribed on the wall stood the Company's motto: 'And ye shall know the truth and the truth shall make you free.' Along the right wall were fifty-three gold stars, flanked by the American flag, representing CIA officers who had lost their life in the service of the agency. Of course, there were many more than that, but the wall wasn't large enough to hold all of them.

Nothing had changed, and it felt like he'd never been away.

Several people went by, pausing before one of five access portals. After swiping their badges across the sensor, they walked into the stark interior. The security guard looked at Price without expression.

"Can I help you, sir?"

"Mark Price."

The guard blanched and bobbed his head. "Welcome to Langley, sir. We heard that you were coming. Can I have some ID, please?"

Price offered him his DHS badge. Although no longer valid, it should verify his identity. The guard looked at it carefully, then handed it back.

"If you would wait for one moment?" He picked up a phone and spoke rapidly.

Price turned away and surveyed the entrance foyer. It all looked the same and he felt like he had stepped back in time. A familiar figure appeared from a room behind the access portals and hurried through. Price smiled and extended his hand.

"Nice to see you again, Adam. They still got you minding the store, I see."

Adam Spiteri, head of the Office of Security, beamed and grasped Price's hand. His grip firm and dry as his eyes traveled over Price with penetrating scrutiny.

"Somebody's got to. It's nice to see you back, although I would say that sentiment will not be shared by everyone."

"I believe it."

"Before I take you upstairs, we need to sort out a few formalities," Spiteri said apologetically and extended his arm toward the portals. As they started walking, he held out a white visitor badge. "This is just to get you in."

Price swiped the badge across the sensor. It gave a beep, a gray triangle turned green and he walked into the broad corridor on the other side. Spiteri ushered him into his office where Price needed to sign papers. DCIA or not, the paperwork never ended. He then pressed the palm of his right hand against a flat gray pad. When the thing turned blue, leaving an outline of his palm print, he pulled back his hand. After fiddling with his computer terminal, Spiteri extracted a laminated silver access badge and attached an alligator clip.

"You know the drill, sir. Wear it at all times. I don't have to tell you not to lose it. Not that anyone will come down on you if you do, except I'll lose some sleep," Spiteri said with a genial smile. "But it will make my life a whole lot easier if you don't." He reached into his desk drawer, pulled out a gray cellphone and held it out. "A modified BlackBerry. Totally secure, enhanced military encryption, and the signal is untraceable. I'll show you how to set your PIN and use some of its special features later."

Price glanced at the slim instrument with its black glass screen and keypad, and slipped it into his jacket pocket.

"I thought we used High Technology Computer PDA smartphones?" Price queried and Spiteri shrugged.

"We still do, but we give all senior level executives BlackBerrys with our special modifications. The HTCs are first rate, but we don't want to be reliant on the NSA for our communications. Besides, they could be lying to us and are listening in."

Price nodded, understanding fully, a vivid demonstration of inter-service rivalry and lack of trust. In an intelligence organization, lack of trust was a given, but this represented needles duplication and wasted effort, something he would need to discuss with Trent Bruster. Establishing a good working relationship with the NSA director would be invaluable.

"Now that you're the director, there is a question of your personal security. I'm afraid you won't be driving yourself around anymore. You'll be assigned a driver and one of our special executive cars. The driver will also act as your bodyguard. Your car will be driven home. We'd prefer that you lived in one of the upstairs suites—"

"A prisoner?" Price snorted derisively.

"—but I didn't figure you'd want to give up your house in McLean."

"Damn right. You know how much it cost me to get that place?" Price demanded, glaring at Spiteri.

His house not flashy, but comfortable, and in a nice neighborhood, surrounded by open lawns, trees and superb amenities. Being almost next door to Langley, it was also convenient.

"We'll have to install some security devices there. If you could let me have your key and the code to your alarm system…"

"You mean you don't have it?" Price said wryly, dug out his key ring, unlatched the house and car keys and handed them over. He didn't like the intrusion his position would impose on his personal life, but he accepted the necessity. He reached for a post-it note on Spiteri's desk and wrote down the alarm access code. No use getting mad at the poor man for doing his job.

Spiteri escorted him to a bank of two elevators at Building 1A where the executive offices were located. People moved around, usually hurrying, but Price paid them no attention. When the left elevator door opened, he got in. Spiteri pressed the seventh floor button and Price pursed his lips. This was it.

Dark blue carpet covered the floor and the air had a faint lavender smell when Price stepped out of the elevator. Unlike a normal office floor, this one not open plan. Glass-walled reception areas guarded dark, wood-paneled enclaves. Neat white plaques on doors proclaimed their owners. Price had been here before and knew his way around. Without waiting for Spiteri, he turned right and moved quickly down a wide corridor toward the end office.

A trim, serious, middle-aged woman looked up when Price and Spiteri entered. Her short light brown hair framed a pleasant face that could turn severe at any hint of criticism of the Company or the man she guarded in the palatial office behind her. In his time, Price had received more than one of Miss Claire Dobson's caustic tongue lashings and never enjoyed the experience. She stood up quickly, patted down her dark gray business jacket and held her five-foot eight slim frame with regal dignity.

"Good morning, Miss Dobson," Price said with a friendly smile. Getting her onside would help him a lot, especially her encyclopedic knowledge of everything that went on within the Company, provided she accepted him. If not, he still hoped that Mary would decide to come over. "And how are you today?"

"Not too bad generally, sir," she said gravely.

Price looked at her and suppressed a grin. The woman never smiled. Given the business she was in, there might not be a whole lot to smile about. She had served two DCIAs and a change at the top did not guarantee that people lower down would still hold a job by end of the day. Did she worry about hers?

"Good to hear it. Please get me a cup of coffee, black with one sugar—"

"No cream?"

"Not today. Then I want to see Raymond Grant and Leonard Zardwovsky."

"Yes, sir."

Price turned to Spiteri. "See me at eleven and we'll talk. I'll need clueing in about my computer access, among other things."

Spiteri smiled faintly. "Yes, sir." He turned around, opened the door and walked out.

Alone, Price stared levelly at Claire. "One question, Miss Dobson. If you're uncomfortable in any way working with me, let me know now. I won't hold it against you if you are."

She lifted her chin and her deep green eyes looked at him without wavering. "Sir, I serve this agency and your office."

Price accepted that. The Steel Lady could be difficult and a pain sometimes, but her loyalty beyond question. He should not have doubted her, but people change and he had been away for a while.

"Then we understand each other. There will be some adjustments here and I would value your input."

"Sir, it's not my place—"

Price lifted his hand to stop her. "Let's not have any false modesty, okay? You've been here a long time and you know how things are run better than most. I'd be a fool not to take advantage of that."

"You can rely on my support, sir."

"Good! A couple of things I want to see on my desk first thing every morning."

"Yes, sir?"

"The first three pages, original or copy, of *The New York Times* and *The Washington Post*. The editorial pages too. I also want to see the input for the President's Daily Brief before it goes out. When *The Economist* is published, I want a copy."

Claire gave him a puzzled look, then smiled. "I shall take care of it…sir."

"What I need right now is the current organization chart and a list of all in-house and offshore operations. Miss Rosslyn should have it, if she's still working here."

"She is."

He took a step toward the ceiling-high door to what was now his office, but she beat him to it and opened it for him.

"We could use a blast of fresh air here, sir," she said softly, her eyes searching his face.

Price chuckled. "As long as I don't get blown away with it."

The door closed behind him with a click and Price surveyed his new domain. The thirty-by-thirty corner office had plenty of light coming from tall, glazed, specially made windows designed to defeat remote microphone and laser eavesdropping devices. Tucked into the windowed corner stood a rectangular conference table with six padded chairs. Beside the door on his left, a high cabinet/bookshelf filled with bound books, stacked periodicals and three colored crystal decorative vases. Grant's memorabilia? On his right stood a large L-shaped executive desk, its polished dark brown surface bare, except for a phone station. Tucked against the corner lay a 21" flat computer screen, a standard keyboard and a wireless optical mouse. Two comfortable looking visitor chairs were positioned before the desk.

Price took a deep breath and walked to the high-backed black leather chair behind the desk—Grant's chair. He decided he would keep it anyway. He sat down, the leather creaking slightly, slid his briefcase beside the drawers next to the wall and took a deep breath.

A button glowed yellow on the phone pad. "I have your coffee, sir. Shall I bring it in?"

Price pressed the button. "Please."

The door opened and Claire walked in, holding a large silver mug bearing the CIA seal. She placed it on his desk and straightened.

"Mr. Grant and Mr. Zardwovsky will be here in a minute."

"Show them in as soon as they get here."

"Yes, sir."

"By the way, where have you stashed Grant?"

"Down the hall, sir, in the Protocol area. It was the only place with a spare desk. If you want—"

"That's fine. He won't be making any complaints."

Claire smiled faintly and walked out.

Price stared at the closed door. Protocol was one section he would look at closely. What the hell did the Company need a Protocol section for? He had time to take a couple of sips when he heard a knock and the door opened.

"Mr. Grant and Mr. Zardwovsky," Claire announced.

The two men walked in and she closed the door after them.

"Please sit down, both of you," Price invited. "This isn't going to be pleasant for anybody, but I want to steer clear of personalities as much as possible."

If Grant harbored any resentment at being ousted, he hid it well. He took the left chair and eased himself down. Dressed in his trademark dark blue pinstripe suit and heavy yellow tie, Zardwovsky looked a little uncomfortable. Of average height, the bulge around his middle prominent, black hair glossy, temples streaked white, he projected a presence. The man was a skilled field operative and case manager, and knew how to run covert field ops. Unfortunately, once he got into position of power, it went to his head and he became an office politician, forgetting what his job was all about.

Price noted the look of resentment on Zardwovsky's face, a subordinate now his immeasurable superior, and ignored it, not giving a damn. He took a sip of coffee, placed down the mug and stared at Grant.

"Raymond, at one this afternoon, you'll start me off with a rundown on everything that's going on in this place. I mean everything."

"I'll be here," the elderly vice admiral said gruffly. "Did you revoke my access privileges?"

"Mine were also cut." Zardwovsky looked petulant.

Price stared at them. "It wasn't, but it would have been one of my first things to do."

"Why? I've got cases to run," Zardwovsky said.

"Not anymore you don't. Hand over your duties to Mossman until I decide on your replacement."

"Replacement?"

"After you have completed giving me a debrief of your Directorate, you'll be packing your bags. That's not why you two are here. I need a background update on North Korea and the Company's involvement with Kham Chang-uk and Yeum Ling-chol. Details are important." Price did not bother with threats. The two men were professionals and knew the consequences of trying a cover-up, not that a threat would stop them from doing it if it would help their case.

Grant shot a wrathful look at Zardwovsky. "He exceeded his orders! Like I told Stone, we *were* gathering background intelligence, but this fool thought he would do something smart and topple Sung Kang-dae."

Zardwovsky bridled. "Like you didn't know! A successful coup would give you a crowning feather in your cap and a lever with the president. That's all you were worried about."

"Enough!" Price snapped. "I don't give a damn about your individual motives. I only want to know what was done, how, and who is involved…on both sides. Is that clear?"

Zardwovsky clamped his mouth and nodded stiffly. Grant sighed and shook his head.

"Ow, hell, Price. I never liked you much, but that doesn't mean I'm willing to compromise the Company over it because I was kicked out."

"You didn't like me because Zardwovsky here poisoned your mind about me. Instead of taking responsibility when one of his ops went south, he made sure others were blamed for his incompetence."

"Now just a minute!" Zardwovsky snarled and jumped to his feet.

"Sit down," Price said softly, bared steel in his voice. Deflated, Zardwovsky swallowed hard and took his seat.

Grant looked thoughtfully at his deputy. "Maybe it's better for the Company that both of us are leaving." He turned to Price. "How much do you know about the North Korean situation?"

"I've had a session with the Secretary of State and the National Security Advisor, but obviously not about the CIA plot to undermine Sung."

"Well, then you know almost everything," Grant said amiably. "Including the events in the Yellow Sea."

Nice to have a free press, Price thought. "What are the bits that I *don't* know?"

"I know Zardwovsky infiltrated the Workers' Party, the Supreme People's Assembly, and the other two main parties: the Korean Social Democratic Party and the Chondoist Chongu Party. We were also feeling out key ministers on the possibility of a leadership change."

"With Kham and Yeum?" Price prompted.

"And, of course, Tham Pan-yong, the Minister of People's Armed Forces, and the Premier, Tung In-san. Kham and Yeum were our primary targets. Both are part of the reformist faction and eager to affect a change at the top. They helped Sung oust that kid, Kim Yong-un and his ruling committee, but I never authorized any coup." Grant glared at Zardwovsky.

Price turned his head at his former boss. "Well?"

"I want immunity or I'm not saying anything," Zardwovsky declared flatly and crossed his arms over his chest.

Price leaned forward and glared. "I can take you downstairs and shoot you full of shit that will keep you talking for a month. When I'm done, you'll be lucky to get a job as a night watchman at a Burger King. So cut the crap, okay?"

Zardwovsky went pale and seemed to shrink into himself. Regrouping, he straightened his shoulders, gave Grant a pitiful look and snorted.

"All right, but you'll be sorry you asked. Sure, I bankrolled Kham and Yeum. The beautiful part is that Sung knows all about it."

"What?" Price stared at him, unable to believe it.

"Sung's a scumbag, they all are, but he's pragmatic like the Chinese. He is still a hardline ideologue, but he can see the writing on the wall. His country is heading for a revolution because of

Kim Jong-il's moronic Juche doctrine. There is no way that he will embrace democracy or the West, but like the Chinese leaders, to keep himself in power, he's willing to entertain elements of free market economics. Improving the lot of his people will ensure his own survival."

Well, crap!

"He was willing to shut down his nuclear facilities in exchange for telling him who is plotting against him?" Price asked and Zardwovsky laughed.

"Don't be naïve. He knows who the plotters are. His intelligence service, the Reconnaissance General Bureau, has every dissident organization infiltrated. He could round them up whenever he feels like it."

"But he didn't know about Kham and Yeum, did he? What was your price?"

"Ten of his nuclear warheads."

Grant gaped. "He actually handed them over?"

"An exchange on the high seas. One of his subs delivered the nukes to a motor cruiser we rented in Japan. The boxes were then transferred to our naval base in Yokosuka, where they are awaiting shipment here."

Price sat there stunned, although he believed Zardwovsky implicitly. It was not the first time that the CIA had made dirty deals on its own, interpreting the wishes of the White House. Sometimes in the name of plausible deniability, and at other times because they thought they knew better, like the Mossad sabotage of the Valero refinery. Gathering his thoughts, he smirked.

"You sold yourself cheap. Sung's got sixty warheads."

"Sixty-four," Grant said dryly.

"Whatever. Giving you ten won't make a bit of difference to him. For that, you compromised what could be a friendly regime if Sung is toppled. We could have had a unified Korea!"

"You still can," Zardwovsky said smugly. "All you have to do is let Kham and Yeum move in on Sung. You see, they know

Sung is on to them, but he doesn't dare sweep them aside just yet. They've got powerful generals in their corner—"

"Which you helped them buy."

"—and Sung's hold on power is not as secure as he likes to think. He has to tread lightly. At least for now."

"You bastard!" Price hissed and Zardwovsky smiled.

"You'll find out from Grant when he gives you his rundown. Remember that underground nuclear test Iran conducted right after the Valero incident? Guess who gave them the warheads?"

"Warheads?"

"Sure. New in his job, Sung wanted to cultivate friends. He gave President Al Zerkhani four warheads in exchange for cheap oil. Iran held enough enriched uranium to make a stack of bombs, but not the technology to do it, or mount them on a delivery vehicle. Sung gave Zerkhani both."

"And you knew about that without telling me?" Grant looked outraged.

"Tell you what, you old fool. You were too busy sucking up to Congress and the White House to realize what was going on. Somebody needed to execute our charter. Anyway, with a nuclear Iran, Pakistan and Israel are effectively neutralized. That's got to be good for us."

Price raised a hand. "Wait a minute. Pakistan knows that Iran has several nuclear warheads?"

"We leaked the information to their Inter-Service Intelligence. It was in our interest that they know. The Moslems may be fanatical and the Sunni and Shi'ia factions would slit each other's throats given any excuse, except for their mutual hatred of the West. Instead of letting them kill each other off like we should, we spent one and a half trillion dollars and almost seven thousand men killed invading Iraq and Afghanistan following a totally idiotic political strategy. We're out of there now, and the shitty part is that we haven't achieved anything. Today, both countries are as screwed up as before. Three if you count Pakistan, and why did we do it? A grand gesture of liberation, inviting the people to embrace democracy under a Western umbrella. Stupid! We forgot that they hate us much more than they hate each other. They have always been our enemies and we made them that."

"Explain," Price ordered.

"Look at your history. In the eleventh century the Francs organized the First Crusade to stop the European kings from slaughtering each other. They united everyone in a holy cause to liberate Palestine and free Jerusalem, but in reality a license to murder and pillage in the name of Christendom. Afterward, whenever the Europeans got tired of squabbling among themselves, they organized another crusade. To us, it's ancient history, but to the Moslems, it happened yesterday. The rhetoric of our politicians keeps reminding them of that shameful past. A crusade against terrorism, Bush said. It simply played into the hands of Osama bin Laden and others like him. The Moslems see us as conquerors, and everything we've done since the Crusades reinforced that impression. Before the twentieth century they had no power or money to do anything about it, but with oil, they finally possessed the means to strike back at us."

"Like China is doing today with their cheap exports," Grant said softly.

"You got it. They're the ones with money these days and they're waging unrestricted warfare against us, but it's a war fought in boardrooms, stock exchanges, and with cyber terrorism. We might not be shooting at each other, but that doesn't make it any less deadly. If you think that Saudi Arabia and the Emirates are our friends, you're deluded."

Price slowly leaned back against his chair trying to make sense of what he heard. Zardwovsky clearly had a depth to him he hadn't appreciated before, but running a foreign policy agenda of his own? It hardly seemed credible. Compared to the blundering efforts of past administrations, perhaps not too hard to work out why he had done it. Bad administrations or not, it couldn't excuse what the CIA did. It was an organ of government. It didn't make policy, but carried it out! He wondered what other initiatives the Company was involved with, but didn't exactly relish the prospect of finding out.

"All right, we'll talk about it later. How did you contact Kham and Yeum?"

"Through a special BlackBerry cellphone we arranged for them to get."

"And presumably Sung also has one?" Price asked and Zardwovsky chuckled.

"We gave him a Nokia. It wouldn't do to have everyone walking around with the same type of phone, far too obvious and bound to raise comment."

Price looked hard at the man and pondered if he could unravel the mess that CIA had made. No, not the CIA, but a few key people. He only needed to identify them and understand what was done.

"Okay, let's get into the details. Who is the case officer for North Korea?"

"Mannix."

"Jurgen Mannix? I thought he was a field operative?"

"He got hurt in Afghanistan, but still a good man."

"I want to see him at eleven-thirty," Price said. Zardwovsky nodded.

Revolted, Price understood why the Company wore the reputation it did. This man was completely unscrupulous, caught up in his own vision of the New World Order, which he wanted to shape in his image. The fact that he managed to get away with it didn't say much for Grant's executive ability, surprised the president had not gotten rid of him earlier.

"Talk to me about this double-cross you're running with Sung."

Zardwovsky grinned coldly. "If you're harboring any misguided sympathy for Kham and Yeum, I'd get rid of it. Sure, they've got a more progressive outlook and don't see a future for North Korea under Sung, but it doesn't mean they're pro-West in any way. Both are feathering their own nest and happy taking our money to do it. Once in power they might adopt a more co-operative position toward us, not a given, but they're firmly in the Chinese camp."

"What difference does it make as long as they shut down their nuclear weapons program and disarm?" Price demanded with a touch of exasperation. "A nuclear North Korea isn't in China's interest either."

"You don't get it, do you? We don't care about their reactors. We only care about the reprocessing and enrichment facilities. If you haven't caught on, that's where they get their bombs from. Besides, by giving them money, I had them tight in my pocket, and it wasn't a license to buy Porches."

"Why support them if you were prepared to betray them to Sung?"

"I wasn't going to betray them, and I didn't tell Sung everything."

"The names of generals who are against him?"

"That's right. Because in the final analysis, Kham's takeover will actually be a good thing for us."

"When did you last talk to him?"

"When Tanner left Pyongyang."

"Any hint that Kham might be behind the PROK sub incident?"

"It's possible, but he didn't say anything. All he told me, he'd be in touch once Key Resolve was over."

Price frowned. That could have meant any number of things. He appreciated the deviousness of the Asian mind and their penchant for intrigue. Sometimes, he wondered whether they loved the game more than the actual outcome.

"What's stopping Kham from moving in on Sung now?"

"He wants a further fifty million. Some of that is probably for himself and Yeum, the rest is to shore up his support. They know that if this fails, they're all dead men."

"And you're holding out?"

"I'm after some assurance that he'll deliver on his promises."

Price snorted and shook his head. "Hasn't it occurred to you that once Kham engineers his power spill, he doesn't owe you a thing?"

"If he doesn't deliver, he and Yeum won't live long enough to enjoy their money and they know it."

Price understood the pragmatic brutality of Zardwovsky's threat, although it wasn't the best foundation to build a lasting relationship on.

"What do you want from Sung for giving him the names? Ten more nukes?"

"Actually, it's twenty."

"You're an idiot, Zardwovsky. You might have gotten your twenty warheads, but Sung would still walk away the winner, and we'd have nothing. He would destroy his opponents and clamp down worse than anything done under Kim Jong-il. Not only that, he would never want to talk to us again, and I wouldn't blame him."

"You've missed the whole point, Price. I don't want Sung in power anymore than you do."

Staring at him, Price finally got it. "You would take the twenty warheads, and then tell Kham to move in?"

"Now you're talking. At the same time, I would have halved the North Korean nuclear threat."

"And the other thirty warheads?"

"Kham promised to hand them over once they got rid of Sung."

Regardless of how much he loathed his former boss, Price admitted the plan had a certain evil logic. If it succeeded, it would definitely be a positive easing of tension for the whole region and remove a major headache for the administration.

The things we do…

"All right, what's the protocol for contacting Kham?"

"I send him a special SMS and he gets back to me when he can," Zardwovsky said.

"Write everything down and give it to Claire in a sealed envelope. That's it for now. Thank you both."

When the two men left, Price picked up his mug and took a sip, then grimaced. The coffee cold and lost its appeal a while back, like his new job, he mused.

He sat back, still finding it hard to comprehend what Zardwovsky had done. He shuddered to think what else the CIA cooked in other parts of the world. Although the Cold War might be over, there were still a number of disgruntled countries around the world who would love to see something bad happen to America, whether through their own engineering or somebody else's.

One bite at a time, he told himself, and picked up the unsecured white phone.

"Yes, sir?" Claire answered immediately.

"I need some fresh coffee. Then get me the National Security Advisor."

"Of course, sir."

A minute later, she walked in, placed a new mug on his desk and picked up the old one. "Mr. Stone is on line three."

"Thanks, Claire." When the door closed behind her, he took an appreciative swallow of the fragrant brew and lifted the receiver from the secure brown phone.

"Admiral?"

"Hi, Mark. All settled in?" Stone's gruff, but pleasant voice sounded amused, and Price knew why. He no doubt enjoyed the unenviable predicament of the new DCIA.

"Why didn't you warn me, Graham?"

"Warn you about what?"

"That you put a death curse on me."

Stone laughed with obvious delight. "Nothing of the sort, my boy. Don't tell me you've got cold feet already?"

"My whole body has gone cold. I didn't call you to bitch, not altogether anyway. There is something you and the President need to know."

"Oh? Don't leave me in suspense."

"Zardwovsky's been playing a double game with Sung and Kham."

"That's no surprise."

"The surprising part, he got ten warheads from Sung for betraying Kham's overthrow plot, and he's holding out for twenty more for ratting on all of Kham's supporters."

"You're shitting me."

"You wish, but it gets better. He planned to take the nukes, and then get Kham to take Sung down. The price was the remaining thirty warheads in the North Korean arsenal. One more thing. Remember that underground test by the Iranians?"

Price only heard silence at the other end, followed by a long sigh.

"Don't tell me. Sung gave them some warheads?"

"Four."

"And Grant knew nothing of this?"

"Apparently not."

"Asshole. How in the world…never mind. You were right to call me. What are you going to do?"

"I'll leave a message for Kham asking him to contact me. As to what I'm going to tell him will depend on the President. Last night, he told me to reassure Kham of American support, but he won't be supporting us if he is threatened with death for not delivering those warheads."

"Yeah. The last thing the President needs is another shotgun marriage. Okay, I'll talk to him."

"I need something soon."

"Call you later."

The line went dead and Price slowly replaced the receiver.

Well, crap!

* * *

Pacino pecked over his scrambled eggs, pushed the plate away and reached for the mug. Opposite him, dressed in a cream nightgown, Ruth looked up, her own plate almost untouched.

"Not hungry?" she asked softly, her hazel eyes troubled.

A natural brunette, hair falling across her left shoulder, despite recent events, she held herself with poise. Beneath a small upturned nose, full lips framed a generous mouth. When she smiled, it lit her face, highlighting the delicate cheekbones. She did not smile now, and a cloud hung over her Pacino could sense. After twenty-nine years of marriage, he could feel her every mood, gesture, and expression. Of course, she could also read him like tealeaves.

"How's Linda," he asked to break the silence, and took a sip of coffee.

"Still sleeping. It took a while, but she finally nodded off. There are only so many tears you can shed."

"She's taking it badly, poor thing."

"We all have."

"Including you?"

"I'm saving a few tears after you leave," she told him candidly and gave a wan smile. Looking at him, her eyes were bright. "I want him buried at sea, Kenneth."

"Ruth—"

"That has always been his first love…like it is with you."

He reached for her hand and squeezed. "You were my first and only love, and you still are."

She patted his hand and slowly shook her head. "It's okay, darling. I didn't mind being second. Second with you has been more satisfying than most wives got being first. Seawater runs through your veins, my dear, not blood, and it always will. Don't worry. I knew what I was getting into when you swept me off my feet, literally, and it wasn't because of your pretty white uniform and colored ribbons. They did help, though."

"You still remember that night?"

"How could I forget? It was magical and we were both more than a little crazy."

"But what an insanity." He grinned, and then the smile faded. "You've had some tough times along the way, and so did I, but you helped me weather them."

"That's what sailor's wives are for. Men go to sea and wives gaze at an empty horizon. I admit, it's been hard at the beginning, but later it got better and I wouldn't change it for anything."

Pacino took another sip and his eyes turned misty as memories chased each other. "I remember when he stood on *Reliant's* bridge, eyes far away in a private world all his own. He changed then and the sea claimed him. God! I wish I never took him there. He would be alive today." He searched her face, hoping she would understand. "Don't hate me for taking him away from you."

She nodded and her mouth twitched. "You didn't take him away, dear. He was a creature of the sea like you. Sooner or later, it was inevitable that it would claim him, and that's where I want him to go now. To the only thing he really loved. I couldn't hold him back from it even if I wanted to," she whispered, sniffed and dabbed at her eyes with a napkin.

"Linda has a say in this, you know," he murmured, ignoring her moment of weakness.

"We'll sort it out."

"I wish we had a daughter," he said suddenly and Ruth's eyes widened.

"We do, but I understand."

"Linda..."

Suddenly, his world seemed hollow, without purpose or meaning, and Pacino felt old and weary. His family name would die when he was gone and there would be no one to remember. What use rank and power when in the end, the sea or the ground took them all indiscriminately? There didn't seem to be much purpose to it, only senseless, blind procreation. They were all motes of dust carried along by the wind of life.

"What are you thinking?" she asked after a time. "You seem far away."

"Just trying to make sense of it all."

"There is no sense to it. We're destined to die the minute we're born. For some, it simply happens sooner...like with Vin."

He stared at her. "You're not turning fatalistic on me, are you?"

"Me? Women have always been fatalistic, darling, but men are romantics and would never admit to themselves that we're tougher than them."

"I thought women swooned at the sight of a rose or a whispered endearment."

She chuckled. "Fooled you, didn't we? One sight of a bare thigh or an exposed bosom and you're gone."

"Ah ha! That's how you did it."

"Works every time, my dear. It's almost too easy. Men have only one thing on their mind...always."

Pacino slowly shook his head, amazed at the steel beneath such a seemingly delicate creature. For all their external toughness, men were actually softies. Perhaps a good thing. He would hate to see a military dominated by women. There would be wars, it was human nature, but they'd probably be damn short ones, with nothing much to pick over afterward. Still, men had not done such a bad job of it, until he remembered that males were reared by females.

A hell of a world.

He glanced at his wristwatch: 7:55. Time to be going. He finished his coffee and stood up.

"Will you be okay? I'll try to be home early." Perhaps not, but he couldn't tell her that.

"I'll look after Linda. You'll let me know when they fly in his..." She couldn't quite say it. Standing up, she grabbed his hand.

"I'll call you." He reached for her and held her tight, feeling her tremble against him. He kissed her forehead and smiled. "I've got to go."

She followed him out of the small dining room to the front door. He took his jacket off a peg and put it on. Picking up his cap, he jammed it on his head. He walked out without looking back and marched toward the elevators. His mother, a tough navy wife herself, taught him to be manly and unsentimental. 'Men don't cry,' she told him. Much later when he was almost fully grown and heading for Annapolis, she amended that. 'Wives do the crying for them,' she said. He never forgot that.

Outside the nine-story tower at the edge of the housing complex, he could see trees and grass, a pleasant contrast to the concrete and glass elsewhere. About two hundred yards to his right, another cluster of towers. In one of them was Vin's apartment. He took a deep breath of crisp air and automatically scanned the sky. Clear and blue, it promised to be a fine day.

A dark blue sedan with a fluttering red flag on the hood bearing two silver stars pulled up beside the curb. The driver hurried out and opened the rear door. As Pacino approached, the driver saluted.

"Morning, Neil," Pacino said, returning the salute.

"Good morning, sir." The driver slammed the door shut and walked quickly to the left side. Pacino clipped on his seatbelt and the car accelerated away.

The base buildings flashed by, but he didn't really see them. They all merged into a background of images that didn't require his attention. His world had changed from something familiar and comfortable to one without predictability or reason. All his adult life, he firmly believed that he made a contribution to the defense of America and its values. It was not a perfect country by any stretch of the imagination, but there were many more out there immeasurably worse off. Parading its naval might across the oceans proclaimed its dominance to the world, its flag represented all the things most people didn't have and could never hope to have. A great PR exercise—respect through fear and resentment.

Pacino flew that flag in three Key Resolve exercises, steaming boldly off the North Korean coast, challenging them to try something and hoping they would. It was, of course, also an unstated warning to China, which they have now answered. From being a coastal defense navy, they had expanded and modernized their fleet, turning it into a potent blue water force, not exactly what the United States wanted to happen. Action and reaction. Simple. He wondered what bright political genius formulated that piece of asinine U.S. naval strategy.

What was it all for? He wasn't entirely certain, and the irony of the realization did not escape him. As an admiral, he was supposed to know, but he didn't. He thought he had all the answers, but they eluded him now.

He couldn't get Linda's accusing words out of his head. 'What are you going to do about it?' And he still didn't have a coherent response. What did she expect him to do? Shoot the PROK sub commander? That would really solve a lot. As he read the newspaper headlines over his first cup of coffee, it looked like nobody would do anything about it. The Korean Navy Command wasn't giving any indication they were going after Admiral Chin, and the White House walked softly around Pyongyang trying to stitch up a cooperation deal. What happened in the Yellow Sea was an unfortunate incident and everybody advocated restraint. A sensible posture, he had to agree, except that it whitewashed the underlying cost of diplomacy. Linda was right. No one counted or cared about the number of body bags and shattered lives left in the wake of international statesmanship.

A crappy way to run a world.

In a way, Pacino understood that overreaction would be counterproductive for everybody. Calming down the situation was the correct and sensible thing to do. 'Deeply regret' letters would be sent to everyone on both sides. He would probably get one of those form things and life would move on. What about the mangled wounded and their dashed careers, hopes and dreams? Patch them up, discharge them and forget about them. They got a tough break, that's all. Next!

Not long ago, he had thought the same thing.

You cannot consider the individual, they told him at the Joint Forces Staff College, or you'll lose objectivity and perspective. The military must operate like army ants. The individuals are expendable to ensure survival of the whole, but who made up that magical whole? If it weren't for the individual, there wouldn't be any damned whole. If the individual didn't matter, what was the point? People were not ants, and combat wasn't a fancy video game. Somewhere along the line, they have lost it.

So, Admiral Pacino, what are you going to do about it?

When the car pulled outside the Fleet Headquarters building, he got out without waiting for Neil and hurried inside, returning salutes from officers and ratings coming in or going out. Preferring not to notice them to save wear and tear on his arm, he made for the elevators.

On the fifth floor, the atmosphere cool and subdued, befitting the high-rankers who commanded the 7th Fleet. He opened the door to the reception area of his office and nodded to Chief Petty Officer Karter, clicking away on his keyboard. Seeing him, Karter hastily stood up.

"Good morning, Admiral."

"There's nothing good about it," Pacino growled testily.

Karter bit his lip, clearly uncomfortable. "Sir, we heard about your son—"

"Bring me coffee and I don't want to be disturbed by anyone."

"Yes, sir. Admiral Owen—"

"Coffee," he snapped and walked into his office. The last thing he needed right now was sticky sentiment, even from Owen.

Damn it all!

Inside, the tastefully painted green walls complemented two large windows that gave him an unrestricted view of the dock area and the moored carrier USS *George Washington* at Berth 12. Its island loomed above warehouses and workshops like an apartment block. With Key Resolve ships beached at Incheon until everybody got their act together, it might not be a bad idea to send the carrier out and exercise its air elements. They have been languishing here for three weeks and everyone probably getting rusty. That would definitely apply to its F/A-18 squadrons based at the Naval Air Station Atsugi while the carrier lay in port. He would need to run it past Owen, but there shouldn't be a problem with that.

Standing by the window taking it all in, partially detached from the world outside, he contemplated a life-changing decision that could have profound consequences. Apart from destroying his career, would the grand gesture make a difference? Would it change anything? He could only hope so. It could also change things in ways not altogether desirable, a real possibility. However, someone had to make a statement.

Fish or cut bait, Admiral.

A knock and the door opened. Karter walked in carrying a white mug with the 7th Fleet logo embossed on it, and placed it on a black coaster on the desk. Pacino looked at the burly sailor and nodded.

"Thanks."

The man flashed him a small smile and walked out.

Decision made, he pulled back his tooled brown leather chair and sat down. Logging onto the computer, he brought up high-resolution satellite maps of the Incheon naval base. Only some seventeen miles from Seoul, it was a major South Korean military facility. He checked the layout of docks, ships in port, warehouses, fuel farms, and jotted down coordinates.

After taking a sip of freshly ground java, not a hint of salt that took away the bitter taste, he brought up the layout of the Yongbyon nuclear complex situated sixty miles north of Pyongyang. He enlarged the image and stared at the two reactors and fuel reprocessing plant. Taking another sip, he took down the grid coordinates. Done, he sat back, trying not to think too much about what he planned to do.

Mouth hard, he reached for the phone. "Karter? Get me Brigadier General Eugene Picket at Osan Air Base."

"Right away, Admiral. Sir, Admiral Owen is asking you to see him. Something about bringing back our ships from Incheon."

"Get this call in first," Pacino ordered and hung up.

It didn't take long before the phone rang. He took a deep breath and picked up.

"Eugene? It's Pacino."

"Hi, Kenneth. You've been stirring up trouble again? Never let a swabby do a man's job, I always say," Commander, 51st Fighter Wing, commented dryly.

As he listened to his friend, a faint smile touched Pacino's mouth. "That's why we always call on you zoomies to do the work."

"Wise, wise. So, what the hell happened out there?"

"Everyone got eager and overreacted."

"Yeah, prickly lot on both sides. What can I do for you, Admiral?"

"I want to run a live fire exercise with one of your MQ-10 Hawks. Tactical control will be here."

He would have preferred two birds, one to fly CAP, combat air patrol, in case he encountered activity over his second target and he had to fight his way out. However desirable, it would also increase the probability of detection on the way in, and cause

Picket to ask awkward questions. No, his initial choice was correct. He needed to come in quickly and get out just as quickly.

"When do you want to do this?" Picket demanded.

"At twenty hundred hours today. Can do?"

"What sort of load you need?"

"Two GBU-12s and two AIM-92 Stingers," Pacino said immediately. The five hundred pound Paveway laser-guided bombs would be perfect for what he had in mind.

"Sounds like you're planning a penetration job. Endurance?"

"Fuel her for five hours, but the exercise won't last long. You want a tasking order?"

"Nah. I'll bundle it under the Key Resolve code. You'll be in the hot seat for this?"

"I wouldn't miss it."

"Okay. We'll transfer control once the bird is up. Good enough?"

"Thanks, Eugene. I appreciate this. Sorry that Foal Eagle got canned and your boys didn't get to pound some mud."

"That's the breaks. We'll carve up the scenery some other time. See me when you're around next."

"I'll do that." Pacino nodded and punched a yellow button on the phone pad. The Air Force usually delivered.

"Yes, sir?" Karter answered.

"Get me Captain Ormond."

"Yes, sir."

He replaced the receiver and stared at the phone. There was still time to call the whole thing off. Did he want to do this? The ringing phone made up his mind for him.

"Captain Ormond?"

"Morning, Admiral. You got a job for us?" Having been left out of this year's FTX, Ormond was keen for *George Washington* to show its stuff.

"A night exercise with a Hawk only, Captain, but you'll be

going out soon. I suggest you make preparations for getting under way and recovering your squadrons."

"Outstanding! What's the ops for tonight?"

"Osan will put up a Hawk at twenty hundred tonight. We'll be dropping ordnance on two land targets. I'll come on board at nineteen forty-five. I don't want any ceremonial when I get there. Have your operators ready."

"Aye aye, sir. Anything I need to know about this?"

"A routine sortie, Brian. I want to check out some of Hawk's night terrain systems."

"I'll have the men ready, Admiral."

"See you tonight." Pacino replaced the receiver and reached for the mug.

George Washington had run exercises with the old Reaper drones before the new fully combat-configured Hawk inventory was rolled out, and this tasking order would not be unusual. He'd had a couple of simulator sessions himself. Operating the Hawk was like playing a video game, except more boring. Simply flying around in an empty sky wasn't very exciting. Well, tonight would be different for everybody.

One thing left to do.

It took a while to prepare the email. He checked the wording and made some changes, then set Outlook to send it at 2100 hours. He should be done by then. Staring at the screen, there was still time to back out. The phone rang and he picked up.

"Sir, I have the White House on the line," a slightly awed Karter announced. "It's the President."

Pacino frowned and bit his lower lip. He didn't want hollow platitudes right now, but the man was his commander-in-chief. Call or no call, it wouldn't change a thing.

"Okay, put him through."

Chapter Six

Price rubbed his eyes, sighed and sat back. Only seven o'clock, it felt like he had been sandwiched here all night. Hell of a first day. If this was going to be the pattern from now on, he wasn't sure that he wanted to stick around. It had always been rough taking on a new job, except that in this case, he was responsible for thousands of employees and several billion in annual expenditure. Humbling statistics, and a burden that could crush him if he did not maintain perspective.

His debrief with Grant so far had merely given him a skeletal outline of what the Company did. Apart from active operations, which Zardwovsky was still to fill in, he had staffing to review, budgets, issues with Congress, direct and indirect outlays, asset procurement. The list alarming in its length. He needed to know those things, but he needed to be careful not to get too immersed in detail. That's what his department heads were there for. Micromanagement could stifle organizational effectiveness just as badly as sloppy management.

If it were not for his experience at Homeland Security, he would be completely out of his depth.

He probably needed two more full days with Grant before he would be confident that he had a complete mental picture of the setup, albeit only a rough one, but he didn't want the former director underfoot longer than necessary. Besides, he could not devote all his time to Grant. Regardless of how much he detested the worm, he badly wanted to catch up with Zardwovsky and come up to speed with the must-know cases. After all, that was the core of Company business. Then there were the Intelligence

Directorate, Science and Technology, Support and the various administrative arms. He also wanted a summary heads-up from each department, which would enable him to talk intelligently if the President, the Chief of Staff or the National Security Advisor called. He reminded himself to ask Claire to organize it. Until he came up to speed, likely to take a couple of weeks at least, the section heads within each directorate would simply have to carry the load.

He reached for the coffee mug, only to find it empty. Perhaps it was just as well. He didn't know how many refills he'd had, but there were a few. A turkey and salad sandwich might settle his sloshing stomach. Exhaling loudly, he leaned toward the computer screen. Running through resumes of key personnel might be tedious work, but necessary if he was to understand what went on and identify bottlenecks. He had already spotted three possible problems, and Grant had been remarkably frank and objective. Price had no qualms with Grant getting the boot, but in some respects, the older man had not done such a bad job. By withholding operational information, it looked like Zardwovsky had torpedoed more than one career in pursuit of his personal ambitions. Price didn't mind initiative and encouraged it when he saw it, but he drew the line at backstabbing. Hard, as the practice was prevalent in every walk of life.

His BlackBerry phone trilled and he raised an eyebrow when he saw the flashing red icon on top of the little screen. Hardly a day on his job and people were already hitting on him? He pressed the Secure symbol to accept the call.

"Mark Price." No need for code words. Anyone who knew how to contact him using this method would also know who he was.

"Ah, Mr. Price. I am so pleased to have reached you. This is Kham Chang-uk, Minister of Public Security. I received your, ah, summons—"

"Request only, sir," Price amended hastily, flushing personnel data from his mind and dredging up information from Tanner's briefing.

"Yes, of course. Are you able to talk, Mr. Price?"

"I am at your disposal, Mr. Minister."

Price glanced quickly at his wristwatch: 9:15 a.m. in Pyongyang. The man clearly not an early riser or this could be the only appropriate time for him to call. Kham had called, that was all that mattered.

"Excellent! And please, address me Chang-uk. We are going to be friends after all, are we not?"

"I sincerely hope so, sir," Price said carefully.

Kham could be genuinely friendly or probing with a psychological gambit. This early in the game it paid to be cautious. The whole conversation was also somewhat discordant, having to think of the North Korean as a possible ally after years of looking at them as implacable enemies. The world indeed sometimes breeds strange bedfellows.

"Having that out of the way, you will have to excuse my natural curiosity and a measure of trepidation when I learned of your appointment, Mr. Price. I trust this does not herald a shift in the American position. I would find that most unsettling."

Price smiled at the man's guarded approach and regard for his intelligence apparatus. His appointment to the CIA yet to be made public and approved by Congress.

"Mr. Minister, I want to assure you that you have the President's unreserved support, and I'll assist you in every way to successfully execute your plan."

"I am gratified to hear that, and most relieved. The thought of RGB men bursting through my door, should Sung learn what I and my colleagues are up to, would be most disagreeable."

"If something like that were to happen, it will not be through my hand," Price told him firmly.

"That's all I wanted to know. Can I be blunt, Mr. Price?"

"I wish you would, Mr. Minister."

"Fine. Although Mr. Zardwovsky's contribution to our revolutionary effort has been invaluable, we found the conditions he imposed for his cooperation somewhat constraining. However, given the past relationship between our countries, I fully understand the reason for his stance. What is yours, Mr. Price?"

"Sir, I am aware of Zardwovsky's demands. They no longer exist and the President does not seek to establish a lasting dialogue with you based on intimidation or threats. I'm not in a position to say more, and it's not my place to interpret what Secretary Tanner might say on matters of United States foreign policy."

"I understand fully and will not treat your comments as statements of policy, but I would nevertheless appreciate your point of view."

"Very well. Speaking personally, the United States wants a nuclear-free North Korea. That has never been a secret. Giving up your warheads and removing your strategic missile forces would solve many problems for us, and I suggest for you as well, but this agency will not intimidate you or anyone else to see that done. I cannot speak for the President, however."

Price told the truth, but with a broad hint to Kham that reneging on promises would not be viewed favorably. One call to Sung and the man's career would end suddenly, as would his life. Although not versed in doubletalk, he found that he enjoyed the restrained subtlety of veiled diplomacy. A tool he would no doubt need to sharpen.

There was silence at the other end for a few moments, and then Price heard a soft chuckle.

"Well said. Tell me, please. Is Mr. Zardwovsky still involved with our venture?"

"He's had...health difficulties...that forced him to take indefinite leave."

"I see. I trust he will get well soon?"

"One can always hope."

"So. You don't threaten me and you're still prepared to help me. What do you want in return, Mr. Price? What does America want? In my position, I learned that you always pay for everything you get in some form or another...always."

"I'll not irritate you with tired rhetoric, sir. What I learned from Secretary Tanner, America is not extending its hand to usher in democracy and so-called freedom for your people. Our cultures are too diverse for the concept to be meaningful, and our national policies have different objectives, but there is a commonality we all understand—prosperity through personal enterprise. A comfortable population would in turn lead to political and economic stability. I don't have to tell you the state of your country. Disarming, opening up international trade and normalizing relations with your southern neighbor would be to everyone's advantage."

"And profitable, no doubt," Kham said dryly.

"Call it capitalism or market economics if you will, but the socialist communal ownership model has been demonstrably flawed. Even Sung Kang-dae recognized that. People work best when self-interest is involved."

"I cannot argue with you there, Mr. Price. However, such liberalization will take some time to implement."

"You have already taken steps. All we want is your continued commitment to that path."

"A path that some might not be willing to follow, but that's my problem. Although I am prepared to entertain the idea, you must know that our ties with China are strong and we will continue to maintain them."

"That's an internal policy matter, which we have no desire to influence."

"Indeed? That's somewhat surprising and at odds from the position of previous American Administrations."

"This is President Walters' policy now. I need to advise you, Mr. Minister, Sung knows that you and the Foreign Minister

Yeum are plotting to overthrow him."

"I appreciate that information, but it comes as no surprise. We could not hope to keep our plans totally secret, and it was inevitable that the RGB would unravel them. However, we have taken steps to ensure that Sung does not move against us, at least not right away. Nevertheless, our position is precarious and we cannot delay much longer. We must move now, but before we can do so, there were some funds that Mr. Zardwovsky promised. It's vital that I get those funds quickly."

"The fifty million? I'll arrange for their immediate transfer, sir."

"Thank you. I will not patronize you with effusive gratitude."

"When establishing any relationship, sir, trust is paramount, wouldn't you agree?"

"I find no fault with your reasoning."

"You don't know me and I understand your need to be cautious, but I must know something. Did you engineer that incident with our Key Resolve exercise? I'm not being judgmental, but it would help if we knew the truth when the President considers the matter in a broader context. This is not to say Seoul wasn't a willing participant."

"Hah! I'm glad to see you thinking laterally, Mr. Price. Our neighbor has prospered under your protective umbrella, and they have been very adept at manipulating your presence to their advantage, something America seems to have ignored. Very well, it might help your President after all, although he could be annoyed with me. Tham Pan-yong, the Minister of People's Armed Forces, issued instructions to the naval command to be, ah, aggressive. Done against the Supreme Leader's orders, as he did not want to disrupt the formative talks we had with Secretary Tanner. I dare say that Tham and I will have some uncomfortable explaining to do this morning."

Price ground his teeth in frustration. If he could, he would shoot the man himself.

"What did you hope to gain? I understand that Secretary Tanner was making progress acceptable even to you. Your action could have undone everything. It still could if the President gets sufficiently annoyed. The gambit resulted in several American casualties."

"I'm aware that President Walters might not be pleased and I regret the loss of life on both sides, but we had to undermine Sung's position and demonstrate his duplicity. Talking to Secretary Tanner, he made several hardline generals uncomfortable, which weakened his support and bolstered one of our objectives. At the same time, by appearing to order an aggressive posture during Key Resolve, it gave the appearance that he was appeasing the generals, but it also undermined support he got from the reformist faction who wish to accelerate the liberalization program. This might be a difficult concept for your Western mind to grasp, but deals within deals is a common and acceptable tool to use against your opponent. What is not acceptable, if you get caught, that is, is playing both sides against the middle, if I have your terminology correct. I love your American idiom, you know."

"It can be confusing to some, Mr. Minister."

"Your enemies, perhaps? Anyway, instigating the incident in the Yellow Sea showed Sung as someone neither side could rely on and he lost much face because of it. He is our Supreme Leader, but he isn't invulnerable and doesn't have absolute power…yet. That's why we must move quickly before his position does become unassailable."

"Thank you for the clarification. I cannot say how the President will react to this news, but speaking personally, why didn't you simply tell us beforehand what you were planning?"

"Tell whom, Mr. Price?"

Price shook his head. With Zardwovsky pursuing his own agenda, Kham had acted within the constraints of his position. Grateful for the Company's help, but wary of Zardwovsky's end game. He might also have feared America would betray him to

Sung, which it still could. Kham was right when he said that he could not wait much longer to act.

"How safe are you?"

"Safe enough for now."

"But—"

"Engineering the confrontation with your naval forces served our advantage, but it also indirectly plays into Sung's hand. He could use this as a pretext to move against us. Our support is solid, but it might not remain so if he promises his generals more than we did."

"Hence the fifty million," Price said slowly and nodded. Kham played high stakes poker where the loser would not walk away from the table, but be carried out.

"Money will buy us temporary loyalty, but more importantly, it will give us time to consolidate our move. Once Tung In-san is installed as Supreme Leader, we will deal with our mercenary supporters. I hope you're not shocked, Mr. Price. That's how business is done here. We're the same, you and I. We simply achieve our ends through different means."

"I'm not being critical, sir. We also do things in a manner that would not be considered polite even in your country. I'm not speaking only of this Agency."

Kham laughed. "Well said. President Samun has offered an unprecedented apology for causing the incident, which has done much to defuse a very dangerous situation. I know the man. He would never have done this unless forced under extreme pressure. Your President, perhaps?"

"I cannot say, sir," Price said truthfully.

"Although a noble gesture, in many ways it undermines our plans. I fear I must cut this short. This cellphone your organization gave me is an extraordinary device, but I fear the ingenuity of the RGB, and it's not safe for me to talk too long. I will try to get in touch with you tomorrow morning your time to discuss this further. You have given me much to think about."

"I'll look forward to it, Mr. Minister."

"Be careful of the South Korean National Intelligence Service, my friend. They seek to undermine Seoul and force America to relinquish its bases in the country. Not that we would object," Kham added with a chuckle.

Price frowned, deeply concerned. Was there a secret conduit between the RGB and the NIS? He would need to talk to Grant about that. If true, it cast a dark shadow over American/Korean relations.

"I shall have the matter investigated."

"I suggest that Mr. Zardwovsky might be a good source of information. Until next time."

When the line went dead, Price pressed the Secure icon and placed down the handset. After a moment, he picked up the normal non-secure phone.

"Claire? Get me Admiral Stone, and then go home."

"Yes, sir. Thank you."

* * *

After having his ID checked by a grim guard, the heavy gate to the Berth 12 pier slid back and Pacino's official car moved toward the looming shape of the 104,000-ton *Nimitz*-class nuclear carrier USS *George Washington*, tied portside. Its 1,040-foot-long hull towered like a city block. The black water reflected harbor lights in a rippling display. A brightly lit ferry made its way toward Tomaricho. Far across the bay, a container ship glided slowly toward Tokyo. Looking about the almost deserted floodlit dock, work for the day done, those taking liberty or leave would be gradually returning as the ship made ready to sail.

When the car stopped, he quickly got out and stared up at the carrier's lit island. The deck empty, Ormond's birds nested at the Kunsan Air Base. Once the carrier went to sea, his flock of F/A-18 Super Hornets would come home, giving *George Washington* back its teeth. As he walked toward the two guards standing beside the boarding ramp, the white sheet hanging off the rail proudly blazoning CVN-73, he wondered how you conned a big bastard like that. The largest ship he ever commanded was a *Ticondeorga*-class cruiser. In the end it was only a matter of degree, he thought phlegmatically. He gave orders and the tasks were done. Everything was automated, even the people who manned the ships.

The guards saluted him and he walked up the ramp to an entry port halfway up the towering hull. An awfully young lieutenant snapped to attention and saluted when Pacino stepped across the threshold.

"Welcome aboard, sir. Captain Ormond asked me to escort you to flag bridge."

"Never mind that. I want to go to CIC right away."

"Yes, sir. Please follow me."

Clearly nervous at escorting the deputy fleet commander, the lieutenant unconsciously hurried, forcing Pacino to lengthen his strides. Looking at the youngster's back, he smiled. To a lieutenant, an admiral was one rung below God and beyond cares. At that rank, what could possibly worry him? He knew what the lieutenant thought because that is exactly what he thought before he achieved his present lofty height. If only the youngster knew.

A deck below the carrier's island, the Combat Information Center cool and dimly lit. Apart from the manned UAV command consoles stuck into a corner and a youngish lieutenant commander talking to the two operators, the control center stood deserted. Pacino glanced at his escort.

"My compliments to Captain Ormond, and tell him I'll see him in about an hour."

"Aye aye, sir!" The lieutenant saluted crisply and left.

The commander walked to Pacino and nodded. "Welcome to CIC, Admiral. I am Lieutenant Commander Ransom, assistant Tactical Action Officer."

"Commander. Is everything set?" Pacino asked, glancing at the active Hawk screens.

"We just established a comms link with the Osan Ground Control Station, sir. They confirm ready launch at twenty hundred."

"Good." Pacino reached into his pocket and dug out two pieces of paper. After glancing at them, he held one out. "Your first target."

The youngster looked at the grid reference coordinates and frowned. "Incheon?"

"A disused warehouse, Commander. The ROK Navy Command wanted the site cleared for some time. I thought we'd give them a hand."

Pacino watched closely as the young commander considered the coordinates. Clearing out an old warehouse in the middle of an active base by bombing it? After a moment, Ransom slowly nodded. He might not understand what was going on, but orders were orders, no matter how crazy.

"Would you care to observe, sir?"

"Definitely." Pacino walked to the Hawk remote operator station and stood at ease.

Sitting in large padded beige couches, the two operators studied their two small side-by-side screens mounted in front of a keyboard. Both control stations had standard handgrip joysticks. Above the small screens were two thirty-inch displays, showing a camera view from the 360-degree mounting in the Hawk's nose. The right station's screens were for sensor data and combat maneuvering feeds. One operator would pilot the UAV through a satellite link while the second monitored weapons and fought the craft if necessary. A communications console separated the two operators, above which were mounted two large blank screens.

The camera view on both operator stations showed the Hawk's bright headlights against a lit runway stretching into the night. Yellow ground lights delimited the active runway. The

Hawk paused at the takeoff point and the operator glanced at Ransom.

"Sir, Osan reports ready to roll in three minutes."

"Get it moving now," Pacino ordered, not fussy about a lousy three minutes. Committed, he wanted to get it done and over with.

Ransom grinned and tapped the pilot's shoulder. "Tell them we're cleared to roll."

Within seconds the UAV spun up its Williams FJ46 turbofan jet engine and began to move. As it reached takeoff speed the nose lifted and the fat forty-two-foot-long Hawk clawed into a black sky. The sensor operator's upper screen lit up with split windows showing radar, real-time GPS grid position and thermal camera images.

"Ask Osan to consent control handover," Ransom told the operator.

"Aye, sir."

"Once the Hawk is past ten thousand, close the link with Osan," Pacino ordered.

He did not want them to see where the UAV went or what it did. More importantly, he didn't want them taking back control if someone realized what was going on.

After a brief conversation into his headset the pilot gently grasped the joysticks.

"I have consent, sir. Link is nominal."

Ransom handed him a slip of paper with the target coordinates. "Punch these in."

"Aye aye, sir." The pilot keyed in the numbers and handed the slip to his partner, who immediately started typing into his keyboard to set up one of the laser-guided GBU-12s.

Pacino observed wordlessly, marveling at the benefit of unquestioning discipline. Just like that, it was done.

"Flight time is seven minutes at four hundred mph if we cruise at twenty thousand," the pilot announced.

"No." Pacino shook his head. He did not want the Hawk wasting time gaining altitude, not on this leg. "This is a max speed run. Come in at fifteen thousand and release at eight miles."

"Aye aye, sir. Four minutes to target. Link with Osan terminated."

Nothing much to see until the Incheon sprawl opened up below the Hawk. On the left was blackness where the sea met the shore, broken by lights from ships anchored in the inner harbor. A lot of them were probably his 7th Fleet units. With Key Resolve canceled, they would be making ready to depart. Simply looking at the profusion of lights on the land, it was impossible to tell that here lay a major naval installation.

"Coming up on IP," the sensor operator announced, now in his element. "Arming the Paveway...Laser designator on."

Unlike dropping a pure gravity bomb that required the aircraft to be over its target, or close to it, the combat Hawk could release from up to twelve miles away, a great tactical advantage for the attacking aircraft. Once on its way the Paveway would ride the laser beam to its impact point within a foot of the invisible laser dot.

"Target acquired."

A precision surgical strike, Pacino wanted to make sure of his target. The warehouse he selected not disused like he said, adjacent to buildings that carried flammable and explosive inventory. He wanted to leave a message, not destroy the whole place.

"Bring up the image intensifier and IR views," he asked quietly.

Immediately, the sensor operator's lower screen showed the angled roof of a long structure. Even at eleven miles the image remained perfectly steady as the television camera compensated for the Hawk's slight flight movement, locked on the invisible laser rangefinder/target designator point.

"Zoom out a bit."

The image expanded, showing warehouse buildings on either

side of his target. They matched the photos he had studied from satellite reconnaissance downloads this morning. There were no hotspots in the infrared image. Pacino did not want to cause collateral damage on his conscience by having someone killed.

"Are we being painted?"

Probably an unnecessary question as the sensor operator would have told him, but he didn't want to take any chances. After all, he *was* intruding into restricted military space, but his concern were the parked ships of his fleet. They should be maintaining strict CIC watches and one of them might detect the incoming Hawk. By coming overland, he had reduced that risk, but not eliminated.

"Traffic and weather radar from Incheon International Airport only, sir," the sensor operator told him.

Pacino nodded thoughtfully. Exactly what he expected. Incheon would have no reason to light up its search or targeting radars. Even if they did, the Hawk's stealthy skin would make finding it extremely difficult. It might be peaceful down there right now, but that would quickly change once he dropped the Paveway. Then again, perhaps not. When the warehouse went up, the explosion could easily be mistaken for an industrial accident. It would take the local authorities a little while to establish the cause of the mishap, and that's when the *kim chee* would hit the fan.

"You have weapons free," Pacino said.

"Weapons free, aye, sir. Coming up to eight miles…Opening bomb bay doors…Weapon going hot…Paveway released."

The television image rocked slightly as the five hundred pound, ten-foot nine inch stealthy weapon fell from the inboard release coupling. A bomb bay to hold ordnance rather than on exposed wing hardpoints, a major advance on the old MQ-9 Reaper, and dramatically increased the Hawk's survivability in a hostile environment.

"Bomb bay doors closed…Weapon is tracking to target," the

operator announced calmly.

A routine exercise as far as he was concerned, Pacino thought. For excitement, this was a non-event. Computers and technology did their job without fuss. The excitement lay with him, his fluttering stomach and slightly clammy hands, and the realization that he could be influencing the course of events here. No, he *was* influencing events.

Over two minutes later the intensified image of the warehouse suddenly flared in a silent blast as the Paveway struck. The operator immediately zoomed out. A huge column of debris shot upward, bursting through a climbing dust cloud. Everything within a fifty-yard radius stood flattened, and the adjoining warehouses severely damaged, but there were no secondary explosions, Pacino was glad to see. There would be fires to contend with, but he wasn't concerned.

The first part had gone off without a hitch and he slowly let out his breath, not realizing that he had been holding it. Staring at the destruction, he reflected on the conversation he'd had this morning. He appreciated the call, but not the hollow substance. The president was sorry for his loss and Vin would get a Silver Star for his heroism. Big deal. Like that would make up for everything. Was that all a man's life was worth, a piece of tin?

"Well done, everyone," he said warmly and held out the second slip of paper. Ransom took it and frowned, then gave it to the pilot who quickly typed in the new coordinates. "Execute this leg from sixty thousand at five hundred mph and release from ten miles."

Yongbyon only 188 miles from Incheon, it would take the UAV a little while to climb up to its designated altitude.

"Climbing to sixty thousand and going to five hundred mph. Flight time is twenty-seven minutes."

Ransom stepped away from the operator consoles. "Admiral?"

Pacino could see the concern in the young man's face. This

could be a problem.

"Yes, Commander?"

"Sir, those coordinates you gave me. They're in North Korea."

"And you have a problem with that?"

Did the youngster suspect? Pacino wasn't sure, but he would not leave CIC until the job was done. Afterward, it wouldn't matter. If he left now, Ransom might be tempted to query his order with Ormond, but with Pacino standing beside him, cloaked in the formidable authority of an admiral, discipline made him obedient—for now. Pacino had given him a legal order, although an unusual one, and Ransom was compelled to obey.

Pacino waited for the man to decide. In the end, Ransom slowly shook his head.

"No, sir. There is no problem."

"Good!" To ease the atmosphere and chew up time, Pacino sat in a spare seat and leaned back. "Why don't you ring up the mess, Commander, and order us some coffee."

Strictly speaking, drinking or consumption of any food in CIC against regulations, but he didn't think that anyone would object. Rank did have its small privileges.

"Aye aye, sir," Ransom said uncertainly, then picked up a phone and spoke rapidly.

Pacino sipped his coffee as he listened to the muted hum of ship's machinery, surrounded by large dark screens of the carrier's weapons management system, and waited patiently as the minutes crawled by. Ransom did not say anything, which was proper, and Pacino preferred to maintain a shell of solitude. Besides, what could he tell the youngster? Would he understand or even care? Pacino didn't need his understanding, sympathy or forgiveness. Whatever the burden, this was something he needed to carry alone.

He was throwing away his career and landing himself in a shitload of trouble for his pain. Many would think him crazy for doing it, but Linda was right. Somebody needed to make a stand. Passing responsibility up the chain of command served only to avoid action and merely salved one's conscience, comfortable with the thought that he had done everything possible within the limits of his authority. That was the problem. Everybody knew why the system was broken and what needed fixing, but no one wanted to act, not when it meant stepping outside that comfort zone.

Well, he definitely stepped outside his comfort zone tonight.

"Nine minutes to IP," the sensor operator stated at last. "Getting some search radar side lobe from Pyongyang. Nothing within detection range."

The North Korean capital was one of the most heavily defended cities on the planet. It had more than 150 antiaircraft emplacements, SA-16 MANPAD and SA-5 SAM missile batteries, and innumerable ZPU-4 and ZSU-57 AAA guns. The Hawk wasn't getting close to that place and Pacino did not worry. Yongbyon was only sixty miles farther north, and although heavily defended with over twenty SAM sites and multiple AAA emplacements, it represented a far softer target.

He placed his mug on the armrest, got up and stretched. Casually, he stood behind the two operators.

"Paveway armed…Coming up to IP…Laser designator on."

Heart beating slightly faster, Pacino watched as the targeting system locked on from fourteen miles. At sixty thousand feet, this would be a high altitude strike and relatively immune from any counterattack. Going lower would be far too dangerous and he could not risk losing the drone. Although he could release the weapon now, he would not be certain of the accuracy of his target position, and he needed absolute precision here. Hitting the wrong site would be catastrophic, which would almost certainly trigger a major retaliatory response. Not a desirable outcome. The other consideration if he released now, despite its stealthy skin, the Paveway might still be detected by various search and missile radars. Again, not a good thing.

At thirteen miles the high-resolution night camera image closed and centered on a mass of transformers, high-tension electrical pylons and a grid of wires coming from Yongbyon's two nuclear reactors. The vast substation channeled power to a squat rectangular building containing the uranium enrichment plant and reprocessing facility that recovered plutonium from spent fuel rods. A straight line of pylons in twin rows took away the surplus energy supply. Under no circumstances could he risk striking the reprocessing plant. The resulting contamination would make tens of square miles totally uninhabitable and cause countless needless deaths. If he shut down the substation, although not a permanent solution, it would nevertheless deliver an adequately satisfactory message.

"Range to release point, one mile."

"You have weapons free, Commander," Pacino told Ransom.

The young officer stared hard at the screens, then slowly turned to look at Pacino, clearly not comfortable with unfolding events. In the end, he bit his lower lip and nodded.

"Execute!" he said at length, his voice harsh.

"Weapon going hot...Bomb bay doors open."

Pacino clamped his mouth. This was the mission's most critical moment. With its bomb bay doors dangling, every passing moment increased the chance of detection. From a radar cross-section of a bird, the Hawk would suddenly look like a car.

"Search radar hit rate climbing...Paveway released...Bomb bay doors closed...Radar hits dropping below acquisition threshold. Weapon is tracking."

They might have detected the Paveway when released, but the missile radars apparently lost it as the guided bomb reached terminal speed. No one expected an air raid coming from sixty thousand feet.

A long three minutes waiting for the Paveway to strike, but

the pilot did not loiter. He banked the UAV to port and locked in coordinates that would take the craft back to Osan, doing it without shifting the laser designator from the target.

Suddenly, a bright flare, wreckage flying everywhere, and spectacular electrical arcing. Lights throughout the complex immediately failed. Only darkness remained and fires from the burning substation.

Satisfied, Pacino looked at Ransom and nodded. "Excellent work, Commander. A textbook example of a precision strike."

"Thank you, sir." Ransom said quietly, staring at the sensor operator's screen and the silent fires. "I don't quite understand—"

"Not your concern, Commander. Please call Captain Ormond and tell him that I'm on my way up to flag bridge."

"Aye aye, sir!"

It was unfair to leave the youngster in suspense, not knowing what was going on, but he would find out soon enough. Pacino climbed the stairs one rung at a time 150 feet up to flag bridge, a deck above Primary Flight Control, wishing for an elevator. However desirable, on board a warship, clearly not practical. Well, it gave him exercise. Slightly out of breath, he paused at the top of the stairs, clamped his mouth and strode toward polished wood doors with their mounted twin silver stars of the carrier group commander when one was in residence. Right now, it was his flag bridge, if only for a few more minutes. He opened the door and walked into the brightly lit command center.

Captain Ormond turned away from the outward sloping windows that overlooked the four-point-five-acre expanse of the flight deck and smiled broadly.

"Glad to see you again, Admiral."

"That remains to be seen, Brian," Pacino said wryly as they shook hands.

Ormond frowned. "Why? What's up?"

"Captain, I need you to put me under open arrest."

* * *

"Christ, Kenneth! What the hell got into you?" Vice Admiral Owen roared. "You're one of the most rational men I know. What you have done now is completely out of character. You've trashed your career in this man's navy and probably trashed mine with it."

"Admiral—"

"I haven't finished, goddammit!" Owen slammed a meaty fist against his desk and pens jumped. "You're an instrument of policy. You don't make it! Haven't you got that yet? Whatever your reasons, and I don't give a short ass for them, you're part of a chain of command, just like I am. That might not sit comfortably sometimes, but that's the price you pay for not being a civilian. You can't have it both ways. If you had a beef, why in hell didn't you talk it over with me first? You don't decide to blow everybody up because you're pissed off at something."

"Sometimes a pivotal act by an individual can change the course of history," Pacino said calmly, standing stiffly at attention.

"Don't talk to me about history like they found me in a dumpster. You live in an ordered society with rules of conduct. America isn't some Third World dictatorship."

"No, it isn't. Still, with all our rules, somewhere along the line we have forgotten what we're about."

Owen lifted his arm, palm out. "Save me the psychobabble, okay? Let's deal with reality."

"Then let's deal with it."

"You were up for your third star. You know what that means? The CNO, the Joint Chiefs and Congress thought highly enough of your abilities and judgment to give you strategic responsibility. So did I! You've made me look like an idiot. You couldn't have caused more trouble if you were a paid subversive. Christ! What possessed you?" Owen exhaled slowly, glared at Pacino and waved a hand. "Oh, hell! Sit down, will you? You look like a damn midshipman on parade."

Pacino pulled up one of the visitor chairs closer to the desk and eased himself into it. He could tell that his friend was more than a little disappointed and he didn't blame him one bit. If the situation were reversed, he'd be kind of pissed off too.

"You really took out the Yongbyon substation?" Owen peered at him, a twinkle in his eye. Probably a reflection from the overhead lights, Pacino thought.

"I did, sir," he said stiffly.

"For Chrissake, Kenneth. Relax, okay? The shit has already hit the fan. I would never have done what you did, but it doesn't mean that I didn't want to. The rules, remember? I'm not excusing you, mind you, but a lot of people will silently agree with your action. They might agree, but it won't stop them from crucifying you, you know that."

"I never figured I would get a medal," Pacino growled and Owen chuckled.

"You can bet on it." The Commander, 7th Fleet, stared hard at Pacino. "Tell me what went through your mind."

Pacino leaned forward and pinned Owen with his gaze. "You want to know what went through my mind, David? The attack on *Wilbur*? It wasn't the senseless waste of lives lost and people wounded—on both sides—but that nobody gave a crap. We don't count, Admiral. We're chess pieces moved around on a world board by players who don't care how many are lost as long as that nebulous political objective is achieved, and we go along with the charade. When they happen to make a bad move, it's tough shit on the pawn. In many ways the dead are lucky. There is little else that anyone can do to them. It's what we do to those poor bastards left behind that sucks. We ship them home, discharge them and forget about them. The shitty part is, we've been doing it deliberately. When they come crying to us for help, we throw up a barrier of bureaucracy, making them feel like traitors for daring to question authority. We first betray their trust by using them up in senseless conflicts, then we betray them again by ignoring their broken minds and broken bodies."

"It's not possible that you can think in such simple terms, Kenneth."

"It's called distilling the truth. We make things layered and complicated to avoid responsibility and make it easy on our collective conscience. My son died, and for what? Key Resolve is nothing but a flag waving exercise to intimidate North Korea and give China second thoughts about taking us on. Why the hell do we need to intimidate them anyway? It's merely a hollow political gesture without any strategic value at all. Everyone is still stuck in a Cold War mentality that had no credibility even then."

"Whether you like it or not, our job is to execute White House policy. The military is not a democracy."

"We're not ants either." Pacino snorted and crossed his legs.

"You want to debate every order made by civil authority?"

"Not debate, but contribute to the discussion."

"What the hell do you think the Joint Chiefs are for? They are our voice in the White House and Congress."

"Are they? It makes me wonder what we're saying to them. The President called me this morning. Did you know that? And you know what he said? He expressed condolences for my loss, and then told me that Vin would get a Silver Star. I almost laughed at the cruel joke. I like Walters and what he's doing, but I felt insulted by his clinical disposal of my feelings and the feelings of all those affected by Vin's death. Like a medal made up for everything, and you know the scary part? He wasn't even aware how condescending he sounded. He genuinely thought a call from him and a colored ribbon was all it took to take away the hurt. After all, we're the military where unit colors and a few ribbons on your chest is everything."

"What the hell did you expect him to do? Hold your hand while you cried on his shoulder?"

"I expected him to understand. As a former Air Force fighter puke, he should have known better."

"A medal is all he *can* give you!"

"No, David. That was the easy way out. Remember the Hornet driver who shot down that North Korean MiG two years ago? I went to see him and pinned a Silver Star on his chest. I felt real proud of myself, hardly noticing his arm in a brace and a leg in a cast from crashing after the triple-A got him. I didn't tell him that he no longer had a career because he would get a medical down check. It would have spoiled the moment and the photo shoot, but he knew. I walked out from the hospital thinking I had done the right thing. I felt sorry for him, but I was also proud of what he did. Did I bother to find out what happened to him, or that he was all right? Like hell. I've done my duty and he was somebody else's problem now. When Walters finished with me, I knew then how that aviator felt. I promised myself right there that the wounded we created a couple of nights ago wouldn't be forgotten. I cannot take the entire credit for that. It took my daughter-in-law to get me thinking straight."

"Do you believe that bombing Incheon and Yongbyon will change anything?" Owen demanded contemptuously. "You think that anybody gives a shit about your boy or why you blew your stack? It'll be all about political damage and how to clean up the mess you made. In case you've forgotten this basic fact, the military have always been expendable, subordinated to civilian whims, right or wrong. I applaud your misguided sentiments, Kenneth, but I cannot help feeling that you've been more than a little naïve."

"Perhaps, but someone had to cry enough."

Owen snorted and shook his head. "They'll bury this and they'll bury you with it. No one will hear your cry and you would have done this for nothing."

Pacino gave a sour smile. "That's where you're wrong, David. My cry will be heard, all right."

Alarmed, Owen sat up. "What have you done?"

"I sent an email to CNN and *The Washington Post*," Pacino said simply. He didn't have to elaborate. The consternation on Owen's face told him the admiral understood the awful implication.

After a moment, Owen leaned back and his shoulders sagged. "Shit! They'll have it on every network by now. You've blown it properly now, I'll give you that."

"I couldn't take the chance that I'd be whitewashed," Pacino said tightly.

Owen leaned across his desk, picked up the TV remote and pointed it at the 36" LED screen mounted in a side cabinet. A few seconds later the screen cleared and he quickly changed channels.

"…sketchy and we're still waiting for confirmation from our Seoul bureau desk, but we can categorically state that some sort of explosion and fire took place at the South Korean naval base at Incheon. As for Admiral Pacino's assertion that the United States Navy mounted a strike against the North Korean nuclear facility at Yongbyon, we still have no word from Pyongyang."

Pacino recognized the CNN morning anchor, Ralph White. It looked like his email was received and acted on. For CNN and everybody else, this was sensational news. He couldn't be silenced, not now.

White straightened some papers before him and turned to his frigid co-host, Sharyl Knight.

"Sharyl, what can you tell us about Admiral Pacino?"

Looking suitably grave, her mane of golden hair piled up in a bun, she nodded and stared at the camera.

"We're still checking his service record, but—"

Owen snarled and tossed the remote on the desk. The TV turned dark.

"I can't believe you did this, Kenneth."

"What did you expect me to do? Send Walters and Parker a

letter requesting permission?"

"If you think this stunt will get you any sympathy from Parker, you can forget it."

"I didn't do it to get sympathy and you know it."

Owen exhaled loudly and nodded. "Yeah, but I sure hope you get it from somebody, because your ass is in the sling for sure."

"Tell me one thing, Admiral. You're my superior officer, and you've got to throw me to the wolves, no hard feelings about that. Tell me that I haven't screwed myself for nothing."

Pacino waited as Owen thought it over. When his friend looked at him, his heart sank. There was no understanding in those eyes, only profound frustration. Owen was Navy through and through. There was no right way or wrong way, only the Navy way, and Pacino had broken the code. Friend or not, he could not expect any mercy here.

"What do you want from me?" Owen growled. "Give you absolution? As your superior, I've got to throw the book at you, but I won't be the convening authority. You're facing Article 94, 109, and 133...conduct unbecoming, at least, and probably General Article 134 in case the CNO doesn't think those are enough. He might dispense holding an investigative hearing under Article 32, since you've given him a virtual open-and-shut and go straight to general court-martial proceedings. That will depend to a large extent on what I recommend as your immediate commanding officer."

"And what will you recommend?"

"Frankly, I haven't decided yet. Part of me wants to shoot you for gross dereliction of duty, which you deserve, and part of me wants to pin a medal on you, which you so decry. You have created a complex problem that doesn't have an easy answer. Thank God I won't be the one having to decide what to do with you. In a sense, you've put the Navy and our whole policy making process on trial."

"That might not be such a bad thing."

"You know what they say about being careful with your wishes," Owen said gruffly. The desk phone rang and he picked up. "Owen!"

Pacino saw him wince and pull away the handset. Owen pressed a button on the keyboard and replaced the receiver.

"—have him strung up from the Washington Monument! What the *hell* is going on in your command, Owen?"

"Admiral—"

"I want his butt here so that I can personally carve him a new asshole. Then I'll have him quartered! For crying out loud, David, we no longer do gunboat diplomacy. Well?"

Owen looked at Pacino and wagged a finger in warning. Recognizing Admiral Parker's voice, Pacino got the idea the Chief of Naval Operations had seen the CNN newscast and was less than happy. Before the day ended in DC, lots more people won't be happy.

"Admiral, I have Pacino here with me if you want to talk to him," Owen said.

"I got plenty I want to say to him, but I want to do it to his face. You get him here right away. Do you read me, Admiral?"

"Aye aye, sir."

"Call me after you get rid of him." There was a click, followed by a dial tone, suddenly loud in the office.

Owen pressed the speaker button and exhaled loudly. "I guess he's seen the news," he said, looking weary. "I wonder who'll call next. The President? You better go home and pack a bag. Make it a large one, as you're likely to be over there for the duration. Say your goodbyes to Ruth and get yourself to Narita. I'll have a Gulfstream V waiting for you."

Gazing at his friend, down and dejected, Pacino felt slightly sorry for him, then quickly quashed the feeling. Owen was merely covering his own ass and trying to minimize damage to his career. That was likely to be the case with everybody in the Navy, from the Secretary down, he thought glumly. Well, he had not expected hugs and kisses when he hatched this crazy stunt.

"David—"

Owen raised a hand. "Spare me, Kenneth. It's not likely that I'll see you again, but who knows. You were an exceptional commander and I'll be happy to say that to anyone who asks. You can't take Ruth with you, at least not right now, but don't worry about a thing. I'll look after her."

Pacino got the hint that he'd been dismissed, stood up, and held out his hand. "And you were always a friend. I'm only sorry I got you into this."

Owen chuckled and grasped the offered hand. "Hell! Things were getting dull around here anyway. They can't bust me. I've got too many of the right medals and they'd have to take them all back first. Embarrassing all around. Besides, I'm a survivor. Now get out of here. I'll call a car for you."

Pacino stood at attention and saluted. Owen smiled faintly and gave him a sketchy return.

Outside, the air crisp, Pacino pulled his jacket tight about him. Glancing up at the building he just left, like Owen said, he doubted that he would be seeing it again, at least not in his official capacity. As a civilian, he certainly would not be allowed here. Part of his life had closed and he wasn't entirely sure what lay before him. No matter which way he cut it, it would not be pleasant.

Regrets? He looked at the gold braid on his sleeve and pursed his mouth. Sure, there were a number of things he wouldn't mind doing over, like spending more time with Vin, but genuine regrets? He had a job he loved, an adoring wife, and he had a son for twenty-six years. He could have done worse. There were mistakes along the way certainly, but life tests everyone's mettle. He had learned from his and moved on. Like a stew needing salt, life had its little adversities.

No, he had no regrets. As for the future, that was yet to be written.

A dark sedan pulled up to the curb. A heavyset individual jumped out, stood before Pacino and saluted.

"Lieutenant Reece. I was assigned to drive the Admiral to Narita."

"My residence first, Lieutenant."

"Of course, sir."

Reece opened the rear door and Pacino slid into the back seat, the leather creaking under him. As the car pulled away, he suppressed a smile. It was also night when he first arrived at Yokosuka. A moral somewhere, perhaps?

The car stopped beside his apartment block and Pacino got out without waiting for Reece. He leaned against the door and peered at the burly driver.

"Pick me up in half an hour."

"If the Admiral doesn't mind, I'll wait here."

Pacino nodded and slammed the door shut. Did Reece think that he would try to make a run for it? Did he know?

Inside the lobby, waiting for the elevator, he wondered how to break the news to Ruth. More grief and tears? He hoped not, but Ruth was a tough woman. She would understand. At least he hoped she would.

A soft *ting* and the left elevator doors opened. Inside, he pressed the eight-floor button.

Standing before his apartment door, he fished keys out of his pocket. Unlocking the door, he walked in and hung up his jacket and cap.

"Ruth?"

She emerged from the living room, stood there for a second, then rushed into his arms.

"Oh, Kenneth," she whispered fiercely, holding him tight.

He smiled at her and kissed the tip of her nose. "Sorry. I did say that I'd try to be home early."

She pulled back, sniffed and dabbed at her eyes. He was immediately concerned.

"Hey, what's the matter?"

"We happened to catch CNN while flipping channels trying to avoid a commercial."

"Ah."

"I'm proud and mad at you at the same time."

Linda appeared in the doorway and gave him a strange look. "When I said that you should do something about it, bombing North Korea wasn't exactly what I had in mind." Her eyes filled and a tear slid down her cheek. "I'm so sorry. It's all my fault. I never thought you'd actually do something radical like that."

"You were right to remind me," he said gruffly. "Vin shouldn't be forgotten."

Ruth searched his face. "They certainly won't forget you. What are they going to do to you?"

"Nothing nice, that's for sure."

"Will you face court-martial?"

"Probably, and imprisonment more than likely."

Linda slowly walked up to him, hesitated, and gave him a peck on the cheek. "That's from Vin and me," she said firmly, her voice husky. "No matter what happens, I'll never forget this. Never."

He patted her arm and nodded. "I'd love to chat, but I'm under orders to return to Washington. They've got a plane waiting for me at Narita."

"I'm coming with you," Ruth said immediately and Pacino shook his head.

"Linda needs you here."

"I can take care of myself," Linda said, holding her head high.

"I'm sure you can, my dear, but you're not the only one who'll be packing and leaving now. Whatever happens to me, it's for sure that I won't be coming back here." He stroked Ruth's cheek. "Send everything to Norfolk. Owen will look after the paperwork. Talking of packing, I need to throw some things together myself."

Ruth untangled herself and pointed at the entrance door. His battered black leather travel bag stood there waiting for him. He looked at her and sighed.

"Ruth Pacino…"

"I knew you'd be going as soon as I saw the newscast," she said softly and kissed him lightly on the mouth.

"It wasn't a given, you know."

She shrugged. "Then no harm would have been done."

"No accusations or recrimination?"

"Darling man, I stood with you from the beginning, and I'll stand with you now. I understand a little of what you did, but we'll talk about it later."

Eyes shining, Linda looked at him and squeezed his arm. "You can leave us girls to take care of ourselves. We've been doing it for a while."

Pacino cleared his throat and swallowed. This was more difficult than he imagined it to be. "There is so much I want to tell you."

"Later," she whispered.

"You want something to eat?" Ruth asked, always practical.

He squared his shoulders. "Thanks, but I've only got enough time for a quick shower and a change before Owen sends the MPs after me. I'm sure they'll give me something on the plane."

Refreshed, passport in pocket, he stood by the entrance and picked up his bag.

"We'll both see you in Washington," Ruth assured him.

"I'll call you as soon as I find out where I'm staying," Pacino told her and reached for her.

Her soft mouth opened and the kiss passionate as ever. That was one thing he loved about her; no reserve. She was his and always gave him everything she had.

He broke away, opened the door and made his way out without looking back. As he stood in the elevator, he thought he heard her call his name as the doors closed.

The twenty-odd mile drive to the new Tokyo International Airport spent in silence. From the main gate, Reece took the Hancho-Yamamka Road. Over the Bay Bridge and onto the Shuto Expressway B, past Disneyland, having to negotiate several tollgates, Narita airport blazed in full glory. He could see aircraft landing and taking off…little bubbles of light.

Looking at it all as they slowed down to take the Terminal 1 entrance, Pacino never figured he would be leaving Japan like this. *Simply another chapter in his life to be dealt with*, he told himself.

Cars streamed past them as the sedan pulled up at the military entrance. Getting out, he could see the green-lit Central Building and the North Wing. The boxy Terminal 2 control tower loomed above the low building. He thanked Reece for the ride and walked quickly toward the security gate.

Japanese Self-Defense Force MPs checked his ID and passport before letting him through. On the other side, he walked toward another security gate guarded by two marines in dress blues. When he showed them his ID, he was told to wait. A few minutes later, a slender commander hurried toward him and saluted. Apparently, he was expected.

After introducing himself as Logan, his pilot, they walked down a deserted corridor, Pacino's footsteps echoing on the hard gray floor. Logan opened a side door and they were on the tarmac, assaulted by aircraft noises and the pervading smell of burnt jet fuel. The sleek Gulfstream V already had its engines spinning. Without waiting for an invitation, Pacino climbed the four steps and walked into the luxurious executive jet.

"If you would please strap in, Admiral, we'll be taking off immediately," Logan said and hurried into the cockpit.

A young, pretty petty officer, her blond hair neatly tied at the back, retracted the steps and dogged the hatch. She turned to Pacino and held out her hand.

"I'll stow that bag for you, sir."

"Thank you, uh…"

"Sandra, sir. Flight time to McChord Field will be eight and a half hours and we're scheduled to land at 0500 local time. Refreshments and snacks will be served once we clear the coast," she said brightly and walked to the rear.

Pacino stared at her for a moment, then nodded. He took the second wide leather first class seat on the right that faced forward. This was VIP treatment and he wondered if he would see the likes of it again. Buckling himself in, he sighed and waited.

The engines whined and the aircraft began to roll toward the taxiway.

* * *

The Haeju naval base commander read the flimsy delivered to him from communications and frowned. However unusual, it was a valid order. After a moment, he picked up a phone and relayed instructions.

The duty officer manning the coastal KN-01 missile battery replaced his phone and gave his commands. The battery operators keyed in targeting coordinates into the fire control system and brought the battlefield short-range ballistic missiles to ready state. On order to fire, four canisters containing variants of the Russian-built SS-21 B missiles, originally obtained from Syria, spewed their deadly loads into the night sky. Propelled by their single-stage solid fuel boosters, sixteen six-point-four-meter, two-ton rockets climbed quickly, angling southeast.

Converted to use the American GPS system, the missile's inertial guidance package corrected its trajectory. At two-point-four kilometers per second terminal speed, the missiles covered the required ninety-seven kilometers in a mere forty seconds, giving their targets hardly any time to react.

Lying motionless in the black water, Incheon's harbor lights smearing the horizon to port, ships of the U.S. 7th Fleet came instantly awake. Maintaining watch in the Combat Information

Center as per standing orders, USS *Shiloh's* Aegis command and decision, and weapon control system, issued an immediate missile warning. The weapons officer blanched at the blips crawling across the tactical screens and immediately enabled autonomous defense without bothering to call the captain, allowing the computer to respond to the threat. There simply wasn't time for formalities. The Aegis system instantly rippled off four Sparrow anti-air missiles, followed by another four, then another. Two adjoining destroyers added their missiles into the basket.

In their terminal phase, the KN-01 optical correlation system locked in on the available targets. The missiles having minimal countermeasures capability, the Sparrows easily plucked most of them from the air in spectacular orange-white explosions when the huge 485-kilogram HE warheads detonated, making the very air shake. Four seconds later, *Shiloh* engaged with its Phalanx close-in defense system, sending out streams of tungsten penetrator rounds from its Vulcan six-barreled Gatling guns at the incoming threats.

As more ships engaged, the Phalanx rounds accounted for the remaining missiles…except one. Its airframe riddled with tungsten rounds the missile found USS *Stethem*, DDG-63, striking the ship forward of its five inch main gun. The weather deck ripped open in a fan of razor steel, taking out sixty feet of bow almost to the waterline. The gun housing was literally torn off its mounting and hurled against the crumpled forward superstructure already peppered by shrapnel and burning fuel. The blast also threw the ASROC launcher high over the flattened bow into the black water. Fire surged through the empty mess below the shattered deck and adjoining sleeping quarters. Sixteen sailors hardly had time to register what was happening before they died.

They were the lucky ones.

* * *

President Walters strode along the West Colonnade that ran beside the rose garden, Secret Service agents in front and behind him, toward the Oval Office side entrance. On his left, a gardener was trimming the hedge bordering the open lawn. The two gorgeously dressed marines guarding the double glass doors stiffened to attention. The security detail waited watchfully as Walters entered the office, a heavy scowl clouding his face.

He went to bed late and had not slept well. The North Korean situation bothered him. Why the dinky little country should prey on his mind, he couldn't say, wishing they would simply go away. He had lots more serious problems to consider. At least Samun had enough courage to swallow his pride and apologize to Sung, not that he had given him much of an option. It had not repaired the damage done, but it gave everybody time to pull back the rhetoric and look at the situation more objectively.

The unpalatable truth, and he couldn't get away from it, he was mad at himself. He should have tackled Grant and the entrenched CIA culture much sooner. It might have avoided some of the current unpleasantness. Easy to be clever in hindsight.

That Sung actually handed over ten of his warheads and promised to deliver the rest was simply incredible. If that happened, the result would be eminently desirable, but for the CIA to broker a deal like that without anyone knowing about it was infuriating, and embarrassing. Some commander-in-chief he turned out to be.

Earlier, hardly through his first cup of coffee, glancing absently at newspaper headlines, allowing Cathy's distracting chatter to wash over him, he looked forward to getting stuck into his breakfast. During his last checkup, the Navy doctor told him to cut back on fatty foods and exercise more. Install a treadmill in the Oval Office?

When Manfred called, everything was ruined. Didn't the man have a life? Although the chief of staff refused to go into details, Walters knew it was bad news. The only time he called, and still only eight o'clock.

Damnation!

He made his excuses to Cathy, sighed and walked out of the residence, his minders following closely. If he didn't do it willingly, he knew Manfred would come knocking. The man had no respect. He might be the president with power to blow up the world, but he couldn't have fifteen minutes for breakfast.

Manfred already there when Walters marched into the Oval Office. A marine softly closed the door behind him. On the small coffee table set before his desk stood a tray of pastries and a silver pot. Walters ignored the inviting smells and pulled back the chair behind his desk.

"Good morning, Mr. President," Cottard said gravely.

"What the hell's good about it?" Walters growled irritably as he sat down. "Okay, what've you got for me?"

"You want a cup of coffee before I get started?"

Walters looked at him suspiciously, his head tilted. "You figure I'll need one?"

"You will, and maybe something stronger."

"Never mind the chitchat. Why have you dragged me away from my breakfast?"

"I just got a call from General McDonald. CNN is running a story about Admiral Pacino bombing a warehouse facility at Incheon and the primary electrical substation at Yongbyon's nuclear complex."

It took a few moments for the magnitude of the news to sink in. Feeling utterly weary, Walters felt his shoulders sag.

"That's all I need. When did this happen?"

"About an hour or so ago."

"How in hell did CNN get hold of this so quickly? They got spies over there?"

"It appears Admiral Pacino sent them and *The Washington Post* an email explaining what he did."

"Ah, shit."

"That's about right," Cottard agreed and poured a cup of coffee. Without saying anything, he placed it before the president.

Walters glanced at it and took a long swallow. Excellent as usual, but he hardly noticed. "A bourbon would have been better," he groused and Cottard smiled.

"Later. You need a clear head now."

"Anybody hurt?"

"It doesn't look like it, but we're not sure. We don't know about Yongbyon, but it looks like Pacino was very careful what he hit."

"Any idea how he did it?"

"Simple. He used an MQ-10 Hawk out of Osan Air Base. We're still fishing for details."

Walters stared at Manfred, unable to believe it. "You mean, he rang them up and they let him have one, fully armed?"

"Pretty much. After all, Admiral Pacino is Deputy Commander 7th Fleet. He could do just about anything."

"It's his boy," Walters said after a moment, looking disgusted. "I spoke to him last night, the usual bland condolences, promising his son a Silver Star. I must have been an idiot."

"If his objective was to make a statement, Mr. President, he certainly made one," Cottard observed as he poured himself a cup.

"Have you seen the CNN newscast?"

"I caught a bit of it after McDonald called. The channels are running nothing but. He'll be here as soon as he gets more from Admiral Parker."

"Where is Pacino now? I want him over here."

"Already been arranged. He should arrive sometime tomorrow. Ah, do you want to see him?"

"You bet I do. I need an explanation."

"That might not be wise. The Judge Advocate General—"

"Works for me! Arrange for Pacino to see me."

"Mr. President, that's not a good idea. It's important for the

White House to maintain impartiality. Even a hint that you might be condoning his action won't go down well with Korea…North or South."

"I only want to talk to the man. What's next?"

"We'll have to give something to Granger for his morning gaggle."

"What the hell do we tell them? They know more about what's going on than we do!"

"Still…"

"Tell him to handle it. We'll give him something once we know more ourselves. Make sure the Vice President is in the loop."

"I've sent her a note."

Walters rubbed his eyes. "Gods, what a mess."

What he wanted was a vacation with Cathy, and leave somebody else with the headaches. After a moment, he took another sip and looked up. Jaw firm, he sat up straighter. This was no time to fall apart or start feeling sorry for himself.

"Get Stone and Tanner clued in. You better let Price know as well. Hell of a way for him to start a new job."

"Price is tough and smart. He'll handle it."

"Well, I can't hold his hand." Walters studied his friend. Not having to carry the awful load, Manfred often had a clearer perspective on a situation. "What's your assessment?"

"The fact that Pacino bombed both Koreas is suggestive," Cottard said immediately. "He is clearly sore at South Korea for provoking the incident in the Yellow Sea, and he's sore at North Korea for eagerly taking up the challenge."

"Which our friend Kham Chang-uk engineered," Walters said without humor. "Bastard! There's got to be more to it than that."

"To know for sure, we'll have to ask Admiral Pacino why he did it. The fact that his son was killed and we did nothing is a big clue."

"Manfred, it's only been a day since I spoke to both leaders.

What did he expect me to do? Mount an invasion?"

"I'm not criticizing, Mr. President. Granger did a good job expressing your displeasure, but the diplomatic language gave the impression that everyone should pretend the incident never happened. That this time it cost some lives was too bad. Lives are the price you pay for playing international brinkmanship. You can't blame Pacino, though. We send our kids out, use them and forget them—especially those who come back all torn up. Ever since Vietnam, we have castigated our veterans, making them feel like criminals instead of heroes they were."

Walters cocked an eyebrow. "It sounds like you approve of what he did."

"I don't approve, but I understand, if his motive was to highlight that every life matters."

"Hell of a way to make a statement."

"Sometimes, Mr. President, that's what it takes to make everybody sit up and reflect on what we're doing. Talking of doing, what will you do now?"

"We'll do the psychology dissection later. Right now, I need to call Sung and Samun and calm them down before one of them does something dumb." Walters rubbed his eyes and sighed, wondering what the rest of the day would be like. Looking up, he stared at Cottard. "Has *anything* broken our way lately?"

"We got a fairly favorable reaction to the Foreign Ownership and the Strategic Energy Initiative bills on the Hill and across most of the papers. The editorials are cautious, but there is an undercurrent of sympathy."

"I should damn well hope so."

"The *Wall Street Journal* liked the Energy bill, but were guarded about your proposal to revoke China's most favored nation trading status. As expected, the Chinese reaction has been less warm to all three bills."

"We gave them plenty of warning that this was coming."

"They're citing this is as another example of American growing protectionism while demanding a level playing field from its trading partners. There were hints of retaliation."

Walters gave a derisive snort. "You mean that up to now they were playing with us?"

A knock and Unice peered in. "Excuse me, Mr. President. Admiral Stone and Secretary Tanner are here."

"Show them in…We'll talk about those bills later, Manfred."

The two men pushed past her and strode in. Tanner placed meaty fists on his hips and stood before the president

"Tell me it's not true."

"You're just in time, Larry," Walters said brightly, feeling reassured by the SecState's formidable presence. "I was about to call Sung."

Tanner wagged a finger. "If you don't mind, let me handle him. Presumably, you want to call President Samun as well?"

"Both, but why should I leave this to you?"

"Not all the facts are in, Mr. President, and we need to know why Admiral Pacino acted as he did. Do we?"

"We've been speculating," Cottard said and rubbed his nose. "I left instructions for Granger to get a copy of the email he sent to CNN and *The Washington Post*. Hopefully, General McDonald will be able to fill us in when he gets here."

"In other words, we don't know anything right now, except for the fact that one of our admirals lost his mind," Tanner said caustically. "That's why you must let me handle this. Until we get those facts, the objective is to keep everybody from overreacting, right?"

Walters studied his Secretary of State and nodded slowly. Tanner could apologize to the two leaders as well as he could, and he would use all the right words…diplomatic words. Walters admitted he could be too frank sometimes and might commit to something he couldn't deliver.

"Okay, you have a crack at them. Mind you, Larry, at the first sign that they're not happy—"

"They're probably not happy right now," Tanner said dryly.

"If you get an indication that either of them is contemplating blaming the other and threatens doing something about it, I'll finish what Pacino started. Got that?"

"Reasonable, Mr. President, but if the subject does come up, what do I say?"

Walters thought for a moment. "Look, both are probably pissed off at us, and that's fine. Admiral Pacino will be dealt with, but in the meantime, they need to keep focused on objectives that matter. If they baulk, remind them that they created the whole mess to begin with. I don't want them playing the wounded innocent here."

"Sounds good," Tanner said slowly. "Something else we should consider. Kham Chang-uk might use this to trigger his takeover."

"Frankly, Larry, I don't give a damn who is running that country as long as they disarm."

Tanner smiled faintly. "I understand."

"Mr. President, do you want to bring our forces in South Korea to an alert status in case Tanner's talks break down?" Stone asked quietly and heads turned.

Walters regarded his National Security Advisor. A prudent precaution should things turn ugly, but he shook his head.

"Not now, and the move could precipitate the very reaction we're trying to avoid. Let's give Larry a go and see what happens. I doubt that Sung will start shelling South Korea over something we did. I do want you to give Price a heads-up."

"He probably knows already," Stone said.

"Tell him we'll be in touch once we know more. Also ask him to talk to Kham."

"Yes, sir. He's having a hell of a start over there."

"That's what we said," Cottard agreed with a smile.

Walters looked at Tanner. "Make those calls. When McDonald shows up, we'll be in the Situation Room. Check with Unice. Thank you everybody. Manfred, stay a moment."

When Stone and Tanner left, he sighed and sat back against the seat. After a moment, he stood up, picked up his cup and moved to the coffee table. Pouring himself some coffee, he selected a pastry and sat down on the sofa.

"Didn't somebody say that trouble comes in threes? I wonder what's next?"

Cottard made himself comfortable on the opposite sofa, crossed his legs, and chewed his bottom lip.

"You cannot get personally involved with Admiral Pacino, Mr. President."

"I'm involved whether I like it or not. Ever since I came into office, Larry urged me to change our policy toward North Korea from intimidation to reconciliation, repairing damage done by Bush and previous Administrations, and I've been doing it! I thought we were making real progress with Sung, only to find the CIA quietly undermining us, with the South Korean navy lending a helping hand as it turns out. If I'm to believe Price, all this time the ROK intelligence service has been quietly undermining our position over there, and now this. Where did we go wrong?"

"Why are you surprised? Since the Cold War, force has replaced diplomacy as an instrument of our foreign policy. We employed military solutions in preference to negotiation. Interfering in internal affairs of other countries has not brought peace and stability, but generated festering resentment, hostility and a terrorist backlash. You made strides to address that, but people only remember the evils we did.

"In 2007, a poll showed that most South Koreans saw no benefit at having an American presence, and believed the U.S. to be a far more dangerous threat to stability in the region than North Korea. A telling finding, but did we take notice? Our bases in Japan are more than capable of meeting any North Korean threat, yet we still maintain a doctrine of intimidation with our Foal Eagle/Key Resolve exercises."

"You advocate pulling out of South Korea?"

"I've been thinking about it. It wouldn't be a bad move, and you hinted as much to President Samun. If our presence there is meant to contain China, it's having the opposite effect. The problem is that North Korea doesn't know what we want and our military posture is merely feeding their paranoia. Our thinking is still dominated by that idiotic domino theory that sent us there in the first place. Sure, a nuclear-free North Korea would make everyone's life easier, and in 2007 they were almost ready to do it. Believing that they were stalling the shutdown of their reactor, we hit them with sanctions and called them a criminal regime. If we had a more clearly defined and less confrontational policy, it's possible that we could have achieved what we claimed we always wanted; a non-threatening North Korea, a nuclear-free peninsula, peace and cooperation, and maybe even reunification."

"You're not saying it, Manfred, but that policy shift also applies to China and the Middle East."

"It applies to everybody. You need to define what America stands for and articulate it. So far, our responses have been reactive rather than coherent. I admit a partisan Congress hasn't helped and you would be up against a lot of opposition. The real disease that has hamstrung every initiative is everyone's preoccupation with getting reelected instead of executing the policies of constituents who put us in office. No wonder the people are totally disgusted with all of us."

Walters snorted. "You're not going to change that, not in a two-party political system."

"Perhaps not, but *you* don't have to play the party game, Mr. President."

"Damnation! I represent my party."

Cottard's cellphone went off and he hauled it out of his pocket. "Yes?" He listened for a few seconds, face grim, then nodded. "Thank you, General." He switched off, turned his head and stared at Walters.

"That was McDonald. It looks like Sung has preempted. He just launched a strike against our ships at Incheon."

Walters clenched his teeth and slammed his fist against the desk. "I want that piece of shit destroyed, you hear me? Destroyed!"

"We don't want to overreact—"

"Overreact? You call McDonald and tell him I want *George Washington* out of Yokosuka and steaming for Incheon. If Sung wants to play hardball, I'm more than happy to accommodate him. If President Samun has a problem, I'll accommodate him as well. Enough of this shit!"

Chapter Seven

Admiral Pacino stirred as the smell of freshly brewed coffee permeated the cabin. He pushed back the thin blue blanket, removed the black eye shades, and blinked. The little bed Sandra fixed for him against the rear bulkhead surprisingly comfortable and he slept well.

Enticing aromas came from the galley and his mouth watered. He might be a condemned man, but the Navy did not see that as a reason to starve him. When the aircraft climbed out of Narita, true to her word, Sandra brought him a tray of hot finger food tidbits. Accompanying the delicious snack, he tried to relax with a glass of what must have been at least eighteen-year-old Jack Daniels while waiting for the main meal. The eye-fillet done medium rare with mushrooms, potatoes and salad, hit the spot. Not having eaten since lunch, he hadn't realized how hungry he was until the succulent meat melted in his mouth. Sandra looked pleased when he cleaned up his plate, she offered him coffee and desert—baked cheesecake. He declined dessert with regret, as cheesecake was one of his favorite sins, but accepted the coffee. At his age, despite regular hard exercise, it all stuck to the middle, and he hated the idea of appearing portly. A cigar would have topped it off, but that would have been pushing it.

With Yokosuka a long way behind, Commander Logan came aft to check that his important passenger was okay, and Pacino realized that none of them knew he was under technical arrest. He reminded himself to thank Owen for the small courtesy. Not that it would bother him if they knew.

Refreshed after his sleep, he stood up and stretched his arms. Sandra appeared from the galley and flashed him a smile.

"Good morning, Admiral. I trust you were comfortable?"

"Quite, and thanks for the bed."

"You're welcome. I'll bring out the coffee and breakfast in a minute. We're on time and should be landing in about forty minutes."

"Coffee sounds good, but I'll clean up first."

"Of course, sir."

Finishing his bathroom chores, he walked to the center of the cabin where Sandra had laid out a steel carafe on a small table with all the extras. He sat down in the forward-facing wide leather seat and poured himself a cup, mixed in sugar and took a long sip. Strong, yet delicate, a far cry from some of the shipboard java he'd had. He nodded in appreciation, and wondered what the new day would bring.

He tried not to dwell too much on yesterday, the events already fading into another reality. Was it only yesterday? It hardly seemed possible. Owen was right in one respect. When he faced his court-martial, which he certainly would, his son's sacrifice and the sacrifice others had made would be heard. America must not forget, or turn what he did into a futile gesture, an impulsive act by a bereaved father. Still, facing a possible prison term was not the career end he envisaged. What would happen to Ruth? Speaking to him on alternate Wednesdays across a glass partition? The disgusting thought made him squirm.

It was still dark when the Gulfstream scraped the runway at Lewis-McChord AFB located thirty-five miles south of Seattle. The aircraft pulled in at the small nondescript terminal, but remained on the taxiway. Watching the low building from the window, the place looked like a deserted country airport than a medium Army/Air Force installation.

Sandra told him they'd be on the ground for only half an hour, long enough to fuel and kick the tires. Invited to stretch his legs outside, he took her up on the offer and stepped out on the apron, taken aback by the cold. The air was chilly, but invigorating. He rubbed his hands as he walked beside the sleek business jet. Bright floodlights obscured the stars, the night totally black. A pickup towing a small fuel tank rolled toward him, slowed and parked itself next to the port wing. A man in dark coveralls wrestled a flexible hose and coupled it to a fitting under the wing. Feeling a little chilly, he climbed back into the aircraft.

When Logan returned on board, Pacino saw his guarded look and knew the secret had caught up with him, but he hardly expected it to remain a secret. Logan walked up to him and leaned forward.

"Admiral, I've got some bad news. Last night, North Korea launched a missile strike against our ships at Inchoen. DDG USS *Stethem* was hit forward of its main gun. There were casualties. It's all over the TV."

Pacino scowled, trying hard not to show his dismay. The fools! The prickly idiotic fools.

"When did it happen?"

"Around eleven local time."

His first reaction was to talk to Admiral Owen. Then what? Owen would handle it, and Pacino could do nothing anyway. He was out of the chain of command, out of it permanently. He had started it all, and now, he was merely a spectator like everybody else. More lives lost…

Damn it all!

"Thank you, Commander."

"That's not all, sir. Wait till you hear this. It appears there was a coup in North Korea yesterday and Sung Kang-dae was deposed. The former Premier, Tung In-san, is now the Supreme Leader."

Right then, Pacino didn't give a crap who ran North Korea, if it would only stop this madness. He knew that North Korea might retaliate before he made his attack, didn't he? He stared at Logan without saying anything. What could he say to the man anyway?

Logan noted Pacino's scowl, nodded politely, and went into the cockpit, shutting the door after him.

Sandra climbed in and buttoned up. Walking toward him, she gave a sunny smile.

"Have you heard the wonderful news about Korea, sir? How exciting! I hope this will finally bring peace and our boys can come home."

"I hope so too," he said gravely, his mind with the dead and wounded on *Stethem*. When would it be enough?

"I heard what you did, sir," she whispered, her face fierce. "Someone should have done it sooner."

He nodded and smiled. "Thanks, Sandra. I don't imagine it made me popular."

"You hang in there, Admiral. A lot of people are with you, and that includes me. Please strap in. We'll be taking off shortly. Flight time to Andrews is just under four and a half hours and we're scheduled to land at one p.m. local. Time zones, sir. I'll have coffee served as soon as we're wheels up." With that, she walked to the back of the cabin with determined strides.

At least he had one supporter in his corner. Public sympathy might be on his side, but that would mean little against the rigid articles of the Uniform Code of Military Justice.

The rear-mounted engines whined, spooled up and the aircraft began to roll. It reached the end of the taxiway, turned onto the active runway and immediately accelerated, the engines roaring as they built up thrust. Looking out, Pacino saw the port wing lift. The nose came up and he was pressed back as the Gulfstream climbed. In the distance, Seattle-Tacoma International Airport a blaze of lights against the sprawling city glow. The aircraft tilted to starboard and the sky grew black as the flightpath took it across the snowy Cascades.

A few minutes later, the engines whispering now, Sandra appeared from the galley carrying a carafe of coffee and a tray. Pacino unbuckled and stretched his legs. He would not have minded a shower right then. Although the seating was more than comfortable, the idea of another four hours or so sitting down made his butt ache.

Sandra left him with the coffee and pastries and retreated to the back of the cabin. Pacino sipped, wondering what Ruth was doing right now. Probably already in bed, he figured. He wanted to call her, to talk, to hear her voice, to unburden himself, but that would be selfish indulgence. She had enough on her mind right now. He would ring her once she was up.

The aircraft gave a small shudder and he heard the engines surge, then resume their reassuring purr. A moment later the aircraft shuddered again and the engines wound down. The main cabin lights flickered and the Gulfstream immediately began to lose altitude.

"Sandra?" he called out, but she was already running toward the cockpit.

When she reappeared, face pale, she looked calm. "We lost all engine power and the pilots are trying to bring them back up. Please strap in, sir."

"What are our options?" he demanded crisply. She didn't pretend not to understand.

"We can glide for about fifteen minutes. Unfortunately, we cannot return to McChord because of the Cascades. If they cannot restart the engines, we'll try for Fairchild AFB outside Spokane. Portland is closer, but—"

"I know. The Cascades."

She flashed him a small smile, gathered up the carafe and tray and walked quickly to the back.

Pacino stood and took the opposite seat that faced the rear. If they crashed, he would be thrown back rather than against the unyielding edge of the small table. Tense, but not overly worried, he noted that they were losing altitude rapidly. It did not feel like a normal glide to him.

"Admiral?" Logan called over the intercom from the cockpit. "We're unable to restart engines and dropping fast. We've got perhaps five minutes. I'm jettisoning fuel to try and extend our glide time, but we won't make it all the way to Fairchild. They've been alerted to our emergency and are tracking us."

Pacino tried to recall what the countryside on this side of the mountains looked like. He knew it was mostly dry and flat and that Bing Crosby was born in Spokane, but nothing else.

The engines remained silent as the aircraft fell.

Time crawled and the next five minutes seemed like an eternity. He remembered someone saying that the best place to be in an air crash was at the tail. That might have helped if he were in a wide-body jet, but the Gulfstream was a toy. If they went down, he wouldn't be safe anywhere.

Outside, he could see a tinge of red beneath a cobalt sky, but everything else was black.

"Everybody strap in tight," Logan announced. "We're going down."

Pacino pulled his seatbelt tight until it was almost painful and crossed his hands over his chest, amazed that he could be so calm. Life did not flash before him as the throb writers said. Unable to do anything, he could only trust Logan and his skill. Getting hysterical would not do him any good anyway. He had faced shelling and missiles, and did not doubt his physical courage, but this forced waiting was tougher to take. Not knowing what was happening, the lack of control, grated on his nerves.

"Brace yourselves!"

Below them, only darkness and an occasional pinpoint of light. Spokane's glowing sprawl lit the horizon.

The nose came up and the tail hit the ground with a bang. Metal shrieked and the jet lurched as it slid on its belly, the noise booming in the cabin. The aircraft bounced and suddenly swerved right as it struck something with a resounding snap. The main lights went out as the cabin lifted and tilted farther right, and Sandra screamed. Pacino heard metal tear and his body was thrown against the window frame, dazing him. The cabin jumped as the airframe slammed against an obstruction, caving in the port side. Dust and debris flew through the gaping gash, accompanied by a gale of frigid air.

With a final groan, the noise stopped and everything was still.

* * *

With a harsh jangle the bedside phone shattered the remnants of Paul Brenner's fitful sleep. He had watched an old black and white World War II movie last night, a desert action against Rommel. While the commando team were sleeping, a scorpion had crawled up one of the soldier's legs and stung him. His active imagination working, Brenner had jerked awake a couple of times, thinking that a scorpion was crawling up his leg under the blanket. When he managed to sleep at last, the phone's unrelenting noise didn't help his dark mood.

Crappers!

Without bothering to lift his head out of the pillow, he groped for the receiver.

"Brenner," he growled, wishing evil things on the caller.

"Get your pants on, Brenner!" the all too familiar voice of his boss blasted from the phone. "We have a downed Navy Gulfstream V west of Fairchild AFB and I want you there now. Your Go Team has been alerted and a Hawker 1000 is being prepped to fly you over."

Brenner sat up, rubbed his eyes and yawned. Lack of sleep or not, as the on duty Investigator-In-Charge for NTSB, he couldn't grumble at having his nightmare interrupted.

"What do we know so far?"

"The flight was out of Narita, Japan, bound for DC. It made

a fuel stop at McChord AFB. As they climbed toward their cruising altitude the pilot reported engine surges before suddenly shutting down. They dumped fuel and tried to glide into Fairchild, but ran out of luck. No fire."

"That's a break," Brenner said. Most airliner crashes left melted wreckage and ashes to poke over with a stick. "Anybody walk out?"

"Two survivors. Both pilots dead."

"Tough. Who's coming with me?"

"Gould and Mercer."

Brenner nodded. Gould was an experienced airframe and powerplant specialist with over eleven years at the National Transportation Safety Board. Mercer an older guy, in his fifties, and a systems man. He knew just about everything on instrumentation in any aircraft one cared to name.

"Thanks for getting them for me, Dick. What's happened to the survivors?"

"Arrangements are underway to fly the passenger to Washington. The flight attendant will be returned to Yokosuka, Japan."

"Washington?" Flying in an executive jet, the man had to be a big wheel.

"The passenger was Admiral Pacino," Dickery Evans said dryly.

Brenner didn't need to have it spelled out. He had seen the TV coverage of the blasted Incheon warehouse and listened to several chair experts pontificating on the political fallout for President Walters. The Navy had not wasted time hauling in his ass, that's for sure. He frowned as an ugly thought reared its head.

"Is somebody out to get Pacino?"

"You've got a morbid mind, did you know that?"

"Maybe, but the question still remains."

"That's what you're going to help find out. Call me when you get to the crash site so I can make a press statement." Evans rang off and Brenner listened to the dial tone for a second before he replaced the receiver.

Fully awake, he threw back the blanket and made for the bathroom. A cool shower freshened him up and he dressed quickly, already working the skimpy facts doled out by Evans. With no fire and the airframe probably intact, otherwise the two survivors would never have made it out of the small jet, the investigation shouldn't take too long. Engine surge implied fuel starvation, but that didn't sound right, and Evans did say the pilots jettisoned fuel, which accounted for no fire.

It could be a hundred things that brought the thing down. If he learned anything in his fifteen years of poking around all types of aviation disasters, it never turned out to be a single causal element that created a disaster. There were always a series of contributing factors, most of the time, which made his life both hard and fascinating at the same time.

It paid the bills, but his job also threatened to bankrupt his marriage.

Young, vibrant, and with too much time alone, Verena was getting restless. He knew she loved him, but his job kept them apart too often and for too long. Their reunions were passionate affairs and exciting, but it wasn't a marriage. He knew what she wanted: stability, a level of predictability, and a husband in her bed. He knew all that, which made it worse. The problem was, right now, he couldn't give her that. Vicky was growing up fast too, and needed a firm father figure to lean on with predatory boys sniffing around her. Verena was there to guide her, but it wasn't the same thing.

He had been offered promotion to Washington, which would give Verena everything she wanted, but would it give him what he wanted? The rub was, he wanted to keep her and his current job, and he couldn't have both. Unless he chose quickly, it's likely that she would make up his mind for him. He could walk into his house one day and find it empty. That wouldn't exactly make him cheerful.

Can't have your cake and eat it too, boy.

Crappers!

Badly wanting a coffee, he grabbed his pre-packed travel bag and walked out of the small double-story building that served as the NTSB duty rotation accommodation house for the Go Teams. Part of a complex of warehouses and bond stores outside Denver International Airport, it enabled investigation teams to quickly get to any crash site within the Denver Field Office area of responsibility.

Walking toward the side parking lot, he glanced at his wrist-watch: 7:45. Spokane one hour behind, which meant the Gulf-stream came down in the dark. The little fact meant nothing now, but he tucked it away with the other clutter he carried around. Overhead, the morning sky clear and it promised to be a fine day. Spring was usually fairly nice, but a storm could blow in from the north without any warning. Even on a lousy day, he would still need to go if called. He heard engines spool up from a large jet, roaring as the aircraft raced down the runway. The air filled with noises of car traffic and occasional horn blasts as people made for the airport or were leaving.

He climbed into his blue Toyota Camry, took out a packet of gum from his jacket and popped a stick into his mouth. Chewing furiously, he drove quickly toward the private charter terminal. At the gate, he showed his NTSB badge and the guard rolled back the heavy steel gate. The guard knew him, but he always had to show his ID. He drove to the New Flight Charters part of the small terminal, parked in one of the reserved spots and got out.

Inside, Gould and Mercer, both holding a white plastic cup, large brown bags at their feet, nodded as Brenner walked in. Both were of medium height and wore that confident look and bearing of professionals who knew what they were doing.

"Hi, boss," Mercer growled good-naturedly. "Ready for another one?"

"Ready as I'll ever be. Where's our ride, and who's got a coffee for me?"

Mercer reached behind him, plucked a styrofoam cup off the counter and held it out. Sipping thirstily, Brenner saw a chunky New Flight Charters man walk in from the back office.

"The Hawker 1000 is ready to roll, Mr. Brenner."

"That's great, Charles. Let's go, then."

The four of them walked out and piled into a white sedan, the smell of jet fuel strong in the air, mixed with noises of aircraft moving along the taxiways. An Airbus A340 seemed to hover as it glided toward the runway. Charles revved the car and shot across the apron toward a sleek executive jet some two hundred yards away parked in front of a maintenance hangar. A truck dragging a fuel trailer was just leaving. It was more economical for NTSB to hire a private jet on immediate notice than have one or two on permanent standby, most of the time doing nothing while still eating up money. The Go Team climbed into the aircraft, buckled in, and the flight attendant locked the door. Engines whining, the jet began to move.

At least he'll get a good breakfast on board, Brenner consoled himself, sipping his coffee.

Two hours later, having crossed a time zone and gaining an hour, the Hawker 1000 taxied toward the small terminal at the Fairchild AFB. A Bell UH-1N Twin Huey already had its rotors spinning when the jet came to a stop. Bags in hand the team alighted.

A blue jeep rounded a squat hangar and raced toward them. As it squealed to a stop, an Air Force officer climbed out and approached the small group.

"I am Major Fowler. Who's in charge?"

Brenner took a step forward and extended a hand. "That'll be me, Paul Brenner."

The major looked him up and down as they shook hands. "We didn't expect you guys so quickly," Fowler said, hinting that a government agency should not be this efficient. Brenner took no offense and glanced at the waiting helicopter.

"That's for us?"

"Yes. The crash site is only eleven miles from us. The area's been secured, in case you were wondering."

"Good. Where are the survivors? We'll want to talk to them."

"At the base hospital being checked out. Some bruises, that's all, but if you want to talk to them, you better do it now. They're about to disappear for connecting flights. I presume you know who was on board?"

Brenner stared hard at the leering man. "Major, you tell your commanding officer to hold them until my team has an initial look at the downed Gulfstream. That's official from NTSB. Got that?"

"My orders—"

"You got your orders, Major. Please stash this somewhere for me," Brenner said and handed him his travel bag.

He turned to his team, gathered them with his eyes and started walking briskly toward the waiting helo. Damned military! Always thinking that they can play outside the rules.

It didn't take long to reach the crash site. Half a dozen armed MPs kept a vigil to keep the curious out of the way. There wasn't much for them to do. Two men leaned against an ambulance waiting for something to happen. A red fire truck stood parked beside it. A thick hose lay limp on the ground reaching toward the aircraft. White suppression foam covered both wings.

The land flat and empty, clumps of trees and bushes here and there covered a gravelly orange earth. Low hills made a crescent around them. Without road access, it would be difficult for a nosy individual or reporter to get here. Once the news of the crash came out, somebody was bound to try. Brenner hoped to have the wreckage out of here before then. He would have to clear it anyway or the EPA would be on his case. Quick to bounce him, but not so ready to help people who unknowingly happened to build on a chemical waste dump or go after corporate polluters.

A shitty way to run a government, and he was being grouchy.

He gazed down at the mangled aircraft as the Huey prepared to land, and clearly saw what had happened. Following a trail of broken shrubs and torn earth where the jet first pancaked in, the Gulfstream had hit a large tree and swiveled right, causing the port wing to lift, the impact partially shearing off the starboard wing. The nose then slammed into another tree, crushing the cockpit, which accounted for the pilots. As the aircraft rotated farther right, the port part of the airframe came hard up against some boulders, which tore open the cabin.

Brenner shook his head and sighed. If it were not for that clump of trees, everybody would have walked away without a scratch. At night, coming in at a couple of hundred miles an hour, even with wing lights, the pilots had not seen the obstruction. Once the aircraft touched ground, they had no control where the thing went. Crappy luck.

Did they see the trees and realize what would happen? He wondered what went through their minds when death stared them in the face during those final seconds.

Once down, he ordered the chopper pilot to stand by. Before getting back to Fairchild to set things up, he wanted a quick look around for himself to get a mental picture. Gould and Mercer would do the detailed digging and analysis, focused on the most likely causal leads. He didn't want the investigation dragging on and getting the FBI involved. Always messy, he had no time for political turf bitching, although they would stick their nose in if he didn't clean this up quickly. Once the aircraft's data recorders were retrieved, it would hopefully make this investigation short and sweet. The mostly intact airframe and empennage should make recovery fairly simple.

Lugging their bags of special tools, and some pretty ordinary ones, Gould and Mercer walked to the aircraft and started a critical walk around. Mercer tried the cabin door, but quickly gave up on the twisted frame. He eyed the wide gash in the body, the wing resting on boulders, and squeezed through.

Armed with a fresh stick of gum, ignoring the ambulance men and the fire truck, Brenner ambled toward the front of the aircraft and peered through the shattered perspex into the ruined cockpit. The two pilots were slumped forward, blood staining their faces and bodies. It didn't look pretty. Pinned in by the twisted wreckage, it would take some work to get them out of there. He walked back to the helicopter and looked up at the pilot.

"Radio home and get them to send a heavy tow truck with chains and winching gear. We'll have to drag the airframe back to get at the pilots. See if they can arrange a flatbed to transport the thing back to base. We'll also need a twenty-ton crane."

"Yes, sir."

Mercer emerged from the aircraft and held up two orange 'black' boxes, the flight data and cockpit voice recorders. "Paul!"

"Good man," Brenner said warmly as the engineer brought them over. "Stow them in the chopper." Once back in Denver the recorders would be sent to the Office of Research and Engineering in Washington where the data would be downloaded and analyzed. "See anything useful?"

Mercer stowed the boxes on the rear seat and stepped back. "Can't get into the cockpit. The whole front is twisted and jammed solid."

"I've asked for a truck to pull the airframe back," Brenner said.

"That'll help. No fire or water damage, which also helps. Until I can look inside the cockpit, it's hard to say if it was instrumentation failure that brought the thing down. The cabin is mostly intact. Bad luck about them running into those trees."

"Arrange to have all personal effects on-forwarded."

"Will do."

"Where's Gould?"

Mercer shrugged. "I think he's looking at the starboard wing."

With Mercer in tow, Brenner walked quickly around the port side of the plane, careful not to slip in the fire foam covering the ground. Gould stood next to the torn wing wearing a heavy frown.

"Have you found anything?" Brenner demanded.

"Don't know." Gould knelt, reached with his hand into a jagged hole in the wing and held up wet fingers.

"Is that supposed to mean something?" Brenner said archly, working his gum. Even with the tanks pumped dry, some residual fuel always remained.

"I'm not happy with the color and the smell," Gould said thoughtfully as he wiped his fingers.

Knowing the engineer had his own way of doing things, Brenner was prepared to humor him.

"So?"

"Jet fuel is supposed to be clear straw-colored fluid. This stuff doesn't look quite right to me, and it doesn't smell right."

Brenner gazed pointedly at Gould's impassive face. "Contamination?"

"Could be water from normal condensation or foam residue," Gould said, temporizing. "It was pretty cold when they came down, and they could have picked up ice as the aircraft fell. What I'm afraid of, though, it could also be contamination from a FAME additive."

Brenner sighed and worked his gum.

For jet aircraft, it was critical that fuel remained free of any suspended water. It reduces the heat of fuel combustion, causing smoke, harder starting, and reduced power. The biggest problem is the influence of temperature. During flight, the fuel temperature in the tanks falls as the aircraft gets into the upper atmosphere. Any water would precipitate to the bottom of the tank because of its higher density. No longer suspended in the fuel, the water would freeze, blocking the feed inlet pipes, starving the engines and the aircraft would go down. It would crash long before the water could turn into solution again. Fuel tankers carried water-sensitive filter pads that turned green if the contamination exceeded thirty parts per million, and testing was done all the way up the refueling line. At least it was supposed to.

But Fatty Acid Methyl Esther, or biodiesel, contamination? The increased use of aviation biofuels as substitutes was a growing problem in the aviation industry, as cross-contamination can easily occur at several points along the storage and refueling cycle if people were not careful. There were already instances where aircraft were grounded because of this nonsense. A major problem with FAME, it was not a hydrocarbon, and adding it to a standard kerosene-based jet fuel above the permissible five ppm can seriously degrade engine performance or even cause it to shut down, as may have happened with the Gulfstream.

"Air Force pukes are generally pretty careful with fuel handling," he commented slowly.

Gould shrugged. "Anyone can screw up. We could also be talking about good old-fashioned dust. That will ruin an engine pretty damn quick, but in this case, I doubt that's what happened. I'll have the contents of every tank tested, then we'll know. Too bad small jets aren't equipped with fuel inlet heaters and filters like large passenger jobs. It could have kept this aircraft in the air a bit longer," he growled ruefully. Warm fuel would stop the biodiesel contaminant fraction from forming condensate droplets and gumming up the inlet lines, literally.

"Put it in our report as a Safety Recommendation," Brenner said absently. What if it wasn't a screw-up? He was being paranoid and knew it, but he couldn't get the thought out of his mind. Crappers! Everything wasn't a conspiracy and screw-ups did happen.

Gould shook his head. "There have been only five domestic cases of water and biofuel contamination in the past four years,

Paul. Unless we tell the FAA to issue a directive, the manufacturers aren't likely to comply. They won't figure it's worth the cost."

Brenner pointed at the crushed cockpit. "Those two might still be alive if the thing had fuel heaters. Let me have the test results as soon as you can. Call McChord and get them to fax everything they have on that refueling. Type of tanker truck used, amount loaded, name of driver, tests done, the lot."

"You want to secure the truck?"

"Absolutely. No one is to touch it until we get to inspect it."

"You got it. I only hope that it hasn't been used since."

"Have you checked the turbine blades for burns?" Dust in the fuel would show up on the blades in characteristic charring.

"I have and they look normal, but that doesn't mean anything. I'll have to rip one out and do a chemical test and an electron scan." Gould tilted his head, looking amused. "I can hear the wheels turning, Paul. You don't think this was an accident?"

"I've got suspicions, but without evidence, that's all they are. I'm going back to Fairchild and organize a hangar to house the wreckage. You guys keep digging. If you need help looking for pieces, don't be shy using the MPs."

Brenner pursed his lips and marched toward the waiting helicopter, giving the pilot the wind-up signal. Inside, he strapped in and put on his headset, reminding himself to call Evans.

The Huey lifted in a cloud of dirt and blown grass, nosed down slightly, and headed east.

* * *

After dumping its load of rain over Bremerton and the surrounding hills, the heavy black clouds rolled east toward Seattle, to eventually smash themselves against the Cascades range barrier. Bright sunshine stabbed through the gaps to reveal a smudgy blue sky. Raindrops glittered on windowpanes, leaves and parked cars. Tendrils of steam hovered over the roadway to be swirled into nothing by passing vehicles.

Robert Ashton squared his shoulders and stepped out of the little corner grocery store, the doorbell tinkling behind him. Only three blocks from his place, he never bothered to take an umbrella, forgetting how wet this place was. With 260 days of rain a year, Seattle easily took the record as one of the wettest cities in the country. It made everything lush and green and the vegetation thrived, but you had to take protection or risk sprouting roots.

He had forgotten, or rather, preferred not to remember. Having spent three months on the refurbished nuclear carrier USS *Enterprise*, the Big E, cruising the Mediterranean under the Special Agent Afloat program, coming back to Seattle's invigorating spring weather an uncomfortable shock. He had nothing to complain about. Pollard gave him two days to pull himself together and didn't care if it rained on both of them. Yesterday, it rained.

He took out a warm bacon and onion bagel from his bag of groceries, took a bite, and sauntered across the wet street. With occasional raindrops falling on him from overhanging branches, he slowly walked down the hill, flanked on either side of the roadway by stately old weatherboard double-story houses. Most were painted a dirty gray, but some owners feeling more adventurous had splashed on darker colors. It all blended in somehow.

Ashton swallowed the last of his bagel and dug out the keys as he approached his house, another gray double-story. Walking up the driveway, he frowned as he eyed the faded paintwork. Glancing at the lawn, shrubs that had taken full advantage of his absence to expand. He told himself that something would have to be done. Nature couldn't have it all its way. He didn't consider rolling up his sleeves or wrestling with a lawnmower. That was pedestrian work. He liked greenery and the peace and quiet it gave the neighborhood, but that love didn't extend to putting on gardening gloves or wielding shears. He would ring a guy who did this stuff for him and watched him work up a sweat while he sipped coffee in a lounge chair. He considered himself more the thinker-upper type.

The cellphone went off and he mouthed a curse. Can't a guy enjoy a day off without being bothered? He placed down the grocery bag and reached into his pocket.

"Ashton!"

"What soured *your* day?" Albert Pollard demanded.

"Getting a call from you, boss," Ashton replied amiably, hoping this was only a social interruption.

"I need you to pop over to the Lewis-McChord base and chat with Paul Brenner. He's an Investigator-In-Charge with the NTSB looking at a downed Navy Gulfstream V."

"Well, bully for him."

"Right. I'm sure he's having lots of fun. Because he wants to share it, I thought of you. Wasn't that nice of me?"

"It wasn't. Rats, Albert! I still got a day to go before I'm due to report in. Jetlag and all that, remember?"

"You never suffered from jetlag."

"I've got one real bad right now. Couldn't Hollice handle this? Sounds like a cakewalk and I'm hip deep in housecleaning."

"Get married. That'll fix your house chores problem. Hollice *will* handle some of it. He'll be your shadow on this little ops. He wants to see how the famed Ashton does business. Then again, you may clean this up in your usual efficient style and the whole thing will go away."

"You're heartless, did you know that?"

"I did know it. You keep reminding me often enough. So, get your Corvette out of hock and haul ass to McChord."

"Why is NCIS involved, or are you going to make me suffer?"

"I ought to. The pilot and copilot didn't make it. It could have been simple tough luck, except for one teensy detail. Brenner thinks the Gulfstream could have been sabotaged—fuel contamination. They won't know for sure until they finish their tests."

Charged with looking after security, counterintelligence and counterterrorism, the Naval Criminal Investigative Service also looked at purely criminal goings-on inside the Navy, and this incident could fall into any of the categories. Since McChord fell within the jurisdiction of the Northwest Field Office, Pollard clearly wanted to make Ashton's life miserable. Jealousy, that was all.

Although plain criminal investigation had occupied most of his time on board the *Enterprise*, and arguing with an opinionated, but very inexperienced JAG lieutenant, he hadn't had to handle anything more exciting—if he didn't count an occasional sunburn or two.

"Even if it was sabotage, why did you have to pick on me?" he demanded peevishly in a last ditch effort to get himself out of this. "I still got a day to go on my leave."

"Stop bitching, Robert. You had three months of sunshine and rest. It's time to get back into harness and some serious work. You're on a government payroll and I need you on this one."

"You don't have to remind me that I'm on a government payroll. You know, I could get a hell of a lot more working on the outside."

"Sure you could, but you wouldn't have half as much fun doing it."

"The money would make up for it." Ashton was kidding and both of them knew it. He sighed, resigned to the inevitable. "Since you're determined to ruin my day, is there anything special I need to know about this case?"

"You do. There were two survivors, a flight attendant and a two-star admiral."

"Somebody didn't like the admiral?"

"It was Pacino."

"Rats!" That would explain Brenner being suspicious.

"Right. Drop whatever you're doing and get moving." Pollard cut the connection and Ashton slowly nodded. He picked up his grocery bag and walked to the front door, deep in thought.

He was right the first time. Somebody didn't like Pacino. Lots of people in the Navy and out probably didn't like what the guy did, but who would be sufficiently upset to do something permanent about it, if in fact this was sabotage? The list of possibilities daunting, going all the way up the food chain to Washington. If somebody there orchestrated this, he would never find out...maybe. Despite being annoyed at having his day ruined, he did admit to a certain morbid curiosity about the case.

Chewing on a fresh bagel, he stuffed the groceries into the refrigerator and patted down his brown corduroy jacket to make sure he had his wallet and badge. He slipped on the hip holster with the SIG Sauer P299R and walked across the kitchen toward a door that lead to the garage. Some of the new kiddies liked the updated P239 DAK, but he tweaked his piece just the way he wanted it. Like a comfortable glove, he would wear it until something fell off.

Once he got onto Route 16, driving became easy all the way to Tacoma. There was traffic, but it flowed smoothly and steadily. Get married, Pollard said. For some reason the thought kept bothering him. He'd had relationships, nothing serious, but interesting enough to keep him in practice. None of his affairs were really deep, and neither party wanted it any other way. Like many professionals, his current goals were focused on two broad fronts: career and expanding his personal horizons. Sure, it would be nice to find a warm bundle waiting for him in bed when he got home after a tough case, his interest purely diversionary. He never actually gave any real thought to having something permanent. In his mid-thirties, there was still plenty of time, and women liked mature, responsible men. These days, it wasn't a given that the little lady would automatically do all the house chores. Still, something to think about.

His preoccupation got him to Tacoma South where he connected with Interstate 5. From there, a clear run all the way to McChord. At the gate, he showed his badge to a bored Air Force corporal and was directed to a parking lot next to a small office building.

He got out of the car and looked around, but there wasn't much to see: green shacks, hangars, and lots of open grass and concrete. Across the field a squad of grunts were practicing close order drill. He could hear an aircraft revving its propellers. Inside the reception area, he made it to the counter and leaned on it, waiting to be noticed. The sergeant clicking away on his computer keyboard finally deigned to look up.

"Can I help you, sir?"

"I am Robert Ashton, NCIS, to see Paul Brenner from NTSB."

"We've been expecting somebody from NCIS. Hold on, please." The sergeant picked up a phone and spoke softly. Ashton did not try to eavesdrop.

A couple of minutes later an Air Force captain emerged from an adjoining doorway and gave Ashton a quick appraisal.

"Captain Marchinson, sir. Duty officer. Can I have some identification, please?"

Ashton showed him his badge and the captain nodded. "Come with me."

They walked along a narrow corridor that smelled of old newspapers, walls painted a dark green. Ashton didn't care to be working here full-time. He hoped the walls did not reflect the mood and caliber of people here.

Marchinson knocked sharply on a door at the end of the corridor and entered. "The NCIS man is here, sir."

The major inside stood up and Ashton pushed past the young captain. Wearing thick glasses, graying at the temples, belly starting to bulge, the major carried himself with a casual air of bored indifference.

"Mr. Ashton? I am Major Stowell, base adjutant. Glad to have you on board." He swung his hand at a rugged individual reclining in a chair that had seen better days. "Meet Paul Brenner from NTSB."

Brenner heaved himself up and stuck out a hand. "Nice to meet you," he said in a strong voice that conveyed friendliness and a degree of guarded scrutiny.

A glint in his deep green eyes told Ashton that he looked at another maverick, and was glad. He dreaded the idea of getting stuck with a pencil-pushing busybody, but the NTSB guys had a pretty good reputation for being on the ball and getting things done right.

Ashton shook hands and smiled as he felt the firm dry grip. "Got it all sorted out?"

"You wish," Brenner said and gave a wry chuckle. "I left all the hard bits to you."

Ashton nodded. "That'll be right." He pulled up a spare chair and sat down without being invited. "Okay, Major, clue me in."

Stowell scowled at this liberty and glanced at Marchinson. "That'll be all, Captain."

"Yes, sir."

When the captain left, he took his seat and straightened some papers. He placed a pen parallel to the papers, locked his fingers, and frowned.

"I'm not sure why Mr. Brenner felt it necessary to call the NCIS. We're quite capable of handling what is probably a simple case of—"

"When people are killed, Major, there is nothing simple about it," Ashton said softly. "Anyway, he had no choice. It's standard procedure when there is a military fatality involved from a possible criminal act."

Chewing gum, Brenner grinned as he sat down.

"Foul play has not been proven." Stowell cleared his throat and patted the mathematically straight papers. "Well, you're here. What I want—"

"Major, this is my investigation now. Once I'm done, you'll get my report." Ashton saw Stowell's mouth tighten, but he had no time for him. He looked at Brenner. "Is there somewhere we can talk?"

Stowell stood up and planted his hands on the desk. "You can use this office." Scowling darkly, he stomped out without quite slamming the door.

Ashton hooked a thumb over his shoulder. "Must be something I said."

Brenner chuckled. "It was, but I wouldn't worry about it. I don't relish being here either, and he's being a jerk. You've been told that I suspected sabotage?"

Ashton nodded.

"Whoever contaminated the fuel overdid it. What we don't know is whether it was deliberate, but taking into account our passenger and what we found so far, I'm leaning that way."

"It could also be a plain stuff-up, you know."

"It could. The formal test results aren't in yet, but one of my men at the site saw enough to convince me."

"Saw what?"

"The perpetrator added too much contaminant, probably a gallon of biodiesel. It's a wonder the engines took the mixture. What happened next is straightforward enough. Once the Gulfstream climbed above fifteen thousand, the biodiesel fraction precipitated out, forming a condensation nucleus for any suspended water molecules, and there is always some water in any aviation fuel, and the jet went down when the fuel inlets clogged up."

"I didn't know biodiesel and water can mix."

"Ordinarily they don't, but like ethanol, biodiesel is hygroscopic. It absorbs water at a molecular level because of diglycerides left over from an incomplete reaction. These molecules act as an emulsifier, allowing water to mix."

"Well, shit."

"Yeah. The major problem with biodiesel, in addition to the fact that it doesn't dissolve like a normal hydrocarbon fuel, is its tendency to stick to surfaces such as walls, tanks, and pipes. Even though the pilot jettisoned fuel, the jet didn't glide as long as expected because of clogged vents. It just wasn't dumping as fast as expected. After the crash, and they were lucky the residual fuel didn't ignite, whatever fuel remained had plenty of time to drain out the open sump outlets before we showed up on the scene."

Ashton raised his hand. "Wait a minute. Biodiesel doesn't precipitate."

"Not at ambient ground temperature, no. It's a different matter at twenty-five thousand feet where you're in a sub-zero environment. The stuff was never designed to operate at such temperatures."

"There is no chance that this was accidental contamination?" Ashton asked and Brenner shook his head.

"Possible, but not with the amount of biodiesel we're talking about. The storage tanks where the fuel was picked up were tested. They're clean, and the truck was nowhere near a diesel bowser."

Ashton frowned. "You're saying this base uses biodiesel or jet biofuel?"

"They sure do. Almost all ground vehicles use biodiesel, including the refueling trucks. All thanks to the U.S. Renewable Fuel Standard created under the Energy Policy Act of 2005 to save the environment."

"It didn't save the Gulfstream. So, we have this organic diesel stuff lying around everywhere?"

"I'm afraid so. The 62nd Airlift Wing uses aviation biofuel in their C-17 Globemasters, but we can pretty much rule it out as the contaminant. Our tests so far didn't find any in the Gulfstream's tanks, and why would you use it when a can or bottle of biodiesel is so much easier to get and is far more effective."

"I can see now why you suspect sabotage. If somebody wanted to bring the Gulfstream down, why not use a handful of plain old dust?"

"Dust would certainly do the job, but it has to be the right amount. Too much and the engines would crap out when started. Not enough and nothing would happen, not for a while anyway. It also has to be the right consistency. Grabbing a handful of dirt or sand from the roadside wouldn't do it, too coarse. It would simply settle to the bottom of the fuel tank. You need the stuff in suspension. We haven't found any, but we'll know for sure once all the tests are done."

"Are additives ever put into jet fuel prior to refueling?"

Brenner smiled. "The fuel is blended at point of manufacture, but I can see where you're going. Mixing a bit of biofuel with ordinary Jet A1 might not have done the engines much good in the long run, but it wouldn't have brought the Gulfstream down. Before you ask the big question, nobody knows how the sabotage was done."

"Come again?"

"I talked to the refueling crew who were supposed to handle the Gulfstream. When the aircraft pulled up, the corporal assigned to do the job checked that the tanker was full and did the refueling as per SOP. He signed off the duty sheet and that was it. I called in and the tanker was put under guard until I arrived. Luckily for you, it hadn't been refilled or used since."

Not believing it, Ashton stared. "You mean that somebody just walked onto the base, poured a can of biodiesel into the fuel truck and simply wandered off?"

"Pretty much, unless it was one of the refuelers. That's why Stowell is chewing nails. I don't think the base commander had nice things to say to him."

"I don't suppose anybody saw our man?"

"At night?"

"Yeah. How did he get on the base and leave?"

Brenner smiled and held up both hands. "I'm happy to leave that one to you and Major Stowell."

"Thanks. I'm not an expert on this, but I understand that refuelers are supposed to run tests before any fuel goes near an aircraft."

"They did, but done when the tanker trailer was first filled. The thing was then left parked until the Gulfstream showed up. Plenty of time for someone to get to it."

"Rats!"

"That'll be right. Well, my job here is done. Technically, I'm pretty sure I know what brought the jet down. As to why and by whom, if it was sabotage mind you, I'm happy to leave that one to you also. I don't want to deprive you of the pleasure."

"Big of you." Ashton shook his head and smiled. "You have to give our guy credit. It was neat, simple, and apart from the pilots, nobody else got hurt."

"More by luck than design." Brenner leaned forward, his eyes searching. "Whoever did this knew the Gulfstream was coming and did exactly the only thing that could bring it down in the time available, short of blowing it up, of course."

"The thought did cross my mind. Our man was warned. Like I told my boss, somebody doesn't like Pacino."

"I told my boss the same thing."

"Where is Pacino now?"

"On his way to Washington." Brenner reached across the desk, picked up a plastic bag and held it out. "Refueling forms, with all the right boxes ticked. It's a dead end, but it does give you an evidence trail."

Ashton took the bag and rose, holding out his hand. Brenner took it and smiled.

"Don't think it's been fun, because it hasn't. Wish you luck."

As they shook hands, Ashton studied the man, wishing that he had him on the NCIS team. "Where are you off to now?"

"Back to Fairchild. The airframe is being ferried there and we need to do some checking on the turbine blades in case there was dust contamination after all. It looks like an open-and-shut to me, but we have to make sure."

Ashton nodded, appreciating professionalism when he saw it.

Brenner paused at the door and looked at him. "When you find out who did it, drop me a line?"

"I'll do that."

Brenner waved and walked out, leaving Ashton standing in the middle of the cramped room, chewing his lower lip. Sitting down, he glanced at the forms and peered at the signature. A scrawl written with black ink. The form showed the amount of fuel and type, point of aircraft departure and destination, all normal stuff. The corporal did not check for contamination because the fuel sheet had ticks and time stamps when the tanker was last filled. According to the form, a test was not required prior to actual refueling. He threw the plastic folder on the desk in disgust. Whoever did this knew exactly how the system worked.

He would have the fuel tanker dusted for fingerprints and might get lucky, but he held little hope of getting anywhere with that. If he dealt with a professional, and everything Brenner said pointed to that, luck might be in short supply. Sometimes the other guy did all the right things too. A slim thread to hang his investigation on, but at least he had a thread to follow.

There were others.

Considering the flight time from Yokosuka to McChord, his man had at least eight hours, and possibly more, to set himself up, lots of time to plan everything and tick off the details. He might need to ask Stowell about entry points to the joint base, but from what Brenner said, it appeared that just about anybody could walk in and get out without attracting much notice. He was sure the base commander would be looking into that, or looking for another job perhaps.

So, if somebody did give the kill order, there were only two main places where it could have come from: Yokosuka or Washington. Did the Navy want to silence Pacino, or did someone want to remove an embarrassment for the White House? Ashton didn't care. Although possible and something to look into, he pretty much discounted the likelihood of a Korean infiltrator pulling this off.

He scratched his chin and wondered if the sabotage artist intended to finish the job.

* * *

NORTH KOREAN LEADER DEPOSED
BLOODY COUP SWEEPS AWAY OLD REGIME
AMERICA OPTIMISTIC AT CHANGE OF RULER
SOUTH KOREAN FORCES ON HEIGHTENED ALERT
CHINA WARNS U.S. NOT TO INTERFERE

Pacino folded the copy of *The Denver Post* and slid the tabloid onto a small table in front of him. Finishing the remains of an excellent hot roast duck club sandwich, he picked at the cold French fries remnants. He wiped his hands on a napkin and reached for the coffee cup. All he needed now was a shower, shave and a change of clothes to feel human again. After fifteen hours or so of flying time, not counting the stops in between, he felt, and probably looked, more than slightly soiled. Too bad Sandra could not retrieve his travel bag from the Gulfstream. After crawling out through the gash in the frame, he didn't want her going back in, not with the smell of spilled fuel in the air and a real possibility of fire. After seeing the crushed cockpit, he kept her from going there when she wanted to look. She did not need to carry that type of memory.

Leaning back into the comfortable seat, he felt a pang of guilt for not calling Ruth while he remained stuck at Fairchild. Although it would have been midnight in Japan, he was sure she would not have minded hearing from him, harrowing day notwithstanding. Should he call her now? He glanced at his wristwatch, still set to Tokyo time, only 5:40 in the morning. Biting his lip, he decided he would let her sleep a while longer. If he disturbed her now, it would serve no useful purpose, and possibly cause more emotional trauma.

The engine noise changed subtly, muting to a whisper, and he felt the Hawker angle down. His stomach tensed, knowing what waited for him when he landed. The news clips and commentary he had watched on the onboard television screen had given him a pretty good idea. Predictably, some presenters took a harsh stand, saying the military was merely a mindless tool of civilian authority, while others took a more humanistic and sympathetic angle. Perhaps the latest events in North Korea would overshadow the headlines of his attack and the subsequent retaliatory strike against Incheon, but he doubted it. It would certainly keep the president and the State Department busy figuring their position. Four days, that's all it took to write a new history.

He wondered how many more days he would be allowed to add to that history.

Still, the timing of events in North Korea was interesting. The coup could not have been spontaneous. Those things took planning, organization and time. Were the pundits right when they said that the new regime was more pro-West? That clearly remained to be seen, and China didn't seem enamored with the idea. There wasn't much coming from the White House or the Secretary of State, and what the media reported was pure speculation couched in learned terms. No one knew what went on or what would happen next. Those chair experts rarely did.

He finished the coffee and crossed his legs. Apart from the light gray interior and darker gray seats, the jet's layout not all that different from a Gulfstream. Both were eminently comfortable.

After being checked out at Fairchild's base hospital, the commanding colonel baulked at the idea of Pacino leaving, but in the end, he gave in. Pacino's two stars made the argument easy. The New Flight Charters pilot did not mind at all if the Navy wanted to hire his aircraft. He was going back to Denver anyway, and a hop to Washington was easy money. Pacino had no intention of hanging around waiting for the NTSB to interview him. Besides, he could tell them nothing. After dropping off a refreshed and more composed Sandra at Sea-Tac for her connecting flight to Narita, he was on his way to what promised to be a stormy reception with the Chief of Naval Operations.

The civilian attendant walked up the aisle and leaned against the seat.

"We'll be landing at Andrews in about ten minutes, Admiral. The pilot advised me to tell you that you'll be picked up."

"Thank you," Pacino said, slightly relieved not to have that little worry hanging over him.

He was beginning to wonder whether he would need to catch a cab downtown. *Of course* Parker would have him picked up. He was under arrest, for crying out loud.

The attendant cleared away the table and disappeared into the galley. Pacino strapped in and waited. Outside, the sky clear as far as he could see. Below, the landscape changed from fields and patches of forest to suburbia surrounding Washington. Far on his right the Atlantic merged into a fuzzy horizon, glittering in late afternoon sunshine.

The landing at Andrews smooth, the Hawker bumped along the uneven concrete joints in the taxiway as it made its way toward the tall hangars. A row of F-16s glinted in the sun at the far end of the fairway. The aircraft stopped and the engines sighed as they wound down. The attendant immediately unlatched the door and lowered the steps. Pacino put on his crumpled coat, jammed on the cap and stepped off the aircraft. A flag lieutenant emerged from a black Navy sedan and hurried toward him. He snapped to and gave a sharp salute.

"Lieutenant Grisom, sir. Admiral Parker sent me to get you squared away."

Pacino nodded and returned the salute. "Let's go, then."

"We arranged a room for you at the Mandarin Oriental while you're in DC, sir. It's only about a mile-and-a-half from the Pentagon and within easy walking distance from the White House.

Not that you would need to walk," Grisom added hastily.

"You figure I'll be visiting both, Lieutenant?" Pacino teased him. The youngster looked momentarily confused, then his face cleared and he smiled.

"I dare say you will be, sir. I'll take you to the hotel now so you can freshen up before seeing Admiral Parker."

"A shower would be good, but I seem to have mislaid my travel bag."

"We know about your crash. Everything you need is at the hotel. You might as well know now, sir. Your crash, it was sabotage."

"Sabotage?"

"Yes, sir. Somebody contaminated the refueling truck's tank at McChord. Because of the dead pilots, NCIS has assigned an investigator to look into it. Someone didn't want you here, Admiral," the youngster chirped cheerfully and started walking toward the car.

Deep in thought, Pacino followed. The Gulfstream was sabotaged? It hardly seemed possible. But why? What could anyone gain by having him dead? Revenge by the North Koreans? Thin, but plausible. Then again, perhaps not. They had hit Incheon in a fit of pique and maybe wanted his head as well. They could not have known that he would be at McChord, though.

The South Koreans? That didn't fit either. Seoul would rant and rave, which they already did according to the papers, but he didn't think it likely that they would stoop to murder.

Who, then? Someone in the Navy or the White House?

Grisom held the rear door open and Pacino slid into the car. Unbuttoning his jacket, he could smell stale sweat on his shirt. He must look like a bum, *damn it all*!

The car turned and accelerated toward the main gate.

Only ten miles from downtown Washington, the drive in did not take long once they hit Suitland Parkway, most of the traffic heading out of the city. Over the Frederick Douglas Bridge, with the Potomac on the left and the Pentagon building bright in the waning light, only a couple of blocks to Mandarin Oriental on Maryland Avenue. As the car pulled in at the front entrance, Pacino could see the Capitol a bare half-mile up the broad boulevard.

They crossed the opulent marbled foyer, Grisom checked him in, causing the concierge to raise an eyebrow when he recognized his controversial guest. With his minder waiting in the lobby, Pacino took the elevator to the seventh floor, feeling the miles catching up with him. A couple of hours or so of sleep in a comfortable bed would go down nice just then. At least it was afternoon and his body clock would get reset by morning.

Inside the luxurious apartment, he barely glanced at the comfortable furnishings, wide double bed and writing desk tucked beside the window. He pulled back the drapes and gazed at the city spread below without really seeing it or the people, his thoughts elsewhere. They were just pebbles in the sand, and just as insignificant.

Face grim, he made himself a promise.

The bastards aren't going to sweep me *away.*

He threw his cap on the bedspread and peeled off his grimy coat. Striding to the clothes cabinet, he slid back the double panels and chuckled. Arrayed neatly on coat hangars were two sets of dress blues, complete with all the right ribbons, and three spare shirts. Next to the shirts was a dark gray pinstripe suit. The fact it was there implied he would need it. The top drawer inside held socks and underwear. Beside the bed cabinet were a pair of black shoes.

As he checked out the stuff, he reminded himself to thank Parker. It was a gracious and welcomed gesture. Then again, perhaps the CNO did not want to embarrass the Navy by having him face the media in a rumpled two-day-old uniform.

The bathroom was equally well stocked with all the necessary toiletries. A quick shower restored some of his vigor, and a shave made him presentable. Dressing, he glanced at the phone on the writing desk. He finished knotting the tie, stepped into his new shoes, and sat beside the table. Picking up the phone, he dialed. Barely 6:30 in Tokyo, but if he didn't call now, it might be a while before there was another opportunity. What remained of his afternoon was likely to be busy. Besides, he had been putting this off long enough.

After three rings, a familiar, but sleepy voice finally answered. "Hello?"

"It's me, honey."

"Kenneth! Is everything all right?"

"Everything is fine, Ruth. I'm in Washington and my minder is waiting to haul me in before Parker. Sorry to wake you, but I won't be able to call again for a few hours."

"Silly! You can call me any time, and I was about to get up anyway. Where are you staying?"

"At Mandarin Oriental. Would you believe it?"

"A dead man's last wish, no doubt," she said dryly and he laughed.

"You could be more right than you know. How have you been?"

"After a bit of crying and talking to Linda, we stayed up late and saw what happened at Incheon. Oh, Kenneth, all those lives lost."

"I know, honey. How's Linda?"

"Still in shock. It'll take a while, dear…for both of us. And you?"

Pacino's gut churned as the memories came flooding back. Gripping the receiver tightly, he swallowed. It hadn't sunk in that he would never see Vincent again. He took a deep breath and exhaled softly.

"There's a lot I want to say, but there is no hurry, not now. Try not to worry too much."

"With everything that's going on, you're not asking for a lot, are you?"

He wanted to reach out and take her in his arms. Tough girl, Ruth. "There'll be time to talk once we're together."

"Linda and I will be over as soon as we can. I'll talk to Owen in the morning. Love you."

"Me too. Hugs."

"Call me when you finish with Parker."

"I'll do that." He replaced the receiver and smiled, feeling better.

As long as they were together, nothing else mattered. He had deliberately held back mentioning the crash. She would find out eventually and there was no reason to upset her further now. He had no dents or scratches and that's all that counted.

When the elevator doors opened at the lobby floor, a gaggle of reporters wielding cameras and recorders surged toward him, lights flashing. Grisom was trying valiantly to hold them back, but it was a wasted effort. Somebody in the hotel probably tipped them off. Well, he would have to confront them sooner or later, and it might as well be now as ever.

He stepped out and faced them. They immediately crowded around him.

"Admiral Pacino! Can you tell us—"

"What prompted you to attack—"

"Admiral! Can you explain your reckless—"

"Did you engineer the fall of the North—"

Grisom pushed through them and raised his arms. "Fellows, please! Have a heart. Admiral Pacino cannot—"

"It's all right, Lieutenant," Pacino said firmly and the crowd became expectant. Not liking it, Grisom frowned and stepped to one side. Pacino might be under technical arrest, but he was still a two-star admiral.

"I'll make a brief statement, but I won't be taking any questions. Not now. I'm needed at the Pentagon." He gazed at the predatory faces, the cameras and mini-recorders pointing his way, and squared his shoulders.

"You all know what happened in the Yellow Sea, but I'll recap anyway. It was supposed to be a routine and peaceful naval exercise. We've been conducting them every year and this one started off like all the others. Pursuing its own political agenda, South Korea launched a mock attack on a North Korean submarine."

"How do you know that?" someone demanded. Pacino raised his hand.

"No questions, I said. No one was hurt and the situation could have been defused right there. However, for reasons of their own, the North Koreans retaliated with deadly force, which resulted in a totally unnecessary loss of life on both sides. One of them was my son.

"I want to make one point perfectly clear. What I did was entirely on my own initiative, without knowledge or approval of the Navy. I didn't do it because I grieved over my son. He merely served as a trigger. I did it for all the sons who died or were maimed on that night. I wanted to remind both Koreas, the Navy Department and the White House, that the men and women who serve in our military do so willingly and do it for a single purpose...to protect those left at home, to make sure they remain safe. In all that time, no one ever bothered to say thank you. When we finished using them, we simply discarded them. I wanted to create a reminder that our boys cannot be discarded and forgotten. Not anymore."

Pausing, looking at the puzzled faces trying to register what he said, then nodded. "Thank you."

He stepped toward them and they slowly fell back, silent, making way for him. He gathered Grisom with his eyes and the two of them walked deliberately toward the revolving doors, their footsteps clicking on the gray marble floor. The reporters woke up to the fact that he was leaving, they hurried after him, scrambling for the best position around the car, recorders held out, questions following him in a torrent. Pacino smiled, waved and got into the car and peaceful silence. Grisom started the engine and they pulled away from under the portico.

Once across the George Mason Memorial Bridge, it did not take long to get to the Pentagon River Terrace Entrance that faced the city. As always, a constant stream of uniformed and civilian personnel came and went. As the largest office building in the world, housing some 23,000 people, traffic at every entrance the norm. Grisom took him to the E ring fourth floor that housed senior ranking officers. Although not a direct line officer anymore, the Chief of Naval Operations being an administrative posting, Parker was the top ranking Navy officer, and next to the Secretary of the Navy, had a lot to say how the service operated.

The taciturn captain guarding the inner office stood up when Pacino entered.

"Welcome to the Pentagon, sir. Admiral Parker is expecting you."

"I don't doubt it," Pacino growled and glanced at Grisom. "Thanks for the pickup, Lieutenant."

"A pleasure, sir." The youngster nodded to the captain and walked out.

The captain knocked on the polished wood door and peered in. "Admiral Pacino, sir."

"Show him in," came the familiar crisp voice from inside.

Pacino walked into the inner office and faced the CNO sitting behind a cluttered desk. In an unconscious gesture, Parker brushed back his peppery hair and pushed up his rimless glasses.

"Have a seat, Kenneth," he said amiably and waved a hand at a padded chair. "How was the flight in?"

"Long," Pacino said, pulled up a chair and easing himself in.

He removed his cap and held it in his lap. He fully expected a more frosty reception, but what the hell. To yell at him now wasn't going to get Parker anywhere. Waiting for Pacino to arrive, the CNO probably had time to think and cool down. He hoped so.

"Don't know why I asked such a stupid question," Parker muttered testily. "Of course it was damn long. They always are." He tilted his head. "No ill effects from the crash?"

"Just some bruising. We were lucky."

"I'll say. You were told about the sabotage?"

"I got the word, but I still can't figure out why anybody would do it."

"Lots of reasons, which I'm sure you know, but you don't get it, do you?"

"Get what?"

"They failed once…"

Pacino gaped at him. "The thought honestly never occurred to me that I could still be a target."

"I can see that. I got a warning from NCIS about it."

"They didn't waste any time." The wheels turned in Pacino's head and he swallowed hard. "Ruth! She's planning to come here."

Parker frowned. "That one slipped my mind. It might be best if she stayed over there for the time being, although I don't consider her to be in any real danger. Leave it with me. I'll talk to Owen."

"She won't like having to stay there."

"Your problem. The hotel, comfortable enough?"

"Thanks for arranging that, Wayne. I didn't look like much when we landed at Andrews."

Parker chuckled. "I dare say. It's coming out of your pay."

Pacino wondered if the CNO was kidding, but he couldn't tell and shrugged.

"I might as well use the uniforms while I can. I gather it won't be for much longer."

Parker looked speculatively at Pacino, sighed, and shook his head. "You've had quite a time, haven't you?"

"Someone needed to speak out, Admiral."

"But you didn't just talk, did you?" Tapping the desk with his fingers, Parker finally jerked his head at a bank of three screens mounted in a wall cabinet. "That was a hell of an impromptu interview."

"You saw it?"

"Most of it. Between you and me, I agree with what you said, and it will generate a lot of empathy for you on the street, but you're being naïve if you think that you'll change anything. I've talked to Owen and got a boiled down version of your catharsis. Shit, Kenneth! I can't believe you can have such simple ideas."

"Is it simple to value our men, or naïve to expect that we'll look after them once we're finished using them up?"

"We *are* looking after them, for heaven's sake!"

"Sure we are. With a Veterans Affairs bureaucracy that's more interested in paper stacking than dealing with living people. They've got four and a half million paper files! This is supposed to help our men?"

Parker snorted and leaned forward. "We're getting them computerized, damn it! Paper files or not, do you know how many bloodsuckers come knocking on our door expecting a handout because they're suffering constant headaches and see us as the cause?"

"I'm sure there are a few, but I'm not talking about them. What about the people we gassed, poisoned and experimented on? What about the broken minds we created in Iraq and Afghanistan? When we're forced to deal with them, under the glare of publicity more often than not, we solve it by pretending they don't exist and wait for them to die. A great solution, Wayne."

"Okay, the system needs some oiling, but why in the name of heaven did you have to bomb Korea to make your point? We don't take unilateral action without civil authority. You realize the political headache you handed the President?"

"What should I have done? Write you a letter? I like Walters and I'm sorry to have left him holding the can, but he needed to be reminded of what's going on, as you did. I couldn't risk you or the Joint Chiefs burying the issue simply because it belongs in the too hard basket. Somebody had to do something."

"And how does stirring up the Korean peninsula help? Your misguided action might very well upset the President's entire reconciliation initiative!"

"They lost boys too, you know. This might make them think as well."

"Shit! Why you? You were about to become one of the youngest three-star commanders in the Navy, and you've thrown it all away on a crazy gesture of self-immolation. You know how the system works. You use it, but you can't abuse it. I simply don't understand what got into you."

Pacino smiled grimly. "Too late for second thoughts, wouldn't you say?"

"You're right about that. It's far too late. Regardless of any personal feelings or sympathy for what you've done, which I haven't got much of, I have to nail you for the good of the Navy. Hell, for the good of our entire military system."

"I understand, Wayne. No hard feelings."

"Hell, Kenneth. I'd feel better if you weren't so goddam understanding. You threw it all away for nothing, but we'll talk later. Right now, I need to put my official hat back on. Admiral Pacino, under UCMJ regulations, the United States government is bringing charges against you under Article 80...an attempt to commit an offense; Article 94...mutiny and sedition; Article 107...false official statements; Article 109...destruction of property other than military property of the United States; Article 133...conduct unbecoming an officer, and Article 134...bringing discredit on the armed forces. Do you understand these charges?"

Face wooden, realizing he was going to have the whole manual thrown at him, Pacino nodded once. "I do, sir."

"Although there is enough prima-facie evidence to initiate immediate general court-martial proceedings against you, which could very likely see you serving time at Leavenworth, your defense counsel demanded that in the interest of justice and discipline, mitigating circumstances warrant holding an Article 32 hearing. Owen had no objection, by the way. You were not insubordinate when you carried out your attacks, and you didn't disobey any orders, because there weren't any! I'm sorry, Kenneth. I wish there was another way." Parker reached across the desk and pressed a button on his phone keypad. "Ron? Show him in."

"Yes, sir."

A moment later, a knock and a tall, skeletal commander stepped in wearing SEAL trident wings. He stopped in front of the desk and stood at attention.

"Commander Eden Powell, reporting as ordered, sir!" the man said in a deep voice, his mantle of authority palpable.

"At ease, Commander," Parker said and glanced at Pacino. "Kenneth, meet your JAG defense counsel. He'll be on your case through the hearing. I'm told he's one of the best. Between us, you'll need the best."

Powell turned to Pacino, his look serious. "Admiral, I must advise you not to say anything to anyone unless I am present. Is that understood, sir?"

Pacino grinned, liking the youngster's take-charge attitude. "We'll have to discuss that, Commander."

"Sir—"

"Argue it outside," Parker interrupted. "By the way, Kenneth, I know you've had a long trip, but are you okay for dinner? I want to talk more about what you did, and your crash."

"And I want to know what's going on in North Korea."

"It's settled, then. I'll pick you up at eighteen-thirty. Wear your mufti. I don't want the media mobbing us." Parker waved at Powell. "Take him away, Commander."

In the corridor, Pacino paused and gave his lawyer a long stare. Instead of being intimidated, Powell's hard blue eyes looked right at him. Pacino could not guess his age, late thirties perhaps, but the lines at the corners of his eyes showed maturity and determination. The man may have seen action as a SEAL, but that might not carry much weight in a courtroom.

"Well, Commander?"

"The government will seek to wipe the floor with you, Admiral, and the raft of charges against you have not made my job any easier. Of course, you don't need to accept me as your counsel. You can get yourself a crack civilian lawyer, and I know one or two if you're interested. They'll milk your story for all it's worth."

"I don't doubt it, but let's face it. No matter what happens, Commander, my career is pretty much bilged and we both know it. I didn't expect to walk away after what I did. What I do expect is to be heard. You're my counsel."

Powell nodded. "You'll need to tell me what you want to say at the hearing, Admiral, and the circumstances that led to your action, but I don't want you telling me that your career is bilged. By the way, I do expect you to walk away."

Pacino goggled at him, then chuckled. "I like your optimism, but you can't be serious. Each of those charges carries a dishonorable discharge, forfeiture of all pay and allowances, and a minimum of five years confinement. With the mutiny and sedition charge, they could throw away the key."

Powell grinned and gave a dismissive gesture. "They're pulling a long bow there, sir. Your acts were committed against foreign powers."

"It's still sedition."

"Perhaps, and only if those powers choose to bring charges against you, which I don't think will happen. They are also looking at the 'big picture', and we'll use that to our advantage. What's important here, your action did not constitute an attempt to overthrow the government of the United States."

"Whichever way you cut it, I'm still in a shitload of trouble. Tell me, Commander, and no horse crap. How good are you?"

"I consider myself one of the two best litigators in JAG, sir."

"And who's the other one?"

"Greer Fisher. He'll be prosecuting."

"Of course. Why did they assign you? I would have thought the government would want to bury me. A crack lawyer could upset their plans."

"They do want to bury you if the Secretary of the Navy has anything to say about it. That's why Fisher is on the case, but I asked for this assignment, Admiral, and the JAG office doesn't play politics."

Pacino laughed at this amusing absurdity. "And you expect me to swallow that bilge?"

Powell's mouth twitched. "I didn't say we're not subjected to political pressure. The Secretary and Admiral Parker have one problem: Rear Admiral Thorton, Judge Advocate General. The man refuses to be pressurized."

"That must bring him a lot of brownie points," Pacino growled.

"Perhaps not, but the fact that I was assigned to your case should demonstrate our impartiality. Like I said, you can always get yourself a civilian lawyer, sir."

"Commander, I appreciate your candor, but you must know the government will do everything it can to silence me. They might even throw me to the Koreans if the gesture would salvage whatever deal the White House is trying to stitch up."

Powell gave a slow smile, but his eyes were hard. "Don't you think that you better leave that to me? Now, let's find a room where we can talk."

Chapter Eight

Heading north toward Silverdale along Route 16, with choppy seas stirring up Dyes Inlet on his right, Ashton experienced frustration. In his opinion, Major Stowell was an idiot. Not able to explain how someone could simply walk into a supposedly secure military installation, offering feeble excuses. The major took out his inadequacies on Captain Marchinson. Never mind that the luckless individual had not even been on duty then.

Of the two available entry points to the joint base, anyone wearing a uniform and flashing a card easily printed on a cheap computer, could have driven or walked in without being bothered by the gate guards. Once in, getting out became even easier. When they saw an approaching car, the guards simply raised the boom barrier and waved it through. Ashton knew this because that's how he got out. The place might as well be a shopping mall, he mused wryly.

Although catching his guy might be somewhat problematic, if not downright improbable, some of his options were more likely than others. For starters, although possible, he didn't figure that he dealt with an ordinary civilian. His man was either military, law enforcement, or a spook. Of the three, a former law enforcement officer made the bottom of his list. Why former? He did not consider it likely that an active duty officer would have the kind of time on his hands to plan and execute something like this, or have the required balls to nonchalantly walk onto a military base and simply walk off after he carried out the job.

If the guy was military, he was also probably retired, looking for action to spice up his drab life. He would have the required balls and the necessary time to indulge in odd jobs. If he hunted for a spook, probably a freelance, all bets were off. He doubted that an official agency would wish to use one of its own and risk creating an evidence trail. Ashton didn't like the scenario of some agency being involved, because it meant he couldn't ask any of them for help. He wouldn't normally, but when dealing with an international dimension, they sometimes proved useful.

As usual, it looked like he would have to do things the hard way.

An interesting problem, eh, Watson?

Who had the motive, and why was it a motive?

The Navy itself might want to silence Pacino. A senior officer suddenly going off the rails didn't make for good PR. It could also be political and for the same reason, more so. The simple fact that he bombed the shit out of a warehouse and trashed a North Korean electrical installation did not sound much like a reason to kill him. It might make certain people grind their teeth, no doubting that, but murder for it? If not a political decision, that left the personal angle, and murder was always personal, he reminded himself. Was it something Pacino said or what someone told him that set him off? This was information definitely worth fishing for.

Chasing down a spook or professional killer might be exciting, as was the idea of unraveling some dark government conspiracy, but this could also be simply a case of ideological passion. His guy may have seen the TV coverage or somebody told him about Pacino and the North Korean missile strike. He might have hated what Pacino did and decided it was payback time. If his guy was one of the base personnel, it would have been absurdly easy for him to get hold of some biodiesel. Even if he were noticed, nobody would have given him a second glance. A thin thread and an unlikely one, but still a thread to be followed.

Well, if young Hollice wanted to see how things were done

for real, this was something he could start working on. Information gathering might be dull, lacking the glamour of the amusing namesake TV show, but facts made cases, and Ashton needed facts.

There was always something…

Clearing his mind of wasteful preconceptions, he concentrated on driving.

Ashton took a left at NW Luoto Road and steered the car into another left turn at Clear Creek Road. With tall maple, elm and birch all around him, the place had a woodland feel to it. He didn't mind the isolation at all, although some of his colleagues grumbled at the lack of amenities available in downtown Seattle. The problem with having offices in the city, Pollard explained wearily, is that all the Navy bases were elsewhere.

He pulled the car into the parking lot in front of the Russell-Knox Building and ambled slowly toward the main entrance. Through the security portal, he took the stairs to the first floor. The open plan saved space, but left little room for privacy and solitary thinking. To gain an illusion of solitude, agents surrounded their desks with filing cabinets, bookshelves and potted plants. As he walked along a narrow open strip beside the wall toward his corner desk, Ashton figured there was a psychological need for an element of seclusion that Human Resources types somehow never appreciated or ignored. *They* had offices.

Many of the desks were empty, the owners out in the field chasing down leads, or at least pretending to. The faces he could see were staring at computer screens, some having two of the things. He would need to catch up with his team of four investigators to find out what was going on, but not today! This was still supposed to be his day off.

He stopped beside a cluttered desk and waited to be noticed.

Agent Brandon Hollice looked up and his face split in a wide grin. "Well, if it isn't the famous Mr. Ashton himself. Welcome back. Nice tan, by the way."

"You're not likely to get one talking to me like that," Ashton growled, but his displeasure made no impression on the young investigator.

Only two years with the agency, smart, articulate, and ambitious, Hollice had enthusiasm and drive, and the necessary degree of irreverence for his superiors and the system in general not to mind the bureaucratic grind that went with the job, but he lacked the experience needed to make him a first rate investigator. That's why Pollard had him assigned to him, to polish off some naivety and replace it with a hard coating of calculated cynicism. It was a harsh world out there and some of its unsavory inhabitants were short on patience with eager, bright-eyed rookies. Listening to Hollice, the polishing shouldn't take long.

"Ah, you're just saying that. How was Club Med?"

"Just like the commercials. Now, if you can tear yourself away from that porno clip you've been watching, I've got a little job only for you."

"The Pacino sabotage? Mr. Pollard told me that I'd be working with you on it."

"Is that so? And what have you worked out so far?"

"He should have ridden one of those Paveways down."

Ashton chuckled. That *would* have saved a few problems all around. "But then, you wouldn't have anything to do, would you? Which, sadly, I would have to note in my evaluation report."

Hollice's grin faded. "I *have* been busy, chief. The forensic team is on its way to McChord, and—"

"Who did you get?"

"Collander and Miss Prissy."

Ashton grinned with approval. Miss Eleanor Pierson was a character in the lab. With a master's in forensic medicine and a double bachelor's in criminal psychology and police procedures, a formidable young lady who didn't stand fools on any terms. Twenty-six, tall and leggy, with large dark eyes able to melt all male resistance, she remained totally professional, repulsing all advances at intimacy. An intimidating personality, which only made her more desirable.

Collander, on the other hand, was a crusty bachelor of forty-eight whose whole world revolved around forensic science. With a refined dry sense of humor that took getting used to, reserved, he nonetheless sometimes revealed a more jovial side when a case came to a satisfactory conclusion, or when having a rare drink with the team at a social outing.

Between the two of them, Ashton figured they wouldn't miss much at McChord, although he didn't expect them to find anything at all. Then again, the most absurd things sometimes surfaced that made him shake his head.

There is always a clue, eh, Watson?

"Is that it?"

"I'm getting a list of all personnel going into and leaving the base within a five-hour window of the Gulfstream touching down. I also asked Major Stowell to provide surveillance tapes from every gate. In addition, I asked Sea-Tac security to give me passenger manifests of all flights leaving Tacoma within plus twelve hours of the Gulfstream taking off."

"Why not arrivals?" Ashton demanded. "And why not surveillance tapes?" After 9/11 all international airports, hubs and most regional fields were required to either upgrade or install security systems. Paranoid overreaction as far as he was concerned, but God wasn't the only one who moved in mysterious ways.

"They're getting the stuff, but they will only pass it on if we ask for it. There's a lot of data there. I want to see if we can establish a definite lead from McChord first. This is supposing, of course, that our man came from somewhere else. He could be a local, you know."

"I do know." Ashton stared at the young man, genuinely impressed. "Good work, Brandon. What else have you got?"

Hollice rolled his eyes. "What else the man asks? I snagged

Pacino's service record and everything he's written on naval strategy, doctrine, U.S. naval force projection, and two recent revealing articles on the treatment of our veterans. It seems to have become his pet beef. While I was at it, I also dug into Vice Admiral David Owen's profile. He's Commander 7th Fleet at Yokosuka. Interesting character."

"Interesting how?"

"Third generation Navy and a strict regulations man. A former aviator and SEAL before transferring to the surface navy, this man seems to have done it all."

"Except drive a sewer pipe."

"Well, it does take a special breed to crawl into a submarine. Did you know that while he was Commander 6th Fleet in the Med in a joint exercise with the French and Italians, he busted one of his destroyer skippers for exceeding his orders while prosecuting a French nuclear sub contact. He apparently violated the Rules of Engagement by being too creative for Owen's taste. He pulled that gag more than once. He has an exemplary record without a hint of impropriety ever since he left Annapolis. Married into old Boston money, socially and politically connected, the man's a real starched ass." Hollice grinned disarmingly at Ashton's bemused expression.

"A teflon admiral, eh? Since you seem to have covered it all, maybe you'd care to run this investigation?"

Hollice raised both hands and leaned back against his seat. "Oh, no. I'm just a new rookie, remember? I'm sure I still have a lot of wisdom to pick up from your many years of unrivaled experience…sir."

Ashton laughed. "Insubordination is something you seem to have mastered already."

"Is there anything else I should be doing?" Hollice asked brightly, clearly pleased with his efforts.

"You should. Get the email Pacino sent to *The Washington Post* and the CNN. We want to add that to his record and build a psychological profile. I also want to know more about Owen."

"You got it."

"And you think you've covered it all?"

"I…think so."

"He thinks so. Have you considered that we might be dealing with somebody on the base?"

"I hadn't missed such an easy one, but I didn't give it much weight."

"And why is that?"

"Why would someone working on the base have it in for Pacino? The Admiral was based in Japan."

"I can think of lots of reasons, and it might not be Pacino at all, but what he represents." Judging by the boy's chagrined expression, that possibility had not occurred to him. After all, conspiracies were far more interesting.

"Ah, well…"

"I want to know the movement of every man with any knowledge that the Gulfstream was coming. I also want a list of everybody who could have come even close to that fuel tanker."

"Gee, chief! You know how many men work at that base?"

"We only need to know who might have contaminated the fuel tanker, and it must have been done after the thing was filled."

"I don't get it."

"I can see that. Think about it."

Hollice frowned, then his face split in a wide grin. "Because they test the fuel before the tanker is filled?"

"Good man."

"Wait a minute! What if somebody slipped the biodiesel in before the tanker was filled?"

Ashton shook his head. "Nope. And why do I think that?"

"Well…although it could have been done, but if our guy did it too early, the tanker could have been used to fuel a different aircraft. He had to make sure the contaminated fuel went into the Gulfstream."

Smiling, Ashton patted Hollice's shoulder. "Exactly right. Let me know when you come up with anything."

"I admit I missed that one, but it doesn't mean that we're not looking for an outsider."

"No it doesn't, and we'll keep looking, but this makes it more exciting."

"If you say so. While I'm slaving away, you're going to be doing what?" Hollice asked, his spirits restored. "I'm supposed to be your understudy, remember?"

"I'll have my feet on my desk sipping coffee, confident that you have everything in hand."

"Gee, that must be hard work, chief. I wouldn't mind helping."

Grinning, Ashton ambled to his desk, glanced at the leafy scenery outside, and pulled back his chair. He sat down, pleased with young Hollice's organized approach and initiative, taking action without having to be told everything. What the boy did was standard procedure. Time to inject some lateral thinking.

After glancing at his watch and doing a bit of quick arithmetic, it was still early morning in Tokyo: 5:30 a.m. His man wouldn't have crawled out of bed yet, but that didn't mean he couldn't waylay him. Leaning across the desk, he picked up the phone and dialed reception.

"It's Ashton. Get me the NCIS duty desk at Yokosuka...Yeah, I'll hold."

Listening to the international exchanges chirp to each other for a few seconds, the line cleared.

"Special Agent Grant speaking."

"This is Robert Ashton, Investigator-In-Charge, Northwest Field Office. Please leave a message for Morris Fielder to call me when convenient."

"I'll pass on your request as soon as he comes in. Is there anything I can help you with?"

"Thanks, but I'll need to talk to Fielder on this one."

He hung up, nodded and sighed softly. A damned nuisance having to cope with the time differential over there, but like weather, there was little he could do about it. He'll send Fielder his wish list in a lengthy email. At least the man would have a heads-up.

Outside, the clouds were rolling in again and he could see dark lines slanting down where it rained. Good a time as any to start planning his lunch break.

***

Mark Price stood before the polarized armored window, coffee cup in hand, and gazed absently at the crowded parking lot below and the green woods beyond. Sunshine streamed down from a clear sky. Wisps of mist writhed over the trees as it burned away.

He took a sip and allowed his mind to wander. Grant and Zardwovsky were gone, taking with them their blanket of gloom and stifling office politics, to be replaced with a new wave of politicking, of course. With the two men out the door, and with them a certain entrenched way of doing business, he sensed a distinct air of cautious expectation and optimism, especially in the Clandestine Service Directorate. He was still to appoint Zardwovsky's replacement, but he didn't want to rush it. The man running it would hold the most influential position after his own, and his attitude, approach and ideas on how to conduct business would greatly enhance Price's tenure or severely damage it.

What worried him were glaring inadequacies in the Intelligence Directorate. With over two hundred highly specialized and skilled analysts sifting through mountains of photo, HUMINT, SIGINT, and media data from around the world, the President's Daily Brief feeds he had seen so far were masterpieces of literary obfuscation that revealed nothing. It was true what they said about getting better intelligence from CNN. The place still had an Iraq Analysis desk even though the U.S. was out of there, but not a Middle East desk. Seeing how a lot of U.S. foreign policy decisions hinged on what happened there, it wasn't good enough burying that part of the world within the Near Eastern and South Asian desk. There was simply too much to cover to maintain focus. Then there was the Policy Support desk. Why the hell would he need help with setting policy, either for the Company or coping with foreign services? Instead of analyzing and telling it like they saw it, everybody spent time covering their ass, afraid of having it reamed. Well, that shit must stop or they *would* get reamed.

When he looked at Science & Technology, his eyes bulged at the dollars poured down that hole. The place had turned into a full-blown research center! The Company needed scientists, but only to support intelligence gathering and clandestine operations, not thinking up cute gadgets. Too much reliance was being placed on remote sensing, overlooking the best sensor platform they had: the human eyeball and the soft computer that lay behind it.

Threatened with information overload, he forced himself to step back into a more objective mode. He was here to set direction, not be a manager, a critical distinction. His job at DHS had elements of both and he liked rolling up his sleeves occasionally, but with an organization the size of the CIA, rolling up his sleeves risked drowning in overwhelming detail. That would be a surefire way of losing control and a quick end to his appointment, including any future jobs with the government.

Last night, he sent the ever-vigilant Miss Dobson an email to be forwarded to every section head. His question was simple. What policy objectives were they serving? In a sense, he wanted them to justify their existence. He had a caveat to that request, wanting five distilled bullet points, not a PR dissertation. Claire came to see him, wearing a whimsical smile on her otherwise stern features, asking him if he was sure he wanted to send that, especially the demand to have responses from everybody by close of business today.

Turning back to his desk, he looked forward to reading the replies. Any attempt to snow him and that section would vanish, including the parasitic personnel feeding off it. He would probably have to make an example or two before the idea filtered through.

He reminded himself to call Tom Meecham and arrange a round of golf. His friend a hopeless player, but it gave both of them a chance to unwind a little and take in some unpolluted oxygen. Tom could always invite Melissa and make it a threesome. He wanted to give Meecham a heads-up about his appointment and field an invitation to him to become the FBI liaison at Langley. Meecham had hardly settled into his current position, and the FBI Director might be reluctant to let him go, but Price knew how Tom thought and worked, and the move would be a great boost to his friend's career, provided Meecham wanted to come down to Langley, by no means a certainty.

The phone rang and he picked up. "Yes?"

"Jurgen Mannix is here to see you, sir. I told him you were busy—"

"Never mind. Send him in."

Price replaced the receiver and chewed his lower lip. Mannix would not bother him unless important. From the two conversations he'd had with him, the man left a favorable impression. Soft spoken, but with an intensity in his voice that marked dedication and a single-minded drive, unwavering black eyes, thoroughly knowledgeable, Price immediately felt he could trust him implicitly. Mannix had left an impression, all right.

Could Mannix replace Zardwovsky? Probably not, too inexperienced. However, definitely a man to keep an eye on. Besides, bumping him into the slot would definitely upset the Deputy Director, and from what he had learned so far, Mossman was a dogged professional and top-drawer administrator. Price needed broad institutional knowledge in that position, and Mannix simply didn't have it.

The thought made him smile wryly. That made two of them.

Following a single knock, the door opened and Price freshly scrutinized the non-descript individual who walked in. Perhaps five eleven, a slight bulge around his middle, a forgettable round face topped with neatly parted rusty-brown hair, he would not excite a second look in a crowd—a perfect field operative. What betrayed him were his watchful eyes, a reserved bearing and a readiness to sprint into immediate action. An ordinary person would not have spotted it, but Price was a kindred spirit.

"Thanks for seeing me, sir," Mannix said in a controlled voice, not intimidated by his surroundings.

Price nodded to the older man and swept a hand at a chair. "I needed a break from looking at budgets and expenditures."

Mannix smiled faintly as he limped to the chair and eased himself down, holding a blue folder in his lap. "Never my good subject."

"Mmm. You wouldn't spend it so easily if you knew how hard it's earned. What have you got?"

"North Korea has done it. Tung In-san, or more likely Kham Chang-uk, who is now Chairman of the National Defense Commission, is preparing to dismantle the long range missile launchers at Musudan-ni and Tongch'ang-dong. Lots of new activity around both sites. Although Musudan is a much older facility, having it pulled down will make a lot of people in Seoul and the Pentagon sleep easier."

"Evidence?"

Mannix slid the folder across the desk. "Keyhole 13 surveillance shots. We also have real-time imagery if you care to see it."

Price didn't answer as he opened the folder, glancing quickly at the 6" by 9" color glossies. He didn't have time to watch movies and he had to trust what he was being told—up to the point when it failed him. The photos were taken from a low Earth orbit bird, the resolution first class. Trucks, cranes and men crowded around three launch towers. Two shots showed a flatbed carrier hauling away a long, white missile body. He looked up.

"A refurbishment, perhaps?"

"Take a look at the last glossy."

One glimpse convinced him. Price replaced the photos and tapped the folder. "They blew up the launch tower deliberately to make sure we saw what they were doing. They obviously know the orbital periods of our Keyholes. It was a message."

"That's my bet, sir. I have never spoken to Chairman Kham, but from what Zardwovsky told me, dismantling their launchers was one of the conditions for supporting the spill."

"It looks like they're honoring that promise. You said Kham is now the NDC Chairman?"

"That's right. Yeum Ling-chol is the new Premier. A fair number of Sung's men have disappeared, including Sung, which we expected, following the general reshuffle of power. I'll have a detailed brief for you before lunch."

"Why wasn't this in our input to the PDB?"

Mannix looked puzzled. "I don't know. The Intelligence Directorate passed the imagery data to us, so they must have known what's going on. They also get copies of North Korean afternoon papers, including the *Minju Chason* and the *Pyongyang Sinmun*. The new power structure was listed in both."

"So, Intelligence sat on this the whole night?" Price demanded coldly.

Mannix shifted in his seat, suddenly looking uncomfortable. "I hope you don't think—"

"Not your fault. Leave it with me. Anything else?"

"No, sir."

"Let me have the brief as soon as you can."

Mannix stood up and picked up the blue folder. "You'll have it."

Price watched him go. When the door closed, he clenched his

right fist.

Well, crap!

It looked like his talk with the Intelligence Director hadn't penetrated. He picked up the phone and pressed a yellow button.

"Yes, sir?" Claire answered immediately.

"I want to see Casey Purtell, now."

"Yes, sir."

He hardly put the phone down when his BlackBerry trilled. Glancing at the flashing red icon, he raised his eyebrows and reached for the instrument.

He pressed the Secure icon. "Mark Price."

"Ah, Mr. Price, I am so glad to have reached you. I would appreciate a moment if you have the time."

Price quickly glanced at his wristwatch. Just after ten, which meant midnight in Pyongyang. The power spill clearly required some consolidation.

"Of course, Mr. Chairman. My congratulations on your appointment."

"Thank you, although I am beginning to think it might be a dubious honor." Kham gave a fruity chuckle. "We shall see. You must forgive me for calling you like this, but there are matters the Premier wishes to discuss with Secretary Tanner that we hope will strengthen the formative cooperation between our two countries. However, before doing so, I persuaded him and the Supreme Leader that America should have time to digest the substance of these talks before engaging in formal dialogue. I chose you as our intermediary, Mr. Price."

Taken aback at this, Price blinked. "I am honored that you saw fit to talk to me, sir. I will, of course, pass on anything you tell me, but you must realize that I'm not a diplomat. Secretary Tanner, I suggest, would be in a better position to evaluate your message in the context of U.S. foreign policy."

Kham laughed outright. "Your very words betray your skill as a diplomat. I wanted to talk to you precisely because you're not a

State Department official, although you do have a mastery of its nuances. There is another and more personal reason why I chose you, Mr. Price. I feel I can trust you. Given our past history, I find myself surprised able to say that."

Price frowned. After his dealings with Zardwovsky, that Kham could still trust America *was* surprising. Then again, the crafty old devil could be blowing him smoke. It would be a mistake to think that any overtures Kham made were anything other than a momentary convenience rather than a change of ideology.

"I'm flattered, sir. I gather that your takeover was successful?"

"Indeed. Sadly, Sung and some of his closest supporters will not witness our country's new dawn, while a number of my former colleagues will have time to reflect on the benefits of rural living at a correctional farm. Buying support never works as a long term solution, but I digress."

Price smiled ruefully. Kham might be reaching out to the West and aping what he thought was acceptable behavior, but he was still a hardcore communist, comfortable enjoying the privileges of a totalitarian regime, and taking full advantage of its instruments. Of course, that's the way business was done everywhere, wasn't it?

"In recognition of America's support and our hope of realizing the initiatives explored with Secretary Tanner during his visit, my government is prepared to undertake a number of immediate steps as proof of our sincerity. It's the substance of those steps that I wish conveyed to Mr. Tanner."

"I'll give him your message personally, Mr. Chairman."

"I am pleased to hear that, Mr. Price. The Premier wishes to advise the United States that we will take unilateral steps to shut down our uranium enrichment and reprocessing facilities. The United States will be free to send anyone it wishes to monitor the shutdown. Moreover, we will not take any further retaliatory action against your naval or land forces for the attack made by Admiral Pacino. Although I regret the missile response on your ships and the resulting loss of life, the action ordered by Sung Kang-dae. The Minister of People's Armed Forces, Tham Pan-yong, powerless to prevent it. However, the action did act as a trigger for our move against Sung. To a degree, I feel a sense of responsibility, having perhaps been a causal factor during your Key Resolve exercise."

"I understand, sir. Sometimes events take on a momentum of their own whose outcome cannot be entirely predicted."

"I am glad you understand. About Admiral Pacino—"

"He has been placed under arrest and will undoubtedly face court-martial for his action."

"A man of principle, Mr. Price, and speaking personally, I sympathize with what he has done. Officially, we will be demanding a formal apology from President Walters and seeking reparations."

"Given your attack on our ships, the President might not be so willing to apologize."

"This is not a matter for negotiation, Mr. Price."

"I shall convey your message, sir."

"Good. Despite repeated demands by previous American Administrations, we will not be shutting down our nuclear reactors. We are energy poor and our reliance on foreign oil supplies is a crippling economic and strategic burden. With the cancellation of our nuclear weapons program, the reactors will be used solely to support civilian consumption. I do need to make one point quite clear. We're not inviting, nor do we want, involvement by the International Atomic Energy Agency. I consider them ineffective meddlers and an outdated anachronism, quite powerless to execute their charter to stop proliferation."

The phone rang and Price pressed a button, canceling the call. It was probably Purtell, but that matter would have to wait.

"Excuse the interruption, sir."

"Are you sure I am not disturbing?"

"I have nothing more important at the moment, Mr. Chairman."

"I doubt that. As you are aware, North Korea is in possession of a number of nuclear warheads and weapons-grade fissile material. With ten warheads already handed over to Mr. Zardwovsky in a deal made with Sung, we knew about that, we're prepared to hand over a further forty, but not to the United States, at least not all of them. We will hand over fourteen to you, with the remaining warheads given equally to our Russian and Chinese allies. There are certain niceties to be observed with our friends," Kham added apologetically.

"I can well believe that," Price said dryly, taken aback by what Kham said. He had pondered the problem how to obtain the remaining warheads, and this solution would come as a relief to Walters, at least he hoped it would.

"Your unspoken question is very loud, Mr. Price."

"And what question is that?"

"Whether we have more than fifty warheads."

"The United States will simply have to trust you on that."

"Indeed. To avoid unnecessary concern, what we'll be handing over are the warhead shells only without the trigger mechanisms. As for the remaining unprocessed fissile material, that will be handed over to China. Your carrier, USS *George Washington*, is steaming toward Incheon, presumably in response to our missile attack. If it could be redirected to our naval base at Haeju Bay, we suggest it would make an excellent platform for holding the handover ceremony with all parties."

"You discussed this with Russia and China?"

"As an initial proposal only. The steps I outlined should relieve immediate international concerns regarding the erroneously perceived threat posed by our nuclear weapons inventory, which has been the singular stumbling block in our relations with the United States and the Western world. To further demonstrate our desire to ease tensions with our southern neighbor, we're also prepared to stop development of strategic missile technology and begin immediate dismantlement of all Taepodong One and Two stocks, including the launch sites."

"I've already seen evidence of your efforts at Tongch'ang-dong," Price said quietly.

"I'm sure you have," Kham replied softly, clearly aware of American satellite surveillance capability. "This initiative will be supported by a reduction of our standing armed forces by twenty percent over the next twelve months."

"That could not have gone down well with some of your generals."

"Perhaps not, but a retired general represents a hollow reed, Mr. Price."

Price grinned, reluctant to explore Kham's understanding of what retirement meant. That move, although welcome, also meant a considerable saving of badly needed funds for civilian purposes. North Korea wasn't changing its spots because they have suddenly turned altruistic.

"We are a peaceful country. Why would we need a large standing army?"

The irony in Khma's voice didn't escape him and Price laughed. "Why indeed?"

"We want to show America and the world that we stand by our commitments. In addition to these initiatives, the Premier is prepared to enter into preliminary discussions with President Samun Man-shik on easing border crossings to facilitate trade and reunion of families. Moreover, my government is also willing to open discussions with the UN Security Council for the drafting of a peace treaty to formally ratify the technical armistice entered into in 1953."

"That's a significant and courageous gesture, sir," Price said, unable to hide his surprise. It would certainly free up thousands of troops currently tied down patrolling the Demilitarized Zone, something the American public would appreciate.

"But a necessary one if our country is to enter fully into the union of nations."

"Mr. Chairman, the concessions you're offering are overwhelming and will be embraced warmly by President Walters. At least, I would like to think so, but you haven't stated the obvious corollary."

Kham chuckled. "And, of course, there are several. If the United States objects to us handing over the warheads to Russian and China, we're prepared to give them everything. We will also publicize to the world your intransigence. As for our other initiatives, we want the United States to open its markets to us and urge your trading partners to do the same. We will also demand from the IMF and the World Bank loans to help finance the necessary transition period while our economy recovers sufficiently to support an improved standard of living for our people. Loans made under our terms. We will not be subject to crippling conditions that will place our country into perpetual servitude. Lastly, we will demand an immediate thirty percent drawdown of American forces in South Korea, with another thirty percent within two years. The remaining forty percent to be negotiated with President Samun. I've read *The Korean Herald* and *The Seoul Times*. Neither are very happy with Admiral Pacino or America right now. I doubt that a withdrawal of your forces will be contested."

"I dare say." Price frowned as a dark suspicion bubbled and burst. "Mr. Chairman, have you discussed any of this with President Samun?"

"Mr. Price, Samun holds nothing but contempt for our country and its people."

"A convenient evade, but I won't press you."

"Then you relieve me from having to lie to you, which I certainly don't want to do."

Grinning, Price had to admire the wily politician, for Kham must be hiding something. He as much as admitted that he'd had talks with the South Korean National Intelligence Service. Did those talks extend to select ministers while the coup was being engineered? Did President Samun know? A football he was happy to field to somebody else, but he would be remiss to the president if he didn't try and find out, and perhaps Mannix already had an answer.

"Please make it clear to Secretary Tanner our sincerity to follow through with our disarmament program, even if it is done without American endorsement. We'll also sign a peace treaty. If America does not open its markets, I am certain capitalist pragmatism will make Europe more cooperative."

"I don't doubt it. I must point out, sir, with everything you have said, Mr. Tanner will ask an obvious question. If you're willing to proceed with your initiatives regardless of our position, why should the United States withdraw from South Korea?"

"I suggest, Mr. Price, domestic and international pressure will force it to comply. I also believe President Walters will welcome an opportunity to extricate himself from that country, although your military might not. These days the American public has little appetite for sending its sons abroad. I am equally aware of the financial burden your presence there is imposing on your fiscal position. If that were not enough, I have a more compelling argument. We will retain ten nuclear warheads to forestall any possible future aggression—by anyone. The world will know that we're ready to disarm totally, even if the United States continues to regard us as a rogue nation. We welcome ongoing dialogue with Secretary Tanner, and hope President Walters will make the appropriate choice."

For sure, Price mused to himself. "Frankly, Mr. Chairman, I'm overwhelmed by your proposals, and thankful I'm not the one having to make the decision."

"If there is good will between two nations, making the decision is easy. I sincerely hope the United States takes advantage of it. I wish you good day, sir."

Disconnecting, Price nodded slowly and sat back.

Well, crap!

This must rate as one of the most unusual conversations he had ever had. He wasn't going to begin guessing the political fallout for Walters, all positive as far as he could see. Why would the administration baulk when they were getting everything it always wanted. There was still a matter of trust as Kham said, but if North Korea followed through on its promises, it was hard to see where America would have a problem. He doubted that not getting all the warheads would be a hurdle as long as North Korea didn't have them. Well, not all of them anyway.

Would South Korea view these initiatives with equal enthusiasm? He would have to talk to Mannix about that as well.

He pulled at his chin and picked up the phone.

"Sir, Mr. Purtell is here to see you," Claire announced.

"Show him in. Once I'm done, call Admiral Stone for me."

"Yes, sir."

The smallish man who walked in, his olive Latin features topped with straight black hair, wearing a thick mustache, eyes wary, stopped before Price's desk and waited. His stance not exactly defiant, more like that of a busy man resenting having his time interrupted.

"Sorry to have kept you waiting, Casey," Price said, trying to keep his voice friendly. He wanted to try persuasion first before resorting to sterner measures.

"That's all right, sir," Purtell said stiffly, his voice making it clear it wasn't.

"We both have a lot to do, so I'll make this short. Why wasn't the North Korean new power structure in the intelligence summary sent to the Director of National Intelligence?"

Purtell stared. "Is that what this is about? The input we provide for the President's Daily Brief is meant to give a strategic snapshot of major world events, political climate, military threats, and strategic shifts, not trivia."

"A change in the North Korean leadership and the impact on

American foreign policy, especially right now, wasn't a strategic shift?"

"I'm sure the DNI would have added a line about that. Who the hell cares what's going on in that backwater? Anyway, the President can read a newspaper."

"If he has time to read one. A newspaper doesn't always tell him what he needs to know. That's why he has us!"

"If you want to bother him with trivia—"

Price clenched his fists and glared. "We don't determine what is trivia, Casey. Our job is to provide the President with information to support his decision-making process. The PDB feeds that I've seen over the last few days hardly qualify. It's predigested mush full of ifs and buts and ass covering qualifiers. I better see some meaningful substance tomorrow or I'll find somebody who can give it to me."

"Is that a threat?"

"Casey, you don't run this Agency. I do. You exist to provide me and the White House with intelligence. So far, I haven't seen any. I want to start seeing it. If you like, you can consider that a threat."

"I resent your slur against my Directorate, Price. I also resent the implication that I cannot do my job!"

"Prove to me that you *can* do your job and we'll get along. That's all, Casey."

Purtell glared, opened his mouth, and then shut it with a snap. Without saying anything, he turned and stomped out.

Price frowned and shook his head. According to his file, the Intelligence Director was smart and very competent. Grant had allowed things to slide and Purtell had apparently withdrawn into a shell. He was now naturally resentful at being yanked into the spotlight. Price had given him the necessary kick in the pants to remind him about the order of things. He hoped Purtell would take the lesson to heart.

The phone rang and he picked up. "Yes, Claire?"

"Admiral Stone is on the line, sir."

"Thank you." Price pressed a blinking white button. "Hi, Graham."

"What's up, Mark?" the admiral's gruff command voice responded briskly. Price had learned to ignore the intimidation long ago.

"I need to talk to Larry Tanner, and then he'll need to talk to the President."

"Why? What happened?"

"You're not going to believe me," Price said and launched into a summary of his conversation with Kham.

* * *

"Please sit down, Admiral," President Walters invited cordially as he lowered himself into the beige, green-striped sofa. His visitor took off his braided cap and nodded.

"Thank you, Mr. President," Pacino said in a low voice and took the other sofa, the small coffee table between them filled with a tray of pastries, a silver pot, cups and stuff.

Walters smiled as Pacino made himself comfortable as he could under the circumstances. It could not have been easy being in the Oval Office under a cloud facing his command-in-chief. To ease the atmosphere, he picked up the coffee pot and filled two cups, the aroma of fresh grounds lingering pleasantly in the air. He held out a cup and saucer.

"You'll find this different from your usual Navy java."

Pacino's mouth twitched as he took the cup. "The Navy is on a budget, Mr. President."

Walters laughed as he mixed in sugar and cream into his. "Good point, but that's not an excuse for drinking glue."

"Your Air Force brews always gave me a bellyache. Too thin."

Walters took a sip and nodded. "You haven't tried the stuff

line chiefs drink. Guaranteed to peel off the lining in your stomach."

Pacino stirred in a teaspoon of sugar, took a sip and sat back, cup in lap. He made a quick sweep of the room, taking in everything at a glance. Walters smiled faintly and placed his cup on the table.

"First time in the Oval Office?"

"I never expected to be here at all."

"And I never get to see two-star flag officers," Walters murmured pensively. "Perhaps that's part of the problem. The Joint Chiefs feed me strategy and tactics, and see me only when there is bad news or when they need authorization for some clandestine ops. It's all remote and impersonal. I understand why it has to be like this, but maybe it's being carried a tad too far. We have lost the human element, haven't we, Admiral?" Seeing Pacino hesitate, he waved his hand, mildly irritated. "You may speak freely. That's why you're here. I've got to hear what people really think. I won't use what you tell me to exert unlawful command influence on your Article 32 hearing, if that's what's worrying you."

"I was merely ordering my thoughts, sir, but my defense counsel will be relieved that you're not here to railroad me."

Walters chuckled. "There is a line already to do that, eh? Back to my question..."

"A commander, any commander, must wear two hats, Mr. President. He uses one to execute the objectives of his mission, his primary role, employing whatever tools are necessary to achieve it. There are only two tools available to him: technology and manpower. The second hat is to ensure that those tools are not wasted. Used up, certainly, that's the reality of conflict, but not wasted. Unfortunately, as the sophistication of our technological tools has grown, emphasis has shifted to its preservation at the expense of manpower. The human operator has become another throwaway component in a military machine where a hundred-million-dollar air superiority fighter or a billion-dollar missile cruiser takes precedence. But you knew that already, didn't you?"

Weighing up Pacino's words, Walters sighed. "My chief of staff advised me not to see you, Admiral. He felt it might compromise my position and pollute the negotiations with North Korea."

Pacino smiled. "My defense counsel told me the same thing. Except he wasn't so much worried about North Korea. The papers will be rife with speculation over my visit. Your chief of staff may have been right about not seeing me."

"The papers don't control what I do and Manfred tends to be overprotective." Smiling, Walters took another sip and waited for Pacino to do the same. "You heard about the change of leadership over there?"

"From what I understand, this should make your job easier."

"We shall see."

"About USS *Stethem*, sir. I don't know what to say. I didn't anticipate that North Korea would react so violently, even though I had acknowledged the possibility."

"If nothing else, it triggered the power spill against Sung."

"What's the count?"

"Thirty-two dead and fourteen wounded, some of them pretty badly. The ship suffered major structural damage forward of the superstructure and it will take a while to put her back together."

Pacino bit his lip and exhaled loudly. "I *deserve* to be court-martialed."

As a former military officer himself, Walters knew what went through Pacino's head. Regret at the loss of life and the suffering of those left alive or still to die. That needed to be weighed against the end objective. The dead didn't care. The living had to be counted now.

"From what I've read, you have a surprising depth for a career naval officer. Most of the ones I've spoken to are very conscious to be not only politically correct, but wary of offending their superiors or raising opinions that don't conform to accepted doctrine. It's a pain and gets in the way of getting things done. Your preparedness to tell it straight is refreshing."

"I don't have any choice, sir. If I cannot tell you what I think now, what I've done would have been for nothing, a gesture by a deranged officer."

"Some people will still think so. Others are already using it to make political mileage against my Administration."

"I regret that aspect of my action, Mr. President."

"If it hadn't been you, they'd have picked something else. I am truly sorry about your son, Admiral, and I apologize for being patronizing when I called you the other day, as though a Silver Star would have made up for your loss."

"There is no need for you to apologize, sir. You were the commander-in-chief and you made a gracious gesture to a subordinate."

"Let's dispense with wordplay, shall we? I had things on my mind, but I cannot use that as an excuse for the way I behaved. It was tactless of me and you must have been hurt. Admit it."

Walters waited as Pacino sat there looking at him. He wondered what went on behind those penetrating eyes. They were eyes of a thoughtful, complex man prepared to sacrifice a brilliant career to make a cry of protest. As the commander-in-chief, it was not only his duty to listen to that cry, but obligation. As a flag officer, did Pacino regard it as his obligation to voice that protest? Manfred had already said as much.

"I was hurt a little, Mr. President, and angry. I would not have thought twice about it if you were a civilian, but as a former fighter pilot, I expected you to understand. Remember the second hat?"

"Yeah, I left it around somewhere on that day, didn't I?" Walters mused with a wry smile, taking the lesson to heart.

"Your words told me that my son didn't matter. Nobody mattered…on either side. All that counted was minimizing the impact on your negotiations with North Korea. Don't get me wrong. I support your initiative, as does the entire military, but if people don't matter, Mr. President, what's the point? Why are we fighting? Why are we dying? We project power around the world, militarily and economically, but why? To expand personal freedoms? For democracy, whatever that means. With corporate globalization and profiteering, individual freedoms and rights merely get in the way of doing business."

"Under our system of government, Admiral, the military executes the policies of civil authority. Bombing Incheon and Yongbyon doesn't exactly fall within that parameter."

Pacino smiled and nodded. "But it got your attention. The Koreans also have sons, but they were prepared to sacrifice them for their own higher objectives, the same as we were. I had to show everybody that this was a flawed philosophy. A posthumous medal means very little to a grieving mother, whether she is tilling a rice paddy or watching CNN in a New York apartment."

"Was resorting to military force the only way to get your point across?"

"It's the only language everybody understands."

"It doesn't say much about us as a species, does it? There is much about what you said that I agree with, but you must be aware that we live in a complex global environment where there is no single neat solution, but a tapestry of compromises that seldom satisfies anyone. However, they do maintain peace."

"Peace for whom, sir? Us? Who is going to attack us? The Chinese, Russia, the Moslem hordes? We're not facing a military threat, not really, and we haven't faced one since the collapse of the Soviet Union. Our threats are economic, they always were, which you understand very well. Warfare is a breakdown of boardroom negotiations. In the process of protecting our economic interests, those very interests are eroding and subjugating the individual. In our desire to bolster unfeeling corporate power by giving them freedom to do whatever they want, we're forgetting the noble words of our founding fathers and the constitution."

"Damnation, Admiral! If America is economically strong, the individual you're so worried about also benefits."

Pacino placed his cup on the table and leaned forward. "In theory, that's true, but it hasn't worked out like that in the real world. We bankrupted ourselves by bailing out the corporate establishment that drove the free world to the brink of economic ruin in their irresponsible drive for short-term profits. We propped them up only to see them decry a return to a more regulated environment, wanting to screw us all over again. How has the individual benefited? Strength has to be built on prudence and responsibility. Everybody has forgotten that the *laissez-faire* system abhors the human element."

Walters stared at Pacino and slowly shook his head. "I can hardly believe we're having this conversation. If you felt this strongly, why did you stay in the Navy? You should have run for Congress and made your voice heard in the only arena that matters."

"Unfortunately, Mr. President, although my views have been festering in the background for some time, I was foremost a Navy career officer, bound by and obedient to regulations. I trusted the political process, confident that you and Congress knew what you were doing. It took the Key Resolve incident to demonstrate that knowing what needs to be done and doing it were subject to expediency and political opportunism, and I was pissed off."

Walters laughed with genuine delight. If he could have a man like this to advise him, or at least remind him of the human dimension that politics exacted…

"I gathered that. What do you want, Admiral?"

"I'm not here to preach to you about economics. You have advisors to do that for you. The military serves civilian authority, but we're not robots. When you send those kids to die somewhere, don't let them die for a questionable national interest policy. Those who survive, don't throw them into the forget basket."

"Simple enough in principle, but you're in effect asking for a review of our entire social fabric."

"No, sir. Merely saying that bureaucratic red tape shouldn't take precedence over the human element."

"When is your hearing?"

"They've got me scheduled for Friday."

"Two days…not much time for your defense counsel to get his act together."

"The hearing is to determine whether I should face a general court. It shouldn't take them long to reach that decision. The real work will start when I go to trial."

"Mmm." Walters nodded and pulled at his chin. After a moment, he stood and offered his hand. "I wish you luck, Admiral. Your action has given me several headaches, but you've also given me a lot to think about. I'll endeavor that we shall talk again."

Pacino stood up and grasped the proffered hand. Walters felt the steady pressure and a peculiar connection with the man. This was somebody the country could not afford to lose. His career was over, nothing could save that, but there was life beyond the Navy.

"Thank you, Mr. President, and I beg you to excuse my outbursts."

"On the contrary. I should be the one thanking you. You have an intriguing way of putting things, something the people I'm surrounded with could emulate. I understand your flight from Yokosuka was sabotaged?"

A flicker of surprise showed in Pacino's eyes. "That's what

I'm told."

"I'll look into it. When you talk to your wife and Linda, please give them my sincere condolences. Forgive me if my words sound trite, but they're genuine."

"Thank you, sir. I'm sure they will appreciate it." Pacino picked up his hat and walked out.

Standing in the middle of the Oval Office, Walters stared at the closed door, Pacino's words ringing in his ears. It would be easy to dismiss them as naïve and simplistic if it were not for their underlying truth. Somewhere along the way, America had strayed. Its economic system has given people one of the highest standards of living anywhere, but bought with shattered individual lives. He reminded himself that there weren't many votes or money to be made looking after the poor and the discarded.

What Pacino wanted sounded simple enough. He wanted justice. Unfortunately, justice was a scarce commodity these days. It merely got in the way of doing business, and Walters wasn't sure he could do anything about it.

Did that mean he shouldn't try?

Pacino would be court-martialed and cast aside, forgotten in tomorrow's headline. Who the hell would care what he thought or why he went crazy? Wasn't that the problem? Discard the issue simply because he lacked a neat solution?

Suddenly, being the president had gotten a whole lot harder.

He walked to the *Resolute* desk and sat down, deep in thought. Leaning toward the phone station, he said, "You can come in now."

He pressed a glowing white button that cut the speaker input and waited. A few seconds later, Cottard walked in from his office. He stopped in front of the desk and folded his hands across his chest.

"You heard?" Walters asked and the chief of staff nodded, slowly rubbing his nose.

"Not your ordinary Navy man, is he?"

"He is right about one thing, Manfred. We used our military, playing them like poker chips, forgetting that they're also human beings."

"Admiral Pacino may have been misguided in what he did, but it took a certain bravery as well."

"I don't want the man crucified," the president said firmly.

Cottard winced and shrugged. "There isn't much you can do to stop it. Whether you like it or not, he did contravene a raft of important regulations. As the convening authority, the Chief of Naval Operations had no choice but to prosecute."

"This is a man we can use. I don't want him wasting his life in Leavenworth. There's got to be something I can do. Talk to the White House Counsel."

"Are you sure you want to do this, Mr. President? Regardless of any personal sympathy you may have for Pacino, you must allow the disciplinary process to take its course. Bringing undue political influence on the case will not only be illegal, but will set an extremely bad precedent. Anybody with a grievance will feel that it's okay to blow up somebody. If that weren't enough, think of the message you'd be sending to Korea."

Walters bared his teeth and glared. "Screw them! They started this mess to begin with. It's okay for Samun to protect Admiral Chin, but they expect me to nail Pacino to the wall."

"Ah, the two circumstances are not exactly the same. After all, Pacino could have started a war, and he directly attacked a South Korean installation. That's not what allies do to each other."

"I have seen what allies do to each other. Israel wasn't supposed to sabotage the Valero refinery, but they did it in pursuit of their own interests. Admiral Chin did the same thing when he allowed his destroyer to attack the PROK sub. What happened next was an inevitable cascade of linked events. I won't throw Pacino on the scrap heap simply to placate either Korea or cover up sins of past Administrations. We *have* turned our men into throwaway components just like he said, and we've got to do something about it."

Cottard placed both hands on the edge of the desk and leaned forward. "Do what? Turn this country into a regulated economy and welfare state? Stop corporations and financial institutions from making money? Have the Joint Chiefs debate every order that comes from the National Command Authority? Give every veteran a million bucks and a lifetime of free shrink sessions? You start spouting such Utopian gospel and you'd be laughed out of office."

"You're a heartless son of a bitch, did you know that, Manfred?"

Chuckling, Cottard stepped back, his face split in a wide grin. "I heard it mentioned once or twice."

"I'm not surprised," Walters growled, feeling torn by conflicting desires and a seemingly impenetrable wall of obstruction.

"Every politician I've known has gone through what you're going through now, Sam. They get elected on a platform of promises to change things and make everything better. Because the people hate the self-serving incumbents and partisan politics, the idealist gets elected. Once in Congress the establishment machinery eats him up. He either conforms or is silenced. What everybody forgets is that our system of government is not designed to further the interests of our electorate, but to advance personal ambition. If that means voting down a piece of legislation that is genuinely in the national interest, then that's what you do. You said the same thing yourself. The balloon of idealism is firmly anchored by the lead weight of politics."

"I should have remained a plain senator from Michigan."

"Are you feeling sorry for yourself, is that it?"

Walters frowned, his expression dark. "Venting spleen, that's all. I got elected because I promised to tackle some of the very things Pacino talked about. Just because we face a divided Congress doesn't mean that I've given up. Instead of pissing on my ideas, tell me how to get it done."

"Yes, Mr. President."

"Asshole!"

"You really want me to talk to the White House Counsel about Pacino?"

"Definitely. I want options."

"And Korea?"

"Talk to Larry. He'll think of something. Remind me to call Tung In-san and congratulate him on his appointment as Supreme Leader. Put a call to Pyongyang and arrange a time."

"Yes, sir. I'm worried about the possibility that somebody sabotaged Pacino's flight."

"Me too. Call the FBI Director and get him to put a man on it in case the NCIS team needs help. It might also be an idea if they assigned a detail on Pacino. There is always a chance that some radical nut might want to take a crack at him."

"I would have thought Price would be a better bet for that."

Walters wagged a finger at him. "The CIA cannot operate on the mainland, you know that. Exchanging intelligence is okay, but I don't want any of his clowns on this."

"Leave it with me." Cottard rubbed his nose. "If someone is after Pacino, his wife could also be in danger."

The president frowned. "Have a word with Admiral Parker."

"Yes, sir."

Glancing at the digital clock on his desk, Walters sighed. "I'm going upstairs for lunch."

"Want company?"

"Thanks, but I have some thinking to do. With Cathy in San Francisco, I'll have the place to myself."

"And how is the First Lady?"

"Opening buildings and cornerstone laying with the VP, she does well and relieves me of such drudgery. If I acceded to every request for an appearance, I'd never get any work done."

Walters took the elevator up to the residence, two Secret Service agents flanking him, and walked thoughtfully down the broad carpeted corridor that led to the First Family's private rooms.

He hated to admit it, but the conversation with Pacino had undermined his objectivity. He almost regretted seeing the admiral. Everyone has gripes. If it wasn't the weather, the rising cost of living, job security, or lack of it, it was Congressional antics. Everybody was getting polarized. That should have been a good thing, cutting through irrelevancy and getting to a decision. Unfortunately, polarization also brought with it bullish intransigence and an unwillingness to be reasonable out of pure spite.

During the hiatus following Israel's attack on Valero, with Congress cowed, he had pushed through legislative reforms, the Republicans reluctant to be obstructionist after ranting to bomb Iran for the attack. They had gotten over their shyness and were regrouping, getting ready to return to their old philosophy: do it our way or it won't get done at all. The Democratic Party still held both houses of Congress, which made the Republican position difficult, but they never wasted an opportunity to pour sand into the administration's agenda. He wondered what the midterm elections would do to him. As a rule, they never favored the incumbent party. He would have to wait and see. A shitty way to do business.

Could he actually launch some of the things Pacino asked for? The ideas were sound enough, but in a multifaceted social and economic matrix, implementing them might not be possible. There was simply too much vested interest and inertia. Checking that thought, he reminded himself that he could also be looking at the problem from an incorrect point of view. Pacino's innate sense of justice would certainly resonate with the voters, the only criteria that counted. If he were to break the issues into individual programs, he could take his initiatives directly to the people. With judicious campaigning, publicity and marketing, he might possibly pull it off. If Congressmen on either side of the aisle were threatened with dismissal come the next elections if they didn't bow to the wishes of their constituents, he might conceivably convince them that his initiatives would help them keep their seats. There was always a risk of a backlash from the Republicans at a later time, but once the legislation was passed, it would not be that easy to repeal.

There would be the inevitable controversy and outcries from some quarters, but he had faced controversy when he sought the presidential nomination. He made the people feel they mattered and they believed in him. Why couldn't he do it again? It would take time to think things through and draw up legislative bills, but that didn't mean he couldn't start publicizing his vision—Pacino's vision. Reading the papers and watching the commentary on TV, the admiral had already struck a responsive chord. Could that sympathy be stretched into a partial withdrawal from South Korea and NATO? There would be the old cries of retreating into isolationism, but America didn't face a Cold War anymore, and the economic one it fought did not require troops in Europe.

Somewhat reassured, he ordered ham and mushroom soup, a mixed salad with chicken, and fresh juice. As always, the kitchen prepared an excellent meal and he ate with relish. He was into his first cup of coffee after he finished when the phone rang. Glancing at the extension button, he sighed and shook his head. He placed down the cup and picked up.

"Sorry to disturb you, Mr. President, Admiral Stone and the Secretary of State are downstairs."

"Can't you handle it for a change?"

"Afraid not. You need to hear this. It's North Korea."

"They invaded Seoul?"

Walters heard a snort. "Not exactly."

"Five minutes."

When he walked into the Oval Office, the three men went silent and waited for Walters to take his seat. Making himself comfortable, he looked up.

"Okay, Manfred."

Cottard glanced at Tanner. "You tell him."

"Mr. President, around ten this morning, Kham Chang-uk called Mark Price, bearing a message from Premier Yeum Ling-chol. They are proposing a meeting with me, but by giving us a heads-up, they wanted to give us enough time to prepare a measured response."

"A response to what, Larry?"

"They're prepared to hand over most of their nukes, some to us, the rest to Russia and China. They want to draw up a peace treaty to formally end the armistice. They're also willing to shut down their uranium reprocessing and enrichment facilities, but want to keep the reactors going for civilian electricity generation. There is more, but that's the guts of it."

"And the quid pro quo?"

"Opening up the world's markets, an apology and reparations for the attack on Yongbyon, cheap loans from the IMF, and an immediate thirty percent drawdown of troops from South Korea."

Staring at Tanner, trying to take it all in, Walters slowly turned to Cottard. "He's shitting me, right?"

"Unless Price has been lied to, I don't think so, Mr. President. To show that they mean it, they have already started dismantling their long range missile launchers."

Walters waved a hand. "That could be a distraction, ridding themselves of obsolescent equipment."

"I doubt that's the case, sir, not when they're doing it at Tongch'ang-dong. That's their most advanced launch facility."

"Mmm. This warheads exchange, how is that supposed to happen?"

"They want USS *George Washington* to divert to their naval base at Haeju Bay. The handover will be made on board," Tanner said.

"Under the glare of world publicity, no doubt," Walters groused.

"Wouldn't you want the world to see that North Korea is suddenly one of the good guys?"

"Where is the carrier now?"

"As per your order, Mr. President, it left Yokosuka at 0600 our time," Cottard replied, "and should get to Incheon in about forty hours. It took her a better part of two days getting ready to sail."

Walters nodded and looked at his Secretary of State. "Assessment, Larry?"

"It looks good to me, sir. I want to talk to Yeum officially, but apart from their demand that we start withdrawing from South Korea, which I gather you want to do anyway, I cannot see a downside for us. Price did mention one thing that might be worth exploring. Kham hinted that he and Yeum held talks with Seoul before the power spill, presumably to lay the groundwork for these moves."

"And I'm to believe that Samun didn't know anything about it?" Walters queried skeptically. Tanner shook his head and smiled.

"Highly unlikely, sir. I think he simply kept his cards close to his chest in case Sung still wound up on top."

Walters exhaled slowly, his fingers drumming against the desk. It made sense. After a moment, he looked at Stone.

"Admiral? What's your take on this?"

"They're giving us everything we always wanted. That's got to be good, Mr. President. I would want to talk to China and Russia, though, before we all get carried away with euphoria. I don't see them objecting to North Korea finally disarming, but China might not like the perception that their satellite is shifting West."

"Larry?"

"Graham has a point, but I'm happy to talk to both prime ministers and feel their temperature. Before I do that, I want to talk to Kham first. He ran this past them, but apparently not in any detail."

"Call Kham and get those details. If he hasn't thought it through, settle any issues you see that might be stumbling blocks. Manfred? Call General McDonald. I want *George Washington* to drop anchor at Incheon. It's too soon for it to be headed directly for Haeju Bay. Once the handover details are finalized, there is plenty of time for it to get there."

"Sir, we're sending the carrier without its escort screen. All our ships are anchored at Incheon," Stone pointed out diffidently.

"Have a couple of destroyers and a cruiser steam toward it at best economical speed."

"Mr. President, are you actually going to go through with this?" Cottard demanded. "Including the withdrawal?"

"Tell me why I shouldn't." When no one said anything, Walters nodded. "Exactly. Before this runs away from us, I want policy impacts, domestic and foreign. To carry this through, we need to be prepared. Just because it all looks good on the surface doesn't mean that there isn't a catch somewhere. If there is one, I want you to find it. Larry, I don't want this administration embarrassed if it turns out Kham was putting one over on us. If necessary, remind him why the carrier is heading for Incheon."

"You got it."

"Graham? I want impact analysis on withdrawing from South Korea. The Joint Chiefs must have scenarios. Talk to McDonald. I want a brief by end of the day."

"Yes, sir, but his reaction will be predictable—too much too soon."

"He works for me, not the other way around. Manfred? Did you make the appointment?"

"Kham will expect your call at seven tonight."

"You and I will talk to Granger after I'm finished with Kham. Oh, and get the Vice President and the SecDef in the loop. Everything on my desk by five. That's it everybody."

Chapter Nine

"Admiral, you're not listening to me!" Powell announced sharply, valiantly trying to control his exasperation. "You're so caught up with telling your story, you're ignoring what's important right now, which is that we have a hearing on Friday. You'll have your chance to tell it, but you must give *me* a chance, or that story will be about your pending court-martial! Remember that impromptu interview downstairs?"

Pacino bit back an angry retort and pursed his lips. Damn it, he was not used being spoken to like that, but the irritating man had a point. Watching the news last night, he wanted to punch out the TV screen. Even CNN, normally a pillar of objectivity, had cut down his speech to a minute of bare facts of his attack without the message about forgotten servicemen, his main point. Fox News was the worst, an anchor's voiceover about a grieving officer who lost control, using the whole thing as a hook to attack Walters and his administration. If that was the kind of reporting his hearing would receive, his message would be drowned out by sensationalist irrelevancy. What the hell had come over the media? Doesn't anybody care anymore?

Then again, the long flights, the crash and the bruises were taking a toll on him.

He took a deep breath, looked up, and stared into Powell's steely eyes. "You're right and I apologize. You also have a mission here."

Powell's gaze remained stern. "No, Admiral. There is only one mission, but you're creating two conflicting objectives for it. You want to use the hearing as a pulpit to bare your soul and go down as a martyr. That's all very well, except it doesn't work like that. Greer Fisher will steer clear of any sentimentality and hammer the cold facts to prove the government's charges. He won't give you a moment's breath to even launch into your *raison d'etre.* I know how he thinks. I've seen him work...against me. You must approach this hearing like a set piece battle with Fisher sunk. You can say your peace, but to counter him, you must take the emotion out of it. If you're not prepared to listen to me, get yourself another lawyer, because I'm wasting my time here."

Bright sunlight streamed into the room through larger double windows. Patchy fluffs of white marred an otherwise clear sky. Pacino sat back and crossed his legs, Powell's words warring with his preconceptions. He picked up his cup and sipped thoughtfully at the coffee that had grown lukewarm some time back.

"I commanded men and ships, Commander, for what seems like a lifetime, supremely confident in what I was doing and always in control. After all, I'm a two-star admiral, but you're right. I did lose my objectivity. My hearing and pending trial should be treated as simply another tactical warfare evolution, but with one difference. I don't command here. You do, and that realization comes hard. It's been a while since someone berated me like I'm a raw ensign. I guess that in a courtroom, that's what I am. I don't like it, but I'm forced to admit that I'm out of my depth when dealing with the law, and I appreciate what you're trying to do for me. Okay, Mister, I'll behave."

The lanky commander cracked a brief smile. "Like I told you, Admiral. You let me do my job and I'll get you off."

Pacino sighed and shook his head. "You said that before, but you're dreaming, Eden."

"I've never been more serious."

"They have the deck stacked."

"The charge of mutiny is a catchall gambit to insert drama into the proceedings and paint you as a traitor, hoping the Investigating Officer will keep that in mind while the other charges are being heard. They're also doing it for the media, of course. The government knows the hearing will be packed with onlookers and the idly curious, no way to stop that, and we don't want to. Fisher will use them to create an expectation in everyone's mind that you're nothing but a deranged criminal. The media loves sensation and will want to see you roasted, regardless of any perceived justice of your case. We cannot allow that."

Pacino snorted. "I hope whoever sits on that bench will have an open mind, Commander. Because he's the one we must convince, not the media."

"Agreed, but the mob will convict you by proxy if we let them, and your message will never be heard."

"Do you know who'll be presiding?"

"I don't, and it doesn't matter. Our tactics must stand on their own."

"Okay, let's get down to cases, Article 107 and 109. I did make false official statements when I ordered General Eugene Picket to prepare a Hawk for me. I deliberately misled Captain Ormond that this was nothing but a night exercise. If Fisher is looking for facts, he has them."

"You did not waste or destroy any property of the United States, which goes to the crux of the regulations. Damage was done in a foreign country. Fisher can't have it both ways, and Article 109 won't apply."

"What about the conduct unbecoming charge? They'll have me there."

"Although Fisher will try make a big deal out of it, at no time were you ever dishonorable, cruel or behaved immorally. Under the military code, you behaved as an officer of character. As for Article 134, your action in no way prejudiced the good order and discipline of the Navy."

"You're kidding me, right? I illegally used my authority to appropriate a UAV and attacked two foreign countries!"

"Where no one got hurt. Believe me, Admiral, the government stumbled badly on this one. Under the preemption doctrine, Article 134 cannot be applied to an offense already covered by Articles 80 to 132."

"That's lawyer bullshit, but you would know more about that than I do." Realizing the double meaning of what he said, Pacino lifted his hand. "Forgive me. I didn't mean—"

"That's all right. No offense taken," Powell said with a tight smile.

"Okay, hotshot. Talk to me about Article 80, an attempt to commit an offense. What about that? Coupled with Article 107, they'll nail me."

Powell wagged a finger. "It all comes down to intent. That's where we have a lever. The preceding acts committed by both Koreas during Key Resolve and the subsequent political atmosphere contributed to your state of mind. It's all interconnected, even though Fisher will try to sidestep both parts. What you're forgetting is that the UCMJ is designed to address deliberate criminal acts and misdemeanors."

"Mine were deliberate."

"None were within the jurisdiction of the United States. A telling point. You acted from honor and highest moral principles, something the Navy will silently applaud."

Pacino chuckled and shook his head. "They may applaud it, but they don't count. Like you said, Fisher won't care about that. He'll be looking to apply the strict interpretation of the articles."

"That's why you have me, sir, to blunt and deflect his attack."

"What's the worst case?"

Powell shrugged. "If we do go to a general court, you're probably looking at a dishonorable discharge. With public sympathy this case is likely to generate if we pitch it right, I doubt the government will push for confinement."

"You hope."

"Nothing is certain, Admiral."

"You don't have to tell *me* that."

"We can also seek an administrative discharge in lieu of court-martial Under Other Than Honorable Conditions. The CNO can do this as part of his disciplinary option within Article 15."

"I admit guilt and Parker drops the charges?"

"That's it. If you want, I can run this by Fisher."

"Would Parker go for it?"

"It's possible. The Navy won't like having its dirty laundry aired in public, or its legal authority questioned. They would rather bury you than try you. If they have to try you, they'll seek to crucify you, but not before suffering a lot of bad publicity. You're an embarrassment, Admiral, a thinking officer. Not thinking too much helps them sleep at night. You made them think and they don't like it."

Pacino regarded the young man with interest. "That's more than a little surprising, Commander, coming from a career officer."

"Before getting out of the SEALs, I've also had time to think." Powell did not elaborate and Pacino didn't want to pry. Perhaps later the stern commander might care to explain.

"But I would still have to go through an Article 32 hearing, wouldn't I?"

"If Admiral Parker grants you an administrative discharge, that would be it. It all depends on how badly the Navy wants to see you hanging on the wall."

Pacino bit his lip. An attractive option, but taking it would mean he would be silenced. Or would he? Even with a dishonorable discharge, he would be walking free and the media were still very much interested in him. That interest would evaporate in absence of courtroom drama and he would simply become another yesterday's news item.

"Has Fisher decided on his witnesses?"

"Admiral Owen will be called to testify, but that's yet to be confirmed. General Picket, Captain Ormond, and Lieutenant

Commander Ransom, as incidental participants, provided signed affidavits. Of course, you'll be his main witness."

"Of course."

The phone rang, providing a rude, but welcome distraction. He reached across the desk and picked up.

"Pacino!"

"You rat! Why did I have to find out from the TV about your crash?" Ruth demanded with silky smoothness and Pacino winced. Having an argument with his wife never pleasant—for him.

"Hold on." He glanced at Powell. "My wife."

"I'll be outside."

When the door closed, Pacino sighed and sat on the bed. "Damn it all, Ruth. It's two o'clock in the morning where you are!"

"I called earlier, but you were out."

That must have been while he was with the president. "Ruth—"

"First the TV, and then Owen called. I have two unsmiling marines standing outside my door and Linda has a big bruiser with her wherever she goes. We were always open with each other, Kenneth. Why didn't you tell me?"

"Okay, I screwed up. I should have told you earlier, but I didn't want to worry you."

"Worry me? And getting a call from Owen was meant to soothe my nerves?"

"Ruth, nobody knows exactly what happened. I'm fine and you don't have to worry."

"Those marines outside my door aren't here having a rest."

"It's a precaution until they get it sorted out, that's all. You must understand that. If Owen hadn't acted, I would have suggested it myself."

"If someone did try to get you, they might try again."

"Perhaps, but I can't dwell on that. I'm just sorry you're involved, but I would rather have those marines outside your door than have something happen to you in case this is real."

"Linda doesn't like this, you know."

"What do you want me to do, Ruth? Pretend that everything is rosy? It will blow over and we'll be together."

"I want to be with you now."

"I know, honey. Me too. Go to bed and I'll call you in the morning."

"Just don't shut me out again, okay?"

Pacino smiled. "I'll give you a blow-by-blow commentary. Give Linda a hug for me."

"I'll do that. No hugs for me?"

"I'm saving a whole bunch just for you," he growled softly and pictured her smiling broadly. "I've got to go."

"Call, okay?"

"Count on it."

He replaced the receiver and blinked hard a couple of times, wishing she were here right now. He *should* have told her. She would be concerned, but finding out secondhand not only made her fret, but it also made her mad at him. Women!

The phone rang and he picked up. "Pacino."

"This is the Reception desk, sir. I have two FBI…uh…persons, who would like to see you. Shall I send them up?"

Pacino raised an eyebrow, wondering what the FBI wanted with him. It might have something to do with the Gulfstream, but there was one sure way of finding out.

"Ask them to show you their IDs. If they refuse, throw them out."

"Ah, very good, sir."

Pacino replaced the receiver and walked to the door. He opened it and motioned Powell to come in.

"Two FBI men might be coming up, or perhaps not."

The lanky commander merely nodded. He strode to the small

writing table, picked up his briefcase and placed it on the desk. He reached inside and held up a black 9mm SIG Sauer P226 NAVY standard SEAL issue semi-automatic. Chambering a round, he gave Pacino a tight smile.

"I'll check their pedigree. I suggest you take cover in the bathroom, Admiral."

Pacino gaped at him. He wasn't shocked that Powell had a gun, but resented the implication he couldn't handle himself.

"Like hell I will!"

"Admiral, I've been trained to handle such things. You haven't. If our visitors are not what they claim to be, I don't want to be distracted worrying about your safety."

Scowling, Pacino reluctantly gave way, admitting that Powell could be right. Empty-handed heroics wouldn't achieve anything. Still, it cut against the grain.

"And if you get shot?"

Powell shrugged. "Then we'll both have a bad day."

Pacino did not find the thought amusing as he ambled toward the bathroom. Ruth probably would once he got around to telling her.

Some two minutes later, he heard a knock on the hallway door.

"Open it wide enough to throw in your handguns," he heard Powell command. "Then walk in with your hands up."

There were two thuds, then the sound of a door opening.

"Show me your IDs."

It seemed like an eternity before Powell called out. "It's okay, Admiral."

Pacino relaxed and gave a long exhale. He could not fault Powell's caution, but did his counselor overreact? Packing a gun in a briefcase? Damn peculiar way for a lawyer to behave. He opened the door and stepped out.

The two men, one a tall heavyset Asian, dressed in dark gray suits that were almost an FBI badge, were retrieving their hardware off the floor. Sliding them under their jackets, both looked up as Pacino entered the room.

"Afternoon, Admiral," the Asian said amiably. "Not the reception we expected."

"And we didn't expect the FBI to be on the case either. Let's have it," Pacino demanded, noting that Powell still held his SIG, keeping himself flush against the wall.

"We're your protection detail, the first watch anyway. It looks like the President wants to make sure you remain safe. By the way, I am Special Agent Norwood, and my partner, Special Agent Kelner."

"Well, now that you're here, how is this supposed to work?"

"While you're in your room, one of us will be outside at all times. If you're planning to go out—"

"Just about ready to have lunch at CityZen downstairs," Pacino said briskly.

"I would recommend using the hotel restaurant, sir. Even better, have room service deliver everything. Outside, you're only making yourself a target."

"Is this necessary, Mr. Norwood? If a professional wants to get me, he'll get me."

"Probably, but that doesn't mean we have to make it easy for him. If someone is really after you, that is."

Pacino chuckled. "I like your candor. Okay, you have a job to do and I won't interfere, but I refuse to be a prisoner in my own room," he said and turned to Powell. "Commander, let's get some lunch."

Norwood didn't look happy and his face showed it, but Pacino had no intention of being handled. Whoever sabotaged the Gulfstream might not be interested at pursuing this any further. Of course, he could always be wrong. *Damn it all*, he wouldn't hide in the bathroom again.

Flanked by the two FBI men, the little procession attracted

several curious stares when they piled out of the elevator and walked across the lobby. Norwood and Kelner went through the revolving door first, looked around and nodded.

Not sure whether to be annoyed or amused, Pacino stepped out and blinked at the bright sunshine. A light breeze stirred his hair. He tried to ignore the smell of burnt gasoline and traffic noises. Passing pedestrians hardly gave his civilian suit a glance. Powell came out and nudged him lightly. Instinctively, Pacino leaned right slightly. A lance of fire burned through the inside of his left arm and side and he heard a loud crack. Agony twisted his face and he gasped as Kelner shoved him violently toward the revolving door, pushing against the splintered heavy glass panel. Pacino stumbled into the lobby and fell down, catching a glimpse of startled faces around him.

Norwood kept him down on the gray marble floor with a firm hand against his right shoulder.

"Where are you hit?"

Pacino glanced at his throbbing side and grimaced. Blood oozed down the sleeve of his jacket, pooling to the floor. This would not make the concierge happy, he figured. He clamped his right hand on the wound and gasped at the sharp pain.

"Ribs."

Handgun in hand, Kelner talked rapidly into a cellphone. Powell stood beside him, his own weapon pointing down, but ready for instant use, watching everybody with grim suspicion.

Norwood leaned over Pacino and glared. "If you hadn't moved, Admiral, that bullet would have ripped your heart out. How does room service sound now?"

* * *

Robert Ashton pressed the Send icon to shoot off the last email for the day, sat back and stretched his arms. The joints popped and he grunted. Around him, the office quiet, most people waiting for the day to end so they could disappear. He felt a bit like that himself. When they saw him, his colleagues greeted him politely, commenting with mild interest on his tan and adventures in the Med, then drifted away to pursue their work. By mid-afternoon, it felt like he had never been away.

Outside, rain pelted softly against the windows from a black sky. A steady wind whipped tree branches into frenzy and he could hear its thin keening. What he needed was a stiff workout and a brisk jog to loosen him up and get the blood flowing, if he could sneak out early enough. He didn't feel like running in the dark pursued by a biting wind. Staring at the gloomy sky, he was certainly having a hell of a first day, wishing he were back on the Big E, enjoying the warm Mediterranean sunshine.

As expected, Collander and Pierson came up empty, although they were still sifting through their stuff. With the refueling area hopelessly contaminated before Paul Brenner secured the tanker, gate surveillance tapes might give him a lead. At least he hoped so, because right now, all he had was a downed aircraft, two dead pilots and a lot of questions. Chasing Sea-Tac tapes might give Hollice a warm fuzzy, but Ashton saw it as a dead end. A random mug search may yield something, but a long shot at best. Still, the boy deserved his little fun and it was all good training. When the tapes did come in, the sheer volume of data would be staggering and beyond the resources available to NCIS to analyze. The CIA had the manpower and equipment to do the job, but he was reluctant going down that path, at least for now. If one of their men did this job, he would only be giving them a heads-up.

He had not discounted the possibility that a disgruntled airman soured the fuel. Young Hollice was sifting through personnel jackets reluctantly supplied by Major Stowell, and only after pressure from Albert Pollard, that might uncover a disturbed mind or a calculating personality. The problem was, they were working summaries only, not full files. For that, he would have to go cap in hand to the Pentagon. By tomorrow, he would at least have an idea if they had a possible suspect. After his chat with Morris Fielder, he hoped another piece would be slotted into the jigsaw puzzle.

Going over Admiral Owen's personal file, nothing stood out that made him think the admiral had anything to do with this. Sure, the man was understandably pissed at Pacino, which indirectly placed a black mark on his otherwise unblemished record, but that hardly constituted a motive for murder. However, people all the time did some pretty weird things, but the military were usually rational—usually. Ashton could not afford to ignore the sad fact that a uniform merely served to cloak an altogether human personality, and the military were all too human. If it were otherwise, he would be out of a job and could be working for the CIA. The thought made his skin crawl. No, Owen wouldn't risk his precious rank by doing something dumb.

Anyway, it was no use speculating until Fielder came back to him.

Was there anything else he should be doing? Apart from getting out of here to empty his mind and having a stiff jolt of brandy? The brandy wouldn't help him think, but it would get him relaxed, and that's what the old body needed right now.

The phone rang and he wearily reached across the desk for the handset.

"Robert Ashton."

"Glad to have caught you, Mr. Ashton. I am FBI Special Agent Khao Jon Norwood, Washington. You can call me Ken. I've been placed in charge of a detail looking after Admiral Pacino."

Ashton glanced at his wristwatch and blinked. It was seven p.m. out there, for crying out loud.

"Don't you guys have a life, Ken?"

The FBI man chuckled. "Sometimes. Unfortunately, it's been one of those days."

"Yeah, tell me about it. What can I do for you?"

"I understand that you're running the NCIS investigation into the downed Gulfstream V, sir."

"That's right."

"I wanted to let you know that all resources available to the FBI are at your disposal."

Ashton raised an eyebrow. "Somebody must like Pacino."

"It appears the President has taken a shine to him. Regrettably, everybody doesn't share that opinion. Pacino was shot this afternoon."

"Rats! How bad?"

"He was lucky and walked away with a flash wound and a collection of stitches. A long range attempt."

"A professional shooter?"

"We recovered a 7.62mm round from the hotel lobby floor where he is staying. Although mangled a bit, the rifling scars suggest the bullet might have come from an M14 sniper rifle."

"A pro weapon, all right," Ashton mused. Although no longer in general use, the Navy Special Warfare Command kept the M14 in inventory due to its excellent accuracy, effectiveness at long range, and strong takedown capabilities of the heavy 7.62mm round. "The SEALS use those things."

"We know, but you can get that stuff almost anywhere. Copies, anyway."

"Only one round fired?"

"One round only," Norwood confirmed. "I know what you're thinking. With a twenty-round mag and a firing rate of 750 rounds per minute, he could have sprayed everybody when his first shot missed."

"He didn't want any collateral damage. Definitely a pro."

"That doesn't mean I like him."

"Did you figure out where the shot came from?"

"The angle gave us a rooftop across the avenue. We checked the building—"

"And came up with nothing. Figures. If you don't mind me asking, Ken, what the hell were you guys doing while Admiral Pacino was getting shot?"

"Trying to convince the asshole to stay indoors."

Ashton laughed, warming to the man. "Got it. I didn't mean to imply—"

"You did, but I'm used to it. The other reason why I called is to settle jurisdiction. If it's all right with you, I'd like to handle the shooter investigation. Reporting to you, of course."

"I don't mind at all. Glad to have you on board. Right now, I'm thin on leads and still pursuing motive."

"With your Yokosuka office?"

Ashton nodded in appreciation. "It's always nice dealing with a professional."

"Not if next time our pro doesn't miss."

"There is always that. I hope Admiral Pacino will be dissuaded from making further outdoor excursions?"

"He's convinced," Norwood said dryly. "Well, that's it from me. Is there anything I should know?"

"As a matter of fact, there is. Although shooting Pacino has caused me to revise some of my theories, there is one I'm still not prepared to abandon. Not yet, anyway. You guys are required to vet all military service applicants. I wouldn't mind getting a rundown on Air Force personnel stationed at McChord Field, with a particular emphasis on fuel handlers and aircraft service grunts. They've given us files, but they're normal operational jackets and thin on detail."

There was a moment of silence while Norwood apparently digested the information. "I've spoken to Paul Brenner. You're thinking that sabotaging the Gulfstream could have been a crime of opportunity by somebody at the base?"

"It's possible."

"But that would mean—"

"That we have three people in the loop here."

"Three? Ah, yes. The invisible man who gave the order to our shooter."

"That's it. Of course, we could have the whole scenario ass backward and the shooter is acting on his own."

"An interesting slant, Mr. Ashton. I'll see what I can do about those personnel records. Any other ideas?"

"We're getting some surveillance tapes from Sea-Tac, but we lack the necessary resources to do proper ident matching against bad guy files."

"Send them over and we'll run them past our database. You know, the CIA have extensive files on shady operators. It might be worth while running this past them as well."

"I'd rather not do that right now. If we come up empty, maybe then."

More silence, followed by a sigh. "In case it's one of their own? You have a nasty mind, Mr. Ashton. If you got a pencil, I'll give you my number in case you want to call."

"Shoot."

Norwood rattled off the numbers. "If we're done, I'll bid you good night, sir."

Ashton hung up and smiled. Well, not all FBI men were starched asses.

He wondered how the shooter managed to miss an easy target, reminding himself to ask Norwood sometime. Leaning back against the chair, he locked his fingers behind his head.

What do you say now, eh, Watson?

Rain still came down outside.

* * *

NORTH KOREA HANDS OVER ITS NUCLEAR ARSENAL
THE PRESIDENT PULLING TROOPS OUT OF SOUTH KOREA
CHINA APPLAUDS AMERICAN WITHDRAWAL
MARKETS CAUTIOUS BUT STEADY

REPUBLICANS SLAM PRESIDENT'S FOREIGN POLICY

Ashton scanned the headlines, snorted and pushed away the *Seattle Times*. He thought that everyone would welcome what North Korea was proposing, but apparently not. The Republicans seemed to be digging in on principle as usual despite the fact that according to polls, most Americans did not mind the prospect of having their boys come home at all. Personally, the move was long overdue and the deal Walters apparently made with North Korea should make everyone in the region breathe a little easier. Why then would the Republicans be against it? Simply being a pain because they failed to stitch up the deal? Most likely. Our way or no way looked like to be their standing policy. No wonder the evangelical right had them in their pocket. The mainstream population had given up on them. Which, in his view, wasn't good either.

He reached for the remains of his onion and bacon bagel, stuffed with tomato slices and cream cottage cheese, and bit into it. Chewing, he figured that some things would never change, and the GOP was one of them. Bovine morons all as far as he was concerned, but he wasn't about to allow a little detail like that spoil his breakfast.

At least North Korea had not gone into a huff over Pacino's bombing strike. The new regime clearly saw advantages for themselves at turning over a new leaf, even if they were forced into it by circumstances, not to be distracted by something to which they themselves were a contributing factor. Far from appearing weak by withdrawing from South Korea even partially, America had shown itself to be a mature power at a time when its international standing needed a boost. After all, should anybody want to start something over there, the 7th Fleet was still in Japan. Besides, South Korea fielded a sizeable ready army and air force. At any rate, according to the paper, this would not be a full withdrawal. On the face of it, a win-win for everybody.

Driving up Route 16 toward Silverdale was easy. Most of the traffic was going the other way toward downtown Seattle or Tacoma. Despite the fact that Bremerton was less than six miles from the NCIS offices, it was nice not having to fight other cars when going to and from work. Listening to soft jazz on FM 88.5, with the tires whispering on the road, it felt good to be alive this morning. Overnight, the clouds had lifted and the sky now a gorgeous deep blue. Sunshine made everything bright and it promised to be a great day.

As he rolled in, he noted the neat rows of parked cars, more than he saw yesterday, and slid into his reserved space. On the first floor, he snagged a coffee from the kitchenette, exchanged perfunctory greetings with several colleagues, taking a bit of ribbing about his tan, and eased himself behind his desk. Hollice's PC wasn't powered, which meant the boy had not come in yet, somewhat unusual for him. He was regularly at his desk by eight. Ashton didn't worry about it. He would find out soon enough what kept his protégé. Logging in, he opened his email Inbox, blanching at the lengthy list that had accumulated during his absence. Rats!

Paging down, he reminded himself to schedule a meeting with his team for ten. Nobody bothered him yesterday, but that was only because officially, he wasn't in, which he made plain to those wanting to waylay him. Today, however, all bets were off and it was unlikely that he would get much peace. They would figure his holiday was over and time to get back into harness. Well, the building had not burned down while he was away, so things must still be going all right.

He spotted a red-flagged message from Fielder and clicked on the line. Skipping the preamble and Fielder's gripe about being overloaded, Ashton got into the meat. A quick read gave him an overall picture. After a long pull of coffee, he went over the email in detail.

He didn't know how Fielder managed to get hold of Admiral

Owen's full personal record jacket, but he would not be sidelined by irrelevancies. Like Hollice said, Owen was an exemplary officer. A hard charger, prepared to take risks based on all available information, and never spontaneous or rash. The boy paid attention while at Annapolis, coming second in his class on graduation. Somehow the Navy found out that his classmate had secretly married, which was an honor violation, and forced to resign, effectively making Owen top of his class. An addendum note said the Academy commandant was tipped off about the marriage, but it was never found by whom, although there were rumors. The fact that a notation appeared in Owen's jacket spoke volumes.

It appeared that Owen hated coming second.

As Hollice said, the destroyer skipper he bilged in the Med not his only victim. It seemed the admiral regularly dined on an odd commander or captain. Even while a young officer himself, bodies littered his career path. Conclusion? Admiral Owen had reached the top of his career tree and there were no further branches to climb. Interestingly, the observation was made by the previous CNO. There was also a 'Noted' entry by Admiral Parker, the current CNO.

Pausing, Ashton mulled it over. Owen ran tight commands, so what? The Navy liked that, otherwise the man would never have gotten his three stars. It did not necessarily mean they loved him, internal politics notwithstanding. Ah, unrequited love, a real bummer. Along the way, Owen had covered his ass and made sure all the right promotional boxes were ticked. That was nothing unusual. On the contrary, as a commanding officer, it was a sought-after trait. Still, Ashton couldn't get over the fact that a trail of broken careers lay in Admiral Owen's wake.

Did Owen see Pacino's rash act as a blemish on his own otherwise spotless career and an impediment to further advancement? Reading the likely sentiment in the Navy and the general political fallout, had Owen decided to take the offending spot to a drycleaner? It would certainly be in character and gave Ashton a possible motive. Fielder hadn't drawn any conclusions. It wasn't his case, but what he did next clearly demonstrated parallel thinking.

Owen apparently had two phones. An open line for normal daily junk calls, and the other encrypted and secure. Nothing unusual there. Although Fielder could not provide plain text of the secure calls, he did get date/time stamps from the base exchange, something that couldn't be wiped. Owen made two calls yesterday and received two calls between 2100 and 2300 Tokyo time. It was impossible to trace to whom he made the calls or who called him, not with the software that ran behind the encryption system designed to scramble that information. A major inconvenience, Ashton mused, but that's why the thing was secure.

According to Fielder, Owen was also the proud owner of a High Technology Computer smartphone, equipped with customized encryption chips and advanced military-grade software, courtesy of the NSA. If he made or received a call on that device, it would have disappeared into the ether. Those things were totally untraceable and the encryption unbreakable, at least within a timeframe that mattered. Or were they? After all, NSA had issued them, and everyone knew how paranoid they were. Wouldn't they want to eavesdrop on their own equipment? Something Ashton wanted to field past Norwood.

Although possible, he did not believe that Owen would have ordered a hit on Pacino. What was the percentage in it? After all, it wasn't his fault that Pacino went off the rails. It did happen on his watch, he reminded himself. A lead, however faint, and he would pursue it, or young Hollice would. Exactly the kind of thing that would feed the kid's conspiracy mentality.

The second part of Fielder's message an anticlimax. Pacino's record mirrored Owen's career in many ways. Both were go-getters and totally professional, but there was a significant difference. Whereas Owen used the Navy as a stepladder to that top rung, Pacino was much more a people person, and his fitness reports reflected that. He did use people, that came with the job, but he never wasted them, at least not intentionally. His concern for the wounded, the mentally crippled, or just plain in trouble, came through clearly in his recent writings. In hindsight, his action against Korea was almost an inevitable culmination of cumulative events, however shocking to Navy brass. No wonder they found him incomprehensible—a would-be three-star admiral throwing it all away simply to make a humanitarian protest?

Lots of people could be ticked off at Pacino, as the Gulfstream sabotage and attempted assassination illustrated. The trick was figuring out whether the same man had committed the two incidents.

A quandary, eh, Watson?

Ashton closed the email and sent Fielder a polite thank you note with a request to find out if there was any way to crack into Owen's secure phone calls. Thinking about it, he also forwarded Fielder's email to Norwood. With the president interested in Pacino's wellbeing, the FBI might have better luck finding out if the NSA were bugging their HTCs. Norwood would know what to do.

The next email that caught his eye was from Hollice. It contained an attachment of Pacino's message to CNN. Reading it merely confirmed Pacino's concern for men lost during the Key Resolve exercise and the administration's apparent unwillingness to support the country's servicemen. Great public propaganda and CNN had no qualms using it.

What raised his eyebrows was a message from some FBI weenie called Kelner, with a CC to Norwood, containing an attachment. He opened the zipped file and it spilled full record jackets for twelve Air Force enlisted ratings and two officers. Fast work indeed, Ashton noted in appreciation. Poor Kelner must have worked all night to not only sift through the list of McChord personnel, but also identify possible people of interest to his investigation. Amazing what a bit of presidential heat could achieve.

The first file, a captain, didn't get him very far. Some right-wing tendencies, conservative in his political views, religious, holds a racial bias, but nothing extreme. The second file raised a smile from Ashton. Major Stowell, base adjutant, passed over twice for promotion to lieutenant colonel for views not consistent with military doctrine and detrimental to discipline, words written by his commanding officer when the luckless major came up before his promotion selection board. That evaluation also resulted in his transfer to McChord, clearly a career dead end. A man with a possible grudge. Well, well…

However titillating, Stowell did not strike Ashton as someone who would commit sabotage. Then again, he reminded himself that it was those most unlikely to display aberrant behavior that actually did it. Definitely a personality to peel open further.

A brief perusal of other files had not revealed a Ku Klux Klan Grand Cyclops, a neo-Nazi or a socialist leftist, but he would leave the initial analysis to Hollice. The kid would eat this up. Not that Ashton would rely solely on Hollice's input. He would go over each file in detail himself and form his own conclusions. He was interested to see how the boy's thinking paralleled his own. Two heads and all that.

He sat back, reached for the mug and took a sip of tepid coffee. Looking out, the sky was still clear. This was shaping up into one of his better mornings. Dragging the keyboard to him, he forwarded the files to Hollice, including Owen's personal jacket, with a note to see him as soon as he had a body or two at McChord worthy of close attention. The lack of any tangible evidence could still ruin the investigation, suspicions or not. Even without direct evidence, there were interview techniques designed to startle a suspect into providing an incriminating admission. He couldn't beat up anybody, but military personnel did not enjoy all the rights available to civilians, which gave him an edge.

That didn't mean using techniques the Army thugs employed at Guantanamo either.

After considering everything, he glanced at his writing pad, picked up the phone and dialed.

"Special Agent Ken Norwood," the answer came after two rings.

"Hi, Ken. It's Ashton."

"I was looking at your email from Fielder. An interesting character, our Admiral Owen."

"Very. He's interesting enough to follow up. Before getting down to business, I want to thank Mr. Kelner for those files."

"The time difference between us helped, but I'll pass on the message. I hope they'll be useful."

"Me too. What I wanted to call you about was Owen's secure calls. Not from his landline phone, but the HTC."

"Those things are untraceable, Mr. Ashton. Even to the NSA. That's how they were made."

"Rats! Are you absolutely sure about that?"

"Absolutely sure? No. You want me to find out, is that it? Even if the NSA are lying to us, they're not likely to admit it."

"What if the demand came from the White House?"

Norwood laughed. "That would merely give them one more reason to lie."

Ashton grinned. Politicians came and went, but intelligence institutions were there to stay. Revealing a national security secret to a politician was like posting it on the Internet.

"So you think I'm chasing my tail?"

"Not necessarily, not if we approach the problem from underneath. I know somebody in the Cyber Division who used to work at the Puzzle Palace and he might have a clue how to get what we want, if it's possible. He's into this telecommunications shit. Even if Owen's smartphone is untraceable, unless the other party had a device with a similar capability—"

"Something the CIA might have?"

"They use modified BlackBerrys, but yes. The other guy would need to have one of those, otherwise, even with ordinary military-grade encryption, his end would be vulnerable to NSA cryptanalysis computers. Mind you, we cannot trace if Owen received or made calls on his HTC. One of the things the device does is block the switching system's authentication center from recording the event and passing it on to the billing module."

"So we cannot trace the calls directly perhaps, unless your Cyber Division lead can come up with something, but NSA could check for encrypted messages within a given time window. There could be a few, I know, but that's why they got all those computers. Give them a few code words like Gulfstream and McChord to lock on to, they might dig up something."

"Agreed, if Owen or the other party used those words."

"There is always that, but you get the idea."

"You do know that Owen could be as white as his summer uniform."

"I know it, but he was a SEAL and you said the round used on Pacino came from an M14. That's a SEAL favorite."

"Suspected M14. You think he might have called an old buddy to do the job? You're building this on a stack of unfounded suppositions."

"That's all we have right now, suppositions."

"Let me dig into this and I'll get back to you. Always a pleasure talking to you."

"You're just being polite." Ashton chuckled and hung up.

He picked up another load of coffee and got stuck into the remaining emails in his Inbox. Most of them were routine, including the usual junk that came from HR, Accounting, Pollard's own ranting, and who did what to whom in the office. Some actually dealt with cases from his own team. Skimming through them to pick up the threads, he decided to leave the details for the ten a.m. meeting. Jumping into the Outlook scheduler, he booked a conference room and sent out must-attend invites.

With the Preview Pane, he quickly glanced over the entire list and deleted all but two from Accounting that dealt with expenses during his Special Agent Afloat program on the Big E, and one from Pollard demanding a summary report of his trip. As for the ones he deleted, he figured if something was really important, the sender would call him about it. He had better uses for his time than engaging in email warfare or attending useless staff meetings.

Staring at the screen, the phone rang and he groped for the receiver.

"Ashton."

"Hi, Robert. It's Brenda. Pollard wants to see you."

He didn't particularly want to see the boss right now, but an excuse to step away from his desk for a while too good to miss.

"I'll be right up."

He took the stairs to the third floor and stepped into the discreetly lit lobby with its soft brown carpet and wood-paneled walls. It never failed to fascinate him how well the administrative and legal arms of the Northwest Field Office lived while lording over the lesser NCIS mortals.

He padded toward an alcove next to Pollard's corner office. Brenda looked up from her keyboard and smiled. Her desk faced a wall on which hung a large photo of a naval lieutenant standing on a dock, a Trident submarine silhouetted in the background. A row of four steel cabinets took up the wall behind her.

"You can go right in, Robert."

"How is he this morning?" Everyone knew the boss tended to be a bit grumpy until he downed at least two cups of strong milky coffee.

"He was actually polite to me," flashed back the pretty brunette.

"Must be something wrong with him," Ashton murmured with a shake of his head as he stepped to the office door. He knocked once and went in without waiting to be invited.

Albert Pollard looked up from his spacious desk and waved him in. "Ah, Ashton. Grab a seat."

Pulling up a brown cloth-covered chair closer to Pollard's broad executive desk, Ashton sank into its softness. Bright sunshine streamed in through a ceiling-high window, the gauzy curtains pulled back. On his left stood a solid wood wall unit, a crowded bookshelf and bar in one. Apart from a small conference table with four chairs tucked into the right corner, the office otherwise bare.

On the short side, bald, wearing narrow black glasses, bulky but not fat, Pollard could have been a banker for the image he projected, instead of being a highly skilled operative. Other field offices might employ professional administrators, and Pollard was a good one, but Ashton liked that he worked for someone who understood fieldwork.

"You on top of the Pacino case?"

The way Pollard asked the question set Ashton's alarms clanging. "Paul Brenner is pretty much convinced the Gulfstream was brought down deliberately. I've asked the Yokosuka office to trawl for some phone data for me, and we're looking at personnel files at McChord. I'm also liaising with a Washington FBI man on this."

"Yes, I know. Anything so far?"

"Rats, boss! It's only been a day!"

"We're getting heat over this from the White House, Robert."

"So I heard. The President's got to give us time to do this. Even then, we might not get anywhere. Forensics has drawn a blank, as has the FBI with that shooting."

Pollard raised his eyebrows in mock astonishment. "The famed Ashton is giving up? I can't believe it."

"Ah, rack off."

Pollard grinned, then fixed on his official face. "Whatever it takes, okay? And talking of heat, Major Stowell at McChord called me. He's not very happy with you."

"Like I give a toss."

"You met him and I haven't, so I'll let this one pass. Just don't annoy everybody all at once. Cooperation, that's the catchword, got it?"

"What did he want? An apology for being an asshole?"

"Employ a bit of diplomacy, that's all."

Ashton realized that Pollard was right, he sighed and nodded. "Got it."

"Good man. Let me know if you need anything."

"You'll be the first," Ashton said and stood up.

"How's Hollice coming?"

"Fine so far, boss. He's a good kid."

"Just don't turn him into another version of you. The original is pain enough."

Chuckling, Ashton walked out. He expected to be reamed over Stowell, but the boss was a very good judge of character, even over the phone.

Another version of himself? The thought amused him intensely.

When he got down, Hollice sat at his desk peering closely at the computer screen. The boy didn't even see him as he walked by.

He tried to wrap up his ten o'clock meeting within the allotted half hour, but it took over an hour to get his head around what everyone was doing, sorting out snafus and gripes, and giving a few orders disguised as suggestions. After filling in expense forms, starting his Med adventure report and more email warfare, it was close to lunchtime.

He sat back, stretched his arms and gave a soft groan. Hearing a discrete cough, he swiveled his chair and squinted at the hovering form.

"You got something for me?"

Hollice gave a bright smile and nodded. "I've been going over the FBI files you sent me and I think we might have a bite. Two bites, actually."

"And?"

"They are both refuelers, and both were on the base when the Gulfstream was scheduled to come in. One is a corporal, busted from sergeant by a visiting colonel driving an F/A-18. Something to do with spilled fuel during a hot turnaround. Since then, the man has been in hack for brawling and once for taking a swing at an Army captain. Being a joint base, the boys tend to get somewhat exuberant after a drink or two."

"So the man has a chip on his shoulder and hates officers. That's no revelation or a motive."

"True, but get this. He had a brother on USS *Stethem*, a chief petty officer."

"Ah, and he was one of the ones who bought it?"

Hollice nodded, his face expectant.

"And you found this how?" Ashton demanded, already knowing the answer.

"I called Yokosuka."

"Good work, Brandon," Ashton said warmly and Hollice preened. "This definitely gives our man a possible axe to grind. And the other?"

"A good kid on the outside, Airman Second Class, but he failed twice to get into the ROTC program. His old man was a commander who got shitcanned when as executive officer, he ran his frigate onto a sandbar. Our man still a teenager then. He applied for Annapolis, but was turned down. Since the Navy didn't like him, he joined the Air Force. This is the juicy part. Two years ago, a New Flight Charters jet out of Denver carrying some Navy brass was forced to land at Portland after a stopover at McChord. The investigation determined cause as—"

"Fuel contamination," Ashton murmured. "I know. I heard about it. I suppose our boy was on duty at the time?"

"You got it."

"Doesn't like Navy officers, eh? How did you get all this dope on the kid?"

"I talked to Major Stowell."

"Stowell?"

"He was most helpful. Why?"

"Mmm, nothing." Ashton shook his head in wonder. He would have to say something nice to the man next time around. "What about the other files?"

"Malcontents with a mix of right and left-wing tendencies. None of them were on base when the Gulfstream went down."

"That we know of. The way the place is run, anybody could walk in and out." Ashton glanced at his watch: 11:48. "Call Stowell and tell him that we'd like to interview both your men at one this afternoon. That'll give you time to grab lunch and me a chance to go over their files. Names?"

"Colby and Higgs."

Ashton's eyebrows rose. Colby was on the refueling form as the tanker loader. "Make the call," he said. As Hollice turned, Ashton grabbed his arm. "One more thing. Ask Stowell to secure both men's work clothes: gloves, coveralls, boots, the usual stuff. Make sure they bag each item separately and they're to wear gloves while doing it."

Hollice looked at him. "If one of them did sabotage the Gulfstream, no way he'd be dumb enough to hang on to his coveralls if he spilled biodiesel on 'em."

"Maybe, and then, maybe not. Just get the stuff, okay?"

Hollice grinned. "The devious mind of the intrepid Mr. Ashton is revealed. I hear and obey!"

"Asshole."

Watching Hollice push buttons, Ashton chewed his lower lip. A slim thread, two threads, but at least he had something solid to follow. He turned his chair and opened the FBI file on Colby.

On the way to McChord with Hollice driving—after doing all the gofer work, the kid deserved to be at the pointy end—Ashton worked through his salad roll, brushing an occasional crumb off his lap. The day still bright, but in the distance, thick cloud shrouded Mt. Rainier. Finishing his roll, he put his mind in neutral and watched the traffic.

Captain Marchinson met them and led them to an empty, windowless office. A few minutes later, he walked in with a tough looking sulky individual wearing baggy blue coveralls.

"Corporal Colby, Mr. Ashton. If you need anything, call," he said, nodding at the desk phone.

"Thanks, Captain." When the door closed, Ashton smiled and waved at an empty chair. "Please sit down, Mr. Colby."

"I'd like to know what's going on, Mister!" Colby snapped truculently.

"We want to ask you some questions, that's all. This will be much more pleasant if you sat down."

Colby thought it over, pulled back a chair, and gingerly eased himself down. "Ask your questions."

"You know who we are?"

"Captain Marchinson clued me in."

"Okay. Two nights ago, you were on duty when a Navy Gulfstream landed at 0500 to take on fuel. Is that right?"

"Ah, so that's what this is about. You guys looking into the crash?"

"Just answer the question."

"Sure, I was on duty. What's more, I was in charge of the detail that filled the tanker, although I didn't do the actual refueling."

"Who did?"

"Donovan, I think. Say! You guys think that I had something to do with that jet going down? You're crazy!"

"Is it? We understand that your brother was on USS *Stethem*."

Colby's eyes clouded. "Sure, and I'm waiting for the Navy to ship me the body. I'm pissed at the North Koreans for what they did, but I don't blame Admiral Pacino for it. As far as I'm concerned, somebody should have stuck it to those guys long ago.

Just because my brother got killed in the bargain doesn't mean that I hate the Navy or Pacino. I had nothing to do with that Gulfstream crash and you cannot prove otherwise."

Ashton glanced at Hollice, who cleared his throat and leaned forward.

"Perhaps not, but you're in a habit of lashing out at officers, and getting at Pacino, an admiral, would be a big feather in your cap."

Colby snorted contemptuously. "All officers are assholes. Sure, I got busted a couple of times and I flattened an Army captain's nose. The snot deserved it, but the Navy never did me any wrong. Like I said, it took balls for Pacino to do what he did. I cheered when I saw the TV clip. If you don't believe me, check with the guys."

"We'll do that," Ashton said softly. Colby might be a troublemaker, but his sincerity appeared genuine. Of course, it could all be an elaborate front to throw them off. "Okay, Corporal. Thanks for your time."

"Is that it?"

"For now."

Colby stood up, not quite certain he was off the hook. Nodding, he stepped out.

Ashton turned to Hollice. "What do you think?"

"We'll need to do more digging into his past and present, but he put up a good front."

"Yeah, and that's what bothers me," Ashton said and reached for the phone. "Captain? Send in Higgs...Colby is clean for now...You have? That's great. We'll pick them up on our way out, and thanks." He looked up and grinned. "Marchinson has their gear. When we get back, take it personally to Collander and have him go over everything. Check if he has a sample of the contaminated fuel. If he hasn't, call Paul Brenner and have him send us some."

"Isn't it nice when people cooperate?" Hollice said with a

broad grin.

A knock on the door and Marchinson walked in. Beside him stood a pimply youngster in a loose fitting uniform. Ashton's first impression was that with another fifteen pounds on the bones the kid would look good.

"Airman Second Class Higgs."

"Thanks, Captain…sit down, Mr. Higgs."

The kid shuffled to the chair and sat down. Ashton noted that he was not nervous or agitated. He simply sat there waiting. At his age, being interviewed by two NCIS men, a normal person would be at least a little apprehensive. A clear conscience maybe?

"I am Investigator-In-Charge Ashton and my partner, Agent Hollice."

"Marchinson told me who you were."

Marchinson, not Captain, Ashton mused. "We understand you were on duty two nights ago when a Navy Gulfstream landed to refuel."

"I was on the base, yes, but I wasn't on duty when they serviced the jet. I was in the mess watching CNN and how the Navy got plastered."

"You don't care much for the Navy?"

"Since you're talking to me, you must have read my service jacket."

"You tried for Annapolis. Why didn't you enlist in the Navy when you failed your midshipman entrance?"

Higgs shrugged. "I wanted a clean start and I figured the Air Force would give it to me. They treated me okay."

"But you also failed to get into their ROTC program."

"It's hard to put in the required prep work when holding down a job, and the Air Force keeps people like me busy."

"People like you?"

"Enlisted men, Mr. Ashton."

"Were you anywhere near the Gulfstream while it was being refueled?"

"Like I told you, I was in the mess."

"Prior to the refueling?"

"Aircraft come and go here. The first I heard of this Gulfstream was when the scuttlebutt said it went down."

"Can you remember anyone who can vouch for your time in the mess?"

"Sure, I've got a couple of names."

"What did you feel when your father retired after his grounding incident?"

"What did I feel? I'll tell you. At first, I was pissed, but then he sorted me out. Although he wasn't directly responsible, the OOD gave a wrong course change to the helm, my old man had the con and ended up carrying the shit. He convinced me that's how things go and I shouldn't take it out on the Navy. In fact, he was the one who sponsored me for Annapolis."

"It wasn't your idea?"

Higgs shrugged. "I was okay with it. My high school didn't offer the subjects the Navy needed and I never made it."

"And how did you feel about that?"

"I got a shitty deal, that's all. Life is full of shitty deals, isn't it? You just have to learn to hack it."

"And then the Air Force handed you a shitty deal also."

"The ROTC thing?" Higgs chuckled. "Seeing the kind of officers we have here, who wants to be one."

"You wanted to be one."

Higgs shrugged, not saying anything.

"Your record shows that two years ago, you were investigated for a possible sabotage of a New Flights Charters jet that was forced down at Portland."

"And the investigation proved nothing. Sure, I was part of the refueling crew at the time, but I don't have any idea how the mixup occurred."

"Nobody got charged, that's true, but why did you stay on as a refueler for such a long time?"

"I'm not a refueler. That's only a sideline. I'm actually a support and maintenance mechanic on ground vehicles."

"And that includes driving trucks that use biodiesel?"

"Just about all our ground vehicles use that stuff and I drive 'em, but none are used in the refueling area. You must know why. Check it yourself."

"We will. Thanks, Mr. Higgs. That'll be all for now."

Higgs gave a self-satisfied smirk, stood up and marched out.

"Cocky son of a whore," Hollice murmured.

"We might not like him, but that doesn't prove he did it. Dig deeper into his background and check what happened to his old man. Talk to his buddies, the usual stuff. Maybe Collander will come up with something, and then we'll have a different talk with one of our flyboys."

Hollice grinned. "I love watching an expert at work. It gets me all hot and bothered."

***

Shouldering the steep southern swells in a welter of white spray and roiling foam as green water broke over the sharp bow, *Laan Ghae* shrugged and plunged into the next roller. Heavy cloud marred a leaden sky. On the northern horizon, lightning flickered in a scintillating display. Captain Baye Mangjul took a deep breath of the chilly salty air, the wind moaning through the ship's rigging to the whine of powerful diesel engines coming through the blowers, straightened his cap and pulled the collars of his bulky jacket tight around his neck. It didn't make him any warmer. Ahead of the large frigate, a band of black dumped sheets of rain. Two thousand meters on either beam, OSA II missile ships kept station, the small boats making heavy weather in the quartering seas. Their crews would not be appreciating this sortie, Mangjul mused. Not that he cared. They were tools to be used for the greater good of the people.

Leaning against the starboard railing, watching the plunging missile boats, his mouth tightened with anger. For the greater good of the people…how easily the lie slid off his lips. That's how he was used, but he doubted that the people would benefit. The American naval exercise…

He had questioned the dubious wisdom of positioning *Kurung Thae* in the line of advance of the imperialist ships, but his orders came directly from Admiral Takko, Commander West Sea Fleet. It was not an order he could disobey, however illogical. He was furious when the submarine fired a torpedo at the South Korean destroyer, and he ordered its immediate withdrawal, but by then events took their inevitable and disastrous course. Sending *Peryong Lam* to attack the American DDG had also been a futile gesture that resulted in the corvette sunk and his friend Rae Dong-yul killed, with all his crew.

He believed that the People's Navy should never back down to the decadent imperialists, but it also cannot waste a valuable ship and men in a futile gesture. This sortie, it too might be a futile gesture, but this time, he was under nobody's orders. This time, he would strike at the enemy with honor.

How quickly his life had changed, and with it, the face of the Democratic People's Republic. Sung Kang-dae, the Supreme Leader, swept into oblivion by the reformist faction and Tung In-san now the Supreme Leader. The capitalist puppet had not chosen to take on an appellation, discarding it as pretentious and a reminder of things past, now best forgotten. More than his title was discarded in the aftermath when the new regime removed the old guard, and with it, his father, Minister of Agriculture, who had held a protective hand over Mangjul's career. A full captain at thirty-two was a proud achievement, but competence also played a part. He was a good officer and knew it. With his father, others were brushed aside also, including Admiral Takko, retiring at end of the month, supposedly for health reasons. Bad health had suddenly overcome a lot of the senior military cadre.

Wise in the way of things, Takko, a good friend to his father, quietly told Mangjul to make a protest against the imperialists and the new government, should an opportunity present itself. Not liking what was happening to his country, not understanding it all, he took notice.

The frigate plunged into a roller and shook off a cascade of water. Steaming south toward an inevitable rendezvous, fates just might have delivered that opportunity. Turning, he opened the heavy steel hatch to the bridge and walked into the warm, dimly lit interior, the light provided by glowing screens. He took off his foul weather coat and hung it beside another that bore three stripes on the shoulder boards.

Commander Eunji Hwan, a taciturn short man, rarely smiling—his wife played around while Hwan was at sea—he was otherwise an exemplary officer and a loyal member of the Workers' Party. Stern, allowing no slackness in discipline, he was nonetheless fair and the men respected him. Not loved, but that was never a requirement in a naval officer. Hwan issued orders and the men obeyed, as was right and proper.

Mangjul shook the clinging spray off his cap and jammed it back on his head, his stay outside having invigorated him. Rubbing his cold hands, he glanced automatically at the watchstanders hovering around instruments and sensor arrays that made up one long console the length of the armored bridge. Hwan nodded to him and approached.

"Captain, the starboard picket has detected an American screening destroyer coming almost directly at us. Contact confirmed. We're also being painted by their AN/SPS-73 search radar."

"Range?"

"Forty-two kilometers."

"So, the carrier has arrived," Mangjul mused. "Our intelligence was accurate for once."

"It appears so, comrade Captain. Orders?"

"Are you ready for this?"

Hwan straightened. "The ship is yours to command, sir."

Mangjul nodded and patted the smaller man on the shoulder. "Together then. Aircraft?"

"None detected so far, but the Americans must have a CAP operating."

If he were the American carrier's commander, Mangjul thought, he would certainly be running a combat air patrol. After all, it was standard doctrine and the Americans were very good with their doctrine.

"They'll show up eventually," he said comfortably. "Are we still steering two-three-five?"

"Still on course. Captain, the Americans have to know we're here."

"We're in international waters on routine patrol, Commander. They can hardly object to our presence. Maintain course."

"Aye aye, sir."

"Eunji, prepare missiles and torpedoes for firing. Order the OSA IIs to position themselves two thousand meters ahead of us. They are also to ready their missiles."

Hwan remained silent for a moment, then nodded. "At once, comrade Captain! For the homeland!"

As Hwan turned to bark his orders, Mangjul looked at him and slowly shook his head. If his executive officer chose to treat this as a defiant blow by the people against the corrupt imperialists, he wasn't going to disabuse him. Who knows, there might be an element of truth in it. Imagine their gall bombing Yongbyon, and the proud People's Army meekly swallowed the insult. The crew? They took their orders, however illegal, and carried them out. There was nothing to think about. What did *he* think about?

After sending *Peryong Lam* to its destruction, the new Naval Command censured him, citing lack of judgment, an effective career stopper. Never mind that he was obeying Admiral Takko's orders, albeit only verbal, and that was the bitter part. They were blaming him for everything, a blatant excuse to remove a tainted tool no longer protected by his father's shadow. His pending action should prove otherwise. Peace with the capitalists and the decadent southern neighbor? Never this side of hell, as he would make clear to Pyongyang shortly. Somebody had to point out the error of the new way. That his cry of protest might cost him his life and the ships he commanded, he accepted stoically. His duty was to the homeland, not the fat generals in Pyongyang. He would miss his wife and young daughter, but life was simply one long sacrifice. That this time, the prospect that he might be sacrificing everything was merely incidental.

Hwan looked up from his bank of navigation, search and targeting radars. "Sir, we're being painted by a pair of American F/A-18 APG-73 radars. Shall I order air defense action stations?"

"Negative, Commander. We're minding our own business and threatening no one," Mangjul said with a faint smile.

One minute later, two sleek fixed wing interceptors flashed over *Laan Ghae* at three hundred meters, leaving a rolling boom of their supersonic shockwave in their wake. Mangjul winced as the pressure wave squeezed his ears and muttered a silent curse at the American fighter hotdogs strutting their stuff. Well, it won't be for much longer once their nest was disturbed.

"Comrade Captain, the American Aegis destroyer has turned to starboard and is now on one-three-five degrees. They have slowed to twenty knots."

"It's waiting to see what we'll do. Ignore them."

For now, Mangjul told himself. Any divergence from his course would make the American suspicious, at least more suspicious than he was now. The longer he maintained doubt in the enemy's mind, the less time he would have to react. He needed to nurture that doubt to execute his plan.

"Are we still being painted?"

"Search and nav radars only," Hwan responded. "Range is

now thirty-four kilometers."

Mangjul instinctively glanced at the horizon, but the choppy seas were empty. It won't be long before the American showed itself above the earth's curvature.

"Sir, both missile boats report they are at action state. Our ship is ready. We're radiating nav only."

"Very well. Maintain course and speed. Order the OSA IIs to report when the carrier comes into contact."

"Aye aye, sir."

Mangjul watched as the large American *Arleigh Burke* destroyer heaved itself over the horizon, water creaming beneath its clipper bow.

"Bring starboard tubes to firing state," he ordered quietly. "Inform the missile boats to go to ready state, but they are not to activate their targeting radars."

"Aye aye, sir. Lead ship reports they are being painted by the carrier's Mk 91 NSSM guidance and Mk 95 fire control radar. Range, sixty-four kilometers."

"Very well. Order both boats to target their missiles on the carrier using passive acquisition on the enemy's emissions."

"At once, comrade Captain!"

The radio operator emerged from the communications shack located behind the plot table. "Comrade Captain, the American destroyer requests we alter course to port. He advises that should we cross the twenty-four-kilometer exclusion zone, we will be targeted."

"Very well."

Maintaining a steady twenty-five knots, it did not take long for *Laan Ghae* to cross the arbitrary limit line. By now, the American destroyer clearly visible, a solid gray shape that seemed unaffected by the heaving seas. Looking at its sleek lines and palpable power, he lusted to command one like it. Perhaps in some future life?

"Sir, we're painted by their AN/SPY-1D radar. They have

missile lock," Hwan reported, the sound of the warning system's chirp clearly audible.

"Maintain course and speed," Mangjul said quietly. With action imminent, he felt calm and relaxed, in his element. This is what he was born to do. This was right! Kowtowing to an enemy can never be justified.

The radio operator emerged again. "Sir, the American again requests that we alter course. If we approach closer than seven kilometers, we will be fired upon without further warning."

"Very well."

Inexorably, the American DDG closed the apex of their meeting triangle.

"Commander, order the OSA IIs to shift course port to two-zero-zero. Torpedo tubes?"

"Ready for firing. Captain," Hwan said and pointed at the approaching destroyer.

Mangjul could clearly see the American's forward vertical launch system swivel to cover him, white missiles pointing at the sky. Its main 127mm gun slowly rotated toward him. By now, the two ships were barely a kilometer apart. Despite the warning, the American had not fired, but if pressed, would he really fire? He didn't think so. They blustered and protested, but they needed to be goaded into action. However, once goaded, their response was total. He wanted to finish his task before there was a response.

As the triangle closed, *Laan Ghae* swung port slightly to unmask its starboard tube launcher. With three hundred meters between them, the American warship loomed huge, and for the first time, Mangjul felt a twinge of uncertainty. He faced one of the most powerful warships afloat and his frigate suddenly looked insignificant. Then, his tactical sense took over. The enemy ship might be powerful, but its captain had miscalculated, throwing away his overwhelming advantage by allowing *Laan Ghae* to close. Political constraints? Mangjul didn't care, taking his advantages as they came. He had precious few as it is.

"Commander, order the OSA IIs to launch. When you have given the order, you may fire our torpedoes and SY-2s."

"At once, comrade Captain!"

A moment later, four fiery lances stabbed from each OSA II boat as they launched their Yingji-82 anti-ship missiles. Mangjul felt a slight shudder as his ship launched five sleek torpedoes, the weather decks momentarily obscured by a cloud of exhaust from its two SY-2 solid rocket boosters as they leaped into the low clouds. No need for any of the ships to bring up their targeting radars. The American carrier's AN/SPS and AN/SPQ radars provided all the guidance the missiles needed for their terminal attack phase.

"Missile flight time is two minutes and fifteen seconds," Hwan announced with professional detachment.

Mangjul was not interested in the missiles, keeping his eye on the enemy destroyer. Its main gun winked and there was an immediate crash somewhere aft as the 31.75-kilogram round struck. Four seconds later, it fired again, this time right behind the bridge superstructure.

Traveling at fifty-five knots, the torpedoes reached the graceful warship. All five impacted the ship's port side a scant half second apart, raising a wall of creamy water over a hundred meters into the air. The shattering explosion of torpedoes was immediately followed by a single searing detonation as the destroyer virtually disintegrated, hurling torn bits of superstructure and hull plating high into a gray sky. The shockwave slammed into *Laan Ghae*, heeling the frigate sharply to port, the watchstanders immediately clutching the consoles for support, some of them clawing at their ears from ruptured eardrums.

The armored glass that ran the length of the bridge splintered and flying shards filled the compartment with lethal fragments. The wind immediately screamed as it brought in spray and the rolling boom from the dying explosion. The helmsman tore at his face and crumpled to the deck, writhing in agony, blood dripping between his fingers. The weapons control lieutenant stared vacantly at a long spear of glass sticking from his chest before folding wordlessly against his console in silent supplication. Hwan plucked a shard from his left cheek and flung it contemptuously on the deck.

Something heavy plunged alongside the starboard side of the ship, and for a moment, Mangjul thought they'd been hit by falling debris. The roof bulkhead gave a resounding clang, evidence of at least one hit. Eventually the deadly rain stopped, leaving only a roiling sea where the destroyer had been.

Hwan slowly turned away from the destruction, his face pale, blood welling from his cut.

"Unbelievable," he whispered in awe.

"Instead of gaping, bring us hard about! Steer three-four-zero and order the OSA IIs to follow!" Mangjul snarled, anxious to extricate himself from the area, certain the Americans would respond swiftly. "Order the engine room to make revolutions for thirty knots emergency flank!" This would badly overstress the drive train, but right now, he had no time to listen to the engineer's gripes.

"At once, Captain!"

Hwan jumped to the steering wheel and spun it to port, ignoring the body at his feet, and shouted his orders. The frigate trembled as it swung to its new heading, water boiling at its stern.

Face pale, the radar operator looked up. "We have five Harpoon cruise missiles in the air, comrade Captain!"

"Ready the air defense and main guns. You have weapons free. Fire when you have lock," Mangjul snapped crisply.

With minimal defenses, he didn't give the two OSA IIs much for their survival against the sophisticated sea-skimming ship killers, obviously fired by escorting destroyers or cruisers beyond his detection range. For that matter, he did not fancy his chances either.

"Sir, the enemy has activated its AN/SLQ-32 jamming system and launched Sea Sparrow defense missiles…Sir! We have detonation of our SY-2s and Yingji-82s. One could have hit the carrier."

Mangjul wiped flying spray off his face and pursed his lips. Too soon for the missiles to have reached the carrier. That meant only one thing, they were picked off by the screening ships. He may not have struck back at the carrier, no way to be certain, but he was satisfied. Sinking the American destroyer a clear tactical victory and a powerful statement. His father would be proud of him, provided he survived his retirement at the correctional farm.

"Fire chaff!" Hwan bellowed.

The 100mm forward and aft main guns, four 57mm and six 30mm cannons, and six 25mm heavy caliber machinegun air defense weapons suddenly opened fire, the concussion and noise horrendous within the exposed bridge. The enemy had reached for him, Mangjul realized with fatalistic resignation.

A flash to starboard caught his eye and he turned to see orange and yellow fire leap into the sky where one of the OSA II missile boats followed. A second later, he heard the rolling explosion, muffled by distance. Twenty-eight lives snuffed out in a blink, but nothing compared to almost two hundred and ninety on the American destroyer.

"Comrade Captain! Both missile boats are sunk. We have three incoming Harpoons."

Mangjul straightened and clasped his hands behind his back. Fate had caught up with him. He might fight off one, but not all three. He slowly turned to Hwan and smiled.

"You have blood on your face, Eunji."

Hwan brushed his cheek, looked at the red smear on the back of his hand and shrugged. "It was a good contest, my Captain."

A bright flash off the starboard beam was proof that one of the Harpoons was destroyed, but it wasn't enough.

Traveling at 240 meters per second, the three-point-eight meter missile struck the hull immediately below the bridge and the 221-kilogram high explosive contact charge detonated, bodily heaving the bridge superstructure into the air even as the whole assembly disintegrated and its occupants shredded. The second hit midships, breaking the frigate in two to the agonized screech of tearing metal.

Its twin propellers still spinning furiously, the rear part of the stricken vessel pushed away the torn forward segment and drove itself bodily under the boiling waves. The bow section rolled slowly to port, hung suspended for a second, then the frothing waves closed over the gray hull.

Of its complement of 180, there were no survivors.

Two F/A-18s overflew the area, banked east and in perfect line-ahead formation, retreated south toward a pall of black smoke that swirled above the horizon.

* * *

Leaving behind her a broad, pencil straight creamy wake, USS *George Washington*, CVN-73, hardly swayed in the ten-foot swell. White horses marred the choppy waves beneath a dirty sky, but for the 104,000-ton *Nimitz*-class carrier, it was business as usual. Flight operations might be somewhat uncomfortable for crews scrambling around the four-point-five-acre deck, with an occasional rainsquall making people mutter what the hell they were doing in the Navy, but crappy weather was merely another environmental condition.

Two F/A-18F 'Diamondbacks' ready alert Super Hornets belonging to Strike Fighter Squadron VFA-102, moved slowly to cat one and two forward steam catapults. The green shirts directing the aircraft raised their hands when the towbar on the nose gear attached itself to a slot in the shuttle and the jet blast deflector angled up off the deck behind the tailpipes. The yellow shirts twirled their index fingers in the air and the pilots wound up power. They saluted and leaned back against the ejection seat. Both shooters extended their left leg forward in a crouch and pointed down the deck. With a surge the catapults hurled the sleek birds toward the bow. Steam swirled in their wake along the cat slides. In seconds the two fighters were lost in low cloud, only the thunder of their engines marked their passage.

In Primary Flight Control, Pre Fly, 140 feet above the deck in the carrier's island, Captain Brian Ormond sat relaxed in his leather chair watching the Air Boss manage the morning's flight evolutions. The Mini-Boss kept track of what went on deck: refueling, armament, aircraft relocation, and a dozen other chores the carrier had to do to maintain its readiness. Although the inclement weather made life less than idyllic for the crews outside, that's what they were paid for. Not enough, but the excitement made up for it…most of the time. It was hardest on the young, officers and enlisted. Long sea deployments and separation from husbands, wives and family took their toll of troubled marriages and divorces. Seafarers from time immemorial had struggled with that problem, and there were no new solutions.

Ormond had a wife. Plain, barren as a winter tree, his life turned to sunshine when she smiled. His heart was hers and she remained loyal throughout his sometimes-turbulent career. He missed not having children and was devastated when he found that his unusually low sperm count made conception unlikely. She took it well, better than he had any right to expect, women having a possessive slant on these things. She could have left him and he would have understood, however painful it might have been, but she chose to be with him and make it work. He had never forgotten the sacrifice she made and he strived to be the best husband he could. Most of the time it worked.

The phone beside him buzzed and he picked up. "Yes?"

"CIC, Captain. The PROK ships are still maintaining course and speed."

"Very well." Ormond replaced the receiver and frowned.

Having North Korean boats making a nuisance of themselves whenever the American navy prowled about was nothing startling. After all, the Yellow Sea were free waters. Well, as long as they behaved, they could do whatever the hell they wanted. Anyway, they would do exactly that, regardless of what he thought about it.

The North was stitching up a major deal with America and he didn't consider the PROK boats a threat. He had seen the CNN coverage of the pending nuclear warheads handover and pullout of American forces from the South. Admiral Pacino's remarkable action seems to have been swept under the rug for the good of the bigger picture. Everybody was all smiles, so why should he worry about three lousy little ships? They paid him to worry, that's why, he mused sardonically.

He was 160 miles from Incheon, and another four hours would see him safely at anchor with the rest of the 7th Fleet. Too bad there wasn't a major shipping channel between Hanshu and Kyusku. Compelled to go around both islands had added some twenty hours to his steaming time. It wasn't wasted time, though. He used it to exercise his stale wings, something not appreciated by all the pilots who looked on this trip as a gimme cruise. Ormond wasn't buying it, insisting that all his Hornet drivers repeat their carrier quals if they expected to fly.

Thinking about Pacino, he still found it difficult to believe what the formidable admiral had done. So out of the box, it hardly seemed in character. He understood why it was done, and even sympathized, but to actually go ahead and do it, thereby trashing his career, took some balls. Other people thought so too, but clearly not with admiration.

He picked up the phone and punched an extension button.

"CIC, Commander Varnecky."

Although the carrier's Combat Information Center was relatively quiet, nevertheless a watch had to be kept as per SOP. Besides, the executive officer liked the feeling of being in control. Well, Ormond's next fitness report should help the jovial commander get his own ship or fourth stripe. Varnecky would prefer having both, but command was still top of his list.

"Captain here. How far is *McCampbell* from the PROK force?"

"Twenty-six miles, sir."

"Order the destroyer to close and babysit them. I don't want to see them hull-up."

"Standard ROE?" Adrian 'Duke' Varnecky queried.

"Lock 'em up at ten miles and engage at five, with the usual warnings."

"Aye aye, sir."

Feeling better, Ormond exhaled. The powerful DDG more than a match for any PROK frigate and two crummy missile boats. Besides, the CAP Hornets would be keeping an eye on them in case they decided to play.

He watched two fighters trap in, both hooking the three-wire, and nodded. Flying was stimulating, and being a naval aviator also meant the pilot must get his bird down after a hassle in the air. If he couldn't get down safely, he was dead or he killed someone else, and that simply was not an option for Ormond or the *George Washington*. Picking up the phone, he ordered the mess to bring him some coffee.

Apart from sharing the sea with several oil tankers, bulk carriers and general cargo tramps, he had the place pretty much to himself. All in all, not a bad way to earn a dollar. Sipping the remains of his coffee, he watched the Air Boss manage the flights. Another good officer, he mused. He missed flying, but today's high performance birds was no place for a forty-six-year-old geriatric. He'd had his time and his wife didn't mind the extra longevity his current job gave him. Flying with your hair on fire risky at the best of times and better left to the young immortals.

The phone beside him buzzed. "Yes?"

"CIC, Captain. You might want to come down, sir. The PROK boats are being antsy. They have ignored *McCampbell's* warning to keep clear and are sticking to their course and speed."

"They like to see us hopping, Duke," Ormond said with a smile.

"Yes, sir. I simply don't like having CSS-N-1 Scrubbrush or CSS-N-8 Saccades aimed my way."

"You're a worrywart, Duke."

"Guilty."

"Okay, I'll come down and hold your hand." Still smiling, he replaced the receiver.

Varnecky might be a worrywart, but that was perfectly fine with him. The XO was looking after the ship, always a good thing. He stood up and headed for the hatch.

"I'm going down to CIC," he told the OOD.

"Very good, sir."

The marine standing guard snapped to attention. "Captain is off the bridge!"

Ormond clattered down steep stairs a level below the flight deck and entered the fully manned CIC nerve center. Large flat LED screens displayed an array of information; everything needed to maintain situational awareness, and if necessary, fight the ship. Commander Varnecky looked away from the large-scale electronic tactical display map and nodded as Ormond stood beside him.

"Okay, Duke. Talk to me."

Varnecky pointed at three red triangles advancing toward a lone blue triangle.

"*McCampbell* is now nine miles from closing with the PROK ships, Captain. I have them illuminated with our Mk 91 NSSM and Mk 95 radars to let them know we mean business. Our ship is now forty miles from their line."

"Too close," Ormond murmured, studying the display. He cast a quick glance around the dimly lit compartment. "I see you've got all stations manned and ready."

"I don't anticipate any trouble, Captain, but this situation gives us a perfect opportunity to exercise our systems and men under live conditions."

"Agreed." Ormond pulled at his chin. "Order *Shiloh* to take station five miles off our port bow. *John S. McCain* is to position itself off our stern. They are to ready their missile countermeasures. If this turns real, I want defense in depth."

"I concur, Captain." Varnecky turned to the lieutenant manning the communications station and issued quick, crisp orders.

A moment later the lieutenant looked up. "Both ships have acknowledged, Commander."

"Very well." Varnecky pointed at the plot. "*McCampbell* is approaching the five mile limit line."

The comms lieutenant turned. "Captain, *McCampbell* has issued a warning to the PROK frigate not to cross the exclusion zone. They request weapons free."

"They've gone to action state and locked on with the AN/SPY-1D." Varnecky announced. "Sir, if the PROK ship keeps advancing, do we follow the printed ROE?"

The Rules of Engagement were clear. At five miles, the DDG was perfectly free to engage, as the PROK skipper must know. However, the tactical situation was far from clear cut. This was not a hostile engagement and the PROK skipper might simply be looking to stir up the Americans. He had to know why *George Washington* was here. It was on TV and all the papers, including the North Korean ones. Nobody should be looking for a fight. Ormond certainly wasn't. So, a test of nerve, knowing the Americans would never fire first, ROE or not? Besides, if the PROK Navy intended to initiate hostilities for some unimaginable reason, they'd have done it in force, and not by sending in one creaky frigate and two OSA II missile boats. He needed to remember that between them, those missile boats packed eight CSS-N-8 Saccades—potent badasses.

It was in situations like this that being the squadron commander was less than fun. Well, he got paid to make decisions, not pass the buck.

"Signal *McCampbell* that she has weapons free, but not to engage unless the PROK ships light off their targeting radars or they are fired upon."

Seeing the look of concern on Varneky's face, Ormond wondered if he was right not to prosecute immediately. The PROK ships had not made any threatening moves. Blast them out of the water simply because they made him nervous? Man, would that make the political pot boil in the White House and around the world.

"Sir, *McCampbell* has acknowledged."

"Very well."

"They've altered course to port slightly," Varnecky said and Ormond nodded with approval.

The PROK ships were still closing, but by creating a triangle, it postponed the meeting time, giving the PROK frigate skipper an opportunity to reflect on what he was doing. Looking at the tactical display, he wasn't doing anything much, still maintaining course and speed.

The atmosphere in CIC became electric, everyone assuming a more focused posture as the situation developed. Ormond could feel the tension in the air, but not concern. This was still simply an exercise, albeit somewhat more real. He hoped this was as real as it would get.

"Captain…"

Ormond looked at the plot and nodded. *McCampbell* was now almost on top of the PROK frigate, the OSA IIs having moved ahead of it. It looked like the PROK skipper simply wanted a closer look at the DDG. The frigate shifted slightly to port and Ormond's face drained.

"Order *McCampbell* to sheer off!" he snapped to the startled comms lieutenant.

The youngster gaped at him before issuing the order.

Ormond saw the heat blooms coming off the OSA IIs as they launched and knew it was too late. A second later, the PROK frigate also launched, but by that time, his warning would never be executed.

"Vampire, vampire! We have incoming missiles!"

Ormond remembered belatedly that *Najin*-class frigates mounted two fixed five-tube torpedo launchers, one on each side. The frigate had turned to unmask one of them. Staring at the plot, face drawn tight, he waited for the inevitable.

One second, *McCampbell* was a formidable destroyer with two hundred eighty-one officers and men, and the next, she was an expanding cloud of debris. The PROK skipper had played his tactical weakness to perfection—a classic deception maneuver and Ormond had fallen for it.

Jaw clenched tight, he turned to the comms operator. "Lieutenant, order *Shiloh* and *McCain* to Harpoon the bastards!" Committing himself, he looked at Varnecky. "Bring up our SLQ-32A countermeasures suite. Get the Sea Sparrows and Phalanx to ready state as well. You have weapons free, Commander."

Tense, the exec nodded. "Aye aye, Captain."

Ormond watched the tactical display as five Harpoons converged on the PROK force, interpenetrating the flight of ten missiles coming his way. The covering Aegis cruiser and the DDG were already letting loose with volleys of Evolved Sea Sparrows. He didn't feel anything as *George Washington* added its own missiles into the basket, the white tracks in the plot converging on the incoming wings of death were clear to see.

One by one the threats were blotted from the sky despite their sophisticated anti-jamming capability and monopulse active radar. There were simply too many countermissiles for them to evade. One came within a mile from the carrier before it was detonated. Even from that distance, and despite insulation and shielding, Ormond heard it go off.

In the tactical plot, the Harpoon tracks converged on their targets. The OSA IIs were the first to go. The blip from one of the Harpoons disappeared suddenly. Two others closed on the frigate and smeared it out of the water, leaving the sea clear. Only a pall of smoke hung in the air from multiple detonations.

Three minutes, that's all it took to shatter his peaceful world. A bitchy way to earn a dollar. He sighed and his shoulders sagged.

"Duke, download all sensor logs and make ready to transmit to Yokosuka."

"Aye aye, sir. Captain..."

Ormond smiled faintly. "I know. This sucks. I'll be in my sea cabin if you want me. If you hear a detonation, that'll be Owen sending *me* a missile."

As he walked out of CIC, he wondered what he could have done differently. Hashing over it would not bring back *McCampbell* or its crew. The higher-ups and second-guessers would now decide if the lives lost was a bargain for whatever deal the White House had cooked up with North Korea.

A glance at his wristwatch, he found it almost noon. What else could go wrong with the rest of the day?

Chapter Ten

After letting it ring three times, he hoped whoever called would get tired and hang up. When it kept ringing, he sighed and picked up.

"Ashton!"

"And a good afternoon to you too. In case you were wondering, it's seven in the evening here and I haven't seen the inside of my apartment for a while."

"Special Agent Norwood, are all FBI men this cheerful?"

"Meaning that all NCIS Investigators-In-Charge are grumpy faces?"

"Okay, between the two of us, we make a half decent body. I didn't mean to growl at you."

"It's all right. You were merely the latest in a long line today. How's fishing?"

"Had a couple of nibbles, but I haven't hooked anything yet."

"I know the feeling. You dangle the bloody line all day, wear your butt flat, and then walk away with nothing. Less, since the damn fish took all your bait. This is supposed to be fun?"

Ashton grinned. "So they tell me. Seriously, I hope to get a solid bite once forensics checks something out for me. I won't be grouchy, then."

"I wish you luck. About that talk we had this morning? Nothing doing on tracing calls made on a HTC smartphone. My guy tells me those things are unbreakable and swears that even the NSA doesn't know how to get around the encryption protocols. That's why they made them like that."

"Rats! It was worth a shot. Any nibbles from a connecting phone?"

"The Puzzle Palace people are still puzzling. There is a lot of data to sift through, you know."

"That's why they have computers. Got anything on your shooter?"

"Disappeared into thin air. We got nothing, not even a shell casing."

"A pro, all right."

"Or an enterprising amateur who's seen too many movies and picked up a few tricks."

"I had cases like that and they're the hardest to crack. We don't crack all of them either."

"Been there myself. If our man is playing the Lone Ranger, unless he strikes again, we might be out of luck. You got any vacancies up there?"

"Why? Are you thinking of emigrating, Ken? Not enough excitement in Washington?"

"You're mean, did you know that? If I don't come up with a body, I might very well end up breathing some bracing northern air. Probably in Anchorage."

"I feel for you."

"Your sympathy shall not go unrewarded. I'll be in touch."

"Likewise."

Smiling, Ashton hung up. Despite his levity, he understood Norwood's frustration. Sometimes the other guy does all the right things, or is simply lucky, or both. It's the careless ones who usually get caught…and amateurs. That's why he liked the cop shows. No matter how seemingly hopeless, the hero always gets it all solved and tied with ribbon in an hour, which was about as much as he was prepared to put up with. In the real world, cold case files always outweighed the solved ones. Don't call us, we'll call you, the usual response to a relative when a loved one disappears or a body is found floating face down in Puget Sound.

He was getting morbid.

The phone rang again and he sighed. Exhaling loudly, he

picked up. "Ashton."

"It's Collander, Mr. Ashton. If you have a moment, I'd like to talk to you."

"Where are you?"

"In the lab."

"Be down in a minute, doc."

The extensive basement lab smelled of strange chemicals and strong disinfectant. Ashton ignored two technicians and the formidable Miss Pierson clicking away at her computer, as he made his way to a small corner office with waist-high glass on two sides. He walked in without knocking.

"Ah, Ashton, just the man I wanted to see." For a second, Collander looked confused, then his face brightened. "I called you, didn't I?"

"You did," Ashton said as he took a vacant chair in front of the cluttered desk.

The whole place was swamped with books, periodicals and papers, which reflected its owner. Wearing a white lab coat, Collander's hair uncombed, he looked like he had not slept in a week. That was all an illusion, of course. The doctor was always sharp, even though he appeared preoccupied. Probably due to the number of cases he juggled at any one time.

Collander ran an absent hand through his gray hair and pointed at a bulky transparent plastic bag lying precariously on the edge of the desk.

"These belong to your suspect, Colby."

Ashton stared at the bag nonplussed. "He is my man?"

"He might be. In there are his gloves, separately bagged like everything else, and they have traces of the same biodiesel recovered from the downed Gulfstream."

"How can you tell? Diesel is diesel, no?"

Collander gave an indulgent smile. "With hydrocarbon-based products, that would be true. However, even with normal diesel, there are subtle variations between batches depending on the type of raw oil feedstock used, where it came from, whether it was fractionated early in the process cycle or late, stuff like that."

"And biodiesel—"

"Can be identified even more easily. Being organic, it's not too difficult to trace the feedstock. Corn, wheat, soya and the like, all have distinct molecular signatures. Then there are the fermentation bacteria used to convert the raw vegetable matter. Product variation and source of manufacture is easy to trace."

"Rats! You matched the type of fuel in the Gulfstream to Colby's gloves?"

"I had a sample flown in by chopper from Fairchild. Although there was contamination from normal Jet A1, because of its viscosity and tendency to stick to surfaces, I obtained enough to do a mass spectroscopy analysis. The molecular signatures are identical."

"Court proof?"

"Definitely, with an unbreakable evidence chain. You must understand, Ashton, just because the gloves have matching contamination does not necessarily mean that Colby handled the biodiesel container or infected the fuel tanker. What you have is suggestive, but it's not conclusive proof of guilt."

"You know, doc, that kind of logic will do little to endear yourself to me," Ashton pointed out darkly.

Collander gave a small smile. "I often find myself having to dampen runaway enthusiasm of you investigators."

"You're running a DNA test on the gloves?" Ashton demanded sharply and Collander nodded.

"Of course. Miss Pierson is dealing with that. We should be able to get something useful from inside them. I'll get back to you in the morning. If someone else contaminated them, odds are not in our favor at finding any DNA on the outside. By its very nature, DNA doesn't do too well in an acidic environment, and biodiesel is very acidic."

"I'll worry about it once I hear from you one way or another, but what you've given me is still good news. I owe you."

"You always say that, but you never pay up," Collander grumbled and Ashton wondered whether this was one of doc's attempts at humor.

"Next time we go out, the drinks are on me. How about that?"

Collander smiled. "I was only joking, of course."

"The deal still stands."

"Done."

Upstairs, he wagged a finger at Hollice. The young agent sauntered over and sat on the edge of the desk.

"Fates are smiling at us today, my boy," Ashton said, ignoring Hollice's choice of seating.

"Collander had some good news? I overheard you talking to him before you went down."

"It could be Colby. He found the same biodiesel that brought down the Gulfstream on his gloves."

"That doesn't prove he did it."

"And you're raining on my parade, which sadly, I'll have to note in your next evaluation report," Ashton growled. Hollice merely chuckled.

"Just yanking your chain, chief. Although not proof, it's better than what we had this morning. Is Collander checking for DNA?"

Ashton stared at the kid. Was he creating another version of himself?

"In case someone else handled the gloves, yes. We'll know tomorrow."

"Good. I hate having to arrest someone before dinner."

"And what have *you* dug up, Mr. Know-it-All?"

"Not very much," Hollice admitted. "Colby is someone who should have been discharged, but he's good at his job and that's probably why he is tolerated. He is up for sergeant again, you know."

"Is he now? And Higgs?"

"After leaving the Navy, his old man had a couple of odd jobs in Seattle before moving to Denver. He is a senior executive at the Resolute Energy Corporation. With his training, he is a valuable commodity. As for Higgs junior, everybody at the base thinks he is a bit of an oddball and standoffish. Makes like he is an officer. The guys are amused, but consider him harmless."

"What do the guys say about Colby?"

"An extrovert, but everyone who has seen him since his brother died has noticed a change. He is no longer so jolly and keeps muttering about getting even."

"Well, he could be on an emotional down. After all, his brother died under pretty gruesome circumstances."

"And getting even?"

Ashton shrugged. "He could be talking about the North Koreans."

"Or maybe about the Navy. Let's not forget that Admiral Pacino was the single causal factor that resulted in Colby's brother getting killed. All that talk about applauding Pacino could be pure guff."

"Yes, it could. Let's sleep on it until Collander gets back to us."

* * *

President Samuel Walters twirled the brandy in the large crystal balloon and took an appreciative sniff. He rolled the spirit in his mouth before swallowing, savoring the smoothness and flavor of the spirit. Picking up *The Washington Post*, he continued reading the editorials.

Everyone still buzzed about the deal with North Korea and the pending troop pullout. As usual the Republicans were punching holes in the program, chagrined that Walters had pulled off a coup of the century, something that had eluded all previous administrations. Several congressmen on both sides have voiced their misgivings at the withdrawal, but their cries held little conviction when commentators found that those same concerned voices sheltered influential arms, aerospace and missile firms in their districts. An expected and natural reaction, and Walters ignored the protest as wind stirring the reeds.

When he talked to Kham Chang-uk, he found the man sincere and genuinely keen to go through with the deal. There was still an understandable degree of mutual suspicion, which Walters took pains to dispel, and he walked away with a strong impression that he had laid the necessary groundwork to tackle Tung In-san on the official level. Tanner's more substantive discussions with Kham had not done any harm either.

Russia didn't seem to care much one way or another, having domestic problems on its agenda to deal with. The Chinese reaction, although guarded, was nevertheless positive. The proposed peace treaty with South Korea had to be good for everyone. Walters could not believe that China wasn't relieved to be dealing with a more moderate PROK leadership. Sung Kang-dae's belligerent posture and the lamentable state of his country must have been an ideological embarrassment, although Sung had not seen it that way, of course.

He put down the paper and took another sip. Glancing at his watch, almost eleven. For once, he looked forward getting to bed early and sleeping in. Cathy and the VP would be in tomorrow and he would have someone warm to cuddle with in bed. After a stifled yawn, he finished the brandy and stood up.

When the phone rang, he frowned and stared at the instrument with foreboding. It kept ringing and he finally picked up.

"What is it, Manfred?"

"How did you know it was me?" the chief of staff demanded.

"Who else would dare call me at this hour?"

"I'm sorry to spoil your evening, Mr. President, but you need to come down right away. We have another situation in the Yellow Sea. *George Washington* came under missile attack from PROK ships."

Walters felt his shoulders sag. "An attack in force?"

"A frigate and two patrol boats only. Somebody might not have liked what the new government was doing and decided to pour sand into the works."

"Their version of Pacino, eh? Damnation! What's the damage?"

"We sank them, but it cost us a destroyer."

"Why can't they make their protests marching up and down the streets of Pyongyang, waving placards? Never mind. Who's down there?"

"Tanner and Stone are with me. McDonald delivered the bad news."

"Let me put some pants on. Five minutes," Walters said and hung up. He threw off his maroon robe and reached for the cream corduroy blazer.

With two Secret Service agents tagging after him, he took the elevator to the ground floor. On the way toward the Oval Office, the West Wing was alive with people. The government did not rest even while the president slept. With the news Manfred just delivered, he figured there would not be much sleep for him tonight either.

Unice sat behind her desk, busily clicking away at her computer, looking crisp and fresh as though she'd had a rest and shower. She lifted her head and beamed at him.

"Good evening, Mr. President."

"That remains to be seen," Walters growled and walked into his office, his two minders taking station on either side of the door.

Everyone stood as he eased himself behind the *Resolute* desk and motioned to them to sit. He leaned forward and fixed the Chairman of the Joint Chiefs in his sights.

"Let's have it, General."

"The facts are pretty simple, Mr. President. While still some four hours from Incheon, a PROK frigate and two OSA II missile boats intercepted *George Washington* and her escorts. Despite being warned off, they continued to close. Ordered to interdict, one of our destroyers was torpedoed and the PROK ships launched cruise missiles at the carrier. In a defensive counterstrike all the PROK ships were sunk."

"Our destroyer must have been pretty close to get torpedoed," Walters mused.

"Yes, sir," McDonald said in a tight voice. Walters stared at him. "As per the ROE, we couldn't fire until fired upon, sir. Getting that close wasn't the first time this happened. The PROK boats like to see us get twitchy."

"Survivors?"

"None, sir."

"I see. Okay, General. I'll leave the dissection to Admiral Parker. The big question is: why? Did we provoke them?"

"Absolutely not, Mr. President. This came completely out of the box for everybody."

"Any reaction from the PROK Navy?"

"Not even search radar."

"Keep Stone in the loop when you find out more," Walters said in dismissal.

"Thank you, sir."

Walters watched the huge man walk out and ground his teeth. "What the *hell* is going on over there?"

"From what I understand, sir," the National Security Advisor started, "this appears to be a completely off-the-wall operation. With all the talks we had with Premier Yeum and Kham, it makes no sense for them to mount a strike."

"You're saying that someone over there was disgruntled enough to decide to bag himself a carrier?"

"That's exactly what I'm saying."

"Well, if you're going to knock something off, it might as well be the biggest. What kind of a destroyer did we lose?"

"USS *McCampbell*, an *Arleigh Burke* DDG with a complement of 281."

"That's a front line ship, Graham. How the hell did she get suckered?"

"McDonald is looking into it."

"A lot of letters to write." Walters fixed his eyes on Tanner. "What's your take on this?"

"Until we get more facts, I'm sticking with Stone's explanation. I'd like to call Yeum and get those facts."

The phone rang and Walters picked up. He listened for a while and nodded. "Okay, Unice. Put him on." Wearing a bemused smile, he looked at the expectant faces standing before him and pressed the speaker button.

"Mr. President? This is Tung In-san, speaking through a translator. You will have to forgive me, but my English is not up to what I have to say."

"That's perfectly all right, sir, since my understanding of Hangul is nonexistent."

"You must have heard by now of the unfortunate incident in the Yellow Sea, Mr. President."

"I've just been briefed."

"As I have. While I don't have all the information surrounding the event, I want to assure you that no one in my government ordered this tragic attack on your aircraft carrier and destroyer. There is no way I can prove this to you, sir, except to ask that you believe me and accept my profound regret and apology. I did not expect that our first talks would be conducted under such awkward circumstances."

"I accept your apology, sir," Walters said immediately, trying to gauge the mood of the Supreme Leader.

"I am most relieved to hear you say that, Mr. President. However, a mere apology may bring scant comfort or compensation for the loss of your ship and crew, but I will try to meet whatever compensation you see fit to demand. Furthermore, I'll not seek any reparations from the United States as a result of the attack made by Admiral Pacino."

"Sir—"

"I would be honored if you would call me Tung, Mr. President."

"Thank you...Tung. Your gesture is magnanimous and appreciated. However, I cannot accept it. After talking to Admiral Pacino, I understand why he took the action he did. However justifiable, I cannot condone it. America will fully compensate your country for the damage done to the Yongbyon facility. As for your offer of reparations for the loss of our destroyer, I consider your apology as payment in full."

Tanner gaped at him and Stone grinned broadly, holding up his thumb in approval. Walters heard a muffled conversation from the phone before the translator came back.

"Mr. President, I don't know what to say."

"Tung...what happened today is deplorable, but I don't hold you responsible. The lives lost on both sides should not be forgotten, I'll see to it, but I don't want this incident to distract us from the broader objectives you proposed, sir."

"I have no right to expect that you would still wish to entertain a dialogue or seek an agreement, but I am gratified that you're prepared to do so."

"Both our countries stand at a crossroad. A lone voice of dissent should not divert us from the path of honor, and Admiral Pacino's action has given me much to think about. Although justice has been meted out to the frigate captain who initiated the attack on our carrier, perhaps his action was done to voice a similar cry of protest you may want to reflect on."

"President Walters, my navy carries out the policies I set. There is no room for dissent. If you had not destroyed that frigate, I certainly would have shot its commander."

Walters pursed his lips and nodded. If he hoped to engage the North Korean leader in philosophy, it was clearly not going to get him anywhere. Given their respective cultures and history, it was perhaps too much to expect Tung to reciprocate.

"Sir, Secretary of State Tanner has reached a broad agreement with Premier Yeum on the proposals made by Chairman Kham. The United States government is prepared to meet all the conditions set by the Premier. I have some negotiations to do with President Samun, but I don't foresee any difficulties positioning our carrier at Haeju Bay for the handover of your nuclear warhead inventory."

"Premier Yeum is still discussing details with our Russian and Chinese allies, Mr. President, but I also anticipate reaching an acceptable agreement."

"I appreciate your prompt call, sir, and I look forward to meeting you personally on board the *George Washington*."

There was more hurried background discussion while Tanner looked incredulous.

"You're prepared to be there, Mr. President?"

"Should I not be?"

The Supreme Leader chuckled. "I also look forward to meeting you, sir."

"Until then," Walters said and switched off the speaker.

Tanner took a step closer to the desk. "Mr. President, you cannot seriously consider going! Tung may be talking sweetness and light now, but we cannot forget who that son of a bitch is."

"I'm not forgetting anything, Larry. Tell me why I shouldn't be going?"

"The security implications alone—"

"My presence will be the single most potent gesture to Tung that America is sincere at meeting its part of the bargain. Think of it. A photo op of me on the deck of *George Washington* with Tung In-san and a stack of nuclear warheads around us."

"I'm thinking of it, including the part where one of those things goes off."

"Right in the middle of their largest western base? You're being melodramatic, Larry. Even Sung would not have contemplated something that dumb. Besides, didn't Kham say that he's also inviting the Chinese and the Russians to supervise the dismantling of the triggers? As for security, I'll be on a carrier with five thousand sailors around me, not in Pyongyang."

"I'm still not convinced that it's a good idea, that's all," Tanner said stubbornly.

"It's my decision…Manfred?"

Cottard frowned and rubbed his nose. "I can see Larry's point of view, sir, but I can also appreciate yours. It might be a wise gesture to attend."

"I'm glad you see it my way," Walters said wryly.

"Mr. President," Cottard went on unperturbed. "I understand why you refused reparations from Tung, he's got nothing to pay it with, but was it a good idea not to accept his reciprocal gesture? He might have been insulted. Face."

Walters pursed his lips and nodded. "I haven't thought of it that way and you might be right, but I had a reason. We must show not only Tung, but to the world at large, that America meets its obligations and pays its debts. He owes us now, and that could come in handy if we have some tough negotiations down the line."

"We lose a destroyer and we shake hands? That's not likely to go down well with the families of those we lost. The Republicans will eat you alive."

"Damnation! We sank their ships and the board is clean. What do they expect me to do? Bomb Pyongyang? Tung went as far as he could…further. Just because they have a new regime over there doesn't mean they changed ideologies, as you rightly pointed out, Larry. They're still hardline communists who hate everything we stand for. We try and make a big thing out of this, Tung could tell us to jump and renege on the whole deal. Or worse, he could decide to hand over his nukes to Russia and

China, and still insist that we pull out of South Korea, but under hostile conditions and with their long range missiles still in place. Do we want that and face perhaps another fifty years of armistice? Think what the Republicans would make of that! If I'm wrong, I'll find out come the next elections."

Tanner looked at him searchingly. "Mr. President, I never cease to be amazed by your ready grasp of international and domestic politics. You can't be as young as you claim to be."

Walters chuckled. "I've aged a week for every day I've been in this office, Larry. I didn't mean to have a go at you, Manfred, but you do tend to be overprotective sometime. You have to let me do my job. Anyway, we'll hash this out in detail and work out the best spin to put on it before Granger talks to his gaggle."

"It's my job to protect your office, Mr. President," Cottard said stiffly, clearly stung.

"Later, Manfred…Larry?"

"This *could* give us a lever with Tung, sir. You're right about not pushing too hard. Given his background as you said, it's incredible that he's gone as far as he did."

"Manfred, send the Vice President a note and tell her I'll talk to her in the morning."

"Yes, sir."

"Now, how do we spin this for the press?"

* * *

Marchinson brought Colby into the room, nodded to Ashton and closed the door after him.

"Oh, it's you two again," Colby snorted with a smirk. "Well, I haven't got any new answers for you guys."

"Please sit down, Mr. Colby," Ashton said, waited for the airman to make himself comfortable, then nodded to Hollice.

Hollice took out a little pocket recorder, switched it on, and placed it on the desk.

"My name is NCIS Agent Brandon Hollice. With me is NCIS Investigator-In-Charge Robert Ashton and Air Force Corporal Shawn Colby, who is being questioned on the suspicion that on the morning of March 2, he contaminated a tanker containing standard Jet A1 fuel with a quantity of biodiesel. This fuel was subsequently loaded onto a Navy Gulfstream V *en route* from Tokyo, Japan, to Washington DC, carrying two pilots, a cabin attendant and Admiral Pacino. The contaminated fuel caused the said aircraft to crash, which resulted in the deaths of the two pilots. At this stage, Mr. Colby, do you wish to say anything?"

"You guys don't know what you're talking about. I wasn't anywhere near that aircraft. Talk to anybody."

"We did. Although you were at the bar like you said, Airman Second Class Marrick remembers that you stepped out for about twelve minutes. That would have given you plenty of time to drive to the waiting fuel tanker and slip in the biodiesel. I checked."

"You're crazy! I was in the can."

"For twelve minutes?"

"The old insides aren't as good as they used to be, and Marrick is a liar."

"Airman Carmeli remembers you saying something like, 'Back in a sec. Gotta do something.'"

"Like I told you, I was in the can."

Hollice bent down and lifted a transparent evidence bag. When Colby saw the gloves, something went out of his bluster.

"I believe these are yours."

Colby shrugged. "A pair of gloves. They could be anybody's."

"That's right, except they're not. These were found in your locker."

"So you say."

"Your DNA says so, Mr. Colby."

"Okay, they may be my gloves. So what?"

"We found traces of biodiesel on them, and we know that

your work doesn't involve the handling of biodiesel. What's more, it's the same biodiesel used to contaminate the fuel truck for the Gulfstream. We'll be happy to produce the test evidence at your court-martial."

"Court-martial? You guys are crazy! Anybody could have smeared a bit of biodiesel on those gloves and planted them on me. Even Marrick. You've got nothing to go on with."

Hollice smiled disarmingly. "True, but for one small problem." He reached down again and produced a black-and-white photo. "That's an imprint of your left glove on the side of the tanker. It's a perfect match."

"So?"

"You spilled some biodiesel when you poured it into the tanker. You brushed the spill with your gloves, and when you propped yourself against the tanker, you left a smudge on its side. Once we found that your gloves were contaminated, we took a closer look at the tanker. Anything to say?"

Ashton stared hard at Colby in a gambit to intimidate his victim into an impromptu confession. This was the time when Colby would either break or laugh in his face. The evidence they had was compelling, but circumstantial at best. A good JAG officer would get the airman off easily.

Colby sat back and folded his hands across his chest. "You want me to say something? Okay, here it is. Someone is trying to railroad me and you guys have fallen for it. I never handled any biodiesel that night and you can't prove otherwise."

"Well, maybe we can," Hollice said slowly and held up another photo. It was only a partial imprint of a boot, but Colby's face drained, unable to tear his eyes off it. "That's the forward part of your right boot."

"You told us you were nowhere near that tanker, Mr. Colby," Ashton said softly, but he didn't need to shout. He held the man's total attention. "You said you only supervised the tanker refueling. So how did an imprint of your boot happen to get on the loading ledge, unless your foot was in that boot when you opened the inspection hatch to dump in a load of biodiesel?"

"Do you want to claim that somebody else took your boots, wore them when he contaminated the fuel, then replaced them in your locker?" Hollice added with a confident smile. "You know, extracting DNA from a sweat-soaked boot is even easier than getting it off a glove. Guess what? We didn't find anybody else's except yours."

"You guys have been busy little beavers, haven't you?" Colby grated, hate contorting his face.

"It's not like you made it difficult for us," Hollice said indifferently.

Ashton leaned forward. "Well, Mr. Colby?"

Colby sat silent for a while, then grimaced and spread his hands. "What do you want me to tell you? That I did it? I did."

"It was your brother?" Ashton prompted.

"Eric had everything going for him. He was up for Master Chief, but he was always the smart one in the family. Not smart enough to grease for an officer maybe, it takes a corncob up your ass for that, but he did all right. It's the chiefs who run the ships anyway, just like the noncoms do everywhere else. It took an officer to screw up his life, like the one who screwed up mine. When I heard that Eric had bought it, I vowed to make them pay, and getting the guy who caused it would have been sweet. Mind you, I still applaud what Pacino did to those gooks, but he killed my brother doing it. Eric didn't deserve to die. I simply couldn't rest without taking out Pacino, now could I?"

"The problem is, Mr. Colby, you took out two innocent pilots instead and destroyed valuable Navy property," Ashton said.

"Yeah, kinda tough on those guys, but I never figured the damned thing would crash. I thought they'd divert to Portland and Pacino would have shitted his pants. I didn't intend for anybody to die."

"You know, Mr. Colby, they all say that." Ashton picked up

the phone and dialed an extension. "We're all done here, Captain."

"What happens now?" Colby demanded.

"Major Stowell will charge you with two counts of premeditated murder, attempted murder, and sabotage of a Navy aircraft, causing destruction of said aircraft. There could be other charges."

Colby sat up in alarm. "But I told you! I never intended to kill anybody."

"You sabotaged the Gulfstream. By doing that, you must have known the aircraft could crash."

"Well, sure, but—"

"End of story, Mr. Colby."

There was a knock and Marchinson walked in. Two MPs hovered outside. Ashton switched off the recorder and waved at Colby.

"He's all yours, Captain. Charge him and lock him up."

"Okay, Colby. Move it!"

Colby slowly stood up and grinned. "I'll be seeing you guys in court."

"You will indeed," Ashton agreed.

The MPs marched Colby out and Marchinson closed the door. Exhaling loudly, Ashton sat back and grinned at Hollice.

"If he only kept his mouth shut, he would have walked, but guys like that think they're smart and they have to tell everybody how smart they are. You did well, Brandon. Very well. Suggesting to Collander to check for boot prints on the tanker was a neat move."

"Just showing off my own smarts, chief," Hollice said brightly, looking pleased with himself. Ashton frowned.

"A word of advice, Mr. Hollice. You're a bright investigator with a lot of potential, but you don't know everything. Us oldies still have one or two things to teach you. In our business, overconfidence can be fatal at so many levels. You only have to look at Colby."

Hollice sobered instantly. "I apologize, Mr. Ashton. I did not mean to sound cocky. It's just that you allowed me a certain informality—"

"You can be informal all you like with me, but you must be professional, first, foremost, always. Get dazzled by your own cleverness and I'll have no more use for you."

"It won't happen again, sir."

"Forget it." Ashton peered at the youngster and grinned. "It felt good nailing Colby, didn't it?"

After a moment, Hollice relaxed and the old boyish smile was back in place. "I can see how you can get a buzz when things land your way. When the word gets out at the office, everybody will be talking about it. The famous Ashton has struck again."

"Despite the intrepid help of his fumbling sidekick," Ashton added dryly. "This time we won. Next time…"

He hated to pour cold water on Hollice's enthusiasm, but the boy needed a reality check. At the moment, he was justifiably proud and satisfied with a piece of well executed work, but that feeling could all too easily be replaced with arrogance. Very easily. He didn't want Hollice to learn that one the hard way, like he was forced to, until someone who cared took him aside and explained the facts of life in a language he understood.

Ashton shut out the uncomfortable memories, slapped the desk and stood up. "Time we were out of here. We've got a report to write."

Hollice grinned. "You mean, *you've* got a report to write."

* * *

"The number you have called is no longer in service. For further information, please call the Housing Services Center. The number you have—"

Pacino replaced the receiver and frowned. If the phone was

disconnected, that meant Ruth was gone, and probably Linda as well. Why couldn't the woman listen and stay put! To make sure, he dialed Linda's number, only to receive the same canned response. Well, that confirmed it. If the two of them were coming over, why the hell didn't they at least give him some notice? Spring it on him as a surprise? Ruth wasn't like that, but she did enjoy pulling one on him on occasion. Right now, he didn't need any surprises.

Not that he would have minded seeing her, far from it. It would be useful having at least one person cheering for him during tomorrow's hearing. Two, if he counted Linda. Ruth should have called him, *damn it all*!

He picked up the phone again and dialed. These calls would cost the Navy a few dollars, but right then, he hardly gave it a thought.

"Admiral Pacino's office. Chief Petty Officer Karter speaking."

"Good morning, Karter. It's Pacino."

"It's good to hear from you, sir. How is Washington?"

"Cold, and there is still snow on the ground."

"We had some last night. Crazy weather, sir. How can I help you, Admiral?"

"I'd like to speak to Owen if he's available."

"Sorry, Admiral. He took off yesterday afternoon for Washington. I understand he is appearing at your hearing tomorrow, sir."

Pacino nodded. Powell said that he would be appearing. As his immediate superior officer, Owen would be required to testify. Although that could have been done over a video link, it would hardly deliver the kind of impact Fisher wanted for the government. Unless Owen was coming down for some other reason?

"I tried calling my wife, Chief—"

"I thought you knew, sit," Karter sounded surprised. "Mrs.

Pacino and Linda Pacino flew out with Admiral Owen."

"No, I didn't know."

"Women can be tricky like that, sir. Pardon me for saying so."

Ruth should have told him what she planned! Was that revenge for not telling her about his crash? He winced at the thought of what she would say when she finds out that he'd been shot. How could he tell her if her phone was out?

You're making excuses, Admiral.

"What's the situation with the packing and shipping to Norfolk?"

"Housing Services saw to everything, Admiral."

"You mean you saw to everything."

"I was glad to help, Admiral, and Commander Leighton made sure that you're all squared away at this end."

"Thanks, Karter. I doubt we'll be running into each other again and I want to tell you how much I appreciated having you work for me."

"It was a privilege, sir. Don't take no guff off anybody at the hearing, sir. Lots of guys here cheered when the news broke about what you did."

"Thanks for that. If you're ever near Leavenworth one of these days, be sure to look me up. That's likely to be my permanent address for a while."

"You shouldn't talk like that, sir," Karter said firmly. "But, yeah, I'll look you up."

Pacino gently replaced the receiver, breaking the connection, and not only with Karter. He had broken a connection with a whole way of life. Nothing of his past was left there, not even Ruth. Staring at the sleeve of his new civilian jacket, he didn't even have the Navy to fall back on, a Navy that now sought to destroy him.

He stood, walked to the window and gazed absently at Washington's lit sprawl and the twin ribbons of traffic along Maryland Avenue. Was it worth it? He had asked himself that question a number of times and he still had not found a new answer. What he did felt right. He only regretted the lives lost on *Stethem*, and he stood ready to accept responsibility for that despite Powell's adamant order that he must not do any such thing publicly. Powell meant well and was only looking after his client's best interest, but the lawyer wasn't the one haunted by ghosts of the dead and the faces left burnt or mutilated. If anything good comes out of the hearing, he promised himself that those men would be looked after.

If he was to believe the incredible reports that had the entire media buzzing, it had not ended with *Stethem*. He found it astonishing that a powerful, ultra-modern warship like *McCampbell* could have been sunk by one lousy PROK frigate. The details were sketchy, and whatever Parker knew, he wasn't telling.

If the reports were right, the attack appeared to be an isolated incident of revenge, apparently unconnected with anything Pacino did. He wished he could believe that. He did not relish the prospect of having 281 more lives stalking his nights. If it was an act of a lone madman, he could even understand President Walters' position not to retaliate. America had an important peace deal to conclude, despite urging from the Republicans to exact toll for the unprovoked attack. Fortunately for the administration, most of the public seemed to be on the president's side, as were the Europeans in a rare show of solidarity.

Would this latest development and the pending events surrounding the peace deal with North Korea overshadow his hearing, leeching any popular sympathy he enjoyed to date? An impossible question, but Powell assured him that he still commanded considerable public approval. Well, he would find out tomorrow if he'd been relegated to the back pages. As long as he was heard, that was the only thing that mattered.

"Your voice will not be heard if you don't follow my instructions, Admiral!" Powell had said crossly, trying hard to keep his exasperation under control.

Pacino was forced to smile, recalling the frustrated expression on the commander's face as they went through some of the questions Fisher was likely to throw at him.

"No! You only answer the question asked. Don't elaborate or volunteer information. The government must prove its case. You don't have to prove yours."

"Answer yes or no, is that it?" Pacino growled, a little exasperated himself.

"What did you expect, Admiral? A fireside chat?"

"But if I don't say—"

"You'll have your say when I cross-examine you. Another thing. Never answer a question that isn't asked. Fisher will launch into a preamble, then look at you, waiting for you to take up the conversation. You must resist that. Or he might decide to get friendly and chummy, draw you out. Resist that. In that hearing room, he is your enemy regardless of how nice a guy he might appear. He really is a nice guy, but he won't be for you, not in that chamber."

"Will anybody be on my side?"

"I'll be on your side."

"I didn't mean—"

"Remember, Fisher will be pursuing the factual side of the events and how they relate to the specified charges. He will not be interested in the psychological angle or your state of mind. You're an admiral and a senior Navy officer. Your mental competence will not be questioned. It will be assumed. Because it will be assumed, all your acts will be deemed to be made rationally with full awareness of what you were doing."

"They were, but—"

"And because they were, he won't care about the 'but' part. Your actions were motivated by complex personal and social reasons. Explaining them in a coherent, succinct manner won't be easy. If he can get you talking to draw you out, he will twist your words or the intent of your statements, which will force you to elaborate in order to clarify what you originally said."

"Damn it, if I don't get a chance to say why I did this—"

"Admiral, listen to me. He will misrepresent whatever you say until you get sidetracked and your statements become rambling and irrelevant. If he succeeds in doing that, he'll demonstrate to the Investigating Officer that beneath the façade of a responsible naval officer lies a deranged mind who isn't fit to stand in the chain of command. Nobody will care about your son or the lives lost on *Curtis Wilbur*. All they'll see is a tired old man who broke under pressure and caused a major international incident."

"Answer specific questions and don't extemporize. Got it."

"Very good, Admiral. Remember, always stick to the question asked. If Fisher doesn't ask a question, no matter if his statement might sound like one, keep your mouth shut. Don't make flippant responses or try to be amusing. Let Fisher supply the comedy. You don't need to defend yourself. That's my job."

"And if the IO decides I have to face a general court?"

"One battle at a time. You cannot worry about an event that hasn't happened. That's a good way to lose focus on what you've got to do now."

"Always sound advice, Commander. Any development on the administrative discharge possibility?"

"I raised it with Fisher and he passed it on to Admiral Parker. My guess is they want to see how the first day goes before making up their mind. If Fisher can get an upper hand and smell a clean sweep, Parker may risk wearing what you have to say in order to bury you. We'll find out tomorrow, Admiral."

Looking at the flowing traffic below, Pacino wondered how many people cared what he had to say, or cared what was happening with North Korea. Most of them simply wanted to be left alone and not be bothered. They had enough troubles in their dreary lives to be concerned with events on the other side of the world.

That's apathy, Admiral, his inner voice sneered at him.

For someone who had trashed his career to make a point, this was not the time for despondency or defeatism.

Powell was right. Maintain a focused positive attitude and he would get his point across. The president had been sympathetic, but the administration was not a dictatorship. It had Congress to contend with. Still, if Walters showed a degree of political will, change could happen. A battle Pacino could not fight, far outside his level of understanding and competence. He might be a deputy fleet commander, but in Washington's power mill, he was just another piece of raw fodder to be ground up.

He turned away from the window, strode to the bar cabinet, and got himself a bottle of Wild Turkey and fizzy water. Dropping in ice, he sat down at the writing table. Powell offered to come around later to go over the hearing, but Pacino quashed that. He needed time to think and reflect—alone. If he had forgotten something, it was far too late to rake over it now. He could stomach only so much cramming up. Besides, this was only a hearing. Despite Powell's brave words, Pacino was certain he would face a general court. That's when everybody would feel the pointy end. The hearing merely the first round.

He would not have minded dinner downstairs or somewhere outside, but after yesterday's experience, he allowed Norwood to manage him and he had eaten alone, keenly conscious of an FBI man standing outside his door. If he needed a reminder, he only had to flex his bandaged arm and side. Hell of a way to run a country when a man could not eat where he wanted. Right then, he felt sorry for Walters. The president may wield the mightiest military machine on earth, but he was more a prisoner than someone in solitary, gilded cage notwithstanding.

The phone rang and he picked up. "Pacino."

"Hello, darling. You'll never guess where I am," Ruth said brightly and he grinned, the world not such a gloomy place after all.

"You know what you called me the last time we talked?"

"And you're still a rat, you heel. I found out from Owen that you were shot. Why did you keep that from me?"

"It's only a scratch and you were calling in the middle of the night. Did you think I would unleash that on you and give you nightmares?"

"I had nightmares in the morning."

"By then it was old news and you were in a better shape to handle it. Anyway, I would have told you, and I tried, but that was before I found out you had eloped."

He heard her merry giggle and knew everything was all right. Ruth was a staunch girl and the shooting wasn't enough to come between them.

"These aircraft Owen flies around with, I didn't know admirals played with such fancy toys. Had I known, I might have taken advantage of it earlier."

"Believe me, it's not all that's been cracked up to be. Is Linda with you?"

"She's chatting with Owen. We're due to land at McChord at some ghastly hour at night before continuing for Washington. Owen has to be there for your hearing."

"I know."

"Now we'll all be there to cheer you on. If you're worried about our belongings, don't be. It's all been taken care of."

"So I heard. The Navy can still do some things right when it wants to."

"Not mad at me for springing this on you?"

"I've got a big bed and nobody to help me keep it warm."

"Hold on a little longer and it will get plenty warm," she whispered and Pacino smiled. Norwood better not have bugged his room or there would be some embarrassing scenes to explain away—embarrassing for the FBI!

"I can't wait to see you. Give my love to Linda."

"I'll do that. Miss you."

"Me too. Can you get Owen for me?"

"Sure. I'll see you tomorrow."

A moment later, a familiar gruff voice answered. "How you doing, Kenneth?"

"Wishing I was someplace else, David, but I don't want to talk about the hearing."

"And I couldn't anyway."

"What the hell happened with *George Washington*?"

Pacino heard a heavy sigh. "It's the damned ROE. On one hand, I fully agree with the fire only if you are fired upon policy, but as this incident demonstrated all too vividly, it leaves us vulnerable to a preemptive strike, as *McCampbell's* skipper found to his cost."

"The papers were short on detail, but for that destroyer to be torpedoed, it had to be damn close."

"Too close to avoid."

"Why the hell did Kinnock allow himself to get suckered like that? He was a smart skipper."

"All destroyer drivers are hot dogs, as you know, and Kinnock wanted to show that PROK frigate that he wasn't taking any shit off anybody. Ordinarily, there would have been nothing wrong with that tactic. Unfortunately, the frigate captain played by a different rulebook. We don't know quite exactly why he launched his attack, but we can guess."

"He was making a statement," Pacino said softly.

"Like you were, except he won't be facing a hearing. An interesting fact about that skipper. He was the squadron commander during your Key Resolve exercise. His corvette launched the attack on *Curtis Wilbur*."

Pacino made an involuntary hiss. "Bastard."

"I thought that would cheer you up. The good thing is that he's on the bottom now."

"There is justice after all."

"But it came at a pretty stiff price. It cost us *McCampbell*. I'll be seeing you tomorrow, Kenneth, and we may talk again."

"Thanks for everything, Admiral. Especially bringing Ruth and Linda with you."

"Hell, since we were heading in the same direction…"

"Until tomorrow."

"Good luck at the hearing, Kenneth," Owen said and cut contact.

Pacino slowly replaced the receiver, picked up his glass and took a sip. After a moment, he took another. Maybe he would watch a bit of TV before going to bed.

He always kept himself busy, always active, and this enforced idleness was unsettling. At Yokosuka, he had administrative responsibilities to discharge, and when at home, Ruth was there to fill his evenings and nights. Now, he had neither. It was enough to drive one to drink.

He took another sip of the cheap whiskey.

Chapter Eleven

The drive to JAG headquarters in Falls Church, Virginia, made in a heavy black Ford Taurus. Another like it followed close behind, while one stayed in the lead. These precautions struck Pacino as a little silly, but he wasn't going to tell the FBI how to do their job. If that's how they wanted to run things, it was perfectly fine with him.

When they neared the docks area, the car needed to do a bit of maneuvering, but the little motorcade was finally checked through the main gate and they pulled into the visitor parking lot. As soon as Pacino and Powell stepped out, with Norwood and Kelner hovering close by them, the press gaggle surged forward. Taken aback by the frontal assault, Pacino glanced at Powell. The ex-SEAL commander stepped in front of him and raised his hands.

"Admiral Pacino cannot make any statements now!"

"Have a heart, Powell!" somebody cried out. "One question!"

"I've also got a question, dammit!" another voice shouted.

There was a rush forward and Norwood took over. He stood beside Powell and glared at the reporters.

"Clear the way! We need to get inside." His stern voice brooked no argument and the media reluctantly parted.

Powell glanced ruefully at Pacino, a tight smile playing at the corner of his mouth. "I guess you're still news, Admiral."

"Damn it all! I thought I was going to get mobbed. I've never seen anything like it."

"It doesn't happen here all that often. Most of the stuff JAG handles hardly ever makes it into the papers."

Never having been exposed to something like this before, Pacino not sure how to take it. He understood what Powell told him, play the media, but it was not as easy as the laconic lawyer made it out to be. Compared to his ordered navy life, this was total chaos. Well, he was in their world now and he better learn to handle it.

More reporters waited to ambush them on the first floor, but Powell steered him quickly into the relative peace and quiet of the hearing room. At least Pacino thought it was peace and quiet until he saw the hovering press lining the back wall, recorders and cameras waiting to capture every moment of what they anticipated would be unfolding drama. The half dozen rows of public gallery seats were full. It included a fair sprinkling of Navy brass, some of the faces familiar, clearly there as more than mere spectators.

Taking it all in, not prepared to be such a center of attention, Pacino was startled when a pair of arms circled his neck and a cuddly form embraced him.

"Hello, sailor," Ruth whispered into his ear and gave him a quick kiss on the mouth.

He sensed the camera flashes behind him, but he was conscious only of large misty eyes staring into his.

"Ruth Pacino," he said gruffly and held her tight. "You shouldn't be here, but I'm glad you came."

"You thought that I'd leave you facing this alone?"

"Where is…" he started as he lifted his head, but he didn't have to ask.

Linda flashed him a warm smile and squeezed his arm. "Hello, Kenneth."

"It's good to see you again, Linda."

"I wouldn't have missed it for anything."

Beside him, Powell cleared his throat. "Admiral…"

Pacino gave Ruth a peck on the cheek. "We'll talk later."

She squeezed him again and he winced as the sutures pulled

at his side. She saw his discomfort and immediately stepped back, her face full of concern.

"I'm sorry. I forgot."

"It's all right," he said and brushed her cheek with the tips of his fingers. Glancing at the press, they clearly loved every moment of this impromptu reunion.

Pacino stepped past Powell standing behind the left desk and sat down. Facing the empty bench where the Investigating Officer would decide his fate, he slowly turned his head and looked at Fisher. The chunky commander looked back, his eyes and face expressionless. Pacino's two sessions with the government counsel left him with mixed feelings. Fisher had not been in any way hostile toward him. He was simply another case Fisher was determined to win. When he talked to him, Pacino could immediately sense another Powell. Both were skilled professionals who would not ask for or give any quarter.

A youngish captain walked into the room and there was immediate silence. Chairs scraped as everyone stood up. Pacino rose and waited for the presiding Investigating Officer to seat himself. According to Powell, Captain Edwards was a stern by the book juror, but eminently fair, preferring to rule on equity rather than the strict interpretation of the regulations. It did not mean that Pacino could count on any favors from him.

Edwards lifted his gavel and banged it against a wooden pad.

"This hearing will come to order. Everyone can sit down." He waited until the shuffling of feet, the scraping of chairs, and clearing of throats stopped.

"This Article 32 investigation is held to determine whether Rear Admiral Kenneth Pacino should face a general court-martial resulting from his unauthorized action against non-civilian installations in two foreign countries. Namely, South and North Korea. The charges leveled against Admiral Pacino are: Article 80, an intent to commit an offense; Article 94, mutiny and sedition."

Edwards looked up and stared hard at Fisher. "Does the government seriously want to proceed with this charge?"

Fisher immediately rose. "It does, your Honor."

"Very well. In that case, I rule that Article 94 does not apply and is summarily dismissed, as Admiral Pacino at no time sought to usurp or overthrow lawful military or civil authority of the United States. You should have known better than to try that one, Commander."

The comment generated a ripple of murmuring and several snickers from the back. Fisher merely clamped his mouth and took it. Looking at him, Pacino knew why the opposing counsel did not react. The government had a solid case with the other charges and everybody knew it.

Edwards looked down at his notes again. "Next. Article 107, false official statements; Article 109, destruction of property other than military property of the United States; Article 133, conduct unbecoming a military officer; Article 134, conduct bringing discredit on the good order and discipline of the armed forces." He slowly shook his head. "This charge is summarily dismissed. I am amazed, Commander Fisher, that the government bothered to waste my time on this charge. You must be aware that the preemption doctrine prohibits application of Article 134 if an alleged offense is already covered by Articles 80 to 132."

"You Honor—"

"That was not an invitation to comment, Commander. Please sit down."

Pacino saw Fisher stiffen, nod and take his seat. Powell was right when he said the article would not apply. That was two down, but the others more than made up for that little deficiency.

"Commander Fisher. Is the government ready to present its case in support of the other articles?"

Fisher stood up. "It is, your Honor."

"Defense counsel?"

"Ready, your Honor," Powell said promptly.

Edwards nodded and leaned forward. "Admiral Pacino, you have the right to make a statement in your defense. If you don't waive that right, the government can use whatever you might say as evidence to support the charges leveled against you. Do you understand your rights, sir?"

Pacino stood up. "I do, your Honor, and I want to make a statement."

"Very well. The government can begin."

Fisher rose and held up a sheaf of papers. "Due to their military duty commitments, three of my witnesses were not available to attend in person. However, I do have their sworn signed testimonies. Given the incidental nature of their involvement in this case, it was deemed that written testimony would be sufficient."

Edwards turned to Powell. "Does the defense have any objection?"

"No objection, your Honor."

"Very well. You may proceed, Commander."

"The first statement is from Brigadier General Eugene Picket, Commander 51st Fighter Wing, Osan Air Base, South Korea. It states that on the morning of March 2, Rear Admiral Pacino called him, requesting the arming and release of a tactical Unmanned Aerial Vehicle, an MQ-10 combat Hawk. The said aircraft was prepared and released under remote tactical control by the satellite Ground Station on USS *George Washington*, at the time anchored at Yokosuka naval base, Japan. The government wishes to present this as exhibit A-1." Fisher approached the bench and laid the paper before Edwards.

"Comments by the defense?"

"No comment at this time, your Honor," Powell said. "However, the defense reserves the right to rebut."

"Very well. Commander Fisher?"

Fisher walked slowly back to his desk. "The second statement is from Captain Brian Ormond, commanding officer of USS *George Washington*. A request made to him by Admiral Pacino on the same morning to control the UAV provided by General Picket from the carrier's CIC, supposedly for the purpose of making a system check test flight that night. The government presents this as exhibit A-2."

"Does the defense wish to cross-examine?"

"Not at this time, your Honor."

"The final statement I have is from Lieutenant Commander Ransom, assistant Tactical Action Officer in command of the CIC watch on the night in question. He supervised the two UAV operators as they flew the Hawk in the execution of its bombing run on a military warehouse at a South Korean naval installation at Incheon. This was followed by an armed strike against an electrical substation at a North Korean nuclear installation at Yongbyon. The government presents this as exhibit A-3."

"Defense?"

"No questions, your Honor."

"Commander Fisher?"

"Your Honor, the defense counsel refuses to dispute these affidavits because they cannot be disputed. Admiral Pacino did willfully and knowingly set out to cause the destruction of valuable property in two foreign countries. He obtained his weapon by making false statements to fellow officers regarding the intended use of the armed Hawk. He then issued illegal orders to Commander—"

"Objection, your Honor! Leading! " Powell snapped as he stood up. "At no time has Admiral Pacino acted illegally or dishonorably."

"Sustained. As Deputy Commander, 7th Fleet, Admiral Pacino was well within his authority to issue the orders he did, and those orders were perfectly legal, regardless of the intent or effect of those orders," Edwards stated.

Fisher nodded, but appeared unmoved. "I will rephrase, your Honor. Admiral Pacino ordered Commander Ransom to fly the

UAV to two foreign installations where an unprovoked and premeditated attack was made on those installations. Your Honor, the government maintains that it has proven its case for Article 80 and 107."

"Objection!" Powell immediately stood up. "The defense maintains the government has done no such thing."

"Please elaborate, Commander," Edwards ordered.

"Article 107 specifically states, and I abbreviate, any person who, with the intent to deceive, makes an official statement, knowing it to be false, shall be punished. Your Honor, Admiral Pacino made a truthful statement to General Picket when he said that he wanted to carry out a live fire exercise."

"Omitting that it would be done in a foreign country!" Fisher interjected and several people laughed. Edwards banged his gavel.

"Order! Continue, Commander."

Powell cast an amused glance at Fisher. "Admiral Pacino was not required to be specific as to the objective of his request. He was also truthful to Captain Ormond. As the Fleet Deputy Commander, Admiral Pacino is not required to explain his actions to subordinates or the purpose of those actions, however unclear they might be to those subordinates. This is particularly relevant to events that transpired in *George Washington's* CIC and the behavior by Lieutenant Commander Ransom when he carried out those orders. He didn't understand them, but he recognized legal orders and was obliged to carry them out."

"Your Honor, if Admiral Pacino's actions were so admirable, why did he present himself to Captain Ormond and asked to be placed under open arrest?" Fisher demanded hotly.

Edwards banged his gavel. "Order! The government shall present its questions and comments in proper form!"

"No disrespect intended, your Honor."

"None taken, but you raise a valid point. Although Admiral Pacino's statements in themselves were not false, he knowingly used the property of the United States to commit destruction of assets in foreign countries. There is question of intent, of course. Nevertheless, I'm not completely satisfied that the government has unequivocally proven its case for Article 107—"

"Your Honor—"

"I haven't finished, Commander Fisher. However, I reserve judgment at this time until I hear all the arguments. As for Article 109, there is ample evidence to sustain that charge."

Pacino's heart beat faster. That charge alone carried with it a dishonorable discharge, forfeiture of all pay and allowances, and confinement of five years. It didn't look good, and he could not see how Powell could wiggle out of it.

"You may continue, Commander," Edwards said and Fisher cast a satisfied look at Powell.

"Your Honor, since Article 109 has not been disputed, the government contends that Article 80 has also been proven. Admiral Pacino may have issued legal orders, but as you pointed out, they were given under a deliberate intent to commit an offense under Articles 107 and 109."

"Objection, your Honor!" Powell stood up.

"Commander?" Edwards invited.

"Defense contends that Article 109 does not apply."

A ripple of murmuring came from the audience and the press. Pacino looked at Powell in astonishment, unable to believe he had heard right. What could his counsel be playing at?

Edwards banged his gavel. "Order!" He stared hard at Powell. "I am intrigued to hear your explanation, Commander."

"In its rush to prove Admiral Pacino guilty, the government has overlooked an important detail. Article 109 is specific to property other than military property of not only the United States, but in the country where the property was damaged or destroyed. The properties under which Admiral Pacino is charged were military installations, not civilian. Unless South or North Korea wish to instigate military proceedings against the

Admiral, I submit he has no case to answer under this investigative hearing."

Pacino fought to keep his face impassive and resisted an impulse to hug Powell. This unorthodox tactic was something that never came up in their discussions.

Edwards slowly nodded. "Although technically correct, this hearing goes beyond the substance of the charge, but—"

"Your Honor!" Fisher cried out and immediately jumped up.

"You want to comment, Commander?" Edwards said after giving Powell a speculative stare.

"I certainly do! The defense is playing loose with a point of law, your Honor. Knowing full well the whole purpose of Admiral Pacino's prelude was to execute a retaliatory military strike against two foreign countries, he technically committed an act of war! The government is right to charge him with mutiny and sedition under Article 94, which follow from his acts under Articles 107 and 109."

"I already ruled on that, Commander," Edwards said sternly. "The defense has raised an interesting argument, which has the potential to undermine all charges argued to this point. However, I shall reserve judgment until both parties have concluded their presentations. The government may continue."

"Your Honor, the government contends that without further evidence, Article 133 has also been amply proven. Admiral Pacino's conduct, even under the most liberal interpretation, cannot be construed as anything other than dishonorable. In his official capacity, he did disgrace his uniform and the Navy he serves, bringing discredit not only on the Navy, but the United States in general."

"Does the defense wish to redirect?"

Powell stood and stared directly at Edwards. "Thank you, your Honor. Everybody knows the purpose of Article 133. When the government fails to make a specific charge stick, it trots out this convenient catchall clause, an umbrella for all pet dislikes the

Navy might have. In Admiral Pacino's case, as has already been established, he has at all times behaved honorably and with the highest integrity. He has not abused his rank or abused a subordinate, and he at no stage sought personal gain in any form from his actions. On the contrary, he sought to bring honor to the Navy and his country."

A spontaneous round of clapping and cheering sprang from the audience, which Edwards suppressed after some banging of his gavel.

"Continue, Commander."

"The government has tried to paint Admiral Pacino as a villain because he dared make a personal statement which has disturbed several comfortable sensibilities. How does that make him illegible to be an officer and a gentleman? Is it because being a gentleman means conforming to those same rigid sensibilities?"

Edwards chuckled. "We're not done yet, Commander, but I can see that you would love to have this concluded now. Although Admiral Pacino's actions may not have been of a deliberate nature to bring discredit on the Navy, there is compelling evidence that it was nonetheless prejudicial to the good order and discipline of the armed forces, specifically the Navy. An honorable officer does not make an unauthorized strike against foreign countries, regardless of any personal motive."

"Your Honor, if I may point out, you have already ruled that Article 134 does not apply," Powell declared, sounding most respectful.

"You may, Commander, and I did." Edwards turned to Fisher and nodded. "The government may proceed."

"Your Honor, the government calls Vice Admiral David Owen."

The marine guard opened the back door and Owen marched in, dressed in his winter blues. He sat in the witness box and waited. Pacino noted that his friend did not look at him once. Perhaps doing so might have compromised his position. So far the arguments were technical, and to a certain extent entertaining. Now, things were about to get raw.

Fisher approached the box and clasped his hands behind his back. "Admiral Owen, although this is not a trial and your testimony is not required to be given under oath, should this case proceed to a general court-martial, the evidence that you give now will be treated as though given under oath. Do you understand that, sir?"

"I understand," Owen said evenly.

"You are Commander 7th Fleet based at the Naval Base Yokosuka and Admiral Pacino's immediate superior officer?"

"That is correct."

"When did you first become aware of Admiral Pacino's action?"

"Captain Ormond called me and said that Admiral Pacino asked to be put under open arrest after conducting an armed strike package against military installations in South and North Korea using a combat UAV staged out of Osan."

"What happened then, Admiral?"

"I had Pacino brought to my office where I demanded an explanation."

"And did he?"

"Not to my satisfaction."

"Please elaborate, sir."

"Pacino spoke of the loss of his son and how nobody seemed to care that he died from an apparently senseless act committed by the North Koreans during the recent Key Resolve exercise with the units of the ROK Navy. He said he wanted to remind everyone, including the North Koreans, that they also had casualties, and we failed to care for the men and women who serve in our military. His action was meant to remind everybody of that fact."

"By executing a bombing run?"

"It wasn't something I expected from him."

"And how did you react to the news?"

"Frankly, I was astonished. This was so unlike Pacino. For someone up for his third star, his action was completely out of character."

"In what way?"

"Objection, your Honor! Calls for speculation," Powell called out without getting up.

"Overruled. The question is relevant and I will allow a certain leeway, but stick to the facts, Commander Fisher."

"I shall rephrase, your Honor. Admiral, would you consider Admiral Pacino a competent officer?"

Owen gave a wan smile. "The Navy does not give three stars to fools, Commander."

"So, Admiral Pacino is a competent and rational officer about to be promoted. Would you say his action calls his competence and judgment into question?"

"Objection! The question is leading."

"Sustained. Do you have a specific question for this witness, Commander?"

"Your Honor, the state of Admiral Pacino's mind is crucial to determining why he took the action he did. Since this is a motion of discovery, I'm seeking a degree of indulgence."

"This is indeed a motion of discovery, Commander, and your question is more suited to a general court. What I want to determine is whether a general court is in fact warranted, but I'll allow you some latitude. However, if you're seeking to understand Admiral Pacino's motivation, I suggest that Admiral Owen has already answered that. I ask you again. Do you have a specific question for this witness?"

Unsettled, Fisher spent a moment regrouping. Facing Owen, he allowed his hands to fall to his side.

"What did you do after ordering that Admiral Pacino be brought before you, sir?"

"I called the Chief of Naval Operations, Admiral Parker. He

wasn't available and I left a message with his aide to call me."

"Then you had your interview with Admiral Pacino?"

"That is correct."

"And it was during that interview that Admiral Parker called?"

"Correct."

"What did he say?"

"His language was rather colorful."

This caused laughter to ripple through the chamber and Edwards banged his gavel.

"Order! Continue, Admiral."

"The CNO demanded that Admiral Pacino be flown to Washington to face a number of charges."

"Did you specify those charges to Admiral Pacino, sir?"

"As his immediate superior officer, I advised him what he could be facing, yes."

"What happened then?"

"He was taken to Tokyo's Narita Airport where he boarded a Navy flight. As per the CNO's order, I then called Admiral Parker to further discuss the impact of Pacino's actions."

"Sir, did you consider Admiral Pacino's acts unlawful?"

"He considered them unlawful, otherwise he would not have requested to be placed under open arrest."

"Thank you, Admiral. Your Honor, I have no further questions for this witness at this time. However, I reserve the right to recall."

"Very well. Does the defense wish to cross-examine?"

"It does, your Honor," Powell said and walked toward Owen. Standing before him, he leaned forward slightly. "When you ordered that Admiral Pacino be brought before you, did *you* consider his action unlawful?"

"I already answered that question."

"No, sir. You did not. You said Admiral Pacino considered his action unlawful."

"He appropriated government equipment under false pretenses and used that equipment to attack installations in two foreign countries. I'm not a lawyer, Commander, but in my book, those were not lawful acts. The CNO did not consider them lawful either, otherwise we would not be here today. Pacino is a friend and a brilliant officer, but what he did cannot be condoned in any chain of command."

"Did Admiral Pacino violate any orders?"

"No, because—"

"Was he insubordinate?"

"No."

"Did he bully or threatened anybody while prosecuting his attacks?"

"No."

"Was he in any way prejudicing the order and discipline of the Navy?"

"Technically not, but—"

"What exactly is Admiral Pacino guilty of, apart from being an honorable man?"

Owen shifted in his seat and for the first time, Pacino actually saw him looking uncomfortable.

"He attacked two foreign countries out of personal pique, damn it!"

"After South Korea launched an unprovoked depth charge attack against a PROK submarine, which then retaliated with a torpedo strike, followed by a missile launch from a PROK corvette on USS *Curtis Wilbur*, causing a number of deaths and casualties. Among the dead being Admiral Pacino's son."

"Your Honor!" Fisher protested, rising to his feet. "Is the defense counsel going to ask a question or indulge us in a litany?"

"Commander Powell?"

"Getting there, your Honor. Admiral, how did you react when you learned of the PROK attack?"

Owen bit his lower lip. "I was furious at the ROK commander

for provoking the North Koreans, and I was mad at them for striking back after their submarine had in fact already withdrawn."

"You wanted to punish them, is that it?"

"Objection, your Honor!" Fisher growled wearily. "Leading and irrelevant."

"Overruled. You may continue, Admiral."

"I did want to punish them, and I said that to Admiral Pacino when he told me what had happened."

"Why didn't you order him to strike at the remaining PROK vessels? You had the necessary assets in place and a clear tactical advantage. You would have exacted your punishment."

"There were, ah, overriding considerations."

"Political considerations?"

"Yes."

"You wanted to strike back, but couldn't. Yet when Admiral Pacino did exactly what you wanted to do, you brought him up on charges."

"Pacino is in a chain of command and follows the lawful orders of his superiors, who in turn obey the National Command Authority. He executes the policies of civil authority, sir! He does not make them!"

"You're saying that civilian authority and the policies of that authority are responsible for Admiral Pacino's action?"

After thinking for a while, Owen looked directly at Powell. "They were a contributing factor."

That caused an excited ripple of comments from the chamber.

"Order!" Edwards banged his gavel.

Powell stepped closer to Owen. "But Navy policy, sir, does not stem from the Secretary of the Navy alone, does it? The Joint Chiefs, the CNO, and in fact, all senior theater commanders in some way shape policy. Is that not correct?"

"Objection, your Honor. The question is argumentative. The government's policies are not the subject of this hearing."

"Overruled. It goes to the subject of intent, which is definitely the object of this hearing. Admiral?"

"If you want to oversimplify things, Commander, that's to a degree true," Owen conceded.

"What happens if you don't agree with an existing policy?"

"Objection! The government would like to know how this line of questioning is relevant."

"I'll allow the question, but stand warned, Commander Powell. You're dangerously close to straying into matters best addressed at a general court."

"Almost done, your Honor."

"Very well. You may answer the question, Admiral."

"You voice your concern through mechanisms provided for such a purpose."

"And if your protest remains unheard?"

"If your concerns are legitimate, you keep protesting until you're heard, Commander. That protest does not involve taking unilateral action."

Powell turned to Edwards. "I have no more questions for this witness at this time."

Edwards nodded to Owen. "You may step down, Admiral."

As he watched his friend leave, Pacino had expected a damning dressing down, not a reluctant agreement with his objection to several government and Navy policies. Grateful, although he could not see how that would help him, he was puzzled. Owen did not have to come all this way from Yokosuka simply to appear at the hearing. He could have provided an affidavit. There had to be more. Was he here to hash over the *George Washington* incident with Parker, or something else?

When the door closed after Owen, Edwards turned to Powell. "Is the defense ready to call its first witness?"

"It is, your Honor."

"Very well. This hearing is adjourned until 1400," Edwards said and brought down the gavel with a bang. Everybody stood up as he walked out.

Across the aisle, Fisher turned and grinned ruefully. "You've put on a pretty slick show, Eden, but I've got you and you know it."

Powell gave a miniscule nod of acknowledgment. "You know what they say about battles and wars."

"I won this war, regardless of this morning's battle. Your client is going to trial."

"We shall see."

Pacino grabbed Powell's arm and turned him around. "He's right, you know."

"He's playing with our minds, Admiral. Don't worry about it."

"Worry? I cannot believe what you did. You managed to nullify all the charges."

"Not quite, but it's got my learned opponent concerned, and that's always a good thing."

"What was all that stuff with Owen?"

"The Investigating Officer must be cognizant of two potentially exclusive elements here. One is the obvious letter of the charges brought against you. We've already made strides to neutralize them. The other component, of course, is the political environment, ours and of the two Koreas, which led to your action. We had to emphasize that."

"You want to shift the blame to the Navy and the White House?"

"At least show them to be significant contributors as Owen indicated."

"You're nuts! The IO is never going to fall for it, and neither will Fisher. The political dimension might be relevant, but I ordered the strikes, and I'm the one they're blaming."

"True, Admiral, but this is not a black-and-white case and everybody knows it. We're playing to a wider audience than just the IO. Edwards is not the only one listening to what's been said here."

"Are you going to put me on the stand this afternoon?"

"You don't want to?"

"I do want to."

"Be careful with Fisher, sir. I got him blindsided, but technically, he still has a strong case."

"Commanders, I have for relish."

Powell grinned. "He may wear the stripes, but they are those of a tiger, and he's stalking. Keep that in mind and you'll be fine."

"Kenneth!"

Pacino heard Ruth call, turned and nodded to the two burly marines keeping the gallery at bay.

"Admiral! Care to make a statement?" a voice called from the back.

Pacino waved at the press, and with a smile, shook his head. Then Ruth was beside him and they embraced. Linda stood there, not quite sure whether she was intruding. He gathered her in with one arm and hugged her. Cameras flashed to an ongoing buzz. Ruth pulled back and looked at Powell.

"That was quite a performance, Commander."

"Thank you, ma'am, but we've only been shuffling the chips. It'll get more interesting this afternoon."

"Will this be finished today?"

"The hearing part could be, but the IO may take the weekend to write up his report for the CNO. We'll know on Monday. If you're up to it, Admiral, we can have some lunch."

"With them hovering at my elbow?" Pacino hooked a thumb at the press and Powell chuckled.

"We'll use one of the meeting rooms and have stuff brought in."

"Let's do it."

After showing them to a room down the corridor, Powell left, but not before posting a marine outside. Moments later, a knock and Linda opened the door. A pert young ensign stepped in and smiled.

"Good afternoon, Admiral...ma'am." She nodded to Ruth and Linda. "I'm afraid lunch will be fairly basic. I can have coffee brought up, soda and juice, and several types of hot sandwiches with fries and salad."

"What do you have?" Pacino demanded.

"Pastrami, chicken, and turkey."

"I'll take turkey," he answered immediately and turned to Ruth.

"I'll have chicken."

"Make that two," Linda added.

"Coffee and juice for everybody?" Seeing the nods, the ensign withdrew.

Pacino eased himself into a chair at the head of a medium-sized conference table, waited for Ruth and Linda to do the same, and took off his cap. He searched Linda's face and frowned.

"You look tired, my dear. Is everything all right?"

"Long flight from Tokyo," she said with a wan smile. "With three of us on board and only two bunks, Ruth and I slept okay, but Owen had to stretch out in one of the forward seats."

"He'll live," Pacino said without showing much sympathy. "He's a tough old bird."

"Kenneth! What a dreadful thing to say!" Ruth admonished him.

"The other thing is," Linda went on, "I'm flying to Norfolk this evening. I'm staying with my parents until they fly back Vincent's body. I know Ruth wanted him buried at sea and I have no objection, but Owen has other plans. He wants him buried at Arlington with the others from *Curtis Wilbur* and *Stethem*. Besides, Ruth will be much better company and I'll simply be in the way."

Pacino reached for her hand and squeezed. "You'll never be an intrusion, you know that."

"Because I do know it, I hope you will understand that my parents also want me with them right now. We'll all be together for the ceremony."

"And then?"

Linda gave him another small smile. "Life goes on, doesn't it? Even if Vin will not be part of it," she whispered, trying hard to hold back the tears that shone in her tragic eyes.

Pacino patted her hand and nodded. "Yeah, life does go on." He glanced at Ruth, trying to say it all with his look. They had lived together long enough that words were not needed, although there would be words later...from both of them.

"What about you, Kenneth?" Linda asked. "I couldn't follow everything that went on in there, but it seemed to me that Commander Powell had Fisher on the ropes."

Pacino chuckled. "He certainly did, but we're dancing around technicalities right now. It all depends on how Captain Edwards, he's the one on the bench, will take it."

"What if you have to go to a general court?"

"We'll face that one as it comes."

Lunch went by too quickly. Pacino wanted to talk to Ruth, but he did not want Linda feeling shut out. He understood her need to be with her parents, but wished that she could at least stay for the weekend. He also understood that right now, she shouldn't be left alone, and that's what would have happened had she stayed. It would be impossible having her in the same room with Ruth, understandable practicalities notwithstanding. Alone in her own suite, she would brood, recalling everything that might have been, going over all the regrets and reliving the pain of her loss. That would not be good.

The hearing room fell silent as Powell led in his small procession. Someone clapped and the room broke into general applause and impromptu cheering. Touched by the outflow of goodwill more than he cared to admit, Pacino waved to the audience and took his seat. At least the media were not looking to crucify him, even if the Navy sought to do so.

Fisher was already there, but showed no outward reaction. Silence returned as everyone waited for the Investigating Officer to appear. At precisely 1400, Edwards walked in and everybody stood. He seated himself, nodded and chairs scraped as the gallery resumed their seats.

"You may call your first witness, Commander Powell."

"The defense calls Rear Admiral Kenneth Pacino, your Honor."

Pacino squared his shoulders and took a deep breath. He stood and made his way to the stand. Sitting down, he saw Ruth give him an encouraging smile and he nodded to her. This was it. Powell had gone over the type of questions he intended to cover, but to a certain extent, the trend and atmosphere of the hearing would dictate what he would do.

Powell approached him and stopped. "Admiral, you're an officer of long service. Thirty-four years, I believe. Is that right?"

"Something like that," Pacino said, mindful of his instructions to keep his answers to the point and not elaborate, even for Powell.

"You're familiar with Navy regulations?"

"All of them."

"Then you understood perfectly well the charges leveled against you?"

"I do."

"Did you consider during the planning and execution of your strike against Incheon and Yongbyon that your actions contravened any of the regulations? Specifically, the charges subsequently brought against you?"

"I did not."

That produced the expected buzz from the gallery and Edwards banged his gavel.

"Order! I'll not have gratuitous exhibitionism displayed during this hearing. You may continue, Commander."

"If you did not consider your actions illegal, why did you ask to be placed under open arrest by Captain Ormond?"

"Although I felt that technically, I had not contravened any regulation that prejudiced the United States Navy, I did initiate an unauthorized armed strike against two foreign countries. I believed the Secretary of the Navy and the State Department would not look favorably on my action or my interpretation of the regulations."

This generated a general round of laughter and chuckles. Order was restored after more banging of Edward's gavel.

Not showing any outward reaction, Powell gave Pacino a minute nod of encouragement.

"My next question goes to the heart of this whole hearing, Admiral. Why did you initiate those strikes?"

Fisher immediately stood up. "Objection! The question calls for a narrative answer. Moreover, despite any argument over intent, the government is not interested at dissecting Admiral Pacino's motive at this time. He admits asking that he be placed under arrest, thereby acknowledging the validity of the charges laid against him. I submit that those are the only facts relevant to this hearing, your Honor."

Not daring to look directly at Edwards, Pacino wondered if the Investigating Officer would quash him now. Fisher had made a telling point. Only the clinical facts of his actions were relevant here.

"Technically, you're correct. Commander," Edwards said. "However, this is a hearing and I will allow the defense a certain level of latitude, as I allowed you. You may answer the question, Admiral."

Pacino forced himself not to fidget as he gazed fixedly at Powell. This was complicated and he wondered if he could reduce a wealth of personal factors set against Navy tradition and the prevailing political climate to several succinct statements. Well, he wanted his day in court…

"I lived under the regulations of the Uniform Code of Military Justice for most of my adult life. They promote a necessary degree of discipline, order and a degree of behavior that enables the military to execute lawful directives issued by the civilian arm of government. I do not and have never questioned the subservient role of the military to civil authority."

"But you *have* questioned it, haven't you, sir?" Powell demanded and Pacino wondered on whose side he was on. He wanted to wipe his clammy hands, but that simply wouldn't do. He lifted his chin.

"I never questioned duly authorized orders. What I questioned was inaction by civil authority. For far too long, they have forgotten, or chosen to ignore, that while the military is there to implement government policy, real people have to pick up arms, fight and sometimes die."

"But isn't that exactly what happened during the Key Resolve exercise, Admiral? People died in the execution of their duty."

"And they died with honor, Commander," Pacino retorted calmly. "Instead of acknowledging their sacrifice, civil authority has failed to care for them or those who have been maimed in the execution of government policy. The incident in the Yellow Sea has provided a vivid demonstration of the lack of due care."

It all came rushing back; the pain, the hurt and the loss. Damn Powell anyway. He thought he knew what his counsel was doing; clarify his motive now rather than wait for Fisher to tear into him. He pushed it all back, swallowed and cleared his throat.

"My son died as a result of a foolish act initiated by a South Korean destroyer captain, which prompted an equally foolish attack on my son's ship. No one needed to die that night, but people did die, and not only on our side. Incidents happen and they will continue to happen in the future because we're all fallible men. We serve civil authority, but that authority does not extend to blatantly wasting the lives of people sworn to serve their country and then pretend nothing had happened in the name of some higher big picture objective. Such behavior is inexcusable. My son and others who were lost or maimed were treated with such indifference. They were promised a medal and promptly forgotten, as though an award solved everything." Pacino snorted and clenched his fists. He suspected he was ruining it, but he didn't care, not really. At least he had a chance to be heard.

"In any conflict someone has to die, Commander, and this one cost the life of my son. He should not be forgotten or ignored, none of them should, and treated as an embarrassment after an act of misguided foreign or domestic policy. I was determined to remind the Navy, our government, and the governments of both Koreas, that all life is valuable. Some may consider the method I used somewhat extreme, but I used the only language everybody would understand. I'm hoping they've taken notice," he said quietly and allowed his shoulders to sag.

The entire chamber remained silent for several seconds. Even Fisher looked thoughtful.

Pacino had given them a taste of what he meant to say. He wanted to say a lot more, but the court-martial would see to that. In the meantime, he hoped that Parker, the Secretary of the Navy, and President Walters would hear this. Powell was right. The Investigating Officer wasn't the only interested party here.

"Way to go, Admiral!" someone shouted and the room erupted into applause.

Ruth and Linda stood up as one and clapped. In moments, everyone stood, clapping and cheering madly. Edwards banged his gavel repeatedly, but the outflow of emotion needed to run its course. Eventually, order was restored.

Powell looked at Edwards. "I have no further questions for this witness, your Honor."

Edward turned to Fisher. "Does the government wish to cross-examine?"

"It does, your Honor." Fisher stood and walked to Pacino and paused. "A stirring speech, Admiral. You served in the Navy since entering Annapolis at eighteen."

Pacino looked at Fisher and said nothing.

"I asked you a question, sir," Fisher prompted, showing a flash of annoyance.

"Oh, I thought you were making a statement," Pacino said blandly.

Fisher waited. When it became clear that Pacino was not going to answer, he jutted out his chin.

"Well?"

"Well what?"

"Did you begin your naval career at eighteen?"

"I did."

"Did they teach Navy regulations at Annapolis?"

"They did."

"During your career, you must have been called upon to lay charges against enlisted men and officers under those regulations. Is that correct?"

"It is."

"Have you ever questioned the validity of those regulations and how they were applied?"

"I did not."

"In your previous testimony, you stated that you were intimately familiar with all the Navy regulations. Now, you state that you don't question their legality. How is it then that you can dispute the legality of the charges laid against you?"

"Because I don't consider that I contravened the spirit of those regulations."

"The spirit of those regulations...Attacking two foreign countries is not an illegal act?"

Powell immediately rose. "Objection, your Honor. The question calls for speculation."

Fisher turned to Edwards. "Your Honor, Admiral Pacino's action may have been prompted by a highly personal interpretation of civilian and military policy, and the regulations he served under, but the government cannot sanction what has been a technical declaration of war on two countries."

"Objection sustained. Although Admiral Pacino's action might not be in the best interest of the United States, that's a political dimension, the charges brought against him only deal with articles of the UCMJ. He has not been charged with inciting to war. Restrict your questions to the charges, Commander."

"Very well, your Honor. Admiral, when you requested General Picket to prepare an armed Hawk, it was with the intent to carry out a strike against Incheon and Yongbyon. Is that correct?"

"It is."

"When you ordered Captain Ormond to have remote operators standing by in *George Washington's* CIC, it was for the express purpose to execute those strikes. Is that correct?"

"It is."

"In other words, sir, with deliberate intent to deceive, you knowingly issued orders and used United States property to commit an illegal act."

Pacino remained silent.

Fisher colored and bit his lip. "Please answer the question, sir."

"What was the question, Commander?"

Fisher bit his lip again. "Did you deceive fellow officers to procure military equipment?"

"I did not."

"Knowing that you intended to use the Hawk to bomb two countries, you don't consider that asking General Picket to give you one was deceitful?"

"I made a legal tasking request. At no stage did I sign any false record or other official document, or make an official statement knowing it to be false. I made a legal request to General Picket and he provided the Hawk."

"But your strike was not a simple live fire exercise, was it? You made a false statement, didn't you?"

"Objection! The question is leading."

"Overruled. You may answer the question, Admiral," Edward ordered.

"A superior officer is not required to explain his orders or actions to a subordinate, provided the orders are legal, as mine were."

"Regardless of the liberal interpretation you place on what is legal, Admiral, wouldn't you consider that by omission, your actions were not becoming an officer and a gentleman?"

"Objection! The question is leading."

Smiling, Fisher turned to Edwards. "I have no more questions for this witness, your Honor."

"Does the defense wish to present further witnesses or testimony?"

"No, your Honor," Powell said.

"Commander Fisher?"

"No, your Honor."

"In that case, this hearing is adjourned until 1000 on Monday." Edwards banged his gavel, stood up and walked out.

Pacino looked at Powell, smiled and extended his hand. "Whatever happens, Commander, you put up a good fight."

Grinning, Powell clasped the offered hand. "We're not done yet, Admiral."

Ruth stepped to Pacino and hugged him. "Thank you for what you did and what you said, Kenneth, and not only for Vincent."

He patted her back and kissed her. "As long as he's not forgotten."

Standing beside him, Linda gave him a tight little smile. "Judging by the reaction from the press, I doubt that anyone will forget him now."

"Admiral, if you'll wait here, I'll have the FBI bring up your car and take you back to the hotel," Powell said and bowed to Ruth and Linda. "That will include the ladies, of course."

As Powell turned to leave, Fisher walked up to Pacino and nodded. "It's my job to bring you to trial, Admiral, but as a fellow

Navy officer, you have my sympathy and condolences, sir."

"Thank you, Commander."

The young man nodded and pushed through the standing gallery. Seeing Pacino alone, the press surged forward, kept back by the marine guards.

"Admiral! How do you think the hearing went?"

"What did you discuss with President Walters when you met?"

"Admiral! Are you saying that Veterans Affairs has failed to look after our servicemen?"

Pacino lifted both arms, suppressing an involuntary wince at the pain that shot through his side. "One at a time, boys. First of all, we'll find out on Monday how the hearing went. As for the substance of my discussions with the President, that's privileged. However, we did go over some of the things I mentioned in my statement, including my concerns with Veterans Affairs."

"Admiral! Will the President act on any suggestions you may have made?"

"I cannot answer for the President, but I would like to think the Administration will consider favorably the salient points of our talks."

"Do you think the attack on *George Washington* and the sinking of USS *McCampbell* are related to the strike on Yongbyon?"

"I'm no longer in the Navy chain of command and don't have access to intelligence that's now dealt with by Admiral Owen. I understand, however, the attack was initiated by the PROK frigate's commander on his own initiative."

"Like your attack?"

"I explained my actions, gentlemen. Unfortunately for the North Korean captain, we can only speculate what motivated him."

Powell appeared in the doorway and Pacino raised his right hand. "Thanks for your support everyone, but I've got to go."

"Admiral! Has the FBI identified the person who shot you?"

Pushing through the reporters, Pacino shook his head. "They haven't told me."

In the corridor, flanked by two FBI men and the marines, Powell led his little group toward the elevators.

* * *

ADMIRAL PACINO SLAMS GOVERNMENT
THE PRESIDENT WILL NOT AVENGE *McCAMPBELL*
AMERICA SMILES WHILE OUR MEN DIE
ADMINISTRATION TAKING A MEASURED STAND
NORTH KOREA APOLOGIZES FOR SINKING OUR SHIP

"Admiral?" President Walters looked closely at the Chief of Naval Operations standing before him. Cottard hovered close by, observing everything and ready to step in if necessary.

Tall, unflinching, cap under his left armpit, Parker returned the gaze. "Mr. President, you saw the news coverage this afternoon. Admiral Pacino and his defense counsel made a good case. Legally, some of their arguments are questionable and can be dismissed, but what counted was the emotional impact and reaction from the media." He pushed back his rimless glasses that had slid down his nose.

"I can tell you, sir, the public is not terribly interested in legality here, and if I read the scuttlebutt right, most of the Navy isn't either. We can win this and send Pacino to face a general court, and we will be justified at doing so, but regardless of the strict interpretation of regulations, what he did has stirred the national conscience. We can proceed and the Investigating Officer will do the correct legal thing, but will it be the moral thing? That, I'm afraid, is outside my terms of reference."

"In other words, you're leaving me holding the can," Walters mused wryly.

"Sir, as the Commander-In-Chief, you're the final authority as to what happens here."

The president gave a small smile and turned to the Chairman of the Joint Chiefs of Staff. "General McDonald?"

The imposing officer lifted his chin. "Admiral Parker is right, sir. Whatever his motive, Pacino broke regulations and should justifiably stand trial. We cannot have an officer or an enlisted man taking policy decisions into his own hands. That's not our role. Admiral Pacino should be punished to the full extent of the law. Any show of leniency will not only be detrimental to the discipline of the services, but would also set a particularly bad precedent."

"A good by the book answer, General, but that's not what I'm looking for right now. Where do you personally stand on this? The truth now."

"The truth, Mr. President? Pacino is right on every count. The military *has* become a tool and a plaything for past Administrations. I'm yet to see how your Administration ends up using us, sir. As a tool, we were used and thrown aside. We became disposable. I'm not whitewashing the Joint Chiefs, sir. We must carry some of the blame, but if I learned anything during my career, men should never be merely disposable. As a former officer yourself, I would like to think that you understand this."

"I do understand, General. Should this case go to a general court-martial, it will expose some very dirty Navy laundry and several questionable policies of this and past Administrations. I don't need that, not right now. Admiral Pacino's concerns will be addressed, but I need time to examine the extent of the problem and come up with workable solutions. I don't want him crucified, regardless of what the regulations might call for. So, what are my options?"

McDonald glanced at Parker and nodded. The CNO shifted in his seat.

"As the convening authority, I can give Pacino a dishonorable discharge in lieu of a general court."

"Provided he pleads guilty."

"Yes, sir. In view of statements he made to Admiral Owen and to me prior to the hearing, he might not accept that. He could be prepared to face a term of imprisonment, which he certainly will if this goes to trial, in order to make sure his views are heard. As you pointed out yourself, sir, this could be damaging to the Navy and your Administration."

"Rather than going to a general court right away, you brought him up before an Article 32 hoping that I would act?" Walters demanded with a smile.

"Do you want me to dismiss the charges, Mr. President?" Owen countered.

"I cannot order you to do that, Admiral, without prejudicing the due process, but this Administration would find it helpful were you to do so." Walters glanced at McDonald. "General?"

"It's up to Admiral Parker, sir, but as his superior, I'll support a dishonorable discharge. You realize, of course, the negative reaction this decision could prompt from the two Koreas."

Walters looked grim. "They're already in enough trouble over this, General. I doubt that President Samun will raise more than a token protest. In any case, they're not something you should be concerned about. That's my problem."

McDonald nodded. "In that case, I believe we're done here. Admiral Parker will talk to the government JAG officer and a formal announcement will be made on Monday when the hearing reconvenes."

"Thank you, General...Admiral," Walters said and the two officers immediately walked out of the Oval Office. When the door closed after them, he turned to Cottard. "You can have your say now, Manfred."

Cottard stepped closer to the desk and slowly rubbed his nose. "There is nothing to say, Mr. President. McDonald is right. You *are* setting a bad precedent, but I doubt it will be tested anytime soon. Politically, the people will stand behind you, as will most of the Navy, because you'll be doing something that's right. Hard to say how the Republicans will react, but they should be able to read the tealeaves and not buck what would obviously generate them bad will. They might still criticize you out of pure spite. Importantly, no one will be able to level a charge of undue political influence against you, even though everyone will know you wanted this."

"Well, I couldn't fight you and the White House Counsel. On Monday, once the hearing adjourns, I want Pacino brought to me. You'll have to clear my schedule and make me available."

"What do you have in mind for him?"

"Special Advisor to the President. He'll be working with Stone, but will report directly to you and me."

"Mr. President, as the National Security Advisor, Stone may not like someone muscling in on areas that are legitimately his turf."

"Stone tells me things about national and international security. It's not his job to opinionate on military related domestic policy, not directly anyway, which Pacino will be called on to consider, but I agree with you. There will be some overlap, which cannot be helped. That's why I want them working together. If Stone has a problem, handle it."

"And Pacino's terms of reference?"

"I'll leave that open for now. There are enough things to sort out in what he and I talked about to keep him busy for a year. I'm sure he'll have other pet beefs to air. What I do want him to have is unrestricted access to SecDef and Tanner. Pacino will have to tread lightly, but I don't want him starved of information."

"What if he decides to throw the offer in your face? Always a possibility with a man like that. The government hasn't done him any favors, you know."

"Perhaps not, but he's not mad at me. He's mad at the system, and this is his chance to do something positive about it. Throw this back at me? I don't think so."

"We'll find out on Monday who's right," Cottard said evenly and rubbed his nose.

"Anything new on the assassination attempt?"

"The FBI has drawn a blank, but they're still digging. There is one bit of good news."

"Oh?"

"NCIS have identified the person who sabotaged Pacino's aircraft. It turned out to be an airman at McChord. His brother was one of the casualties when USS *Stethem* was hit and he blamed Pacino for it. A spur of the moment thing."

"Damnation!" Walters sighed and shook his head. "The whole thing stinks."

"Claims he never intended for the Gulfstream to crash."

"But it did and he killed two pilots, that's the difference. At least the families I talked to who lost boys on *Stethem* and *Curtis Wilbur* don't seem to blame Pacino. If anything, they're more sore at South Korea."

"That's good, Mr. President. If they're mad at them, they're not mad at you."

"Yeah. Has Larry got all the arrangements done with Premier Yeum?"

"Weapons handover is scheduled for next Thursday. He spoke to the Russian and Chinese prime ministers, and both will be in Seoul on Thursday morning. Osan's 51st Fighter Wing will provide a helo and covering fighters to fly them and you to *George Washington*. The Secret Service has men already on the ground and Osan will be buttoned down tight when you land."

"Good. Make sure Larry is on top of President Samun on our pullout. I don't want any last-minute complications when I announce our timetable."

"From what I gather, sir, Samun is not resisting at all, and Price might be right about Kham having sounded South Korea on this. It makes one wonder to what extent the entire Key Resolve incident may have been stage-managed by both sides."

"If they did prearrange everything, it showed a remarkable degree of maturity by both," Walters agreed pensively, then smiled wryly. "And to think Kham and Yeum used the CIA to fund the whole thing. We must have looked like bumbling amateurs to them."

"It doesn't make the Chinese look too good either."

"Frankly, Manfred, when all is said and done, I really don't care. We got there in the end and that has to be good for everybody. We have another market to exploit and businesses to develop. The Republicans cannot be sore at that. If we don't overplay our hand, Yeum and Kham will remember who helped them. They won't be biting the hand that fed them."

"I wonder," Cottard murmured, his eyes far away.

"Price and Kham seem to have hit it off well," Walters added equitably.

"That could be very useful for us in the future," Cottard agreed. "An informal communication channel might be exactly what we need if Tanner strikes a diplomatic reef. Despite this deal, we cannot afford to forget who they are. Tung In-san may be tractable right now, but once he gets what he wants out of us, it could be business as usual."

"I haven't overlooked that possibility, Manfred, but I'll take this one step at a time. Talking of steps, Price seems to have weathered his at Langley."

"It appears you picked the right man, Mr. President."

"It appears so. While you're talking to Larry, get an update on his discussions with President Al Zerkhani. I want to know what Iran intends doing with the three remaining warheads they got from Sung. If Israel finds out about them, Prime Minister Abdon Sayar will have hives."

Cottard looked thoughtful. "It's bound to come out sooner or later, but that's not what's worrying me. How do we know that

North Korea is handing over all its nukes?"

Walters shrugged. "We don't, and the sticky point is, there is no way for us to find out. We'll just have to trust them."

"That could be asking a lot, Mr. President," Cottard said woodenly.

Chapter Twelve

Pacino folded the *Washington Post*, laid the paper to one side and picked up his cup. Holding it between both hands, he felt its warmth and took a sip.

"How does it feel to be a hero?" Ruth asked from across the breakfast table, her eyes bright and mouth twisted in a lopsided smile.

"I don't feel like a hero."

"You're a hero to me," she said softly.

Looking at her, seeing the love shine in her eyes, he never failed to be amazed by her. A striking woman, her beauty had matured, filled out with confidence and poise. Never beautiful in the traditional sense, it took a double-take to appreciate her clean lines, subtle cheekbones, slightly upturned nose and full lips. When she parted her mouth with laughter, her eyes seemed to light her face, bathing it with inner radiance that had totally captivated him the first time he saw her.

Last night, cuddled together, her head resting on the crook of his arm, it felt good having her warm body touching him. She had always kept her figure trim and desirable, something he appreciated. It was not the slim gracefulness of her youth, but that of a fully mature woman. She did not allow her hips to spread or her breasts to sag. In pillow talk, she confided that this kept his eyes from straying. They did stray, he admitted wryly, but it was only window shopping that all healthy males indulged in. Because she understood that, she was sure that his eyes did not stray too far.

He stroked the smooth skin of her arm and side, he felt content. The hearing, the verdict on Monday, the ache of Vin's loss, they all receded into a part of his mind he had locked and kept those thoughts from intruding—at least for a while.

When she lifted her head, he could only make out her outline in the darkness, but he could feel her sweet breath as her lips brushed his. Enfolding her in his arms, her breasts hard against his chest, he kissed her deeply. Without saying anything, she rolled on her back, taking him with her.

Their lovemaking slow and tender, making up for lost time, the words that were never said, a sharing of emotions and loss they were not able to do together. Neither of them had talked about Vin, not in fullness, but both were conscious of his presence. There were memories and that would have to do now.

Content to be close, Pacino softly told Ruth about that grim night in the Yellow Sea where he watched the whole drama unfold on the glowing screens. Seeing the missile tracks reach for *Curtis Wilbur*, the dread of knowing what could happen and his utter helplessness to change anything, kept him frozen until the missiles vanished. He told her of his twisted insides, anger at the South Korean admiral and the stupidity of the North's attack. None of it needed to happen, and that was the bitter irony of it all. Then the call from *Wilbur* that Vincent was hurt. It felt like someone had plunged a hot knife into his guts. At least the boy was alive, he kept telling himself. He was alive. Having to tell Linda that Vin lay a cripple, followed by Owen's call…

"When I realized that I would never see him again…" Something went out of him and he swallowed hard.

She cradled his head against her breast and held him tight. "Women sometimes forget that men also feel pain," she whispered and stroked his cheek.

He didn't say anything, content to bask in her warmth and understanding.

"What tipped the scales to make you decide to do something?" she asked after a timeless moment.

"Linda's question kept haunting me. Intellectually, I knew what she felt and I sympathized, but what *could* I do? I was in a chain of command and I believed in following regulations and serving under civil authority. I still do. Protest to Owen? I did after flying back to Yokosuka, but he didn't understand or wasn't interested. He is a friend and I hate saying this, but his only concern was how the night's action would look on his record. What pushed me over the edge was the call from the President. I'm sure he meant well and was sincere. When he told me that Vin would get a Silver Star for saving Captain Woods, that tore it. Was that all a life meant to him, a piece of tin? Everything was set for my strikes, but I could still have pulled back. After listening to him, I knew I had to go on."

She snuggled against him. "We just have each other now. In time, Linda will make a new life for herself and we'll lose her as well."

"At least he died with honor," he said gruffly.

"Will you face a court-martial?"

"Probably. Commander Powell put up good arguments to counter the charges, but that was theater. The regulations are pretty clear and I broke them, no matter what he said. Regardless of my motive, I committed a technical act of war. The Navy and the Administration cannot ignore that. They may be embarrassed by what I might say at the trial, but they'll wear it for the sake of discipline. I cannot see how I'll miss jail time."

"Didn't Powell say that Admiral Parker could drop a general court if you pleaded guilty?"

"I'll be cashiered out of the Navy. Buttons torn off my dress blues and sword broken on the knee. It all depends on how badly the Navy wants to punish me. Or Walters. I threw a pretty large spanner into his negotiations with North Korea. He couldn't be very pleased with me."

"Would you accept a dishonorable discharge?"

"To avoid jail time? Sure. My point would have been made and the media could still be interested enough to ask for an odd interview. At least for a while before my story fades or is buried under new scandals."

"Your career and the sea isn't everything," she told him softly and he stroked her side.

"As long as I have you with me."

They talked some more until both were overcome and the night closed over them.

Reality shifted and he noted her puzzled expression. "What?" he asked.

"Where were you just then?" she asked, a quizzical smile playing at the corner of her mouth.

"Oh, memories."

"Good or bad?"

"A bit of both." Taking a sip of coffee, he grinned. "Thanks for bringing over some of my gear."

"I figured you could use it." Looking around the room, she nodded. "Not bad for a jail. Are we going to be stuck here for the entire weekend?"

"Looks like it. I'll have to check with Norwood. Even if someone wasn't gunning for me, we'd be mobbed if we ventured out."

She reached across the table and touched his hand. "We can use the time to catch up. I haven't seen much of you over the past few weeks. First, it was all the planning you put in for Key Resolve, and then this."

"Are you disappointed that Vin won't be buried at sea?"

Ruth sighed slowly. "I was at first, but I'm over it. In a way it's fitting that his final resting place will be at Arlington. I know Linda said that she didn't mind a sea burial, but that was more to please me. This way, she'll be able to be near him."

"How is she?"

"Taking it hard as you can expect. It will take time, but she will adjust, as I will."

Pacino nodded and took another sip. They would all have to adjust.

* * *

Ashton pressed the Send icon, exhaled and sat back. All the emails were done and he could relax. The one he enjoyed sending was to Brenner. The NTSB investigator deserved to know what really happened to the Gulfstream. The image of Paul, chewing furiously on his gum, wearing a cynical smile, brought a corresponding grin to his face.

Brenner had a news item of his own. He was moving to Washington. It meant a promotion, but more importantly, it would save his marriage. Ashton sympathized.

He had not intended to come in, certainly not on a Saturday morning, but if he left his Med report for Monday, with all the things that happen on Mondays, he would never get the damned thing done. Paper warfare, the bane of his job, and the higher he climbed in the hierarchy the problem would only get worse. At least he finished the Colby report. Pollard could not very well complain, but he did, grousing about his stint on the *Enterprise.* Well, the thing was done.

He sat up and fetched himself a fresh cup of coffee, reveling having the floor to himself. Keener souls normally made an appearance in the afternoon once the morning chores were done. Not burdened with family responsibilities, he sometimes took advantage of the morning peace and quiet to get extra work done, disappearing by lunchtime. As a rule, he avoided coming in on weekends, but he never paid much attention to arbitrary rules.

Although Colby now enjoyed a less comfortable time, Ashton's job was by no means over. Theoretically, finding Pacino's shooter was strictly an FBI matter, but he owed Norwood for McChord's personnel jackets, which helped nail Colby. It was only fair that NCIS returned the favor. Unfortunately, Fielder at Yokosuka hadn't been much help.

The secure calls Owen made and received were all with Admiral Parker, the Chief of Naval Operations. Apart from recording the fact of the call, and that took some string pulling to be disclosed, the comms people at Yokosuka never keep a record of the calls themselves. Parker and Owen could have been exchanging recipes. Security was a great thing and Ashton applauded the need for privacy, but right now, he wished the system wasn't so secure. The greater public good outweighed individual rights? He never subscribed to that dubious ideology. Better that a case remained unsolved than spy on every piece of everybody's communication—in whatever form. This might be an inconvenience for law enforcement agencies, but enough individual freedoms have already been eaten away in the name of protecting those very freedoms.

His phone rang and he stared at it suspiciously. Who the hell would be calling him here? Curiosity got the better of him and he picked up.

"Ashton."

"And a good morning to you too," Norwood said brightly. "Is it a good morning where you are?"

Ashton glanced out the window. "It's clear so far, but they're predicting rain later. How did you know I was in, Ken?"

"I didn't. I tried your house and cellphone. Not getting anything on either, I took a chance."

"I could have been out shopping, you know. I do have a life."

"Then I would have missed you. And you don't have a life. That's what my wife keeps telling me. I'm not interrupting anything, am I?"

"Just about ready to get out of here. You've got something new on Pacino's shooting?"

"A nibble. That suggestion you made about searching for code words? NSA has drawn a blank. That could mean several things, none of them good for us. The shooter may have used untraceable equipment to chat with Owen, if Owen actually ordered the hit, or our man was indeed some lone freedom fighter who took it upon himself to eliminate Pacino."

"That had always been my pet theory," Ashton agreed. "Why would Owen take an enormous risk to get rid of Pacino for very little gain? Still, people do the craziest things."

"That's why you and I have jobs," Norwood said. "What NSA did manage to trace was a call made from one of their older HTC cellphones that lists the nearest base station controller at either end. Although the call itself is totally scrambled, this gave us a heads-up. NSA has eliminated this flaw in their later version, but whoever made this particular call either hadn't bothered to get an upgraded cellphone or wasn't able to."

"All right, what's the bottom line?" Ashton demanded impatiently. "I want to get out of here."

"Testy, aren't we? The call originated from Washington and the destination was—"

"Yokosuka! So it was Owen after all. Rats!"

"You didn't let me finish," Norwood admonished him, not bothering to hide his satisfaction. "The destination was also in DC. Guess where the base station controller was located?"

Wheels spun in Ashton's head as he sorted through the possibilities. When they stopped spinning, he didn't like what they told him. Hollice would have loved this.

"The Pentagon," he said slowly.

"Show off. Get this. The call was made sixteen minutes after Pacino got shot."

"Son of a bitch! It's Admiral Parker."

"If it is, we'll never prove it. NSA deactivated the cellphone's number, but that doesn't make the device inoperable. Our boy could latch onto any valid number to use the thing, which he probably already has. There is one other possibility—two, actually. Don't overlook the Chairman of the Joint Chiefs, General

McDonald, or the Secretary of the Navy. All of them have a vested interest at having Pacino silenced, particularly the Secretary. It's likely that one of them is involved, but did he act on his own?"

Ashton snorted. "You're full of good news. So what do we do now?"

"Wait for our man to resurface and try again. The cellphone gag tends to eliminate a lone vigilante. If it's one of the other three, they might give up. Pacino has had his say and the damage is done. Containment is no longer an option. Taking him out now would serve no purpose and only increase their exposure."

"Perhaps."

"There is always room for doubt." Norwood agreed. "You know that Owen came for the hearing?"

"I saw him on TV," Ashton said. "Strictly speaking, he didn't have to attend."

"A tactical meeting with Parker? It's possible if the two of them were colluding."

"What will you do?"

"Make my report and let the higher-ups do their thing. The President won't like this."

"Unless…"

"Yeah, but I doubt very much that he would want Pacino removed. Again, there would be no percentage in it and an awful lot of risk for him. I simply don't see it. Until I'm told otherwise, I'll keep a protection detail on Pacino and try to enjoy what's left of my weekend."

"Your call certainly didn't help to boost mine," Ashton said glumly.

"Good work on getting the saboteur."

"The files you provided helped."

"Look me up when you're next in Washington, Mr. Ashton."

"I'll do that."

Norwood disconnected and Ashton stared thoughtfully at the

receiver to the background of the dial tone. He replaced it in its cradle and picked up his cup. Sitting back, he took a sip.

After a moment, he smiled and shook his head. Amazing what technology can do, but it only went so far. The thinking and the legwork were still left to a man. Norwood was right. Apart from a suspicion, he had nothing to go on with. The Pentagon was full of four-star admirals and generals, and most of them had a High Technology Computer secure cellphone. He did wonder if Norwood's source was right that NSA could not break their own encryption system. Either way, it was unlikely they would be telling him.

Finishing the last of his coffee, he powered down his tower PC and took a long look around the floor: empty desks, filing cabinets, potted plants, and a lot of memories. His tour on the *Enterprise* had expanded his horizons, literally, and the Pacino case even more so. The prospect of having to deal with more routine Navy petty crime, an occasional shooting, drugs or domestic violence, suddenly made him feel constrained and unfulfilled. He was ready to take that next step Pollard had urged him to do for some time, but he had been too comfortable in his role, too complacent.

Perhaps Norwood would get to see him sooner than he expected.

* * *

"They've got the man who sabotaged your aircraft, but have drawn a blank with the shooter. The FBI is certain it was a professional because the order came from the Pentagon," Powell said and Pacino sat up, a heavy scowl clouded his face.

"Parker?"

"There is no way to tell, but it's possible. At least it wasn't Admiral Owen."

"As far as they can tell," Pacino said darkly. Why did Owen

come down to DC? He had his suspicions, glad to learn his friend was not a direct suspect.

"They may never be able to tell, Admiral. Unless another attempt is made on your life, which is unlikely, the FBI will lift their protection detail."

"Fair enough, I suppose, but that's not why you're here. Is it, Commander?"

"No, sir. Fisher has a deal on the table if you want it."

"What is it?"

"You plead guilty to Article 107 and 133. The government drops the other charges and you get an administrative discharge under Article 15, but no confinement."

"A dishonorable discharge," Pacino murmured, relieved the CNO had made the offer, but also disappointed that he would not have his say in court, regardless of the possible consequences to himself if he were found guilty. Then there was Ruth...

He stared at Powell. "What do you think?"

"It's a good deal, Admiral. Frankly, it's better than we had any right to expect, and I dare say the White House had a hand in this. Like I said, we were playing to a wider audience. Friday was a good day for us, but I only sparred with Fisher. He had us in the box and knew it. Despite my arguments, Captain Edwards never had a choice. If we proceed, he will be compelled to recommend that you face a general court. What's more, sir, you know it too."

"I do, Commander. What happens now?"

"If you accept the deal, I'll pass it on to Fisher and he'll talk to the IO. When the hearing reconvenes, Edwards will order your immediate discharge and you'll be free to walk out."

Pacino pursed his lips and nodded slowly. He would be a free man. Disgraced perhaps, but free. Free to make a new beginning. Ruth deserved to have whatever time they had left. She had been alone long enough. Not over the last few years, but too long anyway.

The other important consideration the deal offered, without a prison conviction hanging over him, his job prospects would not be closed. He had saved and there were a few odd investments, but none of that was near enough to support himself and Ruth beyond a few years. Navy pay was never going to make him rich.

"I accept," he said firmly and felt a weight roll off his shoulders. He might be out of the Navy, but he had a network of influential people who may be prepared to listen and act. If not, he can always go to the papers.

Powell smiled broadly. "I would have defended you, Admiral, even if you said no."

Pacino extended his hand. "I was lucky to have you, Commander."

The lawyer took the offered hand. "You were a challenging case, sir. Besides, I didn't want Fisher to have all the fun."

Pacino laughed as Powell stood up. "Good answer. Okay, let's get this done."

In the hearing room, two marine guards flanked Pacino and Powell past the throng of reporters. Pacino flashed Ruth a smile as he made his way to the front. Linda would have loved seeing him go free, but she was probably watching this on TV. Powell immediately strode to Fisher. After conferring briefly, Fisher flashed Pacino a quick look, nodded to Powell and hurried toward the IO's chamber.

Powell took his seat beside Pacino and leaned toward him. "It's all set. Fisher has gone to inform Edwards."

Fisher emerged a few minutes later and resumed his seat. The press saw what was going on, which caused a ripple of expectant comments. They sensed something was about to happen.

Edwards walked in and everyone stood up. Taking his seat behind the bench, he banged his gavel and glowered at the audience.

"This hearing is now in session." He waited until everybody

seated themselves. "Admiral Pacino and defense counsel, please rise."

Calm, despite the fact that his hands were somewhat clammy, Pacino stood.

"After due deliberation of arguments and evidence presented by both counsels on the charges brought against Rear Admiral Kenneth Pacino, as Investigating Officer, it is my ruling that Admiral Pacino should face a general court-martial to answer those charges."

This immediately generated a wave of excited murmuring. Edward banged his gavel.

"Order! After further deliberation and my previous comments, I decided the government has not proven to my satisfaction charges under Article 80, Article 94, and Article 109, and therefore they are summarily dismissed. Article 107, making a false official statement, and Article 133, conduct unbecoming an officer, are sustained.

"Given the nature of the charges and the circumstances surrounding Admiral Pacino's action, under Article 15, the convening authority has elected not to proceed to trial and exercised his prerogative to apply administrative punishment."

The chamber erupted in an uproar of clapping and cheering as everyone stood, camera lights flashing. Edwards kept banging his gavel in a vain attempt to restore order. Finally, the room settled down.

"Admiral Pacino, having pleaded guilty to the charges leveled against you, I rule that you be dishonorably discharged from the United States Navy, with forfeiture of all pay and allowances. This hearing is now concluded." Edwards banged his gavel, stood up and walked out with long, brisk strides.

In the chamber, everybody stood and cheered. Ruth rushed to Pacino and hugged his neck, her eyes glistening with happy tears.

"You rat! When did you know about this?"

"Powell sprang the news on me just before the hearing," he told her and stroked her cheek. "It's over, my sweet. We can go home now."

"To Norfolk?"

"Anywhere you want."

The reporters and cameramen surged toward them. Pacino looked fondly at Powell. "Thank you for everything, Commander."

"Don't let me see you here again, Admiral," the lanky lawyer said with a whimsical smile.

"Admiral! Why did you plead guilty if you didn't consider your action illegal?"

"When did you know about this plea deal?"

"What are your plans now, Admiral?"

Pacino turned and faced them, his left arm around Ruth's waist.

"My immediate plan is to spend time with my wife. We have some intimate catching up to do."

This raised the expected round of appreciative chuckles as the press looked Ruth over, striking in her cream skirt and brown business jacket.

"In answer to your other questions, I still don't consider what I did was morally wrong, but technically, I did contravene the charges I pleaded guilty to. The government had a strong case, which I would have struggled to win. This way, the Navy and the Administration avoided a messy exposure of some of their policies if this went to trial, and I get an opportunity to pursue my grievances in the public arena. As for knowing about the plea bargain, I got notified just before the hearing."

"Admiral! Do you still fear for your life?"

"I'd feel bad if someone were to take another shot at me, especially if he succeeded." The dry comment produced more chuckles. "But I cannot worry about some unknown possibility."

"Does that mean you will no longer be under FBI protection?"

"I have not been told officially what the FBI intends doing."

"Admiral—"

A somewhat short individual dressed in a conservative dark blue suit, sporting black-rimmed glasses, pushed through and stopped in front of Pacino.

"Sir, I am Adam Howard, White House Deputy Chief of Staff. The President has requested that you see him if you're willing to do so."

"This is not a summons, then, Mr. Howard?" Pacino demanded quizzically.

Howard blinked, and then cracked a faint smile. "You're a private citizen now, sir. Well, not quite. Not until your discharge papers are processed, but you *can* tell the President no."

"Don't worry, Mr. Howard. I have no intention of doing anything like that. However, my wife comes with me."

"Of course. If you would follow me, please?"

"Hey, Howard!" someone called out. "Where are you taking him?"

"Does the President want another chat?"

"Admiral! What gives?"

Pacino glanced at Howard, who smiled at the press and raised a hand. "The President has requested a bit of time from the Admiral. I wasn't told why, only to bring him. Granger will give you the full story later, guys."

Flanked by two grim looking FBI men, Howard led them out of the chamber, the press trailing after them shouting questions. Once in the elevator, Howard peered at Pacino.

"How does it feel to be a celebrity?"

"A dubious honor at best, but I guess I did it to myself. So I shouldn't complain, should I?"

"It wouldn't do you any good even if you did," Howard added without any feeling. "For the ride up, we'll use my car. As of this moment the FBI men are off your case."

The two FBI sentinels standing behind the elevator door gave no reaction to this news, but Pacino figured they must have known. He reached for Ruth's hand and squeezed it to reassure her.

Pennsylvania Avenue busy, but not crowded, the morning crush having ended. Their car stopped at the White House west entrance and the Secret Service checked in the two passengers. Walking through the West Wing toward the Oval Office, Pacino's appearance caused a ripple of urgent whispers in his wake. Never having seen the place, Ruth was understandably curious by the goings-on around her.

At the reception area, Unice looked up as Howard approached. "You can go right in. Welcome back, Admiral."

"Thank you, although I'm not sure what I'm doing here."

"I've had that same feeling myself every time I come in." Glancing at Ruth, she stood up and moved away from her desk. "I'll take care of Mrs. Pacino, sir. An impromptu tour, ma'am?"

Ruth beamed and perked up. "I'd love one, and it's just Ruth."

Howard knocked on the heavily painted white door and walked in. Leaving the two women to get acquainted, Pacino stepped into the Oval Office.

President Walters gave him a friendly smile and stood up. "I see you accepted my invitation."

"Hardly something I could ignore, Mr. President," he growled and Walters chuckled.

"Only if you were prepared to face the consequences." Glancing at Howard, he nodded. "Thanks for bringing him, Adam."

"Yes, sir," Howard said and withdrew.

Walters pointed at a sofa beside the great seal. "Please, have a seat."

Pacino took off his braided cap and made himself comfortable. Walters sat down in the opposite sofa and crossed his legs. Making an inverted V with his fingers, his eyes never left his guest.

"Feels good being a free man, Admiral?"

"A disgraced one, sir, but it feels okay. Although I do seem to be improperly attired."

"Until the moment your discharge papers are signed, you're still a Rear Admiral in the United States Navy. You should wash out of your mind this feeling that you are somehow disgraced. The technical requirements of the charges brought against you called for the penalty leveled at you, and more, but you're not disgraced. The press certainly does not think so and neither do the people. Got that?"

"Aye aye, sir," Pacino said automatically and Walters smiled.

"That goes double for me, although you did give me a few headaches."

"I regret that, sir."

"You relished it, and perhaps rightly so."

"If I may, Mr. President, did you have anything to do with the deal Admiral Parker made?"

"Let me put it this way, Kenneth," Walters said with a sparkle in his eyes. The use of his first name did not escape Pacino and he wondered what was coming.

"The Administration pointed out to General McDonald and the Chief of Naval Operations that a speedy resolution of your case would be advantageous to everyone concerned. You're the last person I need to explain why that is so."

"You don't, sir."

Walters uncrossed his legs and leaned forward. "Last time we talked, you got me thinking and I couldn't rest. That's bad for me as my doctor tells me I shouldn't stress myself. Of course, he doesn't have to sit in this office. However, I do need to listen to him, so I decided you should be the one who is stressed."

"Me, sir?"

"Fitting, don't you think? After all, it was you who prodded my conscience. You raised what you saw were administrative and policy shortcomings. I called you here to solve them. The President is asking you to serve. How about it, Kenneth? Up to the challenge?"

Pacino's mind whirled. Work in the White House? That would certainly be a challenge, and one he never anticipated having to handle. He saw himself somewhere back in Wyoming among the Grand Tetons where he spent his youth. A quiet ranch maybe, or perhaps a teaching position at some unassuming college where he would live down the controversy that surrounded him. They were just thoughts, and Ruth probably had ideas of her own. Whatever, but stepping into the seething cauldron of White House, and by extension, Congress politics? The president was right. He would certainly be stressed.

He allowed himself a lazy smile. "Is this your way of getting even, sir?"

Walters laughed with obvious delight. "I haven't thought of it that way, but now that you mention it, I would get a measure of personal satisfaction getting back something of what I had to take these past few days. So, what's it going to be?"

"What exactly do you have in mind for me?"

"Special Advisor to the President. You'll be working with the National Security Advisor, but you report to me and the Chief of Staff. You'll be free to consult with anyone, and that means anyone. If you need to see the Secretary of State or the Education Secretary, you pick up the phone and tell them when. Manfred will help you find your way through the bureaucracy, but you don't take orders from him. You work for me. I don't expect you to get involved in the machinery of this Administration. Your role will be policy. What I want is clear identification of issues and workable options to address them. I cannot use Utopia solutions. Whatever you come up with will have to stand up to Congressional scrutiny and Republican resistance. The other side will never give us any quarter. Keep that in mind and you'll be halfway there. I have some ideas on which I would like your input, but they can wait. You raised concerns regarding treatment of our military personnel, Admiral. This is your chance to do something about it."

Pacino stared at his commander-in-chief. Walters was decisive, knew what he wanted and wasn't afraid to lay it on the line. The president was right. This was his chance to fix some things and not merely bitch about them. He wasn't that naïve to believe he would be able to wave a magic wand and it would get done. The government and its supporting departments was a complex machine that had evolved over a long time, with many vested interests that would resist change. It would not come immediately, but change was possible, and some things should be solvable relatively quickly, if the political will was there, which it seemed to be.

Did he want this, especially right now? He was still to absorb the full emotional impact of Vin's loss. He needed time with Ruth to grieve a little and accept the realization that their son would never be with them again. Was that merely being sorry for himself? Was he castigating himself for all the missed opportunities and mistakes he made when Vin was around? Parents sometimes demanded too much and didn't understand the natural rebellion of their offspring.

Behind his doubts, he recalled Linda's words. He had voiced his protest, hadn't he? What more could he do? *You are hiding behind technicalities, Admiral*, his inner voice called out clearly. He may have aired his complaint, but he had not fixed the problem. Time to decide, Admiral. Talk, was that the only thing he could do?

He wanted a chance to do something, and now, he was given a big one. So?

Taking a deep breath, he looked unwaveringly at his president. "I'll do it."

Walters smiled faintly. "I thought you would. I seldom misjudge character. You'll probably end up cursing me before you're done, and you'll certainly get more gray hairs. Welcome aboard, Admiral."

"From what you told me, I think I'll reserve my thanks for later, sir," Pacino said wryly. Walters chuckled and stood up.

"You've got a few things to do and I must brief a few people that you're going to be here. Your son's funeral is on Thursday, right? Count on seeing me there."

Pacino gaped. It was unheard of for any president to be at an Arlington ceremony. "Sir—"

"It's the least I can do, Kenneth, as you so pointedly reminded me. Our boys should not be forgotten. The CNO has you and Mrs. Pacino at the Mandarin Oriental, right? We leased a nice terrace house in Georgetown for you. Your appointment falls under a special government provision, which means the Administration will be picking up the bill. If Mrs. Pacino doesn't like it, talk to Unice. She'll find you something else. Otherwise, let her know and she'll arrange to have all your stuff ferried over from Norfolk. Unless it's still at Yokosuka? Talk to her. I expect to see you here next Monday."

Amazed that the president had all these details on tap, obviously well briefed, Pacino stood up.

"I *was* slightly worried where I would find a place to stay. Everybody knows about Washington's murderous rental prices."

"Now you've got one less worry. Please extend my apologies to Mrs. Pacino for not seeing her, but I'll make it up to her on Thursday as my guest."

Pacino picked up his hat, put it on, and stood at attention. "Thank you, Mr. President."

"No, thank *you*!"

Outside the Oval Office, Pacino stood bemused for a moment, unable to accept what just happened. Ruth sat in front of Unice's desk nursing a coffee. She noted his expression and raised her eyebrows.

"Kenneth? Is everything all right?"

He shook off his daze and smiled at her. "The President just gave me a job."

Unice beamed with genuine warmth. "Congratulations, sir. He only picks the best."

"The best? That remains to be seen."

"Does that mean we have to move to Washington?" Ruth demanded, looking concerned.

"We don't have to do anything, honey. Not if you don't want to."

Sensing the two of them needed some time alone, Unice picked up her phone and spoke rapidly. She replaced the receiver, looked up and smiled.

"The Secret Service will drive you back to the Mandarin, Admiral, and I do hope you'll take the job, sir." She reached into a drawer and held out a business card. "Call me when you decide and I'll arrange everything, including a car to take you to your house in Georgetown."

"House?" Ruth queried with a raised eyebrow.

Pacino frowned and leaned forward. "You knew about this?"

Unice shrugged. "The President discussed it with me."

A tall serious individual wearing a dark gray suit walked up, nodded to Ruth and stopped before Pacino.

"Sir, I am to take you to your hotel."

Pocketing the card, Pacino flashed Unice a small smile. "You'll be hearing from me."

"I'll see you on Thursday, then, sir."

Handing in his visitor pass at the security desk, Pacino followed the Secret Service agent to a dark saloon that waited under the portico. He got into the back, buckled up and took off his cap. As the car pulled away, Ruth turned and looked at him.

"Well?"

"Linda asked me what I was going to do about Vin and the others, and I thought I had done it. When I saw the President last Tuesday—"

"You'll have to fill me in about that."

"He wanted to find out why I committed those strikes, and I told him. I told him the current system sucks and he needed to do something about it. Ironic, isn't it? Without realizing it, I echoed Linda's words. Just now, the President threw the ball back in my court. Special Advisor and head kicker, and the job starts next Monday."

"Unice said something about a house in Georgetown. Do you know how much it costs to rent there?"

"The government will be picking up the tab for that, my sweet."

Ruth frowned, uncertainty clear on her face. "Move to Washington? I hadn't expected things to happen this fast."

"Neither did I, but I guess that in this town, you move fast or you get left behind."

"Did you take the job?"

"I did, but I can always tell him no if this will make you unhappy."

She snuggled against him, took his hand and held it to her chest. "Darling man, I followed you wherever the Navy took you, and I'll follow you here. You leave everything to me. Unice is a nice woman and she'll take care of us."

"There is only one woman I need to take care of me," Pacino murmured, stared into her eyes and gently kissed her.

Epilogue

Mark Price stood behind the outwardly sloping armored glass in Pre Fly, the watchstanders keeping a vigil over glowing screens, binoculars scanning the Haeju Bay docks. He pursed his lips and nodded. What he witnessed hardly seemed believable.

Sailors lined the edge of USS *George Washington's* flight deck, rigidly at attention like toy sentinels, the breeze flapping their white uniforms. The forward part of the black non-skid deck empty. Most of the squadrons of Super Hornets that provided the carrier's strike force were struck below or had flown to Kunsan, but he could see a dozen parked behind the island. There simply wasn't enough space below for all of them. Two MH-60s, armed marines standing around them, waited to lift.

Hovering near the carrier's island like circling flies, the press gallery were beaming every developing moment to their respective networks in real-time, who in turn broadcasted to audiences glued to their flat screens.

Stacked conspicuously beside a small dais set before the forward catapults, were three piles of innocent looking pine boxes, concealing their deadly content. They held nothing but lumps of black metal, hardly something to get excited about. If the world had any sense, they would dump all their stockpiles in the Mariana Trench, but Price had found long ago that the world was very short on being sensible.

"It looks like they're getting ready to get on with it," Captain Ormond said dryly, a cup of coffee in his hand.

The dignitaries and security entourage appeared below and assembled around the dais.

"It cannot be very comfortable for your men out there." Price indicated at sailors on the edge of the deck.

"They'll live," Ormond said. "Besides, being able to brag about seeing a major world event unfold before them will make up for any momentary discomfort."

Price admitted the man had a point.

Thankfully, there was little ceremonial and the speeches were brief. No one wanted to stand in a stiff breeze listening to boring oratory. This was business after all. When Walters stepped to the lectern, he pretty much echoed the sentiments expressed by the Chinese and Russian prime ministers. Everyone congratulated themselves and the event that heralded a new beginning for North Korea and a peace that would last forever. Wasn't every peace meant to last forever? All a bit boring, but Price figure a moment of boredom was worth the net gain.

The Supreme Leader, Tung In-san, came last, looking solemn and dignified despite his short stature. Price didn't bother listening to the translated speech, concentrating on the gray silhouettes of North Korean warships tied along the piers. Red rail cranes clustered around the docks, dwarfing warehouses and maintenance facilities. Tung wasn't saying anything new.

Then it was over. The four leaders were escorted below decks for snacks, a few drinks and veiled talks, gratified not to be exposed to the fresh wind any longer. Then again, perhaps not so veiled. Either way, watching men crate the boxes from two of the piles into waiting helicopters, Price would probably never know what went on in there, unless Walters chose to reveal something to him. His immediate concern was to ensure that the two helos made is safely to Pyongyang's airport where the crates would be loaded on board Russian and Chinese aircraft.

The last two boxes from the American pile were placed on a forklift and the job was done. Moments later, the choppers had their rotors spinning. Lifting, they clattered east, each holding a security representative from the four countries to ensure the cargoes were properly loaded onto their respective aircraft without any diversions along the delivery route.

Wispy streams of cirrus cloud marred a pristine blue sky above the naval base. The small choppy seas made no impression on the huge carrier as she stood there like a giant reef. A pair of F/A-18 Super Hornets overflew her in perfect line-ahead formation, while two MH-60 Sea Hawk helicopters sanitized the harbor.

George Washington lay alone in the open port, President Walters insisting that its escorts stay outside the Northern Limit Line. A symbolic gesture that according to Tanner, Premier Yeum appreciated. Until the formal peace treaty with the South was signed, a technical state of war still existed between the two countries. It also reassured the Chinese that North Korea was not going to bed with its old enemy. Today's ceremony went a long way toward easing of tensions accumulated over decades, allowing everyone to let out a long-held sigh.

Thinking of politicians, Price smiled. He enjoyed meeting Kham, even though his mental picture of the man didn't quite match the real person. It seldom did. He found the Korean smooth, polished, if somewhat unsophisticated, but easy to work with. Dressed in a general's uniform, the man had revealed his pedigree. Despite the momentous event, it was worth remembering that North Korea was in many respects still very much an unknown quantity, as was Kham. Price didn't worry about that. The politicians had cooked up this deal and they would now have to handle the ramifications.

His job almost done, he looked forward getting back to Washington.

Although the Secret Service had the overall responsibility for the president's security, which mainly involved making sure that Air Force One would have a trouble free transit to Osan Air Base. Flying into Seoul's main international airport would have been far too disruptive. A helicopter had ferried the president to the carrier, escorted by a flight of six Hornets and a hovering AWACS surveillance aircraft.

Price's role had been more subtle. His men had scoured the harbor, sniffing for a possible clandestine dash by a fast boat against *George Washington.* He could have saved himself the trouble. The Reconnaissance General Bureau, under Kham's direction, had swept the docks clean. There was hardly a person in sight. On the moored warships, RGB men stood beside fire control systems with weapons loaded and ready for use to forestall any 'accident'. Price knew this because his people were standing right beside them, as were the Chinese and the Russians. No one took any chances.

To Price, the elaborate security precautions were somewhat excessive, but the old adage about being safe than sorry was very apt here. The world witnessed a major political event and the involved parties did not want anything to spoil their fun. North Korea might enjoy a more progressive regime, but that didn't mean some hothead wasn't prepared to make a statement for the good old days.

Seeing the Hornets fade into blue specks, Price turned to Ormond. "Everything seems to have gotten off without a hitch, Captain."

"I'll be saying that when I drop my hook again in Yokosuka, sir. I never expected to be this close to Haeju Bay, at least not without missiles flying."

Price grinned. "I know the feeling. Talking to Chairman Kham wasn't something I figured I'd be doing either, but they're living up to their commitments. I have to give them that. How does your crew feel about all this? Especially after losing *McCampbell?*"

The heavyset officer pursed his lips. "Losing her has hit us hard, especially since I was responsible for her. As to why we lost her, that's a policy decision of our standard ROE, which the brass are already reviewing, and I'm happy to leave them to it. The deal we made with the North? I'll tell you this, Mr. Price. Sure, it's a good thing and eases tensions in this part of the world, but for me and the crew who serve this ship, I frankly don't give a toss. I'm happy to leave that to the higher-ups. If you'll excuse me, sir, I need to start making preparations for getting under way." Ormond touched his cap and walked off.

Looking at the retreating figure, Price wondered whether most Americans felt the same way. Korea had always been a tangled mess created by politicians on all sides. The ordinary Joe on the street never wanted to be there at all, and sending men to watch the DMZ, pouring billions down that rat hole, which only benefited South Korea, hardly made much sense.

After watching what went on this morning, perhaps the world had gained a measure of sanity after all. Anyway, his job done, there were plenty of other issues waiting for him at Langley.

Mark Price cast a last glance at the slick flight deck, squared his shoulders and made for the door. The khaki-clad marine snapped to attention as he walked through.

About the author

Stefan Vučak has written twenty-one novels, which include eight SF books in the Shadow Gods Saga. His *Cry of Eagles* won the coveted Readers' Favorite silver medal award, and his *All the Evils* was the prestigious Eric Hoffer contest finalist and Readers' Favorite silver medal winner. *Strike for Honor* won the gold medal.

Stefan leveraged a successful career in the Information Technology industry, which took him to the Middle East working on cellphone systems. Writing has been a road of discovery, helping him broaden his horizons. He also spends time as an editor and book reviewer. Stefan lives in Melbourne, Australia.

To learn more about Stefan, visit his:

Website: www.stefanvucak.com

Facebook: www.facebook.com/StefanVucakAuthor

Twitter: @stefanvucak

More Books by Stefan Vučak

https://www.stefanvucak.com/Books/

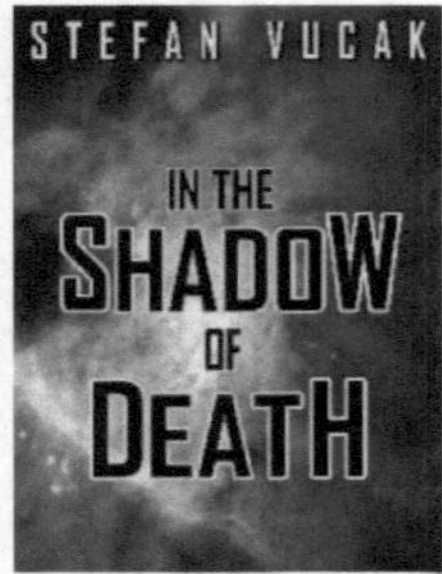

www.ingramcontent.com/pod-product-compliance
Lightning Source LLC
Chambersburg PA
CBHW030647120726
47905CB00001B/91
* 9 7 8 0 9 9 4 2 9 2 3 8 4 *